Time Will Tell

WYLFHEORT
MAGICAL MYSTERY
FANTASY ~ HISTORY
BOOKS

L. J. Hutton

ISBN: 978-1-7396943-5-7

Published by Wylfheort Books 2023

Copyright

Chapter 1

As soon as she saw her mother bustling in through the front door with that look on her face, Fliss knew what was coming. With a sigh, she stopped fussing next-door's cat out in the sunshine and followed her inside.

"Well!" Constance Allcock said, pulling a face as though she had been through the worst trial ever. "Who should I run into but Cath Greyson from the W.I. And you know nothing gets past her! Well I couldn't *not* speak to her – that would have been rude…"

"…I would have," Fliss muttered, knowing that Mrs Greyson was an interfering busybody, but her mother never even heard her.

"…and what does she say the moment I stop? 'Oh, I see your Felicity is still around. Is everything alright?'" Mrs Allcock shuddered. "What could I say?"

Fliss could feel the tension in her jaw mounting. "You could have said that what I do is none of her business."

"Felicity Allcock! How rude! No, of course I couldn't have said that. Good heavens, the very thought of it! But you've put me in a very difficult position, my girl. I said when you came crawling back home that there would be talk, and there is. I told you so, and your father did!"

The stress was rising ever higher inside of Fliss, and already she could sense that tears weren't that far away, but she must hold it together until she could get up to her room.

"For the love of God, Mum! I had a nervous breakdown! You make it sound as though I was walking the streets touting for trade!"

"There's no need to be crude," her mother reprimanded her. "I'm just saying …one minute I can hold my head up, at least as far as being able to say that you had a job in the City." The inevitable sniff followed instantly. "Not as good as Janice Jones' son being an investment banker *and* being married with twins – could you not have found yourself someone like him in the years you were in London? But at least your career was *some* excuse for why we're not grandparents yet, and you in your late thirties."

Fliss tried desperately to keep her voice from wobbling as she retorted, "I'm not your only child! Go and harass Ben over his lack of children and his divorce for a change."

And then her father's voice came from behind her, never able to just leave things be between her mum and herself.

"You leave Ben out of this. You know that the divorce wasn't his fault. Working all the hours God sends in his job, you'd have thought the ungrateful bitch would have been glad of having a man who worked that hard."

Fliss turned to him. "I don't think that was much consolation for spending every evening at home on her own, especially on those nights when Ben was out wining and dining his clients. Ben's paid for you pushing us so bloody hard into high-flying jobs with his marriage, me with my health. It comes with a price – one you don't ever seem to see."

"Price?" Graham Allcock spluttered. "I know what price I paid! A bloody high one, putting you two through university and afterwards! Your mother and I could have had some pretty exotic holidays on what you cost us."

"Funny how you've never been on one since, then, isn't it?" Fliss bit back. "Not one in over fifteen years. And why is it that you never remember that you asked me to pay back every last penny? …And that I did!"

"*Hmph!* Prices had gone up a lot by the time you did," Mr Allcock blustered, never able to admit that they hadn't gone away because he was simply too tight-fisted to pay the going rate. And Fliss knew what was coming next, because it always did. "And you've been grateful enough to come running back home, haven't you? Where would you have been without us, *hmm*?"

Unable to bear a single second more, Fliss turned on her heels and took the stairs two at a time, fleeing first up the main stairs, and then on up the narrow ones to the attic bedroom. When they'd been children, Ben as the favoured son had been allowed to choose that as his bedroom, while Fliss, despite being the older, had been cramped up in the small original third bedroom. Little more than a box-room, it had been cosy when she was little, and a terrible squash once Ben had had to share it with her before the loft conversion was done – because heaven forbid that their parents would let either of them have the other double bedroom. That was for guests. Guests who never came, but who Constance kept the entire house in a state of pristine permanent alert for, scurrying around to plump up cushions the moment anyone moved.

Now, though, Fliss had claimed the attic for herself, rearranging the bed so that it was above the empty room in order that her parents wouldn't hear her sobbing at night. Nor would she have come home if there had been any other option. But her job in the advertising agency had taken its toll on her. It was a cut-throat business to start off with, and one Fliss had never really wanted to go into. However, by the time she had finished university, the one thing she had been certain about was that she didn't want to come back to the Midlands and close to her ever-critical parents. Living in London was more expensive, but with her commissions, she could just about afford a place of her own.

The big problem had been that affordable housing also came with a long commute. Even then, Fliss had only had the top half of what had once been a modest-sized terraced house, with what had previously been the rearmost bedroom in the tunnel-back converted into her kitchen, and one of the main two bedrooms as her lounge. One of everything – hardly living the high life – but at least it had been hers, and she'd just about managed not to need to have a flat mate, which would have meant each of them having a bedsit and sharing the kitchen and bijou shower-room. And indeed while she had still been in her twenties, Fliss had enjoyed the buzz of working in the go-getting atmosphere.

Yet as forty had started to loom on the horizon, Fliss had come to the realisation that all of the enjoyment had gone. Getting up by six o'clock, in order to be out of the house well before seven o'clock simply to get into the centre by nine, was exhausting, and it was a rare work day when she left at five. Mostly she was lucky to be home by eight, and since she needed to be in bed not much beyond ten, there was no time to do anything in her evenings. Weekends weren't much better, because on Saturdays she ran around doing things like washing and shopping, and on Sundays she was so wiped out, more often than not she found herself nodding off on the sofa mid-afternoon. Any pretence at a social life had long since gone, and the friends she'd once had had drifted away, now more wrapped up in their husbands and growing families, and with little in common with someone whom they saw as the career girl.

That wasn't who Fliss wanted to be, though. Her dream had always been of a cottage in the country, contentedly married – not like her mother, who seemed to be forever on edge – and with a couple of kids and dogs running about the place. And it was the kids which had been the tipping point to her breakdown.

It had been such a silly little thing on the face of it. She'd managed to take the time off to go and have her smear test. Not something she was wild about having done, but forced herself to go anyway. And it had been then that the nurse had said,

"Ooh, I see you'll be thirty-eight in a few weeks' time. Clock's ticking, you know. I know women these days have families later, but there's a much bigger risk once you've passed forty. So if you want kids, you'd better think about trying for them sooner rather than later."

At the time Fliss had been rather taken aback that someone who didn't know her would make such a personal comment, but once she'd got home, rather than composing the letter of complaint she'd half thought of writing during the journey back, all she could do was look around her empty flat and feel a terrible panic welling up inside of her. Where had her life gone to?

And as for kids, well she needed to find the man first! Because Fliss had never seen herself as a single mother. She barely kept things together financially as it was with only one income coming in, so there was no surplus for things like nursery bills. And anyway, what was the point in having a baby if she was only going to see it to get it up and put it to bed during the week? Someone else would have all the joy of watching to do the first of things, not her, because she'd be at work. Nor would the weekends be any better, because if she was knackered now, it wouldn't be any easier when there were two of them.

She'd seen that happen to two of the women she worked with. Karen had given up her job, unable to cope with the long hours of separation from her little girl, and was now living in a caravan on a friend's farm somewhere Wales; while Becky had gone back to the husband she hated, because at least he was out most of the time, and with his extra income, she could work fewer hours. Neither of them was exactly happy, though, and Fliss had talked enough with them on coffee breaks before they'd left to know just how hard and heart-breaking their decisions had been.

Yet knowing all of that didn't help a scrap when it came to her hormones clamouring for that little person to cuddle. Maybe it would have been different if she'd had a supportive family, but not only did her parents not want her here, her brother hadn't even considered helping her in her crisis, let alone on a more permanent basis. What her parents refused to hear was that despite being on his own in his spacious penthouse apartment, Ben hadn't wanted his big sister cluttering up the place, because he had a succession of ever-younger women coming home for one-night-stands with him. The spoiled younger child and beloved son had turned into a selfish and demanding man, far too quick to use people when it suited him, and completely unable to face up to when he made a mess of things, and that he was actually to blame for whatever mishap or disaster struck next. That had been the other major factor in his divorce, but was one Fliss had learned very quickly to never mention here in this house.

And for all of her resolve to never come back, after she'd collapsed at work, and then come apart again back at her flat, it had become clear that she was not going to be able to go return to her old job. Not that they'd kept it open for her. Six months to the day from her collapse, she'd found she was being let go on health grounds, and with no money coming in aside from statutory sick pay, all she could do was put her flat on the market and come home, though 'home' was never how she thought of it. After all, 'home' ought to have been somewhere you came to where you trusted the other people there implicitly, yet Fliss couldn't even recall the last point at which she could have said that she trusted her parents to have her best interests at heart. Deep in her heart of hearts, Fliss prayed that if she was ever lucky enough to have a child of her own, that she wouldn't turn into her parents, but would cherish that child as it deserved.

In fact, even now she didn't fully trust them not to turn around one day and tell her to get out, that they'd had enough, and for it to be without a moment's thought as to how she was at that time, or what she might be able to do in the way of supporting herself. No, trust was in short supply in Fliss' life. It wasn't there with her parents, with her brother, and certainly not with any employer. In short, Fliss felt utterly alone, with not a single person she felt she could count on come what may.

If there was a bright spot anywhere, it was that with London prices being what they were, she should clear enough from the sale of her flat to put down a sizable deposit on one here. But that presumed that she had a job up here to be able to pay the rest of the mortgage off with, and Fliss had the sense to know that using what little capital she ended up getting from the sale to rent somewhere short-term wasn't a good idea. Once spent, that lump sum would never be regained, and the closer she got to forty, the bigger deposit she would need to put down on a property. And anyway, if she went the other route, sooner or later she would still need a job to pay the rent once it was gone; which brought her back to square one. She needed a job.

However, coming back home hadn't been good for her. By the time she'd arrived, she thought she'd got past the point of being in tears several times every day, but her parents' dismay upon learning that she might be there for months hadn't done much for her. And since then, their constant harping on at her to pull herself together and just go and ask for her old job back, not to mention their endless sniping and criticisms of every small fault they saw in her, had made things even worse. Having hoped that she could at least reduce the dose of her anti-depressants, she'd instead found herself having to beg the doctor she saw at the local practice not to increase her dose.

"I *will* be alright," she'd forced herself to say, yet not feeling it. "I just need a bit more time. I'll be fine."

But her next check-up was getting closer, and she knew she would be going in looking even worse than she had the last time. At that stage he would up the dose, not brooking any argument, and Fliss knew enough to know that it would be very foolish to just stop taking the pills. Even at the dosage she was on, she ought to wean herself slowly off them, and the higher the dose climbed, the longer and harder it would be to be free of them. And Fliss desperately wanted to be free of them. They dulled the pain but numbed her too.

All of her old get-up-and-go was slipping away in a prescribed fog of absence – absence of pain and misery down to a dull ache, but also absence of any ability to find joy in much of anything else either. What was currently truly scaring her was that she no longer recognised this stranger inhabiting her body. The 'real' Fliss – as she thought of herself – had been able to find a bright side to most situations. You didn't escape from her kind of childhood, get yourself through uni, and then find a career, by moping around and being dismal, she kept telling herself. Up until these last few months, she'd been the person of whom people would say, 'I wish I had your optimism'. Now, though, she panicked every time she found herself thinking, 'is this the last straw on the proverbial camel's back? And if so, will I …can I …heal? When will something like normality come back?'

What frightened her even more was that she was increasingly finding herself wondering whether it wouldn't be better to not be here at all. Not just here in this house, but anywhere at all. An utterly terrifying thought in her more rational moments, but at least then it would stop. All of it! No listening to her parents' endless moaning, no fretting through the night about what was going to happen to her, no painful wonderings about whether she could face a life if it was never going to involve the family she so desperately wanted, just a peaceful nothing. And it wasn't as though there was anyone who would actually miss her.

Why, she wondered, had her parents ever bothered having children? They'd not been that interested while she and Ben had been kids, and her mother had always been so worried that they might make a mess, or create a noise, or generally just be normal, that they'd been forced into a weird kind of pseudo-Victorian childhood a century after that sort of thing ought to have had its day. To be seen but not heard, and preferably not seen that often, either. To be forever reminded that neighbours might be watching and commenting. And worst of all, 'what will I tell your father when he gets home?' Because it hadn't taken long for Fliss to work out that her mother's fretfulness was caused by her father's eternal disapproval.

Her father would have been better staying single and just having a woman he saw occasionally, she had long since concluded. And her mother had deserved someone kinder and more considerate. But by now, with her father having unwillingly taken early retirement from his job, and her mother having somehow turned into a parrot who just repeated whatever he believed, her sympathy for her mother had been eroded away.

A different woman might have decided that it was time to stand up for her daughter at last. A different woman might even have come up to this god-awful room under the eaves and had an adult conversation with her; one in which her mother might have decided that enough was enough, and if they could scrape together sufficient to find a little flat for the two of them at least until a divorce came through, then she could escape along with Fliss. But not *her* mother. Oh, no! The thought of leaving this house had probably never even crossed her mind, Fliss had been forced to conclude. She would rather die miserable but with her own weird version of respectability intact, than take a chance, and maybe find that there was a life out there after all.

Fliss, on the other hand, couldn't wait to get out of here, if only she could find a way to do it. And one thing was for sure, this time – no matter how bad it got in the future – she would never, ever come back. However much the future terrified her, coming back here would be the worst possible option. A tent in some hidden hollow of the Malvern Hills was looking like a brighter prospect just at the moment, even if it was a distinctly chilly and wet spring. And there was a part of her – the tiny part that wasn't repeatedly thinking that it would be better if this was over altogether – that was wondering if she could scrape together the cash for a tent and a sleeping bag, and just take off?

Today, though, all she had the strength left for was to bury herself in her duvet and shiver. Even her tears had reduced to a trickle over these weeks, as if that was another thing she no longer had the energy for. And so, facing the wall on the little single bed, which was preferable to having to look at the shrine to Ben's glory which her mother had made the bedroom into, she didn't hear the footsteps on the stairs until a warm, gruff voice behind her said.

"Oh Fliss, lass! What have they done to you?"

Scrubbing the heel of her hand across her damp eyes, Fliss rolled over to see her godfather and uncle, Bernie, hurrying across the bedroom to wrap her in one of his wonderful hugs. Bernie had married her mother's sister, and he often joked that that was the biggest mistake of his life. Certainly Margot had been as much of a social climber as Fliss' father had been, and had made Bernie's life hell with her aspirations, and Fliss could see what he meant. Margot would have made a much more fitting partner for Graham Allcock and his aspirations, but then she would also have been far less compliant than Constance had been, which was probably why Graham, draftsman and would-be architect, had chosen the younger sister, leaving Margot to decide that the even younger Bernie the builder would have to do, because she wasn't about to be outdone by a sister only eighteen months younger, and being left behind on the shelf any longer than the six months she had already, despite still being only in her early twenties. But at least Margot had had the decency to drink herself into an early grave, thereby leaving Bernie in peace for some years now.

"Bernie," Fliss sniffed. "Oh my God, am I glad to see you! You're the first friendly face I've seen since the last time you came!"

He held her back at arms' length. "I don't like the look of you at all," he said worriedly. "I swear you've lost even more weight! …Well that's it! I'm taking charge of you now. You're coming to live with me."

"Bernie," Fliss protested weakly. "What will your sons say?"

"Jonas and Edmund? Oh, they're not speaking to me anyway, so it won't make much difference."

"No! What happened this time?"

Whatever it was, Bernie didn't seem to be overly upset about it, but then his relationship with his two sons had been marred by his wife for so long there wasn't much left to spoil.

"Ach well, you know that I signed the firm over to them?" Bernie's successful local building and decorating firm had been a considerable legacy to hand on to his sons, now both men in their early to mid-thirties. "Well they want to move into bigger contracts with housing developments. I've told them that that's a precarious way to go. You only need a housing crash and you're in deep shit, but all they can see is the chance to make a mint by throwing up cheap houses."

"Isn't that their decision to make?" Fliss wondered.

"Yes and no. Initially I was still on the board of the company, even if I wasn't hands on in a day-to-day kind of way. They wanted me to invest more money in the company so that they could bid on a risky deal. I said no; they threw their toys out of the pram; I sold them my share of the company – simple! If they want to play silly sods with their inheritance, then that's up to them. I provided them with a manageable firm that would have kept them going for the rest of their lives if they'd not been so greedy. But if they want to go down that route, then I'm not throwing my pension pot in after them."

He suddenly smiled. "Hey, don't look so gloomy! …Look, you know that I've now gone back to doing what I always loved doing, which was working on old houses. I was the one with the accreditation for that – me personally – so now that I'm separated from the firm, I can still work on those kinds of projects. And I can tell you, Fliss, I haven't had as much fun in years!

I'm just taking on the lighter work, the patching up and decorating. A bit of plastering, a bit of carpentry, the odd bit of plumbing, and basically just a lot of knowing what materials to use instead of slapping trade emulsion onto old lime-plaster, and then wondering why it looks like shit. It reminds me of why I got into the trade in the first place. So I was thinking, why don't you come and join me?"

"Me?"

He became serious. "My lovely girl, I've watched you over these last few weeks. You're going downhill, not improving. And it's clear you need a job. If nothing else, you need something to focus on instead of sitting up here dwelling on everything that went wrong. It's hardly rocket science, wielding a paint brush! And what you don't know about the basics won't take me long to teach a bright young woman like yourself. And the thing is, Fliss, you'd be working with just me. No pressure, no boss yelling at you, just a simple manual job with no stress attached – and isn't that what you need right now?"

For the first time in so very, very long, it felt as though a glimmer of light was shining through the gloom for Fliss. A painter and decorator? Not a career she'd ever thought of, but then maybe a straightforward, normal job was just what she needed? And Bernie? He was the one person in the world, she belatedly realised, who she felt she could have some real trust in.

Chapter 2

It didn't take long for Fliss to carry her bags down to Bernie's substantial pick-up truck, in part because she'd only ever unpacked those clothes that she absolutely needed. Even the damp washing went into a bin-bag, with Bernie asserting that his tumble-dryer would soon sort them out.

"Felicity, what are you doing?" her mother had hissed at her, as she and Bernie carried the suitcases, boxes and bags out. "Bernie, you can't do this! She's *our* daughter!"

And for the first time ever, Fliss saw Bernie turn on her parents angrily and retort, "Well it's a bloody shame that you've never remembered that, isn't it! You two ought to be ashamed of yourselves, but you never will be, will you? You're always going to be more worried about what other people will say than whether Fliss is okay. Well I'm not standing by this time. I've learned the hard way with my own boys how toxic you two were when you got together with Margot, and I'm sure as hell not going to stand by while you ruin Fliss' life too!"

He turned to Fliss and helped her up into the cab. "Go on, love, up you get. Let's get you home and a meal inside of you."

And with her mother standing on the pavement wringing her hands in anguish, and yet fearfully looking around in case any of the neighbours were watching, Bernie drove her away.

Mercifully, Bernie no longer lived in the house he'd shared with Margot. That had been sold within months of her passing, and now he lived in a comfortable detached bungalow on the outskirts of Ledbury. So there were no bad memories in this home for Fliss, only happy ones of coming here on her own to visit Bernie on the occasions when she'd been back for a brief visit.

"I don't do posh cooking," Bernie said cheerfully, as he came back from putting her cases into the largest of the spare bedrooms. "Will ham, eggs and chips do?"

"That sounds like bliss," Fliss sighed, collapsing into one of the huge squashy sofas. "If I never see another piece of over-boiled cabbage again it'll be too soon."

Bernie chuckled as he wandered into the kitchen and began clattering pans. "Never going to win Master Chef, was she, your mum? I always had to make some excuse never to eat at their house once I'd realised that she couldn't boil an egg without buggering it."

His down to earth matter-of-factness made her smile in a genuine way that she hadn't done in a very long time, and it reminded her that Bernie was the dad she wished she'd actually had, instead of the one she'd got. What a terrible shame that his two were so much of Margot in personality that they hadn't appreciated what they'd been blessed with, because Bernie was a gem. And it was slowly sinking in that he'd offered her a real lifeline with that job. He'd seen what nobody else had, which was that she needed something to occupy these long empty days and stop her from dwelling on everything, but at the same time something without any pressure attached to it.

Yet for the first few days, all Fliss seemed to do was sleep. No sooner had she got up and had breakfast than she was out for the count again. Whatever nervous energy she'd been running on up until now had evaporated, and instead she was left to just deal with the chronic exhaustion that came with her depression. And bless him, Bernie never said a word of censure over his narcoleptic guest, understanding that the first thing she needed to do was to recover some of her physical reserves, even if her mental ones were going to take a bit longer.

By the end of the first week, she had progressed enough to be able to stay awake for most of the day as long as she had a nap at lunchtime, and it was then that Bernie started talking to her about his work. Not in a pushy kind of way, though. Rather, he showed her the projects he'd worked on in the years since he'd ceased to be involved in his actual building company. And it came as something of a surprise to Fliss to realise that this had been going on for quite a while. In the eight years since he'd stopped being an active part of his company, but had still had a controlling share in until recently, Bernie had taken on a whole string of independent jobs. Some of them were quite small scale, such as the re-plastering of the back rooms of an old house in Powick after it had been flooded.

"Lovely old house," Bernie said affectionately as he showed her the photographs. "The problem was, the lady who owns it had had the initial replastering repair done with the twerps the insurance company said she had to use. Well that was never going to work, because the place hasn't got a damp course – it's too old to have one of those. But worse from the damp point of view, it hasn't got any deep foundations either in a lot of it. It's one of those places that's had bits and pieces tacked onto it, you see, and so the more modern bits – by which I mean late Victorian," and he gave her an amused wink, "– they're okay. They have foundations at least. But this back bit, well, that goes back right into the Georgian era, and might even be really early seventeenth century. So you stick modern plaster onto it, and depending on how many wet years you then have, sooner or later you get these big damp patches appearing," and he showed her the 'before' photos, where large dark patches could be seen on the walls.

"Can't even think of putting paper on those," he said authoritatively. "Has to be emulsion, and even then, you've got to use the right sort, something that will breathe. But first I had to mix up some proper old lime plaster. Nasty stuff if you don't know what you're doing, mind you, but look at this finish …doesn't that look good?"

And it did. So much so that Fliss actually found herself becoming interested. That in itself was a novel experience, because she couldn't remember the last time she had felt even a spark of curiosity over anything. The idea of having something to show for her efforts beyond an anonymous bank transfer of pay was suddenly very appealing. Moreover, she'd always had a good eye for colour – that had been part of what had made her an asset to the advertising company, because she could spot the flaw in an ad's colour scheme sometimes faster than the graphic designers – so she could see straight away how the colours Bernie had picked had flattered. Stark white on those old and uneven walls would have only shown every lump and bump, but the very pale and muted dove grey was enough to keep the room light and airy, and yet also soften its flaws.

"That's lovely," she said and meant it. "I don't think I've ever seen that colour in a house. Did you have to blend the paint specially?"

Looking pleased as punch – though it was because he'd hoped that Fliss would enjoy this, not because of the compliment – Bernie explained, "I used a special heritage paint brand. But you're right, that's not straight off their catalogue. I mixed two parts of their palest grey to one of their softer mauves to get this colour. That's part of the fun of doing this. It's working out what you need.

"Have a look at this old black and white cottage. See how small the windows are? Well to get the room to match up and look right, I had to use three different blends of colour. The basic, slightly muted, almost-cream colour is one the catalogue calls Duckling White, and that's on the sunny wall. But on the back wall I had to add in some proper stark white, and on the dark window wall and the one with the door in it, I had to add in even more. It was weird the way it just didn't look right when I'd put the first coat on all over. It looked for all the world as though I'd used three different colours. That's what I mean about using your brains when it comes to stuff like this."

As they worked their way through what amounted to Bernie's portfolio, Fliss could feel herself being drawn in. It appealed to her in all of the ways her old job never had. Bernie got to know the property owners in advance, for a start off, and if he felt that they wouldn't take his advice, then he firmly but politely declined the job. As he said, the last thing he wanted was to get started and then have them constantly changing their minds over colours and finishes when they got up the next day, or looked at it before the paint was fully dried out and screeched in dismay. So there was no stress there.

And then there was the creative side. That also was becoming ever more attractive, because in her old job Fliss had only ever been able to comment on the designers' work, she never got to do any of it herself. And there was something inside of her that was crying out to have this artistic release. To be able to decide within a basic brief what shades of colour to present to the client for them to choose from – and Bernie was very firm on this point.

"I never give them the whole bloody colour card," he said, rolling his eyes in mock exasperation. "Most of them struggle to decide what to have for dinner that day, let alone whether it'll be a colour they can live with for the next five years. I take photos of what they've got, you see. So if they've got a pair of dark leather chesterfield sofas in a small room, you just know you can't let them pick a bottle green for the walls, or it would be like walking through a dark forest all the time."

"Bottle green for the walls?" Fliss gulped. "Really? People do that?"

"Oh, it can work," Bernie admitted. "I did this lovely old Georgian house's dining room that had acres of decorative plaster around the windows and huge, deep coving, and some up on the ceiling too. Well with that in a nice subtle off-white, and the rest of the ceiling in a muted cream, it was crying out for a darker colour below on the walls to really show it off, and given that the whole of one of the longer walls was ceiling to floor windows, light wasn't a problem there. I put the dark green on the two end walls, and a much paler leaf green on the fireplace wall opposite the windows so that it would reflect some of the light back. It looked really smart, especially as it had one of those big white marble over-mantles breaking up the back wall. But that's what I mean about choosing your place and setting."

"Wow! I'd love to have seen that."

"Ah, well it was before I really went solo, you see, so it was done under the auspices of the company, even though it was only me and the apprentice lad working on it. I had to leave the official photos back with the lads. I know they've copied it more than once, but without taking the time to get the right paints. God knows what the owners of those places thought when they saw the end results, but that's not my problem."

That made Fliss ask, "Bernie, are you okay with the way things are between you and the boys?" Somehow they were always 'the boys' to her, the younger cousins who'd never quite grown up. "It sounds as though things are almost as bad between you and them as it is between me and mum and dad."

Bernie gave a bitter laugh. "Not quite *that* bad! …And no, I'm not happy that we're barely on speaking terms. But you know, at some point you have to recognise that your kids have become adults. You can't be forever trying to tell them what to do. And if they make dreadful choices, sometimes the only thing you can do is shut up and let them get on with it. The way things are at the moment, I'm just staying well out of the way, because then I can't say something that will mean we can never go back.

"But if this all goes base up for them – as I fear it will – then at least one or the other of them will be able to come to me for advice. I can't say help, because my feeling is that it'll be financial help they'll come begging for, at least in the first instance, and on a scale that I can't hope to give them. And just in practical terms, I can hardly have one of them with their wives *and* kids coming to live here in this bungalow, there just isn't room. If they've used their houses as collateral, then they're going to have to sort themselves out. But I'll always be here for them if they want my moral support, it's just that they're riding high at the moment and don't want it. The time will come, though, it'll come."

He reached over and squeezed her hand affectionately. "Don't worry, Fliss, you're not edging the boys out of anything they currently would ever want, much less get involved in. And my relationship with them isn't anything like as toxic as yours is with your parents. I wouldn't dream of kicking either Jonas or Edmund as hard if they were in your position. You're actually ill, not just throwing your toys out of the pram, and I can't understand why Constance and Graham can't see that, I really can't."

"I think they're scared stiff that they might have to actually *do* something for me," Fliss found herself saying with more bitterness than she had wanted to allow to show. "It's so bad for their standing with the neighbours and all of those clubs my father belongs to, to have to admit that your daughter is," and she sarcastically made finger quotes in the air, "'mentally ill.' You'd think it was catching, and I was carrying bubonic plague the way they've gone on."

It was the opening Bernie had been hoping for, and so now he ventured to ask, "What happened, Fliss? If you don't want to tell me, it's alright, but I'm concerned and I'd like to know what on earth it's been to hit you so hard?"

And suddenly Fliss wanted to tell him. He was the first person who'd asked and genuinely meant it, and so it all came spilling out. The horrendously daily journeys, with her getting ever more tired and more isolated, and then the realisation that the family she so badly wanted was slipping over the horizon out of reach, and with there being nothing she could do about it. By the end she was talking between hiccupping sobs again, but unlike her parents, Bernie never interrupted her, just made sympathetic noises until he was sure she'd said all she needed to.

At that point, though, he went and poured them both a stiff gin and tonic. "This probably doesn't mix with your pills, but I think we both need these," he said as he chinked his glass against hers. "Bloody hell, Fliss, I'm not surprised you cracked. You had it coming at you from all sides. There wasn't a single part of your life that wasn't stressful. That damned job was a nightmare – especially with your new boss. You were struggling to keep your head above water financially with a mortgage like that. You'd got no social life left, and then to cap it all your hormones kicked in.

"Well I can't guarantee that you'll meet the decent bloke you so deserve, but working with me, you won't have the work stress for a start off. And I can assure you that while I get up early enough to get to the job – wherever it is – by nine, I finish at four, or five at the very latest. I'm too old myself to be burning the candle at both ends. And I tell you something else, if I'm working a fair way from home, I stop and have a proper meal at a sensible time at a pub on the way back. I wouldn't dream of living like you did, getting back so late that all you could do was microwave a ready-meal and then fall into bed. Nor are my jobs relentless like yours was, they're all short-term, so if I've had a tiring job some distance away, I make damned sure that the next one is closer to home so that I've got chance to recover.

"I know I'm only in my late fifties, but I want to live to a ripe old age, not conking out with a heart-attack at sixty-two! Which also means that I take proper holidays. I don't sting my clients with what I charge them, but between what I've got put by, and what I earn, I've afforded a good holiday every year. I went to New Zealand last year for three weeks, you know. When did you last have a holiday?"

"Holiday?" Fliss sniffed. "I barely made it to a day trip to Brighton on my weeks off in the last year or so. I think the last time I went on anything you'd call a holiday was with my friends while we were at uni'."

"I take proper breaks, and so will you," Bernie said firmly, glad more than ever that he'd stepped in. What the hell had Graham and Constance been thinking to let Fliss carry on running herself into the ground like that? But then he knew the answer to that already. They hadn't given Fliss herself a second's thought. And in their own strange way they were as bad with Ben, because Bernie was pretty sure that in stark contrast, they had given Ben considerable financial help, and consequently, that was partly why there was nothing left to help Fliss out when she'd so badly needed it.

That bit about her so badly wanting a family had him worried, though. It was something he couldn't fix for her, and he knew from talking with one of his former secretaries who'd been in the same position, that it wasn't something Fliss was going to be able to just turn off. To his mind, the only way she was going to even halfway cope was if there was nothing going wrong in the rest of her life. *You're going to have to step up, Bernie, old mate,* he told himself firmly. *One way or another you're going to have to help her get the other parts of her life back onto an even keel, or she'll be scarred for life by this.*

Chapter 3

Monday

It was another week again before Bernie made his announcement.

"We've got a job to go to," he told Fliss cheerily at breakfast on the Monday morning.

She froze with her mug of coffee halfway to her lips. "Already?"

Bernie grinned. "In truth it's been on the cards for a while. I just hadn't said anything because it was all dependent on the clients being able to buy the place. And it's the job I had in mind when I came over to your mum and dad's place to see you …although I thought I was going to have to do a fair bit of grovelling to get you to come and join me. I never dreamt that you were in such a bad way, you see, and it's a big job, so I'd only thought of asking you to come and have a break before going back to your office work by giving me a hand – sort of like a working holiday with built-in recuperation time. Took me all of a few seconds to revise that when I saw you, though. That was when I realised that you needed a permanent change. But right from when I got approached for this job, and then heard you were back home, I'd always had this funny feeling that you'd be joining me on it."

Fliss didn't quite know how to respond to that. It certainly made a bit more sense of Bernie's behaviour if he'd always been intending to ask her to help him with the job, and less of the spontaneous decision. That was something she was rather glad of, because it meant that he'd thought things out more beforehand, and also that he'd already discounted asking his sons or one of their apprentices for help with the work. In turn, that made her feel a bit better in as much as it therefore wasn't anything to do with her being around if Bernie's sons had rejected the job already, meaning she hadn't contributed to a worsening relationship between them. She'd never been close to her cousins, but that didn't mean she'd do them down. After all, she'd had enough of a cross to bear down the years with the endless negative comparisons her parents made between her and Ben, to not want to wish a similar fate onto them.

"What sort of job is it?" she asked tentatively. She didn't want to be ungrateful, but somehow in her muddled state she'd thought it would be a month or two before Bernie asked her to do anything. Of course, common sense said that while he spaced his jobs out, if he'd had the intervals she'd been thinking of, he'd only have had three or four jobs a year, and that wouldn't have been practical.

"Oh, you're going to love this," Bernie blithely carried on, despite guessing that Fliss was having an inner wobble. He wasn't being insensitive, but rather presumed that her confidence had taken such a pounding that she would be doubting her every move for a while. "It's a lovely place out at Bishop's Wood, which is a hamlet of next to no houses off the A449 up towards Stourport-on-Severn. The thing is, it's been split into three for a goodly while. The whole house is what's been up for sale, but a part was let out long-term to the people who've bought it, and the other smaller bit has been a holiday let.

"Now that might sound like a lucrative arrangement – you know, extra regular income from the long-term rental, and then seasonal top-ups – but it didn't quite work out that way. The older couple who owned the main house found the holiday change-overs becoming more arduous, and the previous folks in the long let left it in a bit of a state, despite only being next door. So when Mr and Mrs Davenport took the long let, having come back from working overseas, they soon came to an arrangement with the owners to buy the place that suited them all. The season of holiday lets for last year got to run through, with the understanding that no more would be booked for this coming season. The Davenports stayed in the long let despite its current state, and the Chandlers had time to sort out where they wanted to live, and to decide what they would take with them and what they'd leave behind."

"Gosh, that sounds all very amicable," Fliss said. "What went wrong? I'm guessing something did since you said that the Davenports had to wait and see if the sale went through?"

Bernie grimaced. "The Chandlers' daughter and her grasping husband is what! They as good as demanded first refusal on the sale, offering to swop their rabbit-hutch of a modern semi for the main house."

"Surely there would have been a huge gap in the price?" Fliss guessed. She'd looked at the local property market enough to know that a modern semi, and then the kind of place Bernie was talking about, weren't remotely in the same price bracket.

"And that was the rub. That's what's held everything up. Because the daughter and her husband went to every mortgage lender in town, and few others besides, trying to raise the money."

"I'm guessing no-go?"

"Dead right!" Bernie sniffed in disgust. "The husband can't hold down a job for more than six months at a stretch, so heaven knows why they thought they would get a loan of the kind they'd have needed. To make matters worse, they've twice been in arrears with the mortgage they have, let alone a bigger one, so there wasn't a snowflake in hell's chance that they'd get one for twice that and more. But it's all held up the sale, you see, because they got a right shyster of a solicitor involved who could see his fees getting higher and higher the longer he dragged the legal wrangling out. And then the Chandler's son got in on the act, and said that if his sister was getting her cut of the inheritance early – because she'd tried that trick to get her hands on the place, too – then he wanted his."

Fliss was aghast. "What a charming family …not! Makes even mine look vaguely functional!"

Bernie laughed now. "Well in truth, the son was happy for his mum and dad to move into something more manageable, and to enjoy their retirement. Mr Chandler was telling me that their son only pulled that stunt when the daughter had mithered their mum so much that she looked like caving in as far as letting the daughter live in the house for free, while they kept the rentals going as income – not that that would have worked anyway. Once he legally staked his claim, though, the sale was able to go through, because it was clear that no court was going to uphold the daughter's claim *and* the son's as well, since that would have left their mum and dad homeless.

"So all's well that ends well. The Chandlers are off to a retirement bungalow out this way, and have booked onto an around the world cruise to get away from the daughter while she has her tantrums; and the Davenports are about to finalise the sale, all of which means that this afternoon, you and I are off to Sytchampton House to do some measuring up, and to see if anything additional needs to be done beyond what I've already quoted for."

Fliss took a moment for that all to sink in, then asked, "So what's our brief? …Is brief even the right word?"

Bernie smiled. "It's as good a word as any. As for what they want the quote on, well there is some building work, but it's light-weight stuff as far as I've been able to assess it – primarily restoring old doorways that have been blocked up. The holiday let is the easy one. All we have to do with that is restore the doorway through to its one and only bedroom from the original landing, and in the process take out a modern spiral staircase, then open up its doorway downstairs into the main hall."

His enthusiasm for the project now really began to shine through. "That's actually the really sensitive bit, though, because although the holiday let only had one of everything – a tiny kitchen and bathroom, plus a modest lounge and a bedroom – that's actually part of the oldest part of the house, alongside the bit the Davenports rented. It's a proper black and white property, Fliss! Most likely Jacobean, but maybe even Tudor."

"Really?"

"Oh yes! Because you see the main front of the house is Queen Anne, and a beautiful specimen it is too, probably dating from around 1700, so the little place is the original house by the thick end of a hundred years."

"Good grief, I can see why they want it treated with kid gloves. If I had a place like that I would love it to within an inch of its life…" but then her voice trailed off wistfully, as she realised that the likelihood of her ever getting a house like that was nil. She was brought back to the present by Bernie leaning over the kitchen table to squeeze her hand and say,

"'Course you would! But in the absence of owning it, you can have the fun of playing with it!"

Fliss looked at him bemused. "What do you mean?"

"I've been given carte blanche to pick colour schemes throughout."

"No*oooo*! How did you wangle that?"

Bernie laughed. "Oh I didn't have to wangle much. You see Mr Davenport is colour-blind, and Mrs Davenport declares that she can't match a colour to save her life. She said to me that every time she's picked furnishings in their old houses, it's been an absolute disaster. They've fallen in love with this place, and so she wants it to look wonderful, which means that she's willing to leave things to me. It hasn't helped that they're both ex-forces, and have spent a lot of time in married quarters, where you can't change things beyond the furniture, so for years they didn't have a chance to play with decorative schemes. Then they've been working in Dubai, which gave them huge savings, but again they were in rented apartments where they couldn't change much anyway.

So this is, in effect, their first proper home, despite them being in their early fifties."

"What are we working with, then? I mean, are they bringing stuff they had in Dubai? Because I should imagine the kind of bright colours which would look stunning in that brilliant light will just look garish in English daylight. I'm remembering back to when I was at school, and my Saturday job was in a department store. The buyer for China & Glass used to go to places like Greece and buy up all this stuff that had looked great over there. You know, white houses, deep blue skies and seas, with big pasta bowls in azure blues and rich citrus colours. But under fluorescent lights in the store, they were bloody awful things! Absolutely hideous. They always went in the sale for a fraction of the original price."

Bernie was already laughing. "Oh, you're going to love what Mrs Davenport has, then."

"That bad?"

"Possibly worse!"

"Oh dear." Then Fliss began to feel a giggle building up inside. "I don't suppose we could put all of it into one room? Their bedroom, for instance? You know, limit the damage?"

Glad to see the way that Fliss was already brightening up, Bernie agreed with her, "I think we should seriously consider that possibility," and laughed with her.

Yes, he thought, *this is going to be just what you need.*

The drive out to Bishop's Wood on a sunny March morning was an unexpected delight for Fliss, Bernie tactfully avoiding going through Great Malvern and therefore any association with the Allcock family home or either of Fliss' parents individually. Instead, he took the quieter country roads through Knightwick and Martley, finally swinging eastwards at Great Witley, meaning that they had only a short stretch on the busy Worcester to Kidderminster road before turning off again. It ensured that Fliss was completely relaxed when they began weaving their way down narrow lanes, exclaiming in delight when they saw a 'Riverside Camping' sign,

"Oh wow! Of course, we're right by the Severn here, aren't we!"

Bernie nodded, focusing on the road ahead in case he met a farm tractor head on, but smiling widely as he told her,

"This house is just far enough back from the river to not be on the flood plain." He turned left off the road on to what was little more than a narrow, metalled track which started to go steeply downwards. "See? This is the descent down one of the upper river terraces. You'll see that we don't go down even onto the next terrace, but there are old springs not far from the house. People are apt to call them Roman springs because they've been known of for so long, but in truth I reckon they predate the Romans by thousands of years, because they're completely natural."

"How fascinating. I had no idea that there was such old stuff around here."

In reply, Bernie pulled up and gestured forwards through the windscreen. "What do you think to Sytchampton House, then?"

He'd stopped the pick-up right at the turn into the gateway, giving Fliss a perfectly framed view of the house sideways on. Built in what she presumed were local red bricks, part of the exterior had long since been rendered and painted in white, though it was in dire need of a fresh coat.

"Which bit am I looking at here?" she asked Bernie curiously, as she peered a bit harder through the windscreen. "I can't see any black and white bits here."

He pointed to their right. "See those two windows in the white bit? They're the side of the nice Queen Ann frontage. What you're looking at butting up to it is the long rear side of the bit Mr and Mrs Davenport have been living in, but I think that old house must have originally faced the other way. What we're looking at is actually the original back which would have once given out onto this yard we're pulling into, albeit since rendered over. Wait 'til you see the other side of it, though! It's picture perfect, Fliss!"

He pulled the truck a little further in through the brick piers of the gateway, and then swung to the left to where Fliss could now see that there was a gravelled parking area with a low-slung Mercedes sports car already on it. Leaving the pick-up there, he led the way to the door facing them and knocked loudly. Within moments, the door was answered by a dainty woman with immaculately groomed hair, and the kind of light but perfect make-up Fliss wished she could achieve and never managed. Knowing that this vision was probably at least fifteen years older than herself, and maybe nearer twenty, did nothing for Fliss' self-esteem, but she wrung out a smile as Bernie said cheerfully,

"Hello there, Mrs D! Looking lovely as ever! This is my niece, Fliss, who I told you about. So here we are, come to do a last measure up to double check, and take stock of any extras for the job. Is Mr D in?"

Mrs Davenport gave a radiant smile, which at this point seemed completely genuine to Fliss. "No Eric has gone into Worcester to finish signing things off with the bank, so you'll have to put up with me." She turned the lovely smile on Fliss. "You'll have to tell me if what I'm asking for is hideous, because I'm absolutely hopeless at this stuff."

Instantly Fliss doubted that, given that Mrs Davenport was wearing a beautiful champagne coloured skirt and matching sweater, which perfectly accentuated her silver blonde hair. It probably wasn't natural, that kind of even hair colour wasn't something many women achieved without assistance, and it made Fliss wonder whether there was an ulterior motive for them asking Bernie to choose the colour scheme. Indeed, Fliss now thought that Mrs Davenport was almost flirting with Bernie, and she wasn't sure how she felt about that. It might be that she was the kind of woman who did it without thinking – and Fliss had met more than a few like that over the years, women who flirted as easily as others drew breath. But she really hoped that this couple weren't setting Bernie up for something. She couldn't have said why, but she instantly felt that there was something very off about this woman, something not quite right and false.

As she let Bernie jolly Mrs Davenport along for a few minutes, Fliss took the time to stand back and take a harder look at the house. Even on this, its least prepossessing side, it clearly had the potential to be a stunning property once restored. And that in turn made Fliss wonder whether the Davenports were really that enamoured with the house, or whether they'd spotted it as a potentially lucrative trade-up. That would make more sense of why Mrs Davenport wasn't getting hands-on with the colour schemes. This wasn't being done to create a home – it was to make Sytchampton House into something perfect to be advertised in one of the glossy county magazines, or to have a photo-shoot of, all of which would drive the price up.

Thank God poor old Mr and Mrs Chandler are off on that cruise, Fliss thought sadly. *It would probably break their hearts if they drove down here for a nostalgic look, and saw a 'For Sale' sign on the gatepost. They must think they've handed their beloved house on to someone who'll cherish it for years, not make a mint out of it and then flog it to the highest bidder.* And then the subsequent image of some flash rich couple, with a couple of top-of-the-range BMWs on the drive and an investment portfolio, just using this house to sporadically retreat to from London, or to entertain corporate contacts at, depressed her even more.

She was so lost in her bleak thoughts that it took Bernie actually tapping her on the arm to wake her up to the fact that they were going inside. *Oh God, paste a smile on your face, girl!* she told herself sternly. *Bernie's been so bloody good to you over this, at least try and look enthusiastic even if you don't feel it. You've been faking it for months with your mum and dad, so how hard will it be to at least put on the mask, so that Mrs D doesn't think he's got some surly wench still rooted in her teens trailing along with him?* Unfortunately, the answer to that was: *harder than I thought it would be!* And not least because the moment she crossed the threshold to the house, she fell in love with it.

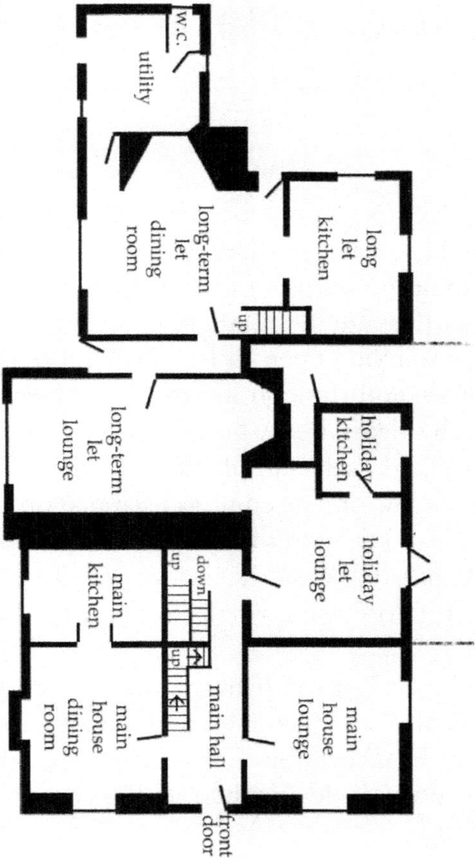

The house as Fliss first sees it

Chapter 4

Monday

They walked in along a dark and narrow passageway, yet Fliss felt the warmth of the past wrapping around her rather than any sense of gloom. A door off to the right was standing open to let a little more light into the hallway, and through it, Fliss saw a beautiful old room with original heavy beams across the ceiling. Or rather it could be beautiful. At the moment it had a revolting acidic orange emulsion slapped on every bit of plaster, and even in that briefest of glimpses, Fliss guessed that they'd be having to get daubs of the ghastly stuff off some of those gorgeous beams as well.

At the end of the hallway, they turned left into what was obviously being used as a dining room, but a voice in Fliss' head instantly said, *this is the kitchen*, and before she could stop herself, Fliss heard her own voice saying,

"Oh, what a glorious room!"

Mrs Davenport turned to her, and Fliss heard the surprise in her voice as she said, "Do you think so? We always think it's so gloomy in here." She gave a sigh which made her next words sound as though this was the biggest trial ever. "We wanted Bernie to knock a wall out and put patio doors in, but it seems we're not allowed to do that since it's a listed building. Only Grade 2, but listed nonetheless."

"Good grief…!" Fliss gulped, just about managing to bite back the words 'you bloody vandal,' in time. Then found herself quite literally biting her lip to stay quiet as Mrs Davenport added,

"I know. These planning men are quite impossible at times. Bernie, dear, I do hope you're going to be able to do *something* with this place in spite of them?"

"Don't you worry, Mrs D, it'll look the cat's whiskers by the time Fliss and I have done with it!" Bernie cheerfully assured her, but Fliss felt that nagging warning again.

Funny reaction for a woman who's supposed to love the place, she thought. *They've lived in it for long enough to know the drawbacks, so why put in a bid for it if you already don't like big chunks of it? You know you can't do what you want with it, so why spend all this money on it?* It certainly added credence to her thought that the Davenports were probably going to sell the house on at speed. Please God, Bernie wasn't totally taken in by them, because if the husband was like this too, Fliss wouldn't have trusted them further than she could have thrown them. Or was that her own scars skewing her viewpoint too much?

Mercifully, Mrs Davenport had already turned her back on them and was going through to a modern kitchen, calling back, "Tea or coffee?"

"Tea for me, please," Bernie replied, and before Fliss could even answer, Mrs Davenport was already replying, "Right, I'll get the pot going, then."

You've written me off! Fliss thought indignantly. *I don't fit your idea of what a career woman would be, and so now I don't even have a say in what I'm going to drink!* Before getting to Bernie's that would've had her excusing herself in a hurry, and then fleeing outside to weep even more tears – if she could have summoned any more up. But for the first time in months, Fliss felt stung enough to make at least a show of fighting back. She'd certainly had enough practice at dealing with snotty clients in the past, who'd thought that they'd be better off with a man handling their advertising account than a mere woman, and although she was a long way from being that old assertive self – indeed wasn't entirely sure if she would ever get back quite that far – nonetheless Fliss tucked her hands in her lap as they sat down at the table to hide the tremor, and decided she was not going to play the mouse.

When her mug came, already swimming with milk and the first sip revealed it to be laden with sugar, Fliss firmly pushed it away from her.

"Oh, sorry, didn't you want a drink?" Mrs Davenport asked, the smile slipping slightly. "You should have said."

Fliss pasted her best executive smile on and replied, "I love tea. I just don't take milk or sugar in it."

"Oh!" Mrs Davenport clearly realised her gaff and went faintly pink. Then compounded the insult by saying, "I assumed a working girl who was on her feet all day would want all the calories she could get. You certainly don't need to lose weight."

"That's because I've been unwell," Fliss riposted before Bernie could say anything. "I've had to give up my position as an advertising executive in London for now while I build myself up again. Bernie wanted my input because I've handled client accounts with some of the glossy county magazines and property portfolios."

Her jaw was aching with tension as she fought to keep the smile she was far from feeling in place, but it was worth it to see Mrs Davenport lost for words. Fliss also heard the amusement in Bernie's voice as he said,

"I told you I was bringing someone on board who would be an asset, Mrs D. Our Fliss isn't just a pretty face, you know."

God bless you, Bernie, Fliss though gratefully, *even though I'm probably nothing remotely like what Mrs D thinks amounts to pretty. The way I feel at the moment, 'pretty' isn't a word I'd use for any part of myself, but it's nice to hear you say it without even pausing.*

And with great tact, Bernie was already moving the conversation onwards and away from the danger zones, while Mrs D sashayed back through to the kitchen on her kitten heels to get Fliss a fresh cup. What came through was now rather stewed and bitter, but at least it wasn't so sweet as to make Fliss want to gag, and she drank it gratefully, happy to keep her face hidden behind the mug.

"Eric and I have decided that we don't want to be here while you're doing the rough work," Mrs Davenport was announcing, "so as of now we're going to go for an extended stay with my sister." The practiced smile was there again, and Fliss was now much surer of the artifice of it. "We haven't seen one another in so long. Family visits from Dubai to Cornwall really weren't that practical, as I'm sure you understand. She's invited us down there, and then we're going on to see one of Eric's old army pals in Hampshire, so we'll be away for quite a while.

"Of course, you've set things up with Eric about payments and so forth, haven't you, Bernie? …I'll be giving you keys to all the doors today before you go.

I don't need to remind you to set the alarms at night, do I? …No, I didn't think so."

You patronising bitch, Fliss thought, lifting the tea mug up for cover again, though only the dregs now remained. *God, I'm glad you aren't going to be here when we're working all day. I'm not sure my tact has enough strength left in it at the moment to not put my foot in it with you. And well done, Bernie. You really are a pro at handling clients. You haven't batted an eyelid at her insults, and you're not so daft as to not realise what she's said, but you've certainly got her charmed.*

As Bernie finished and got up to go, Fliss couldn't resist a parting shot of, "Don't worry, Mrs Davenport, we'll have it fit to grace the pages of *Homes & Gardens,*" and saw the way the woman's eyes lit up as if she could already see the inflated price tag.

"Come on through to the holiday let," Bernie said, as he led the way out of the back door of the dining room into the yard. "At the moment we have to go around via the gardens to get to it. There's no linking door from the Davenport's part."

"Thank God!" Fliss breathed, and found Bernie looking back at her and grinning.

Much more softly he added, "I see you've got the measure of her. I wanted to see your reaction, which was why I didn't say anything beforehand. But I guessed that you must have handled enough clients to still have a good built-in radar for people."

"They've got no intention of keeping this place, you know," Fliss said equally as quietly, alert to the fact that they were coming back around to just over a garden fence's distance from the modern kitchen's window, and that although it wasn't open, that still didn't mean that they might not be heard. "They want it pimped up to sell, not to keep."

Bernie nodded, putting a key into the French window and letting them into the tiny cottage. With that door firmly shut, he spoke more normally, reassuring Fliss with,

"The kitchen to this bit of house, plus its yard, is now between us and the Davenport's kitchen." He huffed. "I'm so glad you've said that, though, Fliss, because at first, I thought I was simply getting the wrong impression. He's not a bad bloke, actually, and I think he probably genuinely would like to stay here. But she's got aspirations, and I don't think he's been given much of a say in this. I'll be interested to see what you make of Eric Davenport when you finally meet him, and what you think of them as a couple."

"Oh? Do tell!"

Bernie grimaced. "I think they're splitting up."

"Good grief!"

"Hmm, quite! The first time I met them they were with the Chandlers, and I've got to hand it to them, they put on a good show of being the devoted career couple who had been happy flitting around the world, just the two of them together and no kids. But then the next time they were on their own. She kept the picture-perfect image going, but blimey, Fliss, some of his expressions at the guff she was coming out with! I wish I was better with my phone camera, because what a story those photos of them would then tell."

"So do you think that's why they're throwing money at this place, then? They've got a reasonable amount of dosh behind them, but probably not enough to let them both live the kind of lives they want. They're looking to make a killing out of this house so that they both come out of it fairly well off?"

"That's exactly the conclusion I've come to. And after what she's just said, I reckon it's more that she's going to her sister's, and he's going to stop with his old army mate. I've only got mobile numbers for them, not the landlines to the places they're supposed to be staying at, which already felt a bit odd if they're going to be away for weeks, not just a long weekend as I was first led to believe. I've taken this job because the house is a dream, not because I swallowed their fairy-tale wholesale. And somebody was going to get the job, because the poor old Chandlers were totally overwhelmed by them, so it might as well be me who can do the place justice."

Fliss breathed a sigh of relief. "Thank God for that, because I was praying that you hadn't been taken in by her. I tell you one thing for a start off: it's total bollocks that she can't put colours together. Nobody has that sort of perfect make-up on a daily basis, along with that kind of expensive hair-do and matching clothing, if they can't colour match. Nobody!

"If there were some gaudy bits and bobs about the place before they got packed up, I'd say they're *his* choice and *his* mementoes he's brought back from abroad – not hers. And that makes sense if he struggles to tell reds and greens apart, which is the most common form of colour blindness. Very few people are reduced to just black and white, so he probably sees the rich blues quite clearly, for instance, but doesn't realise how they jar with vivid oranges, and some greens might look muddier than they are too."

Bernie grinned at her. "I think you've hit the nail on the head. And you've just said all the things that I was thinking when I met them on my own. …But the thing is, Fliss, that means that they aren't going to complicate our job by asking for their favourite colour in this bedroom or lounge, or whatever. We really can make this house shine in all of its glory, and that's something I love doing."

His obvious enthusiasm for the house, if not its clients, was enough for Fliss, and she now began to look about her at the former holiday let.

"This really is glorious, isn't it!" she breathed in awe, as she took in the original wattle and daub in-fills and the heavy old oak beams. "The only thing that bothers me about all of this, you know, is that I want someone to cherish it for what it really is. Not to see it just as some damned cash cow."

Bernie came and put his arm around her shoulders to hug her. "Me too, kiddo. I'm half thinking of buying it myself, you know, that's why for once I broke my own rule about not working with clients I don't like."

"Bernie?" Fliss was amazed. "I know it's not my place to pry, but could you erm…?"

"Afford it? …Yes, if I cashed in one of my investments. That bungalow of mine is in a good position for people who need decent schools for kids – and that adds on a lot to the price of a house. I couldn't buy this on that sale alone, mind you, but I bought, extended, and tarted up that place with the specific intention of selling it on. It was never the place I wanted to spend my proper retirement years in. But this place I could truly love. It all depends on how the property market is at the time this goes on to it, though."

"I'd willingly come in with you on this, you know," Fliss surprised herself by saying without hesitation. "That flat of mine in London isn't much more than a rabbit hutch by comparison, but it will still fetch an insane price for what it is, and I was there for long enough for the prices to rise and to pay off a respectable amount on the mortgage."

"Would you?" The way Bernie's eyes lit up was enough for Fliss.

"Too right, I would! I have no idea what on earth I'm going to do job-wise and in the long run, but the one thing I am sure of – I'm not going back to my old job." She took a deep breath, deciding to share what had been bothering her for longer than she cared to admit. "The future bloody terrifies me, Bernie. All I could see while I was in my old job was long years ahead, with me working myself to the bone, and everything I ever really wanted in life just slipping away while I fought simply to exist.

"Well, I don't know what I *am* going to do, but it's not *that*! I want a *life*, even if it's not with the kids I desperately want. I want to *live*, not *exist*! I need to be somewhere where every penny doesn't go in cost-of-living, but where I have a bit left to go out with and make friends again, and that simply isn't viable in London. It means that whatever I do, it will be back up in this area, albeit a long way from my parents, so why not live around here?"

Bernie grinned. "Well even putting the house back together the way that it was, I can tell you that there's plenty of space here for you to have a generous suite of rooms for yourself, where you could live quite independently of an old codger like me."

"Bernie, the last thing you are is an old codger!" Fliss protested. "My father, now he's already an old codger even before he's got old. He's living with some kind of weird faux Victorian morality and a set of social mores that probably never actually existed outside of his head, and he's got a shocking attitude towards women – doesn't think they belong in politics, and that sort of twaddle, because they don't have the mentality for it."

"He surely hasn't said that out loud?" Bernie was aghast.

"Oh, more than once!" replied Fliss, wincing. "It's embarrassing if he's talking when we're out somewhere, because he never lowers his voice, but when he says stuff like that to my face, it's bloody hurtful. It's as though he always expected me to fail simply because I'm female, and therefore I'm automatically less than Ben. The fact that I was operating at a corporate level far above anything he himself has ever had to handle, and with all of the associated pressures, has never so much as percolated into his brain, let alone that I held those bloody awful jobs down for over a decade – not just a few months, which is how he always makes it sound when I hear him talking on the phone to one of his cronies. No, Bernie, you're far from an old codger!"

A twinkle came into Bernie's eyes as he mocking ran a hand over his thick grey hair. "More of the 'silver fox', then?" Then chuckled and patted his obvious tummy. "Although silver grizzly bear might be closer to the truth," and they both laughed.

He turned and waved at the room. "This was the lounge for the holiday let, and through that door over there is the little kitchen. I'm not sure as yet what to do with that," but he rapped his knuckles on the separating wall. "This, though, is modern plaster-board and could come down without much trouble, although there could always be original walls underneath it. I think that once upon a time – and I'm talking here about an era when this was the main house, and before that newer frontage – that it was all one room, and that what is now an open space beyond the current kitchen door, was actually a roofed corridor connecting both of these rooms to the modern kitchen of the part we've come out of, which was probably the scullery back then." He sighed wistfully. "I wonder why they took that part of the original house down?"

"Could it have become structurally unsound?"

"A bit unlikely given that the rest of the place is made of what even then must have been well-seasoned oak beams. No, it's more likely, given the size of the chimney breast in that dining room/kitchen we were sat in, that that began its life as the main room, built on to here quite soon after this was finished. Then a generation of so later, when the family got a bit more money together – or a new owner came in – they built that orange hall you saw a bit of on the way in. I know it looks vile at the moment, Fliss, but if you can ignore the current eye-watering colours, that's the more handsome room of the two."

Fliss nodded. "I'm no expert, but from my wanderings around National Trust houses on those weekends when I had enough energy to move, even I can tell that the big window in there is more like Jacobean than Tudor. Am I right to think that it would've had to be a much fancier building than this to have had that amount of glass in it during the Elizabethan age, for instance?"

Bernie beamed with pleasure. "I knew you'd be a quick study! Yes, a lot higher up the social scale, back then, to have a near ceiling to floor window if it was Elizabethan. This is little more than the local squire's house, not a member of the real nobility's."

Fliss could feel herself getting swept away imagining the house's past. "I could just imagine the Bennett family living here," she said, with a huge smile. "God, I love that old BBC version of *Pride & Prejudice* with Colin Firth as Mr Darcy!"

Bernie wagged a stern finger at her. "If you ever tell any of the lads at any of the builder's yards we go to about this, I may have to kill you …but I loved that too!" He sighed. "I know life was harder back then than we like to imagine, but you can't help but wish that some of the manners from that era had survived."

"Oh, tell me about it! Like holding a door open for someone. The number of times I've had a door swing back in my face when I've had my arms full of papers or equipment! A bit of old-fashioned courtesy would go a long way with me, I can tell you. …So is the newer front more of the Jane Austen period?"

"Depends on what you mean. If you're talking about Austen herself, then no, or at least I don't think so if I'm guessing her dates right, which would be around the time of the Napoleonic Wars. Remember those soldiers in *P&P*? They definitely date to around then if I'm recalling my military history right. So even the front of this place would have been old-ish by the time she was writing. On the other hand, if you're talking about many of the kinds of houses that she was writing about, then yes, she would have been familiar with houses like this.

"The Bennetts weren't living in a brand-new house, were they? Theirs had already been handed down through the family, and like the owners of this place, they wouldn't have had the money to make every new-fangled alteration that came into fashion. They would have tarted up what they had in newer paint colours, and added the odd new piece of furniture, but that's about all."

Fliss felt a shiver of excitement running through her. "So essentially, we could go for a *Pride & Prejudice* look here and it wouldn't be out of place?"

"No, that'd be fine, especially in the front rooms. So come on, let me show you the rest of the place. That door you can see in the back wall still goes through to the hall of the main house – it's just that it's been kept locked for most of the time. And that modern metal, spiral staircase going up to the bedroom of this bit won't take long to take down either."

He fished an extensive bundle of keys out of his pocket and went over to the door at the back of the lounge and unlocked it with a flourish. "So, Miss Eliza Bennett, what do you make of the main house?"

Chapter 5

Monday

"Oh Bernie!" Fliss gasped as they stepped through into the hallway. "It's just gorgeous!"

She turned around and around, looking back into the oldest part and then into the Queen Ann frontage. "It's like two wholly different houses!"

"Well, I suppose you could say that they are," he agreed, "apart from the fact that this newer bit had no working parts." He saw Fliss' frown of bemusement and expanded, "No kitchen, you see, not ever, not in this part of the house. And don't forget that when this front was built, nobody had plumbed-in bathrooms. Your servants hauled hot water up and down the back stairs in buckets for the master or mistress' bath, and took the dirty water back out the same way."

"What about other stuff? I mean, did the family use the privy in the yard? Which is what I presume the poor servants had to use?"

Bernie pulled a face. "Poor sods had to carry out the chamber pots with their master's or mistress' 'leavings' in them, and then empty them in the privy. No midnight flits to the privy for the upper classes – actually no daytime ones either if the weather was bad."

"Yuk!" Fliss exclaimed.

"Quite. Flush toilets weren't introduced until 1778, and even then, wouldn't have been known of in lesser households like this for quite some time. So a proper water-closet wouldn't have been part of the initial design even for this part of the house."

"God Almighty! I'm glad I never lived in those times! But what on earth did they do when they were entertaining, for instance?"

"Oh, this you're going to love! There was a screen in the corner of the dining room, and the men just used a communal pot as and when needed. They don't show that on TV, do they?"

"*Nooo!* You mean even while the food was on the table?"

"'Fraid so."

"Oh God, that's disgusting! You never get that on the costume dramas, do you? …You said the men, what about the ladies? How on earth did they cope with all those yards of skirts?"

Bernie grinned at her. "I got a bit interested in the history of bathrooms, and I found out that the ladies often wouldn't eat or drink much at big banquets precisely because they couldn't easily relieve themselves. It was a huge social gaff to get up and leave the table before the end of the meal, you know. It's thought that part of the convention of men leaving the ladies to go for a supposed brandy and a smoke, was in part to give the female guests a chance to use the pot – which they had to do standing up, of course."

"Jeepers! How ever did they manage?"

"Probably quite badly," Bernie answered with a chuckle, "although you have to remember that they wouldn't have worn knickers, so no struggling with your panties in that department."

"No underwear?" Fliss was feeling faint just at the thought.

"No, not according to what I was reading. However, they did have specially shaped potties that were more gravy boat-shaped, so that they could hold them up to themselves, apparently. It was called a Bourdaloue, and some of them were made in rather nice porcelain. If you want to see one, there's one up on the first landing window with a plant in it."

Fliss' jaw dropped. "No way! Oh, I have to see this!"

"Well, we'll pass it on the way upstairs. But you do see what I mean now about the front having no working parts originally. It really was just a show frontage in its first incarnation. Of course, it didn't take the Victorians long to install a couple of bathrooms, and another one and an en-suite have been put in since."

"Thank goodness for that!" Fliss giggled. "I was starting to feel positively queasy about those communal potties!"

However, she now did another couple of turns back and forth to look into both halves of the house, and then said thoughtfully, "You know, Bernie, I think we're going to have to be quite careful about what colours we choose."

"What do you mean?" He was silently keeping his fingers crossed that Fliss had seen what he had, and was delighted when she continued,

"This Georgian half is very light and airy – even this hall, with its roof-light up there right at the top, and only the fan-light over the front door. I know it doesn't let a huge amount of light into this hallway, especially not back here, but even so, it seems very light compared to the old part. So, if we do the

Georgian half all in lovely pastel colours, it won't matter what the heck we do with the old part, it will still look gloomy."

"Blimey, I hadn't thought of it like that," Bernie congratulated her, wanting to build up her confidence, even though he had long been thinking along those lines himself. "Well spotted, Fliss. I'd have got to that when I came to put the first coat of paint on in the old part, but possibly not before I'd put some paint on the newer bit beforehand." It was a small white lie, but worth it as he saw her startled look of pleasure.

"I mean, it's not incurable," Fliss added hurriedly. "I was thinking more that we can use slightly richer colours in here, and then pastels in the old half so that it evens it out a bit – you know, like that pale room you told me you needed three versions of colour on." She waved a hand at the hall. "Obviously, in here we still can't go too dark. It's okay at the moment because it's all in white, albeit rather grubby, but don't you think that the all-white doesn't show the lovely plaster moulding off to its best, either?"

"No, it doesn't. I'd definitely got that far in my planning, but I was a long way from returning to bottle green, too!"

"Don't look so anxious, Bernie!" Fliss laughed, blissfully ignorant of Bernie's ulterior motives. "I used to spend my Sundays flaked out on the sofa, and if there was nothing on TV – which there usually wasn't – I'd look at pretty pictures on Pinterest, or at one of the glossy homes and gardens type of magazine I'd brought home from work once they were well out of date. I've got whole boards on Pinterest of pictures of lovely houses to work from. One of the colours I always liked in places like this was a very pale teal –

you know, that not quite blue, not quite green colour. It looks so elegant with white plasterwork. And mauve, or a dusty pink of the crushed raspberry kind or old roses, can also look stunning in these high-ceilinged places. Don't worry, I can show you them as soon as we get back and near a computer. I don't imagine we'll be given access to any wi-fi here."

"No," Bernie agreed dryly. "Old Mr and Mrs Chandler weren't the kind to be online for anything, and I don't imagine the Davenports would have paid out more than absolutely necessary. …Right, come on then, my budding little interior designer, let's see what you think of the rest of the ground floor."

It was at this point that Fliss realised that the Georgian front was really only one proper room deep, albeit very generously proportioned. On its left, and in front of the holiday let, was the room the Chandlers had used as their lounge. A beautiful, full-length window let in plenty of light, but the room was nonetheless dingy and had a carpet which must have dated to the late seventies or early eighties, plus some ghastly dated wallpaper of a similar era.

Across the hall, their dining room wasn't much better. Waving a hand to the double doors leading out of the back of the room to what Fliss could see was a galley kitchen, Bernie explained,

"I think these two rooms must always have interconnected, even though through there would never have been a kitchen when it was built. I tried to find the old plans but without success. My best guess is that it would have been something like a music room, but whatever it was, it was built as part of the new frontage, which had to have been a very flattened L-shape, dovetailing into the old building."

He took her back out into the hall, but before leading the way upstairs, pointed back to the far end of it. "See that line in the wallpaper? If you knock on it, it's wood, not plaster. I think that's the old doorway through to what's currently the Davenport's revolting orange lounge."

Yet Fliss barely heard his words because all of a sudden, she felt as if a ghost had walked over her grave. Something – and she couldn't have begun to say what, let alone why – had goose-bumps running up her arms and shivers down her spine. Desperately trying to pull herself together, she asked,

"Why can't we see straight through to there? What's behind these posh stairs? Another room?"

"No, just the servant's stairs. I suspect that having had to get through the thickness of that wall for the doorway when this was built, they thought better of trying to install a staircase there. Or maybe the wall between the two halves there is so thick because it needed shoring up to support the Georgian first floor. There's a bedroom over the Chandler's kitchen which must go out over the thickness of the same wall, and that has a nice Georgian window in it, but I don't think originally there was anything more than a ground floor in the first phase."

"Could there have been a staircase going out of the old hall in between the two halves? You know, from the Davenport's lounge in the thickness of the wall?" Then wondered whatever had made her think that, because it was hardly an obvious thing to come up with.

"Might have been. I haven't yet discovered where the original staircase to the old house would have been, because the one going up out of the Davenport's dining room – the old kitchen in a previous incarnation – is modern. Doesn't preclude it being in the same location as a previous one, mind you. And there might even have been two separate staircases – one for the rooms over the original kitchen and its scullery, and then another one put in when the second phase went in and they put the newer hall onto it."

"I hope we don't find any bodies in there," Fliss said with a shudder, then wondered where on earth that had come from as Bernie hurriedly said,

"Good Lord, no! Heavens, Fliss, it's just an old house! Just a normal old house."

And yet that Fliss found herself wanting to riposte with, 'Oh no it isn't!', even if she managed not to say it out loud.

Valiantly trying to squash those inner warnings, Fliss followed Bernie up the main staircase, joining him in amusement at the fancy chamber-pot on the landing windowsill which had a very wilted Christmas cactus in it.

"Good grief, a Royal Doulton potty!" she managed to genuinely giggle. "How the other half lived!"

"No expense spared," Bernie agreed with a chuckle. "Now then, what do you think of this?" and he threw open the door into the bedroom which had to be over the Chandler's lounge in the front part.

"Oh, what a lovely room," Fliss breathed again, not daring to say that this time it was in part her relief at feeling nothing spooky in here.

There was only the one window in the wall at right angles to the door, but like in the room below, it was large – almost ceiling to floor – and let in a huge amount of light; and if she couldn't enthuse about the Chandler's choice of décor, she could certainly see

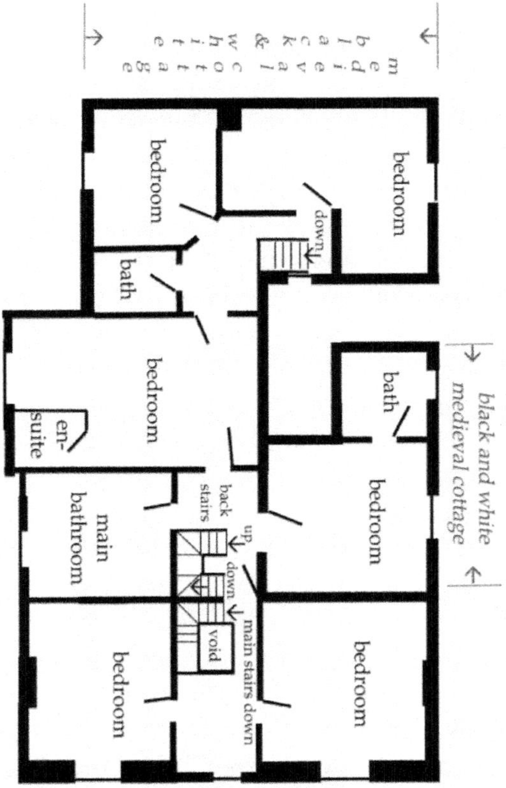

The first floor as Fliss first sees it.

that this would be an easy room to restore to beauty. The same went for the bedroom opposite it across the landing, and when Bernie took her around the stairwell to see the bathroom which had been installed, she couldn't help but be delighted by the lovely old claw-footed bath which dominated the room, even if she wouldn't have wanted to use it – the bottom looked very roughed up and scratchy! Another bedroom lay opposite that, but at the moment was sealed off as being the bedroom to the holiday let.

"Once we've got that spiral staircase out of the way, it'll be easy enough to just unblock this doorway," Bernie said with confidence.

"Hmmm," Fliss intoned, "but that's going to be part of the old building again, isn't it? So again, we'll have the old part opening straight onto the new, so that bedroom is going to have to be in very delicate colours so that it doesn't look gloomy compared to the ones we've just looked at."

"What do you think of this one, then?" Bernie said, opening the door ahead of them.

Immediately, Fliss knew that they were crossing over into the room above the orange hall just by the shiver which ran down her spine again. What on earth was it about this middle part of the house that was giving her the creeps like this? It wasn't an ugly room – far from it. Lovely old beams formed a pent ceiling, and thinking back to what she'd seen on the outside, Fliss now realised that this had to have a separate roof to the rest of the older house, let alone the Georgian one, even if it did butt up to the Georgian wall on the outside.

"Can't say I'm a fan of the en-suite," Bernie was saying, pointing to a door and some obviously modern plasterboard which carved a chunk out of the corner of the room. "I think that can go, don't you?"

Peering in and seeing a dated avocado-coloured shower and toilet, which must have gone in during the seventies, Fliss was quick to agree; especially when Bernie took her out of the room's other doorway, and she saw that there was a small bathroom made out of what had probably been a store room, right next door. Two more bedrooms sat cosily under the eaves of the old house over the Davenports' dining room and kitchen, and in these Fliss didn't feel so much as a twitch.

"Let me show you the top floor, and then we're done," Bernie said, heading back through to the main landing, and again Fliss got that weird shudder as she crossed over the threshold between the two parts, but was determined to ignore it. Bernie had been good enough to give her this chance, and she wasn't going to have him thinking she was coming unravelled by wittering on about spooky atmospheres when he obviously didn't feel a thing. Plus there was her own fierce determination to try and get back to normal, and that didn't include jumping like a flea over every twitch in atmosphere.

Now she could see the servants' staircase, and that it went up another floor.

"Why only the servants' stair going up?" she asked.

"I think this must have been where the children slept and played," was Bernie's answer. "I mean, they're good-sized rooms, as you can see, but we're definitely up under the eaves of the newer part here with those shallow sloping ceilings," and as they had reached the top of the stairs, pointed up to show Fliss the way the ceiling curved to accommodate the roof.

"I don't think they'd have put any guest of significance in here. In many ways, the bedroom over the older hall is more imposing than this, and I would suspect a lot warmer in winter, too. Either that, or because the floors of the two halves are really out of step by now because of the different heights of the rooms, it was just too complicated for the local builder to reconcile elegantly."

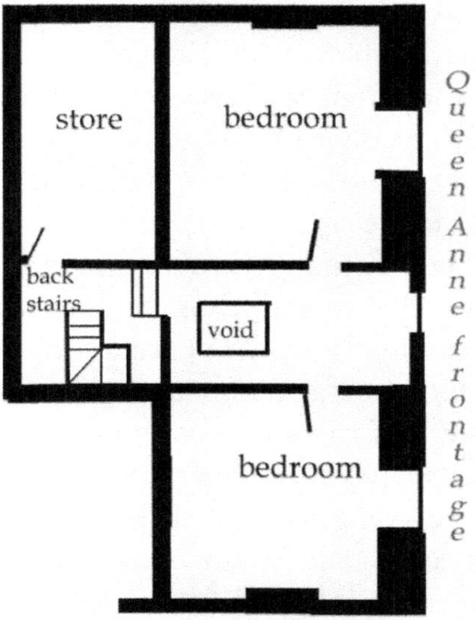

The top floor as Fliss first sees it.

"No, I see what you mean. Not a trace of any decorative plaster up here, is there?" in saying which, Fliss was quite proud of the way she managed to keep her voice even, because here it came again, that weird creeping feeling across her flesh. Yet there wasn't anything remotely odd or gloomy about these two rooms. Granted, the windows weren't as large as the first floor's, being more dormer windows, and the one on the landing was a cute little eyebrow design, arched to fit into the frontage's design and which didn't open in any way that she could see.

For the love of God, get a grip, girl! she told herself sternly. *Heavens, you'll be jumping at shadows next. It's hardly as though someone could have opened one of these and thrown themselves out in a fit of Gothic despair.* Then wondered where *that* thought had come from, because it certainly wasn't the normal kind of thing which popped into her head.

"Of course, all these floorboards are going to have to come up – or at least some of them will," Bernie was saying. "One of the first things that's going to have to happen is that the whole place will need rewiring. I wouldn't want to plug in a single power tool the way things are at the moment. Luckily, my mate Phil can come in and do that pretty much straightaway, so it shouldn't hold us up much. But you and I are going to have to get these bloody awful carpets up as one of our first jobs. I've got a skip coming first thing tomorrow morning, so brace yourself for a lot of dust and fluff!"

Dust and fluff, Fliss said to herself. *See? Nothing more mundane than dust and fluff, is there?* before asking Bernie, "Where will Phil start? Which bit of the house, I mean."

"I presume from the meter and work outwards. It's such a minefield to get qualified to all the modern standards that I leave electricity well alone nowadays. Once upon a time I would have tackled a job even as big as this, but it all has to be properly certificated now. Phil's the specialist, he'll do it how he sees best and I won't argue. That said, the meter is in the cellar which is under the front of the house, so I think we need to make sure he can get to that as our priority."

"I think I'm going to need overalls," Fliss said, mentally wincing at what the rubbish of ages would do even to her jeans.

"And that, my girl, is why our next stop is one of my suppliers to get you several sets," Bernie said cheerfully, and led the way back downstairs.

By the time they'd had a look into the cellar, Fliss was glad that Bernie had also said that they'd be getting her protective footwear, because there were some hefty looking old cupboards and things down there, just about visible in the gloom by torchlight. However, Fliss was cautiously optimistic that if some hadn't been ruined by the damp, that they might scrub up well and be useful if brightened up with a coat of paint. So it was with some dismay that they ran into Mrs Davenport as she walked out with an expensive suitcase trundling along behind her.

"I've arranged for a local house clearer to come and take all that junk away, by the way," she called over her shoulder, and Fliss saw Bernie's face darken in anger for the first time.

"What junk, Mrs D?"

"Oh, that old furniture, or rather the bits and bobs the Chandlers left behind. It really was bad of them not to get that done themselves."

"Who did you call?" Bernie asked, Fliss marvelling that Mrs Davenport was oblivious to the danger in his tone.

When she replied with a name, Fliss could have sworn she saw Bernie wince, even as he ground out, "I think not, Mrs D. They're a bunch of rogues, those lot. They'll take everything that's not nailed down and flog it at a profit."

Mrs Davenport's false charm also slipped a bit, and Fliss saw the nasty twist to her mouth at being contradicted as she said, "But it's just filthy rubbish! *I* don't want it in *my* house, so there's an end to it." And putting the case into the boot of her car, she slammed the lid shut and flounced around to the driver's side. As the Mercedes sports disappeared out of the drive in a flurry of gravel, Bernie let out a very uncharacteristic growl.

"Bloody woman! I can see why Eric wants shot of her."

Fliss thought that view might be heavily coloured by his miserable years of marriage to her aunt, but tactfully said nothing on that score, asking instead, "Do you not think it's junk, then?"

"I think that there's a very fine Elizabethan dresser in that dining room of hers, for a start off. And the mirrors that were left in a couple of rooms only need restoring. If you tried to buy them, proper period pieces like that would cost a fortune. Worse, we haven't really had a chance to assess what's what. They've obviously had their own stuff put into storage since the last time I went upstairs with Eric to assess the job, because the garish bits and pieces I was telling you about weren't there today, along with any of their modern furniture. And I certainly don't think the likes of Mrs D slept on the floor, not even for one night, do you? So they must have moved out a day or so back, and she just came back today to hand over to me and get that last enormous suitcase."

Fliss was thinking furiously. "You say that these people she's called in are rogues?"

"That's putting it politely! Outright bloody thieves might be closer! I know for a fact that several of their 'family' have been put inside for receiving stolen goods. I doubt they've ever even come across any morals they wouldn't subvert."

"Well then, do you think they'd have any scruples about taking Mrs D's money, but not doing the job? She's hardly been truthful with you, has she, so she's not got much room to complain if you equally aren't wholly so with her."

Bernie looked at Fliss in astonishment, then grinned hugely. "Genius! Oh, I like that! Yes, I'll give them a ring in the morning and explain that they're not needed, but to not bother ringing Mrs D on account of her already being gone. I can't imagine they'll twitch a hair over taking the money she's already paid them and running. They quote cheap just to get jobs like this. Then they make their profit on selling on the gems they find that people have thrown out in ignorance. They almost certainly quoted dirt cheap rates in anticipation if they looked inside at all, which would also be why she picked them.

"If we find some more lovely pieces, we can clean them up and put them into the appropriate rooms to make them look great for a photo shoot. She can't complain about that, can she? Especially if it helps increase the value of the house while saving them the cost of having to buy 'stage' pieces. And I'd feel differently about doing something like that if I wasn't already getting a feeling that she'll quibble over every bill I present them with – even though it'll only be what I've agreed with Eric already. I'm rapidly reassessing Mrs Davenport, and I'm not liking the conclusions I'm coming to!"

Chapter 6

Tuesday

When they arrived back at Sytchampton House the next morning, with Fliss kitted out in her new overalls, it was clear that nobody had been there since they'd locked up the previous afternoon. Mrs Davenport had definitely left the building, and that all by itself cheered Fliss up. Her confidence had also been given a boost the previous evening when she'd settled on the sofa beside Bernie with her laptop, and had shown him the images of various houses and their interiors that she'd collected, and which ones she thought might be good models for this house. Once he'd seen what she was thinking of, Bernie had enthusiastically handed over the choices of colours to her, which meant that she felt she was contributing a bit more to this odd partnership than before. Had she picked something garish, he could have made the final choices himself, but right now he knew Fliss' confidence needed that boost.

However, the first task for today was to start getting the stuff up out of the cellar. It was made a whole heap easier with the use of Bernie's portable generator and a couple of large and powerful work-lamps, and for the first time Fliss realised that the cellars ran under both front rooms.

"There's a massive amount of storage space down there," she said as she puffed past Bernie, lugging what had probably been an old log basket out to the newly arrived skip. "I suppose we should be grateful that the Chandlers got too old for taking stuff down there, and that there's not even more to move out."

It took until lunchtime to move all the smaller bits of detritus out of the way, and as they sat down to eat, Fliss realised why Bernie had made so many doorstep sandwiches – she was famished!

"Oh my God!" she mumbled, as she attacked another one. "I forgot food could taster this good!"

"It's only cheese and pickle," Bernie replied, puzzled.

"I know, but it's proper cheese and proper pickle! Not like the readymade sandwiches I only had time to grab at work. And why does it taste so much better sitting out here on the doorstep?"

Bernie laughed. "I think it's because you've worked up an appetite. You'll be a whole new woman by the time a couple of weeks are out."

"I'll be the size of a house if I keep eating like this," Fliss protested, only to have Bernie shake his head and say,

"Nah, you won't. You'll have worked that lot off by the time we go home for dinner."

As soon as Fliss felt as though she could lift anything after wolfing down the sandwiches, the next items they fetched up the stairs were three old tables, none of them anything special, but as Fliss said, with a bit of scrubbing up and a coat or two of paint, at least one of them would be good for in the kitchen or the utility. The next item to come up was a good deal heavier, and turned out to be an apothecary's dresser with all the attendant small drawers. Luckily, all of the multitude of drawers came out with a bit of persuading, despite having got damp and swelling enough to be very tight fits, and then the top lifted off. It was still hard going for Fliss, and she knew that her arms and legs would be aching like mad by the end of the day as she used muscles she hardly knew she had. The base had to come up the stone steps very slowly, with Fliss taking a break halfway as they rested her end on one of the steps.

"I'll give Kevin a ring tonight," Bernie said sympathetically, as he caught Fliss rubbing her upper arms. "The rest of that stuff's too heavy for you to try and move with me. Bloody Davenports! Why didn't they say there was this much stuff down here?"

"Do you think this is what Mrs D wanted the clearers for?"

"Hell, no! She was just thinking of the stuff up in the house, I'm sure. I bet it never even dawned on her or him to come down here and take a look. Far too dirty and unpleasant! And I'm still glad I managed to put the clearers off. For a start, this dresser is potentially a lovely piece. Why don't you take the drawers and things around to the old lean-to garage at the end, so that they're out of sight of the drive? We'll store the stuff we want to keep down there where it'll at least be out of the rain."

"Kevin?"

"One of the lads who used to work for me. Went his own way within a month of my boys taking over the everyday stuff," and Bernie's expression turned forlorn.

It had to be hard, Fliss thought, having to sit back and watch your sons making a mess of everything you'd worked so hard to build up.

"Were there many like Kevin?" she dared to ask, praying that the answer would be 'no'.

"Most of the experienced blokes during that first year."

"Oh, Bernie, I'm so sorry." What else could she say?

He heaved a sigh and shrugged. "No going back now. Trust me, if I'd have known then what I know now, I'd have never given up my controlling interest in the company, much less let it get to a situation where all I could do was let it go altogether. Putting a manager in who I could control would have been a better solution. …Hey-ho… hindsight's a wonderful thing, but bugger all use."

"I won't argue with that," Fliss said with a watery smile of her own. "If I'd known just how much I'd be sacrificing for that bloody silly career, I'd have run a mile from it, hopelessly broke or not. I know I said I'll come out of the sale of my flat with a passable amount, but that's about all I *have* got for burning myself out for over ten years and more. There surely had to be a better way to live than that, even with my student debts, and I have every intention of finding it now."

"Good for you!" and Bernie reached out and hugged her to him. "That's the spirit. We'll get by together, eh? …Now then, why don't you start shifting those drawers around to the garage bit, and I'll go and lug up those rolls of tatty old carpet that are mouldering away down there."

"Don't overdo it, Bernie," Fliss pleaded. "What goes for me goes for you, too. If you do your back in, we're really in the mire."

However, Bernie promised to leave the heaviest

bits until he could get help, and vanished down into the gloom of the cellars again.

Left to work at her own speed, Fliss took the largest drawers one at a time to what masqueraded as a garage, even though it was little more than a pent-roof on four posts. As she carried them around, she realised that they were made of good solid wood.

This would make a really nice piece of furniture cleaned up and with a nice coat of paint on it, she found herself thinking. *The grain isn't good enough for it to look fabulous with it just being polished, but maybe a nice sage green or a soft blue and it would look great.* Memories of looking at photographs of pieces of furniture in magazines and on Pinterest which had been stencilled came to mind, along with the thought of, *how hard can it be to do that?*

She found that if she 'walked' it, she could also move the top piece all by herself if she took it steady, and so felt quite proud of herself for only having to wait for Bernie to move the bottom part. It was therefore as she sat on the doorstep waiting for him that she realised that she could see something inside the shell of the base.

"Whatever is that?" she wondered aloud, getting up to go and crouch before the cabinet base.

On first inspection, she thought it must be just some paper that had been used to line one of the drawers, which with use had wrinkled up, and then got shoved backwards until it was behind the drawer rather than in it. But as she teased away at it with her fingertips, she suddenly realised that it was several pieces of paper. What finally came away in her hands turned out to be covered in childish writing, and she was so absorbed in trying to lift it out without ripping it, that she didn't hear Bernie's footsteps until he was behind her saying,

"What on earth are you doing?"

"Ouch!" she exclaimed, as she jumped in fright and banged her head on the top of the cabinet.

"Sorry, Fliss," Bernie apologised, but failing to keep the chuckle out of his voice. "Didn't mean to make you jump like that. But seriously, what are you doing?"

Fliss struggled to her feet, holding the pieces of paper carefully in her hands. "These look like kids' letters. I wondered if some poor little soul wrote to Father Christmas, and got told that if they posted them in the dresser that they'd get to him? Whoever it was – or maybe more than one – they can't have been very old. Look at the way they're struggling to form the letters."

She looked at Bernie's face and knew that part of him wanted to tell her to just throw them into the skip. But Bernie was nothing if not kind, and instead he patted her on the arm and said,

"Go and put them in the truck, then. You can have a look at them this evening."

"Thanks, Bernie," and she knew that he was thinking back to the conversations they'd had about how much she wished she'd got a family of her own. Bless him, Bernie really was sensitive to that and how she felt about small kids.

She didn't think any more about them until they had finished for the day. However, once back in Bernie's comfortable bungalow, a good meal inside her, and Bernie transfixed to the TV with a football match, she decided to move to the other end of the lounge where it was quieter, and have a look. As they had dried out a bit more in the truck's cab, they'd become easier to peel apart although were still very fragile. In the end, Fliss moved into the kitchen and sat at the table there, carefully peeling them apart and putting each one onto part of a clean tea-towel. She had thought of using paper towels, but then wondered whether they might then stick to that, thereby obliterating anything that was on the back. She would just have to wash the tea-towels thoroughly for Bernie once she was done.

When she'd got them all apart, she realised that without reading them there was no way to tell which one had been written first. She would just have to read them all and then try and decipher the sequence. However, what was clear right from the start was that these were no childish pleas for toys. The first one was in a looping hand, but written in the quite large letters of a child who wasn't yet fully fluent in writing.

> *Dearest Mamma,*
>
> *I do not like it here. I do not like school. All the other boys pick on me. Why do you not tell me when we can come home? I want to come home to India, and so does Ishwar. Ishwar does not like being called Iain, and I do not like being called Nenius. I know who I am. I am Nilmani and I want to come home.*

"Oh you poor little soul!" Fliss gulped, grateful that she had a glass of wine to hand and took a swig of it. What on earth were a couple of Indian children doing here in England? And when was this?

She turned the small piece of paper over, but the child hadn't thought to date the letter, undoubtedly believing that of course his mother would know when it had been sent. The next letter she read wasn't much better – or at least the page of it that had survived, because there was no preamble to this one, no 'dear mamma.'

> *Father says we must learn to become proper English gentlemen. I do not want to be a proper gentleman if it means I have to be friends with boys like Charles. Father says I must be nice to him because his father is important. But I do not like Charles. He is a bully. He picks on me when Mr Garfield is not looking. Father says I should tell Mr Garfield and Miss Morton if he does this in class, but they say I am a liar. They say that my sort are always liars. By my sort they mean Indians. I do not like it…*

But here the letter writer had run out of room on the page, though Fliss didn't need to read his next words to know that it would be something to the effect of England and those who were in control being racist. Feeling her throat tightening, and struggling to keep the tears back, Fliss read more of the similar bits of letters, each one an echo of the others, until she could put them into some kind of order based on the development of the handwriting and what they said. It was a grim catalogue of two little boys who must have been complete fishes out of water in this rural backwater in the past. Yet how far in the past it must have been she never got a clue about. The little boy was too busy pouring out his heart to his much-missed mother to ever give a thought to mentioning who was prime minister, or what was going on in the wider world. But the last letter chronologically, as best she could tell, was by far the worst emotionally.

Dear Mamma,

Father says he will write to you himself but I do not believe he will. I am all alone now. Ishwar died on Sunday. The doctor said it was pneumonia (he'd spelled it wrong, but Fliss guessed that was what he meant) *but I know it was from a broken heart. He has not been well for over a year since we got here, and though I begged and begged Father to send us home to India so that Ishwar could get well he would not. But I know that if Ishwar could have got warm again he would have felt better. It is always so cold here. The sun is never warm and Ishwar never liked the food. I am sure this place poisoned him.*

Father says I must go away to school now. He says it is not good for me to mope about the place on my own and that I should have the company of other boys. But I do not like the other boys here. So I have decided to run away. I have saved my pennies and I will go to London and find a ship for India. I am not afraid. I will do anything to get back home to you.

Your loving son,
Nilmani

"God Al-bloody-mighty!" sobbed Fliss. "You poor little sod! What an evil shit your father must have been to not realise how miserable you were here. And why on earth did he separate you from your mum? She must have been going crazy in India being separated from her children like that. What a bloody cruel thing to do!"

"What's a cruel thing to do?" Bernie's voice asked from the kitchen door, making Fliss realise that she'd said her thoughts out loud.

"These letters," and Fliss tapped the spread lying across the kitchen table as she snuffled into a tissue. "They're from a little boy called Nilmani back to his mum in India. Why on earth he got dragged all the way over here I don't know, but he was most horribly homesick, and he and his brother missed their mum terribly. But in this last letter he says that his brother has died. I'm guessing that it was a younger brother, because the way he talks, you get the feeling that he feels responsible for him. It's so terribly sad."

"Were they servants, perhaps?" wondered Bernie.

"I don't think so, if only because Nilmani says in more than one of them about having to become an English gentleman, and that it's something he doesn't want to be. He doesn't actually use these words, but I think part of him despised the brutal upper-crust way of doing things. He sees it as nothing more than cruel. And you can tell that he just doesn't trust his father anymore; that he thinks he is lying when he says that he's written to their mother back in India.

"But what really upset me with this last letter is that he's talking about running away. Heavens, Bernie, he can't have been more than nine or ten, if that, but he's so desperate that he's saved his pennies and is talking about getting to London and finding a ship back to India. Jeez! I walked around the museums in London often enough to know that it was no safer in the past than it is now! A little kid like that on his own was just asking to be set upon. Bloody Fagin in *Oliver Twist* might have been a fictional character, you know, but he was based on real villains who preyed upon kids back then."

"You think he was Victorian?"

"I don't know. Maybe. But he could equally have been earlier. I mean, the British had a major interest in India long before then, didn't they?"

"No other clues?"

"Not really. The paper is pretty thick, and it looks as though it was written on in pencil before this, and then got rubbed out. This kid was using whatever scraps he could get his hands on, but I'm no archivist and I can't tell the paper from one era from another, beyond the fact that it's not modern."

Bernie came and wrapped an arm around her shoulders. "I know it's not easy, but don't let this get to you, Fliss. Whoever this poor kid was, he's long dead and buried, regardless of whether he survived running away or not. There's nothing you can do to change his fate now. Even if he lived right at the end of the Victorian era, he can't possibly be alive, not even as an old man. So don't go breaking your heart over him, alright? It's sad, but look at it like you were reading a sad book."

"I know," Fliss sniffed, fishing another tissue out from her sleeve and snuffling into it. Yet in her mind she knew it was different. This wasn't some fictional character she'd got caught up in the story of. This had been a flesh and blood person who had suffered terribly, and that made the world of difference to her.

Chapter 7

Wednesday – Friday

Fliss surfaced when her alarm clock beeped, feeling ragged rather than rested, but had known even as she'd gone to bed that the letters would plague her dreams. Two small boys with huge, pleading brown eyes had pursued her through her subconscious, demanding to be heard even if they were long past rescuing. However, one thing she realised upon waking was that the little boys ought to be traceable. If they were destined to become gentlemen, then that implied that they had to be the owner's children, or at least very close relatives, and in the past, there couldn't be that many owners of Sytchampton House who had connections to India. Not that she would be able to do it any time soon. She owed Bernie her full support and input for the immediate future, not least because she was still immensely grateful to him for rescuing her from her own parents' house. Quite what life would have been like there by now didn't bear thinking about, but it wouldn't have been good, of that she was certain.

And so she dragged herself out of bed and into the shower, and even managed to take over the making of the lunchtime sandwiches from Bernie as he answered a phone call. When they got to the house, she discovered that not only had Kevin turned up, but he'd brought another of Bernie's old employees, Sean, along with him. With both of them being fit younger men of a similar age to herself, the process of emptying the cellar went considerably faster, and to Fliss' silent relief, none of the other old piece of furniture which came up into the light had anything at all buried in their depths. Even better, both men seemed like nice guys – nothing like the opinionated and often egotistical young men she had run into at the agency – and there was plenty of light-hearted banter without it ever getting personal, let alone nasty.

By the time they'd cleared both cellars, the garage area was already stacked half full, with Kevin and Sean having the sense to put smaller items on top of the bigger pieces to save some room for whatever else might need to come out. And it was at this point that Fliss realised why they'd avoided putting much in the skip.

"Come on," Kevin said cheerfully, "we'll give you a hand with those manky old carpets, too. They look like they're welded to the floors with the muck of ages!"

The carpet which had been put down in what everyone was calling the 'orange room' really was disgusting. But it was only as they started to lift it that Fliss found out why. She was watching from the doorway as the three men began dragging up and folding the carpet from the window end, and was astonished to see what looked like mud beneath it.

"They laid it on soil?" she gasped in disbelief.

"Nah, not soil," Sean replied, scuffing at the mud-like stuff with his sturdy workman's boot. "See? There're old tiles underneath this."

"But where's the mud come from?" Fliss asked, wondering if Mrs Davenport was actually too haughty to dream of using a vacuum cleaner.

Bernie stood upright and flexed his stiffening shoulders. "It's actually just the normal stuff that gets walked in. The problem is, these old quarry tiles really *were* laid straight onto the soil – no damp courses in those days. So whenever it's damp outside, they get damp. It's not a problem until you cover them over. If you let them breathe, they're fine. But once you cover them with modern manmade stuff, they start to sweat, and that's what turns normal dust into this layer of what looks like compacted mud on top of them."

At this point the three men had got the carpet folded up as far as the door, which was roughly the midpoint of the room, but as Fliss stepped into the room and closed the door to allow them to roll it past it, Sean shook his head.

"No, don't worry, Fliss. We'll cut it in two here. With it being damp, it'll be far too heavy to carry if we do the whole room in one go," and he produced a Stanley knife and began sawing across the carpet, which gave up the fight remarkably easily.

As Sean and Kevin lugged the first roll out to the skip, Fliss noticed that Bernie wore a worried frown.

"Is something wrong?" she asked.

Bernie grimaced. "When I quoted for this job, I was told that the carpet was on a flag-stone floor – one like the former kitchen has. But the thing is, Fliss, I couldn't inspect this one, because there was so much furniture in this room there wasn't anywhere where I could lift up an edge to check. So I had to take Eric Davenport and the Chandlers' word for it that it was onto flagstones, and I quoted on the basis of this floor being sound. The Chandlers said that they'd put this carpet down only a few years ago, you see – and on my visit, the centre bit was covered up by a huge rug, so I couldn't see it – so I presumed they knew what was beneath. I guess it must have been longer ago than they thought and the Chandlers had forgotten."

He shook his head despairingly. "But this? This is going to have to come up. There's no way around that. The tiles will have to come up and be chucked away because they're now rotten and crumbling, and then this whole area will have to be dug out to allow for a waterproof membrane to be put down. And the thing is, I'm going to have to ask Sean and Kevin to do that, because there's no way we could get something like a mini digger in here – it's going to have to be done by hand, and I can't do all of this by myself. So that's immediately going to be adding on their hourly rate to the cost."

"Is it going to come to that much more?" Fliss had no idea how many man-hours this was likely to take, but it was a big room, well over twelve feet wide and easily double that long.

Bernie sighed. "Well, yes, it is. Especially when you factor in needing to put some kind of proper floor surface in, whether that's floor boards with carpet, or the modern version of flagstones. And with a different client that wouldn't be a problem. If it was someone who wanted the job done right in order to live here, they'd be likely to stump up the cash. But the thing is, Fliss, my Jonas was the one who sent the Davenports to me. They'd approached the boys, you see, but one-off jobs like this don't interest them anymore. Jonas sent them to me saying that I'd do it on the cheap."

"Oh Lord!" Fliss could immediately envisage another row brewing between Bernie and his sons.

"Exactly! Even before this, it was never going to be a cheap job, and I had to argue my case over every step with the Davenports, pointing out that anyone else they went to wouldn't do it any cheaper, and many would charge a lot more," and he grimaced as he added, "and I think they phoned a few before they believed me.

"But if I now have to add even more onto the bill, it could lead to arguments, even though I made them sign a document saying that I had quoted the price on the basis of what they'd told me, because I'd not been able to do a full inspection of the property. Laying the membrane and a new floor isn't that expensive in terms of the materials – it's the labour cost that's going to push it up – and Mrs D is likely to go and start bawling and shouting at Jonas and Edmund that their old man is ripping them off, and I know my sons well enough to know that they'll be down here having a go at me quicker than you can say 'knife'."

"Oh, Bernie, I'm so sorry."

"And me," came Kevin's voice from the doorway. "Don't worry, Bernie, we'll come and do the heavy work for you, and you can pay us when you get paid. But don't you dare take any crap off your sons! They've dropped you in it with this job, and if they get some of the flack for it, they ought to man-up and take it."

Bernie smiled wanly and thanked him and Sean, but as they ripped up the rest of the carpet, Fliss could see that it was playing on Bernie's mind.

With it being a bit late in the day for the two men to start digging today, Fliss therefore suggested that they go and rip up the rest of the carpets. In what was the Davenport's dining room which had been the original kitchen, as Bernie had said, there really were lovely flagstones on the floor, so that needed no attention. The holiday let's lounge floor turned out to have very substantial oak floorboards under the underlay, and they at least were pronounced to be in good condition. So it was as they turned their attention to the later part of the house that they once again found oddities. Happily, beneath two layers of carpet, the hall floor turned out to be more quarry-tiles but of a much better quality. These too would have to be lifted and re-laid once cleaned up because of being uneven, but Bernie was much more confident that they had originally been put onto a proper base, if only because the walls of the stairs to the cellars going down from the hall showed no signed of sagging or bowing. In the lounge, however, they lifted an aging nineteen-seventies carpet which had once been sculpted – but was now nearly bald – and found a parquet floor underneath.

"Ooh!" Bernie exclaimed in admiration. "Now that's a nice bit of beech-wood! It'll have to be got up and checked for woodworm and things, but given that it's over the cellar, at least we know that it's sound underneath."

The dining room also proved to have similar parquet flooring, and so they were all rather disappointed to find that some vandal had ripped it up in what had been most recently the Chandlers' kitchen. On top of that, at some point something very heavy had been dragged over the main room floor, rather than having been lifted, and several of the parquet blocks had deep gouges in them.

"God knows what they hauled over this," Sean said in disgust, "but these are too deep to sand out without making the blocks much thinner. I reckon you'll have to ditch those blocks."

"I was thinking that," Bernie admitted. "I think the best thing we can do is get up all of the blocks, and then find the best of them to re-lay right the way through on this side once we've got the kitchen out, and removed the pipes and drains." He turned to Fliss. "Now that's something you can definitely do. We'll set you up in the garage, and you can scrub all the blocks off and find us all of the good ones."

"What about the lounge?" Fliss wondered.

"Oh, we'll go to a reclamation yard and find some more parquet," Bernie said confidently, "or even for this bigger space, if needs be. Lots of public buildings used to have parquet floors because they were so hard wearing, and as they've been pulled down, there's usually somewhere that's got a house floor's worth in storage. And the good thing for us with that is that they've usually been for much bigger spaces than we've got here, so even if some are damaged, we'll get a room of this size out of them."

And with Bernie sounding more cheerful, Fliss was only too willing to volunteer to drive so that they could all go and eat at the local steak-house-style pub with Kevin and Sean, and allow Bernie to have a couple of pints with them. She was silently blessing the two younger men, because they obviously had a huge regard for Bernie, and were more than willing to help him out. Without them, Fliss could see that they'd have very quickly become stuck as the job turned into something way bigger than Bernie could have allowed for. And privately, she was seething at both the Davenports and her cousins, because she could see that the Davenports had wanted something for nothing, and Bernie's sons had been spiteful enough to promise that on their dad's behalf. That made her angrier than she would have thought. Having had a father who didn't care less what happened to her, the fact that her cousins would blithely try to scam a loving father like Bernie both baffled and infuriated her, to the point that she would have given both of them a good telling off, if not a slapping, had they been within reach.

However, she said nothing, not wanting to upset Bernie further by hearing her criticise his sons, and allowed Sean and Kevin to jolly Bernie along until the evening became quite convivial. They didn't linger late, everyone aware that they needed to be back at work early the next morning, but Fliss was relieved to see that Bernie was more of his normal cheerful self when they got home. As he flopped in front of the TV again, she picked up her laptop and went looking for inspiration for colour schemes which would work with the slightly orange tints of the beech-wood parquet, inwardly sighing over the fact that it wouldn't have been her first choice for flooring because of the colour, but that if Bernie said it fitted the house, then for now she would have to go along with that. At some point in the future, hopefully she'd be able to suggest putting some more subtly coloured rugs down over the most visible parts, but tonight it was all about supporting Bernie after the way he'd supported her.

Luckily, the next day was spent with Kevin and Sean helping Bernie rip up the carpets in the upper part of the house, three of which some idiot had glued to the floorboards. And so Fliss found herself on her hands and knees, kneeler pads protecting her knees from the hard floor, with a scraper in her hand, trying to get the remnants of the carpets' undersides up off the floorboards. It was quite a relief to hear Bernie say that up on this first floor, it would be a case of laying new underlay and putting new carpets in, so she didn't need to get the boards to an absolute pristine finish. Even so, she was decidedly creaking in her back by the end of the day, and was more than a little relieved to realise that tomorrow was Friday. In her old job she'd longed for Fridays to roll around as the end of the inevitably stressful weeks. This was very different, and it was the unaccustomed physical exercise which had her gratefully realising that, come Saturday, she could have a proper lie-in.

In the meantime, while the men began lifting the orange hall's rotten quarry tiles, Fliss' task for Friday was to go and clean the floorboards up on the top floor. It was a gloomy day, with heavy showers scudding in regularly, and so up in these two rooms with their smaller windows, it was dark enough for Fliss to need the lights on. The original light bulbs were so feeble they were barely worth having on, but Bernie had brought several much stronger, low-energy bulbs with him, and Sean, as the one who was tall enough to reach them, was good enough to come and put one in each of the two top rooms for Fliss.

She was very glad of the starker light, because once again she got the shivers just stepping up onto the tiny top landing. With the old bulbs casting shadows into the corners of the rooms, she would have been jumping out of her skin every time something caught the corner of her vision. And there were more nooks and crannies up here. For a start off, the sweet little attic dormer windows might have looked attractive, but because they projected outwards, on the room's side they only threw light in a direct line from them. To the side of each of them facing the front, there were deep shadows, not helped by a whole family of spiders having woven their webs across the angles of the sloping ceilings on that side.

At the back of the rooms, things were slightly better in that there was more headroom, but although the landing in between them had the eyebrow window for light and a skylight above the void of the main stairs, the moment you went down the four steps to reach the servants' stairs, it was incredibly gloomy. Off to one side at this level, Fliss now realised that there was a door, and before she got down on her knees and started scrubbing again, she plucked up the courage to open the door and peer in.

As she looked in, suddenly there was another woman staring back at her in the half light, and she let out a squeak of shock, then almost as fast realised that it was her own reflection she was looking at.

"Bloody hell!" she gasped, leaning against the door jamb as she waited for her heart to stop pounding.

"Fliss? You okay up there?" Bernie's voice echoed up the stairwell.

"Yep, fine! Just scared myself to death, that's all!" Then she realised that in the nightmare of discovering all that extra work to be done, that Bernie, Sean and Kevin couldn't have looked in here, possibly assuming that it was merely a cupboard. But this was a proper small room, albeit one without any visible window, and it was crammed with furniture! Was all this what Mrs Davenport had wanted thrown out as well?

Groping at the side of the doorway, she found a light switch, and when she flicked it, it spluttered into life revealing that the room went across every bit as far towards the side of the Queen Anne frontage as the room in front of it did, going by what she could see of the ceiling. And if it had a light in it, what was the betting it might have a plug somewhere too? That would mean it was connected to the rest of the house, and would need to be rewired alongside it. Phil was going to need to get into here.

"Bernie?" she called down. "I think you'd better come and look at this!"

"What have you found?" she heard him saying with a chuckle, as he plodded up the stairs. Then when he got to the turn in the servants' stairs where he could see the doorway Fliss was standing by, "Oh bugger! Where did all of that come from?"

"I thought you might not have realised this lot was here," Fliss apologised, "but it struck me that if there's a light, then it must be part of the lighting ring up here, and therefore connected to all of the other electrics. Phil's going to have to get in here, isn't he?"

Bernie groaned but nodded, complimenting her with, "Well done for finding that. I thought it was just some cupboard under the eaves. Nobody said anything about it being a full room. Mrs D said it was just a cupboard and at the time I was worrying about the bigger picture, not some cubbyhole, but you're right Fliss, this is going to have to be emptied."

By this stage Bernie had come to stand by her and was looking into the room. "You know, the Davenports and the Chandlers have been a bit remiss in dismissing this. This is genuine antique furniture, not just the old stuff we hauled out of the cellars. I don't think we ought to be sticking this lot out into the damp of the garage."

Fliss was already thinking hard and wondered aloud, "If I can get the floors scrubbed up here, could we move this stuff into the two front bedrooms, or whatever they were originally? If we make sure that Phil has access to whichever floorboards he'll need to lift, surely he won't be needing to do that much up here when there's only the two front rooms and this cupboard-room?"

Bernie brightened visibly. "That's actually a really good thought. I'm sure that Phil will run these lights off the same ring as the floor below. It's hardly a huge electrical ring by modern standards, and in answer to your question, no, he won't need to do much up here once he's got the lights for down below sorted."

"That's all good then, isn't it?" Fliss said encouragingly. "So if I crack on and get at least one of the rooms scrubbed up before Kev and Sean leave, they can help us move most of this stuff into that room. Some of it can still stay if it's not in Phil's way. Once they've helped us get it up those three steps onto the bedroom level, it wouldn't be as hard for us to shift a few pieces through to the other room on our own if we need to, or even leave a couple of bits on the landing."

With that thought in mind, she set to with a vengeance at scrubbing the floorboards, getting the dust of ages up off them. When she'd done the one room, Bernie was able to easily identify which floor boards would need to come up for Phil, in no small measure because it was clear which ones had been lifted in the past, probably for similar work. And so as the light began to fade, Kevin and Sean came upstairs and helped moved the furniture out into the bedroom.

The first wardrobe, which had the mirrored door which had startled Fliss, was a gentleman's wardrobe – very nice with its walnut veneer, but not a piece Fliss would ever want, being rather heavy and brooding. However, the next wardrobe they brought out had Fliss gasping in delight.

"Oh, isn't that lovely!" she exclaimed. "Look at all of the painted scenes on it! How fabulous!"

"Is it?" Bernie said, perplexed. "It's a nice bit of early Victorian or maybe Georgian, I'll grant you, but not that special."

Fliss felt herself blushing as she confessed, "I know, but I loved *The Lion, the Witch and the Wardrobe* as a kid, and I always imagined the wardrobe they walked through to Narnia looking something like this." She didn't dare add that there had been so many times she had prayed for a way out of her bedroom at home into somewhere like Narnia – or even better, Middle-earth. That wasn't a confession she wanted to make in front of Kevin and Sean.

Sean laughed, and with a cheeky wink to her, opened the door. "Sorry, Fliss, no back way out of this one. Just a lot of old spiders' webs."

Fliss felt her blush deepening at his teasing, even though she knew there was no malice in it. "I know," she confessed, "I just meant that I always hoped that one day I'd have a lovely piece like this, not just some grotty flat-packed thing which fell apart after ten years, if I was lucky enough for it even to last that long."

Bernie had obviously said something to both men when she hadn't been around about what she'd been through, because she immediately got a hug around her shoulders from Sean, with him saying,

"Well since the Davenports have said they've had all their stuff out of the house, and the Chandlers left it behind, I'd say it's a case of finders keepers. You grab it, Fliss, if you want it that bad. Who the hell else is going to care?" Then couldn't resist adding, "But if you vanish one day, we'll know where you've gone!"

Chapter 8

The weekend

One thing Fliss had already learned after living at Bernie's for a few weeks was that Saturdays were dominated by the sporting fixtures for him, and she would never have said a word against that. Bernie had worked hard all of his life, and if this was what gave him his relaxation time, he'd well and truly earned it. However, Fliss had never had the remotest interest in sports, but whereas previously she'd gone and found somewhere quiet to sit and read, or to listen to her own music, for the first time she felt it would be nice to get out. And so assuring Bernie that she was feeling much more confident again, Fliss decided she needed some retail therapy. Or at least, not so much spending her currently limited money, but going around to the places where they sold the paints to see what they looked like off-screen.

She was also now feeling the tug to go and have a look at some things like rugs and curtain material. It would be disastrous to pick a lovely paint colour, but then find that it was near impossible to get any of the soft furnishings to match, whether it was for an as yet unknown buyer, or for her and Bernie. And it had been so very long since Fliss had had any need to purchase anything like that, she had no idea what was readily available, as opposed to the high-end ranges she'd seen advertised in magazines.

Of course, down in London there would probably be no problem in finding a huge variety to choose from, but Fliss was alert to the fact that out here in the shires there wouldn't be as many wealthy clients, and also that she and Bernie were working to a definite budget. And although there was a wonderful fabric shop in Malvern, which she knew from past visits had a glorious selection for home furnishings, she wasn't feeling quite strong enough yet to venture onto her parents' territory, not least because there was the strong possibility of walking into her mother on Saturdays. So instead, she decided to venture first to an antiques place she'd seen out of town on the Bromyard Downs, and then maybe head up to Bromyard itself, or even Leominster.

Luckily, Bernie kept a compact little car for just running about in, as Fliss wouldn't have felt confident driving the big truck into packed car parks on a Saturday. So she was soon heading out into the countryside, singing along to one of her favourite artists on the car stereo, and thinking that this was the best weekend she'd had in far too many years. What felt odder was a growing certainty that Sytchampton House was *her* house. Common sense told her that at best she would have something like a third share in it with Bernie, because while she would definitely get a good price for her London place, it wasn't going to buy her more than that with what the house would fetch once renovated. And while she was intensely grateful to Bernie for even offering her a part ownership – if he did actually buy it, which was by no means certain – then she would have to stand back and let him choose which parts he wanted for himself, since he was paying the lion's share.

He's had enough with his sons making all sorts of brattish demands, she thought. *I absolutely can't start saying what I will and won't do. That would be too horrible for him for words. So why is it that I can see myself taking on the front half, when I would have expected to want the older bits? I love all the old beams and the flagstone floors, and I know Bernie does too, but this is more than me already accepting that he will probably have first call on those. What is it about those upper rooms, especially, that keep calling to me? And why am I still getting the shudders walking between the two halves on the first floor, and up on that top floor, but not anywhere else?*

She was no closer to answering her own questions by the time she reached her first destination, and although it was surprising to see the price tags on some of the pieces of furniture similar to those they had discovered in the storeroom, and to realise that they must be far better quality than she'd realised, nothing really grabbed her eye there with the paint range they had on offer. Moving on, she went exploring various shops and showrooms, yet never quite finding what she was looking for. Some of the paint ranges had lovely colours, and were obvious very good quality, but she couldn't see anything that she instantly thought, 'ooh, that's right for the one front bedroom,' or, 'that would look so good in the old kitchen!' The modern paints were just too bright for the old house, even the pastels. And she was also taking into account that Bernie had said that they would need to use paints designed to go over old plaster. Some of the brands did that kind of range, yet she just couldn't find quite the right colours, and what was in a way worse, no colours she thought she would be able to match with any colour of soft furnishings except perhaps grey.

Why do you 'know' that that particular blue is too cold for those first-floor bedrooms? she questioned herself. *You loved the soft blue you had in your bedroom in the flat. You never thought that looked cold. Where are these thoughts coming from? Why can you keep seeing a soft yellow on the walls of the one attic room, and a warm peachy kind of colour on the other one? They aren't colours you've even seen on your Pinterest boards in houses like that. So why are you so certain that they'll work?*

The one thing which she took away from her journey around the wider district was that she had vastly under estimated how dark most of the furniture of the period was, even when seen under modern lighting not the gloom of the storeroom. While it wasn't the black oak of the beams in the older half of the house, nonetheless much of it was still heading into the deep and dark browns. Whether all of the hardwoods had been quite as dark originally, or whether they had been darkened by generations of ardent polishing, she wasn't able to tell, but in almost all of those pieces she saw, the wood was far too nice to cover up with paint. Therefore although it was very much the current trend to paint dark furniture, she also accepted that it was one thing to see a superb job by someone who'd had lots of practice, and that it would be a wholly different thing if she did it herself. Wielding a roller at a wall under Bernie's strict supervision was one thing. Achieving the kind of flawless finish that most of this furniture deserved was another, and over the course of the afternoon, Fliss developed an abiding dread of wrecking a beautiful piece with her amateur and probably ham-fisted efforts.

It's no good, she thought as she turned towards Ledbury again, *you're going to have to decide where you're going to put the furniture you're both going to keep. If it's in the old part, then all well and good. The plan can still go ahead to do that in light, pastel colours. But if you or Bernie decide that some of those big pieces are staying in the Queen Anne end, then you might have to revise the idea of doing that half in warmer, richer colours. If you carry on with those colour schemes with dark furniture too, it's going to be as dark as a pit in the bedrooms!* And of course, if the house needed to be furnished rather more than it was now for a photo shoot – should the Davenports want to market it through the county magazines – then the way to show it off to its best would be with a few carefully selected antique pieces from what they'd found. But those would still pose the same problem of being dark wood.

Yet once back at Bernie's she had to stop, realising that Bernie found it much easier to switch off to the week than she did – which was probably a lot healthier, but old habits were still lingering with her.

However, once they'd breakfasted on Sunday morning, she felt she could legitimately bring up the subject of colour schemes, if only so that they could get the paint ordered. The one brand of paints Fliss had eventually picked potential colours out from was a brand leader for period properties, and available through some of the big DIY stores. But another was very much more specialist, working hand-in-glove with the National Trust, and although there were local stockists, one look at their online lists had Fliss doubting whether any of the local places were big enough businesses to be carrying the whole range. If they were going for these paints, they would have to buy them direct, and that might mean placing an order this week just to get them in time.

"How soon do you think we're going to be starting to put paint on?" she asked Bernie, as they looked at the online colour charts of paints, plus the colour cards Fliss had picked up. "I know that you said that Phil will have to do his thing with the electrics first, and there's all that digging to put the membrane in in the oldest hall. But surely I could be doing some preparation and then painting in the rooms that don't need that much work on them? I'm thinking of the bedrooms in particular, and especially in the Queen Anne bit. If you think that the plaster is sound in some of those rooms, then I might as well make myself useful. After all, I can hardly help with the digging and stuff – I'm just not fit enough yet for that."

Bernie was nodding thoughtfully. "Yes, that's a good point, Fliss. Mr and Mrs Chandler had the roof inspected only a few years ago, and the front bit was fine. They had a bit of a leak in a couple of the gullies on the older bit, and those I shall have to do some plastering on where it's dried and flaked. At the very least some will need a new skim over them. But if you can carry on on your own in other parts until I can get around to that, it would help move things on a lot."

"Great! So which brand of paint do you favour?"

However, Bernie's reply of, "If you mean which is the better one technically, there's nothing to choose from between them. They'll both do equally as well on old plaster. It rather depends on what you were thinking of for the colour schemes," didn't help Fliss much.

"Okay… I'm thinking that we don't go too far off the expected norms. After all, we can't absolutely guarantee that we're going to be the ones who end up buying this place, can we?"

"No, I think that's sensible. And if we want to get paid for the work before the Davenports have agreed a sale – whether us or someone else – then it's got to appear to be sellable."

"I was looking at things like bedding and curtains in some of the stores yesterday, and at the end of the day, people are still pretty conservative for the most part over what colours they want things like their duvet covers and sheets in. Okay, you might get one with lots of flowers on it, for instance, but in that kind of case you can bet that the base colour will be white or cream."

"I see what you mean," Bernie agreed. "Okay, so what colours were you thinking of for the bedrooms?"

"Well, I think we shouldn't go too far from pinks, soft blues, or greens, and of course creams and ivory shades, and maybe a pale peach shade – so definitely keeping to the conventional pastels. Grey is an 'in' colour at the moment, but could both date badly, and doesn't really fit the house time-wise – I can't ever recall seeing just plain grey on any walls in National Trust houses. I love yellow, and that imperial yellow is certainly of the time, but it's awfully hard to match bedding to unless it's a nice pale colour that's almost cream anyway."

She had seen how Bernie flinched at the word 'pink', hurriedly adding, "Of course when I say pink, I don't mean we have to stick to some awful sugar pink that a teenage girl might pick. This one, for instance," and she tapped a colour chart, "is a nice faded dusty rose colour. And I'd probably only do one wall in that just to warm it up," Fliss hurriedly added.

"For the rest of it I'd go for the paler Calamine, which is barely pink at all, with this very soft Great White on things like the ceiling."

"Very nice!" Bernie complimented her. "Yes, I can't imagine many men balking at sleeping in a room in those colours. It's feminine, alright, but not sickly sweet.

He was rather more surprised when she chose a colour called Orange Coloured White for the first of the top floor rooms.

"Didn't you say that you didn't want to go too pale in the front of the house?" he queried.

"Yes, I did until I looked at how dark so much antique bedroom furniture is, and to be honest I would have liked something like a warmer, apricot colour. But nobody seems to do that colour in the right kinds of paints for the old plaster. I'm trying to get some variety in the colours between the rooms," she told him, hardly able to say that her senses were screaming at her for apricot shades somewhere up on that top floor, even if she couldn't quite pinpoint where as yet.

"So many of the yellow paints are heading for the acidic kind, and you tend to get full-on orange or nothing in the brochures, not just this one. But the only yellows you get in any sort of bedding tend to be towards the pastel lemon shades – they just don't match – so in that case it needs to be something that goes with cream. And I'd been thinking of some of the warmer Indian colours you can get in cushions and fabrics nowadays, but they don't necessarily go with these paint colours either."

"Indian colours? You're not still fretting over those two little boys, are you?"

Good grief, there was no fooling Bernie! Yet Fliss was able to say in truth,

"Not exactly. It was just that knowing about them, I wondered whether the owner of the time might have brought richer coloured stuff back from India with him? I mean things like rugs, not as a decorating style of itself. And I thought that something warm and cheerful would suit those attic rooms."

And where the heck did that thought come from? she silently demanded of herself. Because as the words had left her mouth, she'd had a distinct impression of lying in bed under one of those sloping ceilings, and seeing a very strong yellow colour, which had felt almost oppressive. But whose thoughts were they? Not the Indian boys' presumably? They would have been far more used to strong colours, and anyway, that had felt more as if it was an adult, and someone sleeping in a bigger bed than a child would have.

"Fliss?" Bernie's voice cut through her musings. "I said, would this First Light be a better choice?"

"Yes, it would," Fliss hurriedly replied, not wanting to have to confess any further mental wanderings. "Yes, that's nowhere near as strong, and yet it's still got that element of warmth about it."

"Fine, well if you're sure about those, I'll check that they're in stock in the morning so that we know we can get them fairly quickly. As long as the bedrooms are liveable in, I can't imagine anyone is going to protest about the colours. It's the main living rooms that tend to make or break sales, and unfortunately, we're going to have to get an agent into value the place before we make an offer. And I daren't risk Mrs bloody Davenport accusing us of making it unsellable just to drive the price down. This really has got to look its best."

"I'll work on the ideas for the downstairs rooms as we go," Fliss promised.

"And I'll order a bulk lot of this near-white Flint distemper for the bedrooms in the older part to start off with," Bernie decided. "If we've prepared the old panels between the beams with that, if we want to add some colour in at the end, then it'll be easy enough to paint over something as neutral as that. I'll show you how to cut into the nooks and crannies when you come to paint those rooms. You'll be quite the pro once you've finished!"

Yet for all that Fliss smiled brightly back at him, she couldn't help the thought sneaking in that she didn't really want to work on any house other than this one. *You've found your home*, her rebellious thoughts insisted. *Why would you bother with anywhere else?* To which the other practical part of her said sternly, *because I can't guarantee that I'm going to keep it, and anyway, at some point I'm going to have to start earning my keep*. Then felt a strange shiver run down her spine as her other inner voice said, *not if you stay in the house forever.*

Chapter 9

Monday

In typical workman fashion, when they started up again on Monday morning, Fliss discovered that Sean and Kevin had brought a radio with them, which blasted out one of the local radio stations at a volume so that they could hear it as they wielded shovels. Phil also turned up and had his talk-show radio of choice going in the cellar, all of which meant that Fliss was glad to retreat to the quiet upstairs, after showing willing and making the first of no doubt many batches of mugs of tea. Having been used to the quieter hum of office life, she really did find the blasting radios an assault to her senses, so it was with something akin to relief that she shut the door of the one attic bedrooms and felt the quiet descend.

"Phew!" she breathed, putting down the portable heater and its power pack on the floor, and going to open the dormer window a crack. It was another chilly spring day, and since she was going to start washing down the walls, Bernie had suggested that a bit of warmth in the room might help both them to dry, and Fliss to not catch her death from cold, despite the extra jumpers she had on under her overall.

As she opened the little sash window, she felt an impulse to lean out of it. Something felt so familiar about leaning on the sill and just looking out over the frost decked garden to the countryside beyond. And it wasn't just that it was the kind of view she had always dreamed of having from her bedroom window. There was a strange 'you've done this before' sensation …or was it, 'you're going to do this soon,' accompanied by the strong and distinctly weird feeling that it would nevertheless be in the past, not her current future?

Utterly disconcerted by this, Fliss moved smartly away from the window and focused on the bucket of hot water she had also lugged up the stairs. With all of the electricity off now, so that Phil could work on putting a whole new fuse board in as his first priority, she was going to have to go up and down stairs to replenish her bucket, since the only hot water was currently coming from the kettle run off Bernie's portable generator.

You're going to be nothing if not fit, going up and down three flights of stairs all day, she mentally sighed, and wondered why she had volunteered to start at the top of the house. *Damned fool!* she chided herself. *Why didn't you start your cleaning in part of the old house? You'd have had far less walking to do with a hefty bucket.*

Because this bit is more important, that irritating little voice in her head immediately responded.

"Oh go away!" she muttered sternly under her breath, as she began attacking the spiders' webs.

With as much as possible cleared away with a dry cloth, she pulled on some sturdy rubber gloves and began the washing down process. She was so absorbed in what she was doing, and having to squint a bit in the poor light to see if she'd got the dark marks off, that she wasn't really aware of what she was hearing until she stood back to survey her work. Very faintly, she could hear someone singing.

Puzzled, she went to the window and looked out, expecting to see someone delivering something and singing along to their car radio. But as she looked down at the drive and saw nobody, she was immediately mentally kicking herself. Who on earth would be delivering here? Because that was a woman's voice, of that she was sure. Yet in her still rather city-orientated way of thinking, she had immediately thought of the girl who had brought readymade sandwiches around to the offices in the block where she'd worked, who'd always walked around singing cheerily.

Don't be an idiot, she told herself, *who could make a go of a business like that out here? The cost of driving around to far-flung places would wipe out the little profit you'd make on the food. Get a grip, Fliss, you're not in London now.*

Moreover, as soon as she'd leaned out of the window of the south-east room where she'd been scrubbing, the voice had immediately vanished. But as soon as she'd returned to the room and closed the window to just a crack once more, she could again hear it. Whatever the tune was, it wasn't anything she was remotely familiar with, but even odder, she suddenly heard a sound as if of someone shaking out fabric.

What? …Fabric? …Why? …And why up here?

"Oh you idiot!" she muttered. "Sheets! It's the sound of someone making a bed. You heard that enough times at Granny's," thinking of her much-loved and missed paternal grandmother, who had been as perplexed as anyone over her son's coldness towards his children, and who had done her best to compensate for that in the years she had been alive.

Nice crisp cotton sheets, that's what that sound is, she told herself. But then frowned in confusion as it dawned on her that there was nobody up here besides herself, and there wasn't even a bed to make up here, much less any sheets.

For a brief moment she wondered if someone was trying to deliberately freak her out. She'd known one woman a few years ago who'd gone through hell with a husband who'd tried to gaslight her into think her grip on sanity was slipping just to get an easier divorce. *But you don't have a husband!* her distraught subconscious chimed in with. *That's why you're such a mess at the moment. If you'd had a husband, you'd have had kids, and then you wouldn't have had the bloody breakdown! …Oh, for the love of God, stop it, Fliss! Nobody's trying to gaslight you! Who the hell would have any reason to? Certainly not Bernie, and Sean and Kevin have no motive. For pity's sake, stop doubting everyone! Not everyone's hand is turned against you like your parents and brother. …But then why can you hear it?*

Yet as soon as she'd thought the words, the voice vanished.

It's a radio, she lectured herself sternly. *Phil was listening to a talk show, so maybe he's a bit more of the intellectual and likes listening to plays on things like* Radio 3*? Or maybe he was just retuning the damned thing and picked something up in passing?*

Shaking her head at her own gullibility and foolishness, Fliss went and replenished her bucket with clean water, being very careful to not say a word of what she thought she'd heard to the men downstairs. When she went back up, Phil followed her, and after some grubbing around under the floorboards, and also peering up into the limited space under the roof ridge, declared that the lighting ring would begin in the room she was currently working in.

"The wires from here go out onto the landing and then into the other bedroom, before going back into the store room and coming to make the return down the stairs just by here. I'm sorry, Fliss, but I need to start in this room."

"Oh, that's okay, I can make a start on the other bedroom up here until you need to move through into there."

Phil looked relieved, but then asked warily, "Can we move this big wardrobe back towards the wall a bit? I need to get my stepladder in here," pointing up to the central ceiling rose.

"Sure," Fliss agreed readily. "It won't hurt for these walls to dry out a bit. I don't want to scrub too hard unless I really need to, and I can't tell what's damp from washing and what are marks at the moment. We should be able to move the wardrobe between the two of us, even though it's a bit of a monster."

To her surprise, far from them struggling to get the tall wardrobe back into the space by the landing wall, it actually slid into place as if it had been made for that space.

"Well I never!" Fliss gasped. "Look at the fading on the paintwork. It's the exact shape of the wardrobe! No wonder nobody ever struggled downstairs with it. It was probably made for this room."

Dusting his jeans off, Phil nodded. "Bernie would tell you more if that's right or not, but from what I can see, I think you might have a point. There's a bit where that moulding on the top of the wardrobe pokes out, and it matches the paint fading a bit too well to be accidental, doesn't it?"

He disappeared to go and bring his steps and tools up, leaving Fliss alone and with the chance to look inside the wardrobe briefly.

"*Phwar*! Mothballs!" she coughed, as the unmistakable smell hit her full on as she opened the double doors. The bit she was looking into had a hanging rail across its width, so it had definitely been for clothes, not bed-linen, so that wasn't connected to what she'd heard. The biggest drawer underneath might once have possibly held blankets, but somehow Fliss thought that a house of this size would have had a specific linens cupboard, not be using part of the family's clothes storage. So where had that sound of sheets come from, unless it was all a product of her overwrought imagination?

Investigating further, above the hanging space there was a small upper shelf, which Fliss guessed might have held things like hats, but remembering the child's letters, she reached up and patted around as far as she could stretch to until something stabbed her finger.

"Ouch!" she gasped, pulling her hand back sharply and seeing to her amazement a large and ornate hatpin still caught in her skin. It wasn't embedded deeply, nor anything serious, but a bubble of blood was already seeping out.

"Good grief, Fliss, you're bleeding!" Bernie's voice came from behind her, and she turned to see him holding Phil's steps, while Phil had his tool box and a large roll of electrical cable.

"Hatpin," she explained, brandishing the offending object. "I was just making sure that the wardrobe was empty and it was on the top shelf."

Turning it over in her other hand she realised that it was quite magnificent thing. "I bet someone missed it. It looks a bit too good to just randomly lose. Some of the stones in the pin end look like they might be gemstones, though hardly diamonds or sapphires."

"Well just be a bit more careful," Bernie admonished her, fishing a plaster out of one of his pockets and expertly wrapping her finger in it. "I never thought to ask if your tetanus vaccinations are up to date, so maybe that's something we need to get done. I don't want you getting sick again on my account."

Fliss smiled at Bernie's fussing over her. Her own father had never done anything like that, not even sticking a plaster on when she'd fallen over as a small child, which made it a novel but pleasant experience. What would it be like to live with someone who truly cared about what happened to her? She couldn't change the past, but was it too much to hope that the future might be different?

"Thanks, 'dad'," she teased gently. "Now as you're up here, what do you think – did this wardrobe always live in here?"

Bernie's eyes went wide. "Oh yes! Blimey, this must have been made for this room. Look at the ornate moulding on the top. That's been made to look like some architectural fancy, but in fact it mirrors the slope of the ceiling. And speaking of mirrors, those aren't original to the doors. They didn't know how to make mirrors lightweight enough to hang like that back then. Those must have been put on it later on in something like the late Victorian era. Shame really, because that will detract from its value."

"Then shall we leave Phil in here to do his stuff and go and have a quick look to see if any of the other pieces are like that? Made for one of these rooms, I mean. If they are, I can try and work with them in terms of design. It happens that if I just swop the colours I picked for these two top rooms over, then the warmer tones of the wood on this one will work with that soft orange-white we picked out. It doesn't matter that much which room is more peachy than yellow, but we need to be sure about furniture for the other rooms now, don't we? Especially as you said about downstairs being crucial in terms of making or breaking a sale."

And so, leaving Phil taking out wiring that had him sucking through his teeth in professional dismay at its age and state, and muttering darkly that it was amazing that the whole place hadn't gone up in smoke years ago, they went first to the couple of pieces out on the landing.

"Do you know, that big old chest might well have been a linen chest which always sat under the window here," Bernie said thoughtfully, making Fliss' stomach lurch.

Thank heavens he wasn't looking at her to see her jaw drop at that statement, because it echoed far too eerily her earlier experience. Could she have heard someone getting sheets out of that? It had been close enough for her to hear. Then she shook her head in frustration at herself. Of course she couldn't have! That was just plain stupid. She'd have had to be hearing things back through time for that to happen, and that was a ridiculous notion. *Yes, but it's more than a bit spooky the way it links with what you imagined you heard, isn't it? You had no idea that this was a linen chest when it got hauled out, and you didn't even touch it then because it was too heavy.*

Then her thoughts were broken as she realised that Bernie had opened the box's lid and was exclaiming,

"Good Lord, there's still some stuff in here! No wonder it was bloody heavy!"

"Really?" Fliss peered in and saw that what the men had assumed in the half-light was the bottom of the chest was, in fact, old brown paper impregnated with mothballs, under which was a layer of folded cloth. Or rather several pieces of cloth.

"I think I'd better go and get some of the bin bags we brought with us, and carefully lift those out. If they're really old, we don't want them getting steamed up as I scrub, do we?" She leaned in and gently felt the fabric. "Gosh, it's really good quality stuff! I was expecting quite coarse cotton, but this is lovely. It should probably go to a museum somewhere, or maybe the National Trust could make use of it in one of their houses? It's far too good to throw out," she said, hoping like mad that her voice wasn't shaking as much as the rest of her over this discovery. How and why had she thought of crisp cotton sheets when she hadn't even known that they were right here already? That was too spooky for words!

Bernie gently closed the lid. "Well let's go and see if there are any more surprises. Then I can get back downstairs, and you can empty the chest."

Sure enough, another large wardrobe in the other bedroom looked as though it belonged there, and had Bernie teasing Fliss,

"Are you sure you're not psychic? Because it was you telling us where to put the furniture we got out of the storeroom, and it's too weird for words that we should have got both wardrobes in the right rooms."

And in truth, that disconcerted Fliss more than she was prepared to let on, because it really had been she who had made those choices. She had been the one flitting between the bedrooms, working out which and how many pieces they could fit into each one without impeding Phil's work, while Kevin and Sean did the heavy lifting. Bernie had mainly been shoving the furniture around in the old storeroom, checking for any sockets, and making sure that the right floorboards were accessible. Nobody had influenced her decisions, and thinking back to that afternoon, she realised that in all of the hurry to get things shifted, she hadn't had to think twice about what went where, she had *known*, and that now scared her. *How* had she known? How could she have known? *Oh God, I hope I'm not cracking up again*, she prayed.

Something which sent an even bigger shiver down her spine was realising that the beautiful wood veneer on this old wardrobe had a distinct yellowish tint to it. She had no idea what the wood was – possibly something exotic – but there were what she thought of as veins within the grain which went much closer to yellow than the orange tints of the other piece. It was ornately carved at the top, but not so much that it wouldn't appeal to modern tastes, and was in remarkably good condition.

"I reckon this is French, you know," Bernie said thoughtfully. "And on consideration, I don't think this was made for this room in particular like the other one was. It just happens that it fits this room's end wall nicely. Nice bit of oak, too."

"That's oak? I wouldn't have thought that. It's more the colour of pine."

"Oh, it all depends on what they did with it in the first place. Oak doesn't have to be dark. But on the other hand, this could be walnut, just of a different origin to the other furniture. It's completely natural stuff, Fliss, wood doesn't come in one uniform size or colour any more than people do." He turned around and looked at the other wardrobe in the room.

"Now this could be pine underneath the paint."

This was the wardrobe which she had fallen instantly in love with. There was no big bottom drawer on this one, just an attractive plinth and then two large doors, which kept calling Fliss to open wide and step through, even though she knew she would only see the inside.

"And I reckon this is French, too," Bernie continued. "See? That scene on the top panel is surely Paris, even though it was done long before the Eifel Tower was built. And I reckon this other scene is Marseille's port of the time."

"Is this Rococo?" Fliss asked, wishing that she was better informed about periods of art history.

"With these pictures of ladies in pink dresses on swings hanging from trees? Oh yes! When we get home, have a look online at the art of the period. This, I'm guessing, is a local artist trying to copy the paintings he's seen in some grand house further afield. It's nothing like well done enough to be valuable, and certainly not in the same league as say Poussin, or Claude Lorrain – who are the two famous artists of the era I know of – but it's a damned good stab at reproducing the style. And I suspect that this wasn't done the moment that style became fashionable. This is after it's filtered down to the masses over a generation or two, because it took longer to spread back then without modern mass media."

"But even so, isn't this all a bit cosmopolitan for that time? I mean, we've got an Indian connection and now a French one, too. Isn't that weird for a place we've said was just an English gentleman's house, not one of the nobility's?"

"Oh no," Bernie said confidently. "You've got to remember, Fliss, that before the Napoleonic Wars – and to some extent afterwards, too – it was quite the 'done' thing to send your teenage son off on the Grand Tour. It was supposed to polish them into young men of the world, but I've always thought that it was more like the Ibiza club scene of the day – you pack your kids off to let them run wild for a bit, without having to suffer them coming home off their faces, and puking up everywhere in your own house," and he laughed.

"Wow! You're very knowledgeable about all of this. Where on earth did you learn it?"

Bernie grimaced. "Too many years of being married to your Aunt Margot is the short answer in this case. Oh, she had grandiose ideas of sending Jonas and Edmund off on an equivalent tour after watching some costume drama. One look at the state they arrived back in after a fortnight in Ibiza was enough to put the tin hat on that! Not to mention the hole in our bank balance after we'd had to foot the bill for repairs to their hotel room."

"Blimey!" Fliss hadn't realised that her cousins had been quite such spoiled tearaways. "If I'd ever done something like that, my parents would have thrown me out, and sent me back to work at the place until I'd paid the bill myself!"

There was another wince. "Aye, well I did suggest something of the kind, though not anything quite that drastic, but Margot wasn't having it. She was just determined from then on to keep her precious boys tied to her apron strings. Nothing I said would convince her that they'd done all of those things of their own accords, you see. She was adamant that some 'bad boys' had dragged her darlings into trouble."

"Oh Bernie, I'm so sorry, I had no idea."

"Ach, it's all a long time ago now, don't upset yourself over it. But in answer to your question, I know about this because the other thing about being married to Margot was that the only time I got the chance to pick what was on TV was on a Saturday afternoon, when she went out shopping."

That explained Bernie's passion for sport, Fliss thought. It really had been his only escape.

"But I couldn't stand the mindless drivel she had on most of the time," he continued, "so I used to read. In the early days, when the boys were small, it was anything to help me switch off from work and help me sleep. But over the years I got really interested in history. Diving back into a past era helped me to switch off to the present, and I started fairly predictably with military history. Then as time went on, I started wanting to know about what had gone on around that, not least because there came a point when I was working on an old building, and suddenly realised that it was from the same period as I'd been reading about only the night before. That kind of thing gave it a real immediacy for me."

"Goodness, yes, I can see that it would. You don't think it's odd, then, to find French furniture in a house like this?"

"I'm not saying that every house had some, Fliss, but you have to bear in mind that quite often the son of a household like this might have been in the army.

That would account for both the Indian connection and the French. Even a humble lieutenant might have fathered sons on a native girl, or brought souvenirs home from a campaign – after all, France isn't that far away, and you need to also bear in mind that back then the River Severn was navigable to up beyond Worcester to quite large vessels. It might have been as easy as having these pieces shipped to a wharf in Worcester, and then just being brought by cart up here. Some men even stayed on to live in France for a while after that war, so this could have been legitimately his having actually bought it, and then brought it home with him a few years later."

There you go, Fliss told herself sternly, *a perfectly sensible and down to earth explanation for all of this. Stop jumping at shadows or you will make yourself ill again.*

Chapter 10

Monday

With her inner trembling squashed, Fliss felt more capable of focusing on the task at hand once more, and pulling herself together said,

"The good thing is that both of these pieces could stay in this room. They'd look great against that First Light colour we picked out. It's creamy enough to show them to their best."

Bernie was scrutinising the floorboards. "You know, we could just sand these down and then varnish or wax them. With a nice thick rug in here, with those wardrobes it would be very in keeping. Thank God that idiot didn't glue the carpet down in this room."

"I really like that idea," Fliss enthused. "Given that it's a bedroom, and at the top of the house, I can't imagine many people will traipse through here in outside shoes, so it could even be a cream rug. That wouldn't half lighten this room up."

Feeling much more settled and in the present, Fliss helped Bernie ease the yellow oak wardrobe over to almost against the wall which backed onto the landing.

"We're going to have to put a stopper on the floor to prevent the door crashing back into it," Bernie observed, "and I'm guessing that that's what that hole in the floorboards is from. Someone in the past did the same. So where do you want to put your Narnia wardrobe, Fliss? I know that down at floor level, this room's probably about sixteen feet either way, but by the time you take out the window wall with its sloping ceiling, which also makes the right-hand side of the fireplace too low as well, you haven't got a lot of wall space left if you also think about getting a double bed in here. Regardless of what we want, we're going to have to present it to an agent as a viable double room, I fear."

"I was thinking more of a single or queen-sized, to be honest," Fliss admitted. "But wouldn't the wardrobe go into the other fire-side alcove? I don't mean straight in – I can see that it probably wouldn't fit that way – but sideways on? Surely there's room for the one door to open in that alcove?"

Bernie waved a cautionary finger. "Before we break our backs shifting it across the room, then, let's have a measure up," and he fished a steel measuring tape from a pocket. "Here, you hold this end against that end of the wardrobe and let's see how wide it really is."

Yet as Fliss put her hand with the tape firmly against the wardrobe, it was like getting a strong static shock. Mercifully her gasp of pain was covered by Bernie saying,

"Four feet six …hmmm, might just do it, you know," and him walking over to the alcove trailing the tape, and leaving Fliss to scurry after him on distinctly wobbly legs. "Well would you look at that! Straight in, and with an inch to spare! And that will cover the thickness of the skirting board on either side at the bottom. …Right then, let's flex those muscles of yours and get it roughly over here. We won't fully push it back until we've painted behind it, but it can come over by the fireplace and not be in Phil's way."

Scarcely able to bring herself to touch the wardrobe again, Fliss gritted her teeth as she grasped either side, but to her relief this time, although she got a definite tingling through her fingers, the shock and pain were nothing like as bad. With care they walked the wardrobe backwards, not wanting to scuff the boards the way the parquet had been damaged downstairs. And so Fliss immediately halted when Bernie's muffled voice called out,

"Hang on! We've got a wonky floorboard here!"

"Is it one Phil's going to need to get up?" Fliss asked, walking around to Bernie at the back in order to see.

"No," Bernie said confidently, pointing toward the centre of the room to where Fliss could now see that two boards were obviously loose. "That's where he'll need to get to. See? There's a socket over by the window, and then one opposite on the back wall. Phil's said he'll move both of them a bit towards the fireplace, which is why I've lifted the next two boards for him, and he'll put another double one in over by the door too. Modern houses need far more electrical points than in the past, even in bedrooms if you allow for bedtime TV watching and things. People who'll buy posh houses like this will want that." He was fumbling with his sturdy knife, getting it under the edge of the board and then lifting it.

"Well I never," he said, sitting back on his heels. "Somebody's been using this as a hidey-hole!"

Fliss peered in and instantly clasped a hand to her mouth to stop herself from crying out. In the space between the two joists, a variety of things had been wedged in, but the thing which instantly caught her eye was a small carved and painted elephant. *That's Ishwar's,* that terrifying inner voice told her without pause, and she could feel the tears starting to well up. The sad little boy who'd never wanted to come to England must have treasured this link with the place and people he thought of as home, and before she realised what she was doing, Fliss had bent down and picked it up, a rush of sensations threatening to overwhelm her.

"Fliss? Are you okay? You've gone ever so white. For heaven's sake, sit down for a moment."

"The little boy in the letters who died," she managed to croak out. "This is Indian, surely?"

"Oh bugger," Bernie sighed, immediately grasping why it had hit Fliss so hard. He reached in and pulled out various other little bits which could only have been put there by a child – no adult would have thought them important enough. Along with the carved elephant, there was a carved snake and a tiger, plus a piece of cloth which might once have been a small scarf and in vivid colours. Two pairs of small, thonged sandals were hidden down there, and even Bernie could see that they must have belonged to the two brothers.

"How terribly sad," he sighed. "I bet some well-intending servant threatened to throw these out, thinking to get rid of the memories of home to help them settle here, and the boys hid them."

"They thought they would go home one day," Fliss sniffed, having to resort to a tissue, and glad that she'd brought plenty with her anticipating the sniffles from dust, not tears. "I bet they thought they'd need them at some point."

"Poor little blighters," Bernie sympathised. "They must have been such total outsiders in those days. There'd have been nobody like them around here."

"I think I hate their father without even having met him," Fliss gulped, trying so hard not to descend into full floods of tears. "What a cruel thing it was for him to do to bring them here."

Bernie carefully slipped a small bundle of what looked like children's drawings out as Fliss was dabbing her eyes. There was no way that he was going to let her see those right now, but he would keep them safe, because even he was starting to be affected by the plight of Nilmani and Ishwar, if only because he could see the contrast between what their lives must have been like and the childhood of his own two sons.

"I wonder what they thought of the wardrobe?" he said instead, desperate to change the subject to something more positive. "I wonder if they thought these scenes were of some magical place? After all, they look nothing like the countryside around here, and they'd be completely alien to two kids from India. Do you think they thought the fairies lived there?"

That made Fliss give a watery smile, which relived him, and she agreed as far as, "Well India is full of rich mythology. I don't pretend to know anything but the barest outlines, but I'm sure two young boys' imaginations could have filled in a few gaps."

Eager to keep that train of thought going, Bernie added, "I bet they played hide and seek in that wardrobe. It's ideal for little kids to hide in, especially if there were some long, adult length clothes in there – you know, old coats that nobody wore anymore, or at least not regularly."

Yet although Fliss dredged up another smile for Bernie, guessing what he was doing, her own inner voice was adding, *Or hiding from anyone wanting to find them. How many times did they try to bury themselves in there to avoid going to a school they hated, or from a parent they were scared of?* Because those were the images that were pounding in on her.

"Let's go and look at the storeroom," she suggested, struggling to her feet despite still feeling rather wobbly. At the moment she just wanted to get out of this room which kept overwhelming her. There surely couldn't be anything in the storeroom to shake her this badly, could there?

"Okay," Bernie agreed with more cheer than he felt, but willing to do anything which made Fliss forget those two lost kids.

Amongst the remaining furniture in the store room, there was a rather beautiful escritoire and an inlaid bookcase, which Bernie immediately suggested might also both be French and which had clearly been together. There was also a lovely burr walnut desk, complete with top piece for storing things like envelopes in, plus a gloriously curvaceous set of drawers in a similar wood. Other pieces lurked in the gloom, but hinted at being every bit as good.

"We could put these in any of the downstairs rooms," he said, and Fliss agreed, going as far as to suggest that the older part of the house might be best since they would look stunning against a plain cream wall.

What had also become apparent, now that there were fewer tall items in the storeroom, was that the room actually had a skylight window, and that had Bernie musing,

"You know, we could put another bathroom in here. It wouldn't be hard to do with modern plumbing, and it would be a definite plus to have a loo up on this floor. A modern Velux window would be easy enough to install and would let a lot more light in. What do you think?"

"I think that's a great idea," Fliss finally felt able to enthuse. "There are what … six bedrooms down below? And if we get rid of that awful existing en-suite, that only leaves the two shower rooms with their loos in the old holiday let and over the kitchen, and the house's main bathroom for the whole house. If you had a houseful of people in here, these days you'd definitely be struggling. Another full bathroom would be almost a must, or at least that's what I think an estate agent would say."

"And this room runs the full width of the bedroom in front of it," Bernie declared, "so it must be the thick end of sixteen feet wide, even if it is only about eight or nine deep. That's still big enough for a full-sized bath and a separate shower."

"Oh yes! Maybe even two skylights to let the steam out?" Fliss enthused, stepping backwards as she looked around, visualising a lovely modern bathroom with marble tiles. Then felt her head swim violently as she backed unwittingly up to the burr walnut desk, colliding with it. *Look inside!* the inner voice practically screamed at her.

"Woops!" she gasped to cover the totter. "I think you're right, Bernie, I must definitely be burning off a load of calories, because I'm feeling positively faint for want of something to eat. Is it too greedy to get stuck into another mug of tea and some biscuits?"

Bernie chuckled. "We'll make a builder of you yet! Come on then, tea and biccies it is. I can't imagine Phil will say no, nor Kev or Sean. Let's go and put the kettle on."

I'll look at the desk another day, Fliss told herself firmly. *Not today! Today I'll fall apart if I find something dodgy in there,* and she gladly went to take on the role of chief tea maker for the workers, glad to be doing something she would once have thought rather beneath her.

However, Bernie had one more thought on the furniture which did surprise her.

"Do you know, I think all of that in the old store room might be French," he said, as he dunked a ginger biscuit into his tea.

"French?" Phil said in surprise, having come to join them on the camping chairs they'd set up in the big kitchen which had been the Davenport's dining room.

"Mmm," Bernie intoned as he munched the last bite of a second biscuit. "More farmhouse than chateau, I'd say, but nice quality. Those wardrobes were what set me off thinking about it, and having realised that they're most definitely French – especially the one that Fliss loves – it wasn't so hard to place the others as that too. Somewhere along the line, somebody brought a whole load of rather good furniture across, and the likelihood is that there was once more of it, but it's probably got sold off in the intervening years."

"Ooh err!" Kevin laughed, "Wonder if they brought any kinky French knickers over with them?"

"Don't be a peasant," Sean reprimanded him with a playful swipe, and desperate to keep the playful atmosphere going, Fliss chimed in with,

"Bernie was telling me that back in those days, ladies didn't even wear knickers."

There was instant ribbing of Bernie for knowing such a thing, and a lot of slightly smutty insinuations, although Fliss was grateful for it never getting outright vulgar as it almost certainly would have done if she'd not been there. But at least she could laugh along with them and at some of Sean's truly awful puns, which released a lot of the internal tension she hadn't realised had been building up until it went.

"Right, time to get back to work!" Bernie declared, as everyone emptied their mugs. "We've just got time for another hour or two before we lose the light."

Go get another bucket of water and get back to sugar-soaping the walls, Fliss told herself firmly, despite the quiver inside at the thought of returning to the bedroom. And with the background noise of Phil's radio as he worked across the landing from her, at first, she felt a lot more grounded.

Deliberately working where she didn't have to look at the hidey-hole under the floorboards, she was able to ignore its presence for quite a while. But there came a point when the chimneybreast alcove was the last place to be divested of its spiders' webs, and after getting her last bucket of water for the day, she braced herself to tackle it. Resolutely singing songs she remembered from her teenage years, when she'd been so much more optimistic, she ruthlessly rendered the spiders homeless; then began scrubbing the walls where the webs of many years had also trapped the dust, leaving dark smudges across the plaster.

"Oh, come on," she muttered, as she tackled a particularly obstinate mark and stepped backwards to see if it really had faded at all from another brisk rubbing. In an instant she was stumbling, having stepped onto the edge of the hidey-hole. Just about saving herself from diving head first at the wardrobe, she sat down with a bump, feeling incredibly foolish. What on earth would Bernie think if he came up and had to hoist her out of the hole if she got her foot stuck down there? Even at his most charitable she'd be starting to look like an accident-prone liability.

"For Heaven's sake, Fliss! Watch what you're doing," she breathed softly. "Phil's only next door. He'll think he's working with a bloody chicken if he hears you squeaking and squawking all the time!"

She got to her knees, rubbing her hip where she'd landed hard, but it put her in a position where she could see right into the hole. What was that shoved back beyond where the board was lifted? There was something else in there.

She had to lie down to be able to wriggle her arm into the hole, but then realised that it wasn't as far back as she'd feared, because it must have been only as far as one of the boys could reach. Carefully pulling it out, she gasped when she saw what it was, because during her time at the agency, one of her few friends in the early days had been a bright Indian graduate who had shown her an antique copy of the *Bhagavad Gita* he had just bought as a present for his father. If this wasn't the same thing, then it was very close, of that Fliss was sure. Like that one, this was more pieces of manuscript than a book, and had the same beautiful decorations around the edges of each piece, which had reminded her then and now of some of the lovely Indian carpet designs she'd seen.

Sitting back against the wardrobe to stop herself from keeling over again, she carefully lifted them closer to her face. At that point she realised that she could still smell the fragrance of incense clinging to the delicate sheets, and with that whiff of scent came the most vivid image.

Two small boys were kneeling in the bedroom where she was, but it looked different. The walls were a much brighter yellow than she'd been contemplating, and a vivid rug covered the floor where the boys knelt. The older one, who she knew must be Nilmani, was reading from one of the parchments, and it broke Fliss' heart to realise that they had to be trying to remember the prayers they'd been taught in their mother's community.

"Oh, you poor little souls!" she sobbed, then jumped nearly as much as they did when Nilmani shot up and asked in very accented English,

"Who is there?"

But then his gaze darted towards the door, and Fliss also heard the heavy tread of someone older coming upstairs. In a flash, Nilmani was gathering up the parchment and stuffing it under the bed, while dragging his little brother to the bedside. They just managed to kneel beside the bed in time before a very broad local accent said,

"Ah, you'm bein' good lads, sayin' your prayers proper like your papa taught you."

It was a woman, and for a moment Fliss' view was blocked by a broad back dressed in brown, homespun woollens, at which point she realised that she was viewing the room as if from the wardrobe and looking across towards the room's door, except that her view was partly blocked by the wardrobe door, which itself was partially open. What she could see was the blank incomprehension on the younger boy's face. He clearly hadn't understood a single word, but his little face was creased in misery.

"Into bed with you both, now," the local woman said, and Fliss could tell that she was trying to be kind, but hadn't the first idea of how hopelessly lost the two children were in this strange world.

The two of them crept beneath the sheets and the woman picked up the lone candle which had been lighting the room, taking it away with her. The moment her footsteps faded, the youngest boy dissolved into sobs, and Fliss didn't need to understand him to know that he was sobbing for his mother.

"Oh sweetheart, don't cry," she heard herself saying, "I'm sure your mother wants you back as much as you want her. If you were mine, I'd love you and never let you go."

She saw Nilmani's head come up and look straight at her. "Are you an angel?" he asked half in awe and half in fear.

"No, I'm no angel," Fliss sniffed, way past even remotely wondering why or how she was speaking across time to the two boys, or how they could possibly hear her.

"Can you help us?" Nilmani asked.

"No, my lovely, I can't. I can't come into your world, but if I could I would."

"Will you stay a while? I'm so frightened in the dark," and Fliss realised that the trees outside were now throwing flickering shadows across the room, so there must be quite a bright moon in their time for that to happen in a world where there were no street lights – not even gas ones yet.

"I'll stay as long as you want, sweetheart," and she meant it. Any thoughts of where Bernie might think she had gone to had vanished in her blaze of maternal longing for these two children.

Yet it wasn't just the terrible yearning for a child that was doing this to her, there was also the memory of being scared of the dark herself as a child, back in the days when her mother was too busy doting over Ben as her beloved baby boy to bother with the daughter who'd been shoved off into the tiny bedroom, and who was also frightened silly of the strange shadows which flickered across her bedroom walls. It had taken many years before Fliss had conquered that fear, finally realising that it was the street light in the alleyway behind her parents' house which lit the trees up, and sent the dancing dark tendrils across her wall. And so that total identification with the child's fear was doing nothing to help her pull back.

"It's just the trees, sweetheart. Just the trees and the moon shining through them that's making the strange shadows. Don't be frightened of them. They can't hurt you."

"Promise?"

"Promise!"

Then little Ishwar said something, and Nilmani translated for him, saying, "Our mother used to sing to us. Will you sing to us?"

"Of course I will," though the only song she could think of at the moment was George Michael's 'Careless Whisper', which was about as weird a choice of lullaby as she could get. But as she warbled her way rather tunelessly through that, and then on through the other pop songs she could remember, she felt more than saw or heard Ishwar fall into an exhausted sleep. But it was as Nilmani finally dropped off to sleep that she was suddenly disconnected from the past.

With a jolt she came to, aware that her tears had dried on her cheeks. In horror she pulled down her rubber glove on the hand not holding the prayer sheets to look at her wrist watch, and then was even more disconcerted to see that it was only a few minutes after she had last looked at it. Where had that time gone to? Going back over the number of songs she'd worked her way through, it ought to have been at the very least half an hour, yet in the here and now nothing like that long had passed. What had happened to her? Was it some dreamlike state where she'd imagined all of that? Some intense micro-nap where she'd experienced a very vivid dream?

No! her inner voice screamed, *it was real! It was real! You could smell the incense much stronger then. You don't smell things in dreams. Something very real happened when you smelled that parchment. You couldn't have got all of that just from some faded scent. Why didn't it take you to memories of Carrie at university stinking your shared flat out, when she lit a whole pack of incense sticks at one go, eh? That would have been more reasonable to expect. …Oh no, you were leaning against the wardrobe again, weren't you, that must be why! Yet why would you have imagined that Nilmani could speak English, when his little brother – who could only have been a couple of years younger – didn't understand a word? Surely you would have assumed that both would speak English, or neither? No, this was real, this was very real even if you don't understand how.*

Chapter 11

Tuesday – Wednesday

Fliss could only be glad that this time they went straight back home after work, and so she didn't have to keep up the pretence of being sociable, and covered not having to talk to Bernie by faking falling asleep in the truck on the way home. By the time they'd reached Ledbury, she was more able to hold things together while they cooked dinner. After which she raided Bernie's extensive bookshelf for something on the era, and settled down to read about the British army in India until her eyes refused to stay open.

So having gone to bed far earlier than previously, she woke up feeling refreshed, and if she'd had any vivid dreams, they certainly hadn't woken her or lingered to be remembered in the morning, for which she was grateful. She had brought the carved toys home with her, reluctant to remove them from the place where they belonged, but also worried that they would get broken during the renovations. The elephant now stood on the chest of drawers facing her bedroom door – as she'd been told by her grandmother that elephants always should, and though it was just superstition, right now she wasn't feeling up to challenging that. The tiger and the snake followed along behind it, and just seeing where little fingers had rubbed some of the natural dye off the toys made her smile. At least Nilmani and Ishwar had had toys they loved to play with, and to remind them of home.

And that thought had her wondering how traumatic it had been for them to be forced to leave their Hindu faith behind and conform to Victorian or Georgian Christian practices? Clearly, if what she'd 'seen' yesterday was true, they had been desperately clinging to it, and that in turn made her realise that the boys had had what looked like very close-cropped hair when she'd seen them. Had that been another source of dismay, if the tradition where they came from had been for longer hair? Living in a cosmopolitan city, she'd seen young boys of their ages already wearing their hair tied up in topknots which, if it wasn't necessarily universal nowadays, didn't mean it hadn't been the custom for them, and it embarrassed her that she didn't know enough to be able to be sure one way or the other. Politics and religion as topics of conversation had been so heavily discouraged in the name of political correctness at work, that she found herself now woefully uninformed.

Sighing, she went down to breakfast, and then donned her overalls for another day of scrubbing.

"I think I'll make a start on those parquet blocks today," she told Bernie as they drove over. "I'm conscious of being in Phil's way in the bedrooms, and even if I move down a floor, there's the complication of me needing a full set of stepladders for those high ceilings. Not to mention the fact that with bigger walls to clean, each room will take me longer. I could go around with a cloth over a lightweight broom and batter the worst of the cobwebs off the ceiling, but it seems daft to try and do more in there until he's done."

There, that all sounded perfectly reasonable. She'd given Bernie a wholly practical excuse for not going back up to the bedrooms today, and happily, he went with it.

"Sounds fair to me," he said. "I'll set you up in the holiday let kitchen, if you like? It'll be warmer in there than out in the garage, and you can use that sink for your water to save you lugging buckets around."

"That would be good!" Fliss didn't have to fake enthusing over. "Those buckets were getting heavier and heavier as yesterday was going on. I thought I'd come out with arms like a gorilla!"

Bernie chuckled. "You've a way to go before then. But the next time you meet up with your girl-friends, you might have them asking for the name of your gym."

She didn't have the heart to remind him that she didn't have any girl-friends. Had Bernie thought that that had been the depression talking, and that there must be someone somewhere who was still her mate? She couldn't really blame him if he had, because it was becoming clear that even if Bernie didn't have a big group of close friends who were constantly popping over to see him, he certainly had a huge number of acquaintances, all of whom were more like friends to him than anyone Fliss had had around in the last ten years.

Stop it! she told herself firmly. *No wallowing! Life is getting better, not worse. Nobody promised to wave a magic wand over you and make everything right all in one go, did they? It takes time, so keep putting one foot in front of the other. Little steps, Fliss, little steps, you're going in the right direction.*

Therefore she went and got a couple of wheelbarrow loads of the lifted parquet blocks from where the men had stacked them in the open garage, and trundled them around to the tiny kitchen. When she got there with the first load, she could see why Bernie had suggested it. By the kitchen door there was a space where logs must once have been stored, and the whole alleyway between the two parts of the building was covered over, albeit with cheap rigid plastic. Up at ceiling height, though, there were scars in the timbers which hinted that once upon a time this could have been fully enclosed. Now, with kitchen door opening outwards, it meant that even though there was a bit of a sharp breeze today, it was remarkably sheltered in her little corner.

Moreover, with the thickness of the 'orange' hall's huge chimney breast between her and where the men were still digging, it muffled the radio down so that it was just an inoffensive background noise without any definition. And so she passed a pleasant morning sorting and scrubbing the blocks. The tops were almost sticky with wax after so many years, and once she'd got the obvious dirt off, she was trying to think of what to add to her washing water that would cut through it. They also had tongues and grooves cut into the sides so that they fitted together – something that had been quite a revelation to Fliss – and so the grooves in particular needed grubbing out.

She consequently got a system going where she would wash a couple of dozen, and then go back to the previous batch that had been washed, and now that they were a bit drier, used an old chisel Bernie had given her to work the dirt out of the grooves. It wasn't sharp enough to dig into the wood, though Fliss soon discovered that beech was an incredibly hard wood, and she was sure that she didn't have the strength to work the chisel hard enough to do any damage, even if it had been sharper. And it was rather satisfying work, she discovered. Having got half a dozen as clean as she could, she experimented with sliding them together, and realised that there was more than one pattern they could make. *It's like grown-up Lego,* she thought happily, as she went back to scrubbing.

Lunchtime came and went, and Fiss was really relaxing into her work. It felt good to be doing something, and yet it wasn't in any way overtaxing her. And when she turned around and saw the neat pile of well-scrubbed blocks behind her, she was surprised at how many she'd got through already.

As the afternoon light began to fade, she had to ask Bernie for one of the smaller lamps to work by, and it was because of that that she ended up taking one of the blocks outside into the remaining full daylight in order to see it properly.

"What on earth is this?" she muttered to herself, as she poked at the angle of the tongue. "Has someone spilled something over this?"

It was a brownish red stain along the side of the block, looking as if something had dribbled down it. But what would have done that? Surely the blocks had fitted tightly enough together that very little would seep down? She ended up putting the block on one side, but then since she also had a little pile of those blocks too damaged in one way or another to reuse, found herself making a third pile as another appeared and then another, and over the course of the next hour, realised that there was a growing number of the stained ones.

"How's it going?" Bernie's voice called, as he came around to see her.

"Pretty well on the whole," she said with a smile. "I think you're right, by the time we've had to ditch the damaged ones, we'll have enough to go through and make a matching floor for the Chandler's former dining room and into their kitchen. But there won't be enough to re-lay both main rooms, even if we put some of the dodgy ones into the chimney breast alcoves, where they'd be less likely to be seen.

"But what to you make of these, Bernie? There's something on them that I can't identify, and there are more of them than I expected. At first, I thought, 'oh, someone's dropped a bottle of wine on here, and it's leaked down.' But look at how many I've got. That's never just a bottle's worth. And I doubt I've finished finding all of them yet."

"Well I never," Bernie said, puzzled. He picked one up and turned it around in his hands. "You're right, it's definitely something that's come down from above, isn't it?" He angled the block to catch the light. "Whatever it is, it didn't get below either the tongue or the groove, but you can see how it's puddled in the angle of the top part of the tongue, so it must have been stopped from sinking any lower by the tight fit into the groove."

"Yes, but look at the ends, Bernie. There's no tongue and groove on the short ends to stop it, and there you can see a real dribble pattern. What is it do you think?"

Then she nearly jumped out of her skin as from behind her Kevin said in a Vincent Price impression, "It's blood, my dear!" and sucked his teeth dramatically.

However, when she spun around and saw him trying to stick his fangs out, vampire-like, it was so ridiculous that she collapsed in laughter.

"You daft sod," Bernie laughed. "So come on then, smart arse, what do you think it is?"

However, it was Sean who reached over Kevin's shoulder and took the block out of Bernie's hands, moving out into the garden to see more clearly, then saying,

"I hate to say this – and Bernie, I'm not deliberately trying to upset Fliss – but I think it might be blood."

"Blood?" Fliss gasped. "Really?"

Sean shrugged. "I can't say absolutely, but a few years ago I went to work on a house. I do a bit of basic carpentry, you see, and a young couple had bought a house knowing that the old boy who'd lived there previously had died there. What they weren't expecting was to find that there was a great big blood stain actually sunk into the floor boards. The carpet had already been ripped up and thrown away, and they saw the stain on the underlay when they viewed the house, but when that came up, they were more than a bit shocked to see that what they'd thought had just been a spread through the underlay's fibres, was the actual size of the pool of blood-stain beneath it too.

"The poor old chap had had a fall and haemorrhaged, you see. …No, don't look so distressed, Fliss. They said that he'd died almost instantly, according to what the family said that the paramedics told them. What made the mess was that he was there for a few hours before he was found. Certainly long enough for a lot of seepage to have taken place.

"Well, I started sanding the boards, and sanding, and sanding! I reached a point where I told them it would be better to just lift the boards and have new ones put in, because to be honest, I wasn't happy with how much of the boards I was taking away. And it was when I came to lift those affected boards that I saw something like this. Just going at the surface, you didn't see it, but once you got to the sides of the boards you did, and they were marks very similar to these. On the plus side, these look a lot more faded. I reckon whenever this happened, it was a very, very long time ago." He gave Fliss a faint smile. "And just like the house I worked on, it doesn't mean someone met a violent end. It was probably just natural causes."

Fighting to keep the inner scream contained, Fliss managed to smile wanly back at him. Of course, that was the obvious solution, and for once that nagging voice in her head wasn't yelling something else at her, either, although that might be because they were outside of the house at the moment.

"I suspect you're right, Sean," Bernie was saying reassuringly. "Let's face it, in a hamlet like this, if a house had a reputation for some grisly murder taking place, they'd still have been talking about it now, even if it was a hundred years ago! How many local dog-walkers have we had going past in the lane in these last few days saying hello to us, and not one of them saying a word about dodgy goings on? Loads of them!"

And that, Fliss told herself, *is the big difference living in a closer community like this. Stop thinking like this is a big city, where someone can get murdered practically on your doorstep and you don't even know who they were, let alone have anyone but their family remember it barely months afterwards. Out here they might know everyone's business, but that means it's a lot harder to cover things up too. Listen to Bernie and stop scaring yourself with visions of mad axe murderers!*

The next day went very much to the same pattern. Phil was upstairs wrestling with pulling and pushing new wires into place, and installing modern sockets and light fixings. Kevin and Sean finished digging out the 'orange' hall and began laying a waterproof membrane with Bernie, who'd just finished removing the spiral staircase from the holiday let part, and was about to re-lay the necessary floorboards to cover the hole. And Fliss carried on scrubbing at the parquet blocks. But by the end of the day, she'd done as much as she could do. Any further digging into the tongues and grooves of the blocks she was leaving to Sean, because the last thing she wanted to do was to go too deep and wreck a perfectly good block. And so, as the men finished up, she went for a wander around the house, glad to have the chance to see it for herself without anyone else with her.

The stairs up out of what had been the Davenport's part led up to what she could now take the time to see were two lovely bedrooms. Both of these would look gorgeous with an English cottage treatment. If they left the dark beams as they were – and Fliss now thought that it would be little short of vandalism to do something like whitewashing them – then the infill panels would have to be in a light colour, but that didn't mean they needed to be boring.

Duck egg blue, she thought, *that's what would look amazing in here, or that slightly dusty pale green I remember seeing on the colour card. It gets enough of the late afternoon sun to cope with that.* And then as she ambled through to the next and smaller bedroom, *Ooh! And that lovely dove-grey mauve would make such a pretty bedroom in here! Especially with an off-white ceiling.*

All of which meant that she was not remotely thinking of grimmer things as she wandered into what would have once been the main bedroom above the 'orange' hall, after a cursory glance into the first of the shower rooms. She hadn't crossed over the threshold which had formerly given her the shivers, and so she was completely unprepared for what then happened. *What a lovely room,* she now thought, easing herself down to sit on the floor and lean back against one of the huge oak beams. *Gosh, I'd love a bedroom like this!* Yet in the instant that her head touched the beam she felt the room spinning.

She was an onlooker, almost as if she'd become part of the wall itself, and in front of her in the room, a man and woman were arguing. Their speech was old fashioned – not simply 'not modern', but actually archaic – and momentarily Fliss marvelled that she could even understand them. Going by what they were wearing, Fliss couldn't help but wonder whether they were of the generation who had built the Queen Anne frontage.

"I will not be gainsaid!" the man declared vehemently. "I will not have you contradict me, Marjorie. You are my wife, and in this you will do as I say"

"But William," the woman protested, wringing her hands in despair. "He is so young. Does it have to be now?"

"If not now, then when?" the man identified as William demanded. "He is my son, too, and I will not have him becoming some milksop, forever tied to his mother's apron. He must learn to be a man, and a man of the world."

As Marjorie collapsed onto the bed, which was against the wall which Fliss was viewing things from, she saw William's expression soften slightly, although also with some irritation.

"Come, Marjorie," he said in exasperated tones. "You must see sense. Do not forget that it was only your grandfather and mine who were lucky enough to get reparation from the king, and get our claims to our families' lands upheld by the courts. And once again the Stuarts are claiming the throne for their own. King George is not so secure that everything might not change again."

He stepped forwards and patted rather ineffectually at her shoulder. "This new Scottish rebellion …it could go badly, or the king could win. The trouble is, we do not know, and worse, we cannot anticipate it. The rebels have reached Derby, Marjorie …Derby! I know it seems a world away to you, but I have been there with Justice Norrington, and believe me, it is too close for comfort! We must have a foot in both camps, for whoever wins, we cannot be made homeless yet again on the whim of a king or his supplanter. If I go, we risk seeming to have fully backed one side or the other, but if we send our sons to be mere esquires, they cannot be considered to have known anything of what they were getting into. If all falls, we may yet retain this house as custodians on behalf of one or other of our boys."

Marjorie looked up at him, and Fliss could tell by the shaking of her shoulders that she was still crying hard. "But Cuddy is so little," she pleaded. "He's only eight! And even Fanny is only ten. They are too small to be sent away to who knows what!"

William visibly winced. "Their names are Cuthbert and Nathaniel! Stop calling them by those baby names!"

"Well they are *my babies," Marjorie sniffled, "and aside from dearest Flora, the only ones left to me. It is too cruel, William, too cruel to send them away after all I have endured."*

"It was your wifely duty to bear me sons," William retorted. "The parson said so! It is a woman's lot to bear children, and if the Good Lord saw fit to take the other four from us, then you should not question Him! …So that is the end of it. Cuthbert will go to my cousin in London to serve him, and Nathaniel will go north to meet your cousin at Derby, or if not there then to his house in Melrose to await him there, and that is my final decision as the head of this household," and he marched out.

"But you did not bear them!" Marjorie howled, hurling a pillow at the closed door. "You did not feel them kicking inside

you for months as I did! All you bothered about was a small body taken from me at birth. To you it was already gone to the Lord. But not to me, William! Not to me!"

And then the scene skipped. Suddenly Fliss was looking at William who had suddenly gone much greyer at the temples, and she realised that before her in the bed was a body, the sheet pulled up to hide its face, but by the shape she knew it had to be Marjorie, even before William knelt beside her and called her name.

"Why could you not be strong?" he wept. "Why could you not have faith in the Lord as I did? Why, Marjorie?"

And then the door was flung open and a young woman marched in, red-eyed from weeping and yet also furious. "You have not earned the right to be so pious, Father!" she snapped. "How dare you call upon God to excuse what you did!"

"I did what was best for the family," William growled.

"No, you did what was best for you*!" the young woman flung back at him, and Fliss guessed that this must be Flora. "Well, after we bury Mother today, you will never see me again. I go with Uncle John to the north, and when I get there, I will one day travel farther into Scotland and put flowers on Nathaniel's grave, and pray that God will forgive you for sending him there, because I cannot, and neither could Mother.*

"If Cuthbert can ever bear to come home at some point, I hope that his conscience will be pricked for not being here to send Mother to her rest. But I fear you have turned him into a copy of yourself in this last two years, and if you think he will come back here to tend to you in your old age, then you will be very much mistaken. You will reap what you have sown, Father, for I will not return to this house after what you have done, and may you have a long and lonely old age to contemplate your sins against your children, and a wife who was far too good for you."

And with that she stormed out, the door banging shut behind her.

Only when her footsteps had receded did William look up from the bed and whisper, "God forgive me, what have I done? I have saved Sytchampton House for a son who does not want it, and sacrificed my other children and my dearest wife in the process. How did I not see what you were becoming, Cuddy? That you went from being a sweet boy to an almost-man who cares for nobody but himself? May God have mercy on your own children, for I fear you will be an even worse father to them than I have been to you …to all of my dear ones. Is that why God took them from me? Did He remove them from me so that I could not harm them further?"

He pulled the white sheet down from his wife's face and Fliss felt herself gasp in shock. Marjorie was positively skeletal!

"What did you do to her?" she heard herself yelp in horror, and then saw William stagger back from the bed to sprawl on the floor, looking at her in abject terror, and then clasping his hands before him as if in prayer.

"What are you?" he whimpered, and yet Fliss was too shocked by Marjorie to bother that he could see and hear her.

"How did she die?" she demanded. "What did you do to her?"

"I did nothing," the terrified William gabbled. "She just stopped eating. Day by day after the news came that Nathaniel had died, she just ate less and less until she had nothing at all." A thought seemed to come to him, and he went even paler. "I could not tell Parson Jenkins, I could not! I did not lie to him! Upon my soul, I did not lie to him. But had I said what she had done, he would have said she took her own life, and then she will not get buried as the good Christian woman she was." He broke and sobbed. "It was my fault, not hers. I should have cared more for how she felt. I will not have her languish in the Fiery Pit with Demons for my sins."

"She won't go to Hell," Fliss snapped back, "but you might well if you don't mend your ways!"

Then as William fainted away, as before, she was suddenly back in the here and now. And in a not dissimilar scuttle to William's, she crabbed away from the wall and crouched panting, trying to calm herself.

"What the heck was that?" she asked of the empty room when she could finally speak, but no reply came, and down below she could hear the normal sounds of the three men working in the orange hall. "*Phew*!"

Was that why she'd had the creeps walking through to this part of the house before? Was there something spooky going on here? Because, she belatedly realised, this was the same wall in which the doorway lay that kept giving her the shudders. Had she picked up on this earlier? And when had all of what she had just seen taken place? Was this around the time the two little boys were in the house or not? Because as yet she had absolutely no context for any of them. Were they related to that couple – the dead Marjorie and her awful husband William – or total strangers because the house had been sold in the interim?

Then it occurred to her that for the first time she had names, proper English names that she could trace, because surely William had to be Sytchampton House's owner? And if his son did finally come home, then Cuthbert would be the next owner. She didn't need to know their surnames, because the house and their status as owners ought to be enough. And then she remembered seeing an advert on TV last night for a website where you could trace your ancestors.

"Okay," she declared, "so you offer a fortnight's free trial, do you? I reckon tonight it's time to see if you live up to your reputation, because I'm going to fire up the laptop and see if I can find William,

Marjorie, Flora, and Nathaniel, and then Cuthbert as presumably the next owner."

William

1747

As Fliss blinked out of view, William lay insensible on the floor, but when he came to, his first reaction was to look fearfully around him for that strange spirit who had appeared over Marjorie's body. He was still sitting shaking when his brother-in-law came to find him.

"Come now, William, the coffin is being brought upstairs for her," John chivvied him. "Leave this to the women folk to make her presentable for her last journey. …William? Whatever is wrong? You look as though you've seen a ghost."

"I have," William croaked, "but not my dear Marjorie's! It was a woman, John, and she was most angry with me. I fear I have been visited by a spirit who may yet try to haunt me."

Not knowing what to say to this, John Macintosh decided that the only thing to do was to apply some good Scottish sense to the matter. "My dear sister is with the angels now," he said firmly. "Such a good soul as hers could not be anywhere else, could it? And she'll be reunited with all her beloved little ones – even Nathaniel, whose grave none of us can visit to honour him in this life."

Yet the mention of Nathaniel's name seemed to

have the wrong effect on William, who clapped a hand to his mouth to stifle a sob.

"Oh Nathaniel," came his muted cry.

"Aye, Nathaniel," John repeated, wishing that he didn't want to punch William every time he thought of the wee boy, who had been sent north to join his own and Marjorie's cousin just in time to be dragged by that man into the slaughter of Culloden. Even now, two years on, he couldn't understand why William had felt the need to have a family member in the Jacobite army. He, along with his and Marjorie's other brother, Iain, had managed to stay neutral in the whole affair, quietly getting on with the family printing business, and carefully avoiding printing pamphlets for either side. So why, when William lived all the way down here, and about as far from that conflict as it was possible to get, short of somewhere like Cornwall, had he thought that a show of loyalty was so pressing to a prince who hadn't even managed to secure the Scottish throne for himself, much less the English one?

But then John and Iain had never liked William much, and they'd not been as convinced as their father that the young English gentleman farmer, with a glove-making workshop in Worcester, was as smitten with Marjorie as she had been with him. And in recent years, as William had begun to neglect her more and more, they had both written to her secretly, begging her to bring the youngest children at least back up north to live with them. There would be no shame, they had both told her, in leaving such a pious bigot as William, and enough people in Edinburgh still remembered her fondly as to be sympathetic to her plight.

Yet Marjorie had struggled with her conscience over that, not helped, John was sure, by that pompous windbag of a parson and the equally obnoxious rector, both of whom even now were downstairs, and would be telling William much which in John's eyes was scarcely Christian, and certainly not to his beliefs. Why could Marjorie not have fallen for a good Catholic lad from Scotland? Granted, there had been much bloodshed in the previous century regarding the Covenant versus Catholicism, and even now, the family had to be circumspect in their public expressions of faith. But in a way, that would have eased Marjorie's return into their close circle of likeminded friends, for who would have blamed her for wanting to return to the Church she had been brought up in?

Luckily John was saved from having to make further placatory comments by the arrival of the coffin and the local undertaker, and William was ushered downstairs. Yet the damned fool of a man had to tell Flora about what he thought he'd seen the moment he got into the parlour.

"Then I hope it was an avenging angel!" Flora declared bitterly, making Rector Underhill tut in disapproval, though he got no chance to reprove Flora, since she turned on her heels and marched out of the room.

"An angel, you say?" Rector Underhill instead quizzed William.

"I do not think it was an angel," William replied, going to the side table and pouring himself a large brandy. "It seemed more to me an avenging spirit."

"Dear me," intoned Underhill sanctimoniously. "I did warn you about your wife's relapse from the true way. I shall come again after the funeral and do what I can to dispel this foul thing."

"Don't you blame this on my sister, sir!" John ground out. "Marjorie was a good Christian woman, and I'll not hear any man say otherwise, parson or not!"

"*Tsk*, you are a man of violence, I see," said Underhill, looking at the long dirk in its sheath at John's belt. "But be warned, sir, we do not take violence against the priesthood lightly in these civilised parts."

John marched up to him and glared into his eyes. "If I'd wished violence upon ye', I'd have wrung your skinny gizzard years ago for the misery you brought to this household!" he snarled, his accent becoming more pronouncedly Scottish as his temper flared. "It is my respect for my sister's soul that prevents me from filleting ye', and turning your guts into so much rank haggis for the swine to feed upon, not your pompous preaching!"

As Underhill went pale, John knew he must leave this room before he truly did do something he would regret, and so went in search of Flora. He found her weeping in the shrubbery, and seeing her getting soaked in her thin dress from the persistent drizzle that had marked this day since dawn, shrugged off his stout woollen jacket and draped it around her shoulders.

"Steady, lass," he comforted her, pulling her into a hug. "Your father is a weak and bitter man, and that rector an utter fool."

"I know, Uncle John," Flora said, sniffling into her handkerchief. "I am so grateful to you and Aunt Ishbel for taking me into your home. I could not bear to stay here alone with Father now. It was bad enough when I left here to come to you on Mother's behalf after Nathaniel died, thinking that he must be buried near you. But having been in your loving home, this place seems even more stark and cold, and especially without Mother here."

"Ishbel and the children will love having you with us," John told her kindly and meaning it. "Your father will have to reap what he has sown. Have you had word from Cuthbert yet?"

Flora nodded miserably. "Father's cousin, Sir Phineas, is going up in the world of King George's court – or at least that is what Cuddy says in his letter. He says they cannot leave right now because important things are afoot, and that Cousin Phineas says it is vital for them to be on hand should his master need him. I am afraid that I have never bothered to find out who Cousin Phineas answers to at the Hanoverian court, only that Phineas' ability to speak their language recommends him to those courtiers who kept the old king company after his arrival in this country."

"Does he, indeed? I thought King George spoke English?"

"Oh, this one can because he was born here, but whoever it is that Cousin Phineas is ingratiating himself with is much older. What I do not like is the effect this is having on Cuddy. Oh, Uncle, he's only a little boy of ten, yet he writes like an old man! The words he sends cannot be his own, and I fear that Cousin Phineas, or one of his trusted servants, stands over Cuddy as he writes to make sure he is not telling us the truth of what is going on."

"You think that they are mistreating him?" That worried John.

However, although Flora paused before shaking her head, she was sure of what she was saying. "If you mean to do they beat him and keep him short of food and clothing, then no. And I say 'no', because I think their staunch faith would not allow them to do that, not having promised Father that they would care for him as if he were one of their own, anyway. They will take that literally, I am sure.

"No, it is more how they are warping his mind. He already writes as if I am simple-minded purely because I am a young woman. He never learned that here! Not even from Rector Underwood! That one is too beholden to some of the grander ladies around here for their patronage to ever be able to express such views, if only in case they got repeated back to those ladies, even by a servant. I know that the reason why Father sent Cuddy to them, and not Nathaniel, was because he feared they would dislike Fanny's – I mean Nathaniel's – mischievous nature. Cuddy was always more biddable, but that is what I also fear makes him more like clay to be moulded by them. If we should meet in the future, I am so scared that I will not see anything of my little brother in the young man he will become."

There was little John could say to that, for he knew that he had no chance of extracting his nephew from the clutches of Sir Phineas. Flora had been allowed to come to him because of that same dismissal of her as a worthless girl, and in that respect, John was far from as sure as Flora that such views had not at least been planted as seeds in Cuthbert's mind long before he left for London. Sir Phineas had not had to start with barren land, only nurture the seeds already sowed by Cuthbert's father and Rector Underwood.

"Come, lass," he said instead. "Let us go and bid farewell to your poor mother, and then tomorrow we can leave this cold, empty house for good, and your father to whatever that spirit was, may God have mercy upon his soul."

Chapter 12

Wednesday evening – Thursday

After dinner, Fliss picked up her laptop and went and sat at the dining table. It didn't take long to find the website and create a new account, but then felt daunted at what she was about to try and do.

"Oh, come on, Fliss," she muttered under her breath, so that Bernie wouldn't hear her over the TV. "You're a graduate, you should be able to figure this out. I know you did English, not History, but for heaven's sake, this is basic research, you know how to do that!"

After a few false starts, she discovered how to find the census results, but then to her frustration realised that they simply didn't go back far enough. 1841 and the very first English census was surely long after William and Marjorie had lived, and the more Fliss thought about it, the more she was convinced that William had been talking about the Jacobite 1745 rebellion. As an *Outlander* fan, she knew that had been the uprising which had famously reached Derby, and if William was sending a son to Berwick, then that was surely Berwick-upon-Tweed and right on the Scottish border. So it wasn't too hard a stretch of the imagination to think that the cousin might be just a mile or two over the Scottish side of the border, and a Jacobite sympathiser, especially since Melrose most definitely lay in Scotland, albeit in the Borders.

What she wasn't expecting was to get some suggestions thrown up by the website itself. She had created a basic family tree, with William and Marjorie as the parents and some very general dates, and then Flora, Nathaniel and Cuthbert as their children, just keeping her fingers crossed that in that combination there wouldn't be too many duplicates. There wasn't a lot to go on, but someone else from a current branch of the family had been digging already, and up popped their family tree.

Her surprised, "*Oooh*!" had Bernie looking up, and she beckoned him over. "I think I might have found some of a previous family in our house," she said happily.

As he came and pulled up another of the dining room chairs beside her, she pointed to the screen. "Look! William Spink of Sytchampton House married Marjorie Macintosh in 1724. That's nice, isn't it? It gives us a definite date when we know the house was occupied, and William is the son of Greville Spink, squire, also of Sytchampton House, and Marjorie is the daughter of Mungo Macintosh, printer of Edinburgh."

"Do you think this is accurate?" Bernie wondered.

"To be frank, I'm not the person to ask that of. I can fight my way around a website okay, but history wasn't my thing at university, even if I did do a lot of later historical literature. It was a Modern English degree I did – not like my housemate who specialised in all things medieval – which meant I only dipped into other periods during the first-year introductory course. So I rather have to take this person's word for it. The plus side is that other people seem to have come up with similar results, although not in quite such detail – but then maybe this person is the one with the knowhow to find what they didn't? Whoever they are, they seem to have it backed up with all of these listed sources, so it looks right."

Bernie scratched at the stubble on his chin. "Hmm... Here we have William and Marjorie, and then this son Cuthbert inherits, am I reading that right?"

"Yes. Sadly, it looks as though they have Flora, and then the next four children – three boys and a girl – all die very young. But then against the odds, Nathaniel and then Cuthbert seem to survive." How could she tell Bernie that she knew that Nathaniel would die in Scotland without sounding crazy?

She clicked to add all of them to the family tree, and then went to Cuthbert's name, where a new screen popped up. "Okay, so there doesn't seem to be much else on Nathaniel," or rather she knew there was no point in looking beyond this, "but Cuthbert was born in 1737 and married in 1759. His wife looks like Alice Dodsworth ...ooh, daughter of a parson! So it seems very much as if the family was rather declining in importance in the area, because Cuthbert is just a 'gentleman' on his marriage document.

"They have a string of kids ...look at all of those names in this next generation! Poor Alice, she must have been worn out by that many pregnancies, and she died young – no surprise there. First Elizabeth, born in early 1760, then Marjorie in late 1762 – must have been named after her grandmother – then Ingram in 1764, Nenius in 1767 ...Ooh, I wonder if that's why they chose to try and change Nilmani's name to it? Or is he earlier or later – I can't find him yet.

"…Catriona in 1769 …hmmm, wonder if she was named after one of the Scottish relatives? …Caroline – hardly a surprise when it was a queen's name, although this girl was born in 1772, so maybe not named after George IV's wife, because I think she was later than this."

Bernie thought for a moment, then said, "I think the king Georges ran with the first one taking the throne in 1714 – hence the Jacobite rebellion of 1715, and then if my schoolboy history is right, George II was something like the 1720s to the 1760s."

Fliss switched to another tab on her screen and did a quick check. "Gosh, Bernie, you do have a good memory for dates! Here we go: George I, 1714 to 1727; George II, 1727 to 1760; George III – he was the mad one, wasn't he? – 1760 to 1820, and George IV, 1820 to 1830. So no, the little girl we were looking at in the 1770s wouldn't have been named after the future queen, because that Caroline would herself have only been a little girl at the time."

She went back to the family tree. "And after Caroline there's just Aquillia, born in 1775, but if you think that Alice had her first child within a year of getting married, she'd been pregnant off and on for the thick end of fifteen years! And that doesn't account for any miscarriages she might have had between the later children as she got older. No wonder she died in 1778. It was probably after another pregnancy."

Bernie had gone and fetched his reading glasses and now peered at the screen. "Did all of those named children survive?"

"Good grief, surprisingly all but Ingram and Caroline, and they die in the same year as young children, according to this tree, so I suspect that that might be down to something like the flu going through the family."

"Or measles," Bernie said with a sigh. "People forget what a killer than was, even in the mid twentieth century. I remember my mum telling me that it killed one of her older cousins when he was a child."

"Yes, we do tend to forget things like that. …Ah, …now the 1737 bloke, Cuthbert, carries on to live right up to 1816."

"Wow, he had a good innings, didn't he! Just imagine, he was born in time to have memories of the Jacobite rebellion in 1745 and Bonnie Prince Charlie, and then he goes on to live through the rise and fall of Napoleon. What a fascinating life he must have led! We think times have changed fast in our lifetimes, but that must have been equally as dramatic."

However, Fliss was following the other names on the tree, and said in surprise, "Would you believe it, it's actually Auberon Lloyd, a widower, who is the head of the household in the first census in 1841, not one of the Spink family, so probably through a female line. I wonder what happened to Nenius and Aquillia?"

"Doesn't the tree tell you anything?"

"No, it doesn't. Without going through the whole tree, I'm guessing that whoever did this is Elizabeth or Marjorie's descendant …or even Flora's from a generation further back, because looking at the connections they've made, they seem to be working back through the female lines."

"Interesting," Bernie mused, "but either Nenius or Aquillia could have served in France or India. It's the right era for men to have gone out to the East in the army, or even the East India Company – that was very influential pre-Napoleonic Wars, and it would be the kind of thing you might shove a son towards to try and make his fortune, especially if the family was running short on cash by then. It was nothing unusual to have families with lots of minor noble connections, but who hardly had a penny to their names."

Fliss smiled. "We're back to Austin's Bennett family again, aren't we? Not good enough to marry upwards to save themselves, which is why it's such a shock when Lizzie marries Mr Darcy, but desperately trying to hang onto what they've got."

"Are your two lost little boys on the 1841 census?"

"No, they're not. Damn!" She managed to find the subsequent censuses, but the boys weren't on any of those either. "Oh dear, so it looks as though they must have died before 1841. What a shame. Hang on, I'll try putting in Ishwar Spink and see if anything comes up. …No, not a thing."

"Didn't it say in that one letter that they were calling him Iain?"

"So they did, after one of the boys William and Marjorie had who died – possibly a favourite brother of Cuthbert's, do you think? Or maybe Marjorie's if she was Scottish? …But no, nothing for any Ian or Iain Spink, either. I suppose if Nilmani ran away, there'd be no record of him anyway, or at least not here. And if he was that unhappy, he might not have bothered using his father's surname with anyone who found him. I can't find any connection between the Nilmani who got called Nenius and this other Nenius who's the son of Cuthbert. It seems to just be a family name."

Bernie reached over and gave her a hug. "Well you've certainly tried to find them, but it's like I said might be the case, they're so far in the past we won't ever find them."

That didn't feel like much consolation to Fliss, though, and when she went to bed, she gave the toy elephant a little stroke. "I will try and find out what happened to you, I promise. If nothing else, I can go and put flowers on Ishwar's grave."

Moreover, as she lay waiting for sleep to come, she found herself wondering who had died so violently in the house as to leave that blood pattern on the parquet? Had there been some falling out between Nenius and Aquillia? Or had that come a generation earlier between William and his son Cuthbert? Could it have been over Nathaniel's death? That had certainly enraged their sister, so why not his brother, too? She could hardly tell Bernie about that, though, could she? He'd think she'd totally lost the plot if she admitted to hearing not just voices, but an argument. And as she finally drifted off, she thought, *don't forget the desk in the storeroom!* And slightly more scarily, *whose voice do you keep hearing in your head? Don't forget that idea that came out of nowhere, that there's a body in the wall between the two halves. Why on earth would you think that?*

Over breakfast the following morning, she did have the bright idea of perhaps going and looking in the parish church's graveyard for Ishwar, at least. But a swift online search revealed that while the obvious parish church at the time must have been St Andrew's in Ombersley, just a few miles down the main road from the house, the church had been completely rebuilt in the early Victorian era, and Fliss had a suspicion that some of the very old grave slabs might have been shifted to make way for the much-enlarged church.

"Not a chance of finding you there," she sighed, as she went upstairs to put on a fresh set of overalls ready for the day. And she found it disconcerting that she was so deeply bothered about finding the two boys. Why could she not just let it go? Because this was bordering on obsession, and Fliss had never been an obsessive person, not about anything in her life before this.

It didn't help that during the evening, Bernie had asked the killer question of,

"What do you want out of life, Fliss?"

And she had been unable to give him much of a definite answer.

"I never, ever want to be dependent on my parents again," had been an obvious start, but as Bernie had pointed out, that was more what she *didn't* want than an active goal. And it was more than a little disconcerting to finally acknowledge that right now the future terrified her.

"I want someone to want me for my own sake," she'd finally been able to admit, "but I don't think that there's anyone out there for me."

"Oh, rubbish!" Bernie had protested. "Stop selling yourself short, Fliss! You're an attractive woman with a lovely personality. Of course, there's someone out there who'll treat you as well as you deserve."

But Fliss wasn't convinced. "Men want a woman who can have kids, Bernie. So many don't want to get their hands dirty with the looking after of them, mind you, as too many women I know have found out, but they regard a childless woman as some sort of freak.

"Then there's the matter of time. I'm not going to rush up the aisle with the first man I meet on a dating site. I'm not that overwhelmed by my hormones not to see how dangerous that could be. But how long will finding someone take before I could even think of having a child? Do you see, Bernie? We could be talking five or six years before I even reach the starting block, which by then would be far too late to think of safely having a first child since I'd be into my forties. And the worst of it is, right now I'm not sure that I don't want the child more than I want the man."

"Well could you not adopt?" he suggested.

Yet Fliss shook her head. "It's not that simple. I watched a friend and her husband going down that route years ago, and it hasn't got any easier since then. The adoption services want to be sure that you have a good support network around you – and given that that's for the child's sake, I have to agree with them.

"It's not me being single that's the biggest hurdle, you see, but the fact that I have nobody around me to back me up. Can you imagine a social worker sitting down to speak to Mum and Dad? The very thought that they might have to help me out sometimes would have them shrieking in horror! And Ben would be no better. I've no married friends living anywhere within this county anymore, and before you say you would help, the first stumbling block to that is that you are still working, Bernie, and couldn't drop things at a moment's notice if I needed you. And I wouldn't expect you to, either!"

But later that night, the desire to at least take on the care of two children who needed a mum wouldn't leave her be. If she couldn't have a baby, why was it so bloody impossible for her to be a mum to a child who had lost theirs? All the red tape protecting those vulnerable kids was there for all the right reasons, but it didn't make her feel any better about things at all.

So it was as much in an attempt to try and draw her own thoughts away from morbidly fretting over two little boys, who must have died over two centuries ago, that when they got to the house she began asking Bernie about the French furniture. Kevin and Sean wouldn't be with them today, partly because they had to go and finish off another job somewhere else where they'd been waiting for the concrete to set fully, and partly because they were waiting on much the same process in this house. The waterproof membrane had been put down and been covered over, with just a skim needing to be floated over it – something Bernie could do all by himself. And so, with Phil still up in the bedrooms working away on the wiring, Bernie and Fliss had an easier day ahead of them.

"Kev and Sean will be back to help us lay the floors in the rest of the house," Bernie explained. "And there's not much point in me starting on the plaster in the old part until Phil's done. Today we really just needed to come and let Phil in. If you've got an idea of what you want for at least a couple of the rooms, we could go and get the paint if you like?"

"That sounds great," Fliss said, not having to fake her smile, though it was more than a little in relief. "But before we do that, could we go and have another look at that old furniture you were so sure was French?" As they made their way up the stairs, she explained, "I know we can't take it too much for granted that we can buy this place, but was Sean right to say finders keepers?"

Bernie shrugged. "Legally? I'm not too sure. But what I can tell you is that none of it is anything like what the Davenports had. Their stuff was very nice, but distinctly modern. I think Mrs D would regard these items as the most awful old tat – in fact she said so, didn't she? Don't forget, she was going to have the whole place cleared into a skip! And as for the Chandlers, they were a nice old couple, but I don't think they knew or cared what they were leaving behind – they were just so exhausted by trying to keep the house going and their dreadful daughter off their backs, they couldn't wait to get on that cruise ship and see Southampton disappearing over the horizon. I'm not even sure whether they hadn't bought a lot of this old stuff along with the house – I don't think we're talking about their own family heirlooms here because surely they'd have put it into store for when they get back? So if you want it, Fliss, I don't think there's anything stopping you in practice. If you feel at all guilty, I would suggest you give something to the Chandlers, since it's theirs rather than the Davenports."

"That's reassuring, and I'd forgotten about the house clearers. You never said, but I presume you successfully put them off?"

"Easy as feeding a donkey strawberries," Bernie chuckled. "I don't think that lot even know what a scruple is, let alone having one. And you were right – Mrs D had knocked them down so far on what she was prepared to pay, they were already regretting ever having said they'd do it when they didn't know there was a room full of antiques to plunder. They just foresaw carting loads of crap to the nearest landfill."

By now they had reached the old storeroom, and saw that Phil had already been in here and installed the lights, but had avoided putting any sockets in after Bernie had mentioned turning it into a bathroom. There was, however, the wiring waiting for a shower and also a heated towel rail, even if neither was installed yet.

"This furniture is all going to have to come out of here anyway," Bernie declared. "We'll need to be getting the floorboards up to run pipes, which I've got Josh, my young plumber friend, lined up to come and help me with. My days of scrabbling around on my knees, groping under floorboards, have long gone. His joints are a lot younger than mine," and he winked knowingly, then ran a hand lovingly across the surface of the inlaid escritoire. "This really is a lovely piece," he said admiringly.

"What makes you so sure it's French, though?" Fliss asked curiously.

Bernie shrugged. "I can't say for certain, I'm not that expert, but look at it. For want of any other description, it's so 'feminine'. Could you really see any English gentleman commissioning a piece like this? All that fancy inlay? Yes, they would have some lovely pieces in mahogany or burr walnut, but the decoration would be in the grain of the wood itself, not with this extra gilt and inlay and marquetry. Of course, it could be Italian, but somehow, I don't think Italian furniture would have made its way into a small manor house of this sort in such a far-flung shire from the major ports, if you know what I mean."

"So would this have been for a woman?"

"Some lady's writing desk? Yes, it could well have been. What's beyond doubt is that the bookcase beside it matches it, and now I can see it a bit better,

I think that the bookcase behind that one, again makes them a pair. Maybe they bracketed the desk in a previous time?"

"The colours in that wood are just gorgeous," Fliss sighed, letting her fingers drift across the marquetry veneer of the delicate escritoire. "In a plain room they would look stunning, though I can imagine that they would once have been against something like a floral wallpaper, and that would have looked quite overwhelming. …So who do you think might have owned these from amongst the people we found on the family tree? None of them sounded particularly French, did they? Not even the later bloke who wasn't one of the Spinks."

Bernie puffed his cheeks with raise eyebrows. "Not a clue, I'm afraid. All I can say is that they're Rococo in style, so that's really before the nineteenth century."

"So that would put them back in the time of William and Marjorie, or their son Cuthbert and his very normal sounding wife, Alice. We didn't find any mention of a wife for Aquillia, did we? I wonder if the French lady was his?"

"Someone escaping the French Revolution? Now there's romantic for you," Bernie said with a cheeky wink. "All a bit *Scarlet Pimpernel* and stuff."

"Oh, good lord, Bernie!" Fliss protested with a giggle of her own. "I know I read some romance, but I'm not that into bodice-rippers, you know!"

"Nah, you can't fool me. I saw you with that well-thumbed copy of *Dragonfly in Amber* the other night! I've never read the books myself, you understand, but I did watch the *Outlander* TV series."

"Yes," protested Fliss, with a roll of the eyes of her own, "because it's a bloody good story and it withstands rereading! …But actually, you've just poked my memory. After Culloden, a lot of Scots fled to France, didn't they?"

"Oh indeed, if only to save their families from persecution for hiding them."

"And wasn't William's wife, Marjorie, Scottish? So maybe this furniture came from someone on her side, who spent years hiding in France?"

Bernie blinked in surprise. "Yes, I suppose it could. That's a connection I hadn't made, but it's as good a one as any. It would certainly fit in terms of the style."

"And does this match the period for the wardrobes in the one bedroom? Not the one that was built for here, I mean."

"I think it probably does. You have to remember, Fliss, that when it comes to furniture, I'm only an interested amateur. You'd need a professional to tell you for sure. Possibly someone like an auctioneer."

"And this desk, too?" Fliss gestured to the desk which had given her such a jolt before, and which she was carefully avoiding touching right now.

"I suspect so."

"So it does look as though someone packed up a fair part of a complete household and brought it over to England, doesn't it?"

Bernie realised what she was getting at. "Hmm, this isn't just a few random treasured pieces, maybe brought over as part of an inheritance from much loved parents, is it? This is someone moving lock, stock and barrel from France. I wonder who on earth that could be, and why? It doesn't fit any of the family members we know of, does it?"

Fliss shook her head. "No, it doesn't, and where the hell does India fit in with it? Because if we couldn't find the boys in the nineteenth century, then they, too, must have been here in the eighteenth, when this furniture was relatively newly arrived. And that really is a puzzle."

Bernie gave another perplexed huff. "Well let's contemplate that mystery while we go and buy some paint. Phil should be done in this half of the house by the weekend, so we can think about getting the bedrooms at least partially painted, and then moving some of these things out into them for the time being, even if that isn't where they're going to be staying."

Oh Lord, Fliss thought as they walked downstairs still talking about France, *and that probably means I'll be having to handle those as well. I hope I don't disgrace myself and flake out the moment I touch that bloody desk!*

William

1747

It was a week after the funeral when William heard the mysterious voice again. Up until now, he had never been able to bring himself to sleep in the big bedroom which had been his parents at the front of the house. He had always had the unsettling feeling of being watched in that part of the house, though he had never confided that to anyone, not even to Marjorie. And so throughout their married life, they had stayed in the big bedroom in the old part of the house which his father had allocated to them upon their marriage. If it had been intended to remind William that he must defer to the old man, even in his dotage, Marjorie at least had viewed it as a blessing. The lower ceiling had made even a room as large as that one a lot warmer in the winter than the cavernous ceilinged new rooms.

Yet now William felt that he could never sleep easily in his old bed ever again. And that wasn't helped by hearing the spectral voice again in there.

"Do you think it might have been someone escaping the French Revolution?" he heard someone who, had he known it, was Fliss asking Bernie, and Bernie's equally disembodied voice replying. Their language was strange, but William could just about follow most of the words.

"Maybe. Given that the troubles started in 1789, if someone was fleeing from France around then, that would almost certainly be the reason why."

"So maybe they were trying to avoid the guillotine?"

William had no idea what or who a guillotine was until Bernie's voice said,

"Not the guillotine. That wasn't invented quite that early. That came with what's called The Terror, and that's not for another six or seven years afterwards, and that's also after Louis XVI is executed."

The king executed? And Louis XVI? That baffled William. The current king was Louis XV, so did that mean that his son Louis was about to ascend the throne? Was there about to be some sort of overthrow of his father to put him on the throne? All of these thoughts rattled through William's head as he heard the man's voice continuing,

"No, what you get at the start is civil unrest – rioting and things over the price of food. But in those first stages you don't really get many French nobles fleeing to England. They're pretty much trying to stick it out in the early days, believing that the king – or at least the powerful nobles – will squash the rebellions. It's only after King Louis and Marie Antoinette are killed in 1793 that you start to see mass migration of the nobles out of France in fear of their lives. And, of course, a lot didn't make it."

Marie Antoinette? William thought in shock. Who on earth was she? Louis the Dauphin had been married for just two years to the Infanta of Spain until her death last year, and in February had remarried to Maria Josepha of Saxony – or so the broadsheets had said. Had they been wrong? The Dauphin had no male children as yet, so who was this Marie Antoinette, and who was she married to? And *what* year had the voice said?

William couldn't know that the Dauphin he was aware of would die before his father, Louis XV, and never become king. Nor that the grandson who would succeed to the French throne would be the Dauphin and Infanta's son, who was yet to be born in 1754 – still seven years in William's future.

"Does this mean that it was one of the French nobility who came to this house?" Fliss asked, totally unaware of William in the past hanging on her every word. French nobility in his house? How could that happen?

"Unlikely to be high nobility," Bernie clarified, "and you have to take into account that there were trouble spots where even men of means found life far more dangerous before then. Brittany was one place, and then the Vendée around the Loire was another one only a year or two later, although that was with counter-revolutionaries."

Counter-revolutionaries? William mentally gasped, his head now reeling with all of this strange information. So there was to be a revolution and a counter-revolution, or were they going to happen at the same time? And when? In his lifetime, or beyond? What years had the ghosts mentioned? 1793? But that was …that was over forty-five years in the future from now! How could these ghosts know about things that would happen then? Were they one of God's stranger creations or the Devil's? That thought all by itself had his guts churning anxiously. He must get the rector back to pray over the whole of this house in that case.

"Heavens, it does get complicated," the woman's voice sighed, but then William heard no more as footsteps moved away, and the voices became fainter until they disappeared.

That, as far as he was concerned, was that in terms of him spending even one more night in this room, and he ordered his servants to make him up the bed in the bedroom across the hall from the servants' stairs. His housekeeper did suggest the room next door to his present one, which was part of the newer house and over the music room, but William turned that down flat. If the strange apparition could appear in the wall adjoining the servants' stairs in his current bedroom, what was to stop it from simply turning around and coming out on the other side of the stairwell in the other one? No, he was not risking that! Anyway, the one he was going into was over the library, which was part of the original house, and he felt much safer there. If one strange spirit could appear to him, heaven knew whether or not his father might turn up in the rooms he had used most, and William had been scared enough of him in life to not want to face him in death.

However, the next morning he realised that it just would not do for the master of the house to be sleeping in the room to which his father had consigned visitor's personal servants. It just wasn't done. And worse, William feared what gossip might spread around the village, despite his constant injunctions to the servants to hold their tongues about what went on in the house. Already he had heard some quiet whispers about Marjorie's death, and that she had died of a broken heart. Praise be to God that nobody had yet uttered anything to the effect that she might have starved herself to death – that would be such a stain upon his reputation that it might never recover.

And so, despite a terrible inner reluctance, he decided that he must go and choose one of the front bedrooms for his own. Even in the light of a fresh new day, he still couldn't face the bedroom over the music room, and anyway, it was still a touch small for the master of such a house as this to have as his own, so that left the two front bedrooms on the first floor, and the ones above them on the second. All had stood empty since his father's death, rooms waiting on visitors who never came anymore. His father had been the one who had been welcome amongst the higher levels of county society, not him, though William never grasped that it was his permanent coldness towards everyone which had put his own generation off him, not any lack of status. William wasn't a cold fish only to his family, he was like it with everyone, eternally paranoid that they were as disapproving of him as his father had always been, and so saying as little as possible to avoid either making some unforgivable *faux pas*, or giving some clue away of an inadvertent indiscretion which would come back to bite him later on. William trusted nobody because he'd never even had anyone within his family whom he could trust.

Nevertheless, he still couldn't bring himself to use either of the main bedrooms, not just his father's, and instead chose the one on the top floor which had a window which looked over the driveway and the gardens. At the moment the bedroom had little furniture in it, but that wasn't a problem. He could always have the footman and groom bring some of the other furniture across later. The main thing was to seem to be in control of his own house, and to make an understandable move out of a bedroom he could no longer face. Grief for his wife would be sufficient explanation to the servants. They could pass that on to whomever they liked. A grieving widower was socially acceptable, a man who jumped at shadows was not.

Chapter 13

Thursday afternoon – Friday & 1758

With Fliss having chosen readily available paints for the bedrooms she'd started cleaning, it was just a matter of driving back into Worcester to a branch of a big DIY chain and picking up the paint. And in truth she really was enjoying this part of the process. She couldn't wait to start putting the colours onto the walls and seeing whether they looked as good as she hoped they were going to. She was also determinedly putting down the seeing of things to her overactive imagination, and the unexpected chance to have what she couldn't help but think of as a proper home at last.

If the Davenports and the Chandlers didn't want that lovely old furniture, then she certainly did, and it was going to be all the better for not having to pay an arm and a leg for it, as well. To salve her conscience, she might make as large a donation as she could manage to some suitable charity, or even better to the Chandlers – who she felt were the rightful owners if anyone was, albeit by default – but the Davenports were already so dodgy to her way of thinking that she had no qualms over deceiving them at all.

Her decision was helped in no small measure by knowing that she'd had to leave all of little furniture she had in the London flat. She'd scraped together enough money to put a few boxes of treasured possessions into storage, but there was no way she could afford to hold onto a flat's worth, not even one as small as hers. Her parents had outright turned her down over that and so had her brother. Meaning that for once, Fliss was determined to have a proper fresh start that didn't cripple her financially from the outset – whatever happened this time, it had to last, because once she tipped over that magic line in the financial world of turning forty, things like mortgages and big loans for furnishings were going to be nigh on impossible to get. These days everyone wanted to know how long you'd been in a job, to be sure you were stable and likely to stick it out for the term of the loan; so without a very good job where she could pay money straight out of her wages, she was in real trouble.

Whether you end up living in the house, or you have to find a place somewhere else, you'll have a few really beautiful pieces of furniture in there, she told herself, feeling thankful. Okay, the painted wardrobe wasn't what most modern people would want, quite aside from it being her own childhood dream, but if she couldn't afford to buy pictures for on the walls of wherever, then it would be all the better if the furniture was decorative in its own right. And if she could rent nothing more than a stark modern studio-flat with magnolia on every wall, then the two inlaid bookcases and the escritoire would completely decorate a wall all by themselves. None of them were that big that they wouldn't fit into a modern place.

The big wardrobe where she had found the hatpin and which had fitted so well into the other bedroom, however, would look out of place in anywhere modern, and so would the ornate desk with its pigeonholed top. And much as it grieved her to think of them being thrown out, she recognised that they might still have to be sold on if the house was too. It would be better to send them to a sale room and send the Chandlers the money, rather than doing as Mrs Davenport had done, and just abandoning them to the fickle tastes of any new owners. So with all of that in mind, when she and Bernie got back with all of their tins of paint, one of the last things Fliss did for the day was to go and drape the wardrobes in firstly a tough cotton decorator's sheet, and then with a plastic sheet too. It would be a terrible shame if in her less than expert painting, she ended up flicking emulsion or distemper over any of the pieces, and then finding that it wouldn't come off without damaging the delicate old surfaces.

On Friday morning, with Phil now having finished with the top bedrooms completely, Bernie brought up the first of the paint and showed Fliss how best to use a paint roller, and also how to cut into the angles and corners with a brush.

"Better to put lots of very light coats on, rather than a thick coat where the paint dribbles and runs," he explained to her. "You'll probably have to stop around mid-afternoon, because without the lights on, you won't be able to see what you've done and what needs touching up."

"Great!" Fliss agreed with a beaming smile, already delighted with how the Orange Coloured White was going on to the old plaster. It was soaking up the paint like a sponge, but even with the small patch she had covered this far, she could see how the colour was warming up the room. "How long should I leave it between coats?"

"It probably depends on how fast it dries," Bernie admitted. "The way that first coat is getting sucked up, by the time you've finished the last of the walls, you should be able to start going around again. I'll work up here alongside you today, doing the ceilings. There's not much else I can productively do."

And so, with Bernie expertly wielding a roller on a long, extendable handle, and doing the clever stuff of cutting in both paints where they met at the ceiling's edges, they had a pleasant morning transforming the first bedroom. Once he'd put one coat on the room Fliss was in, Bernie moved on to do the other bedroom ceiling, and then to cleaning the landing ceiling and walls. It meant that by the afternoon she was working alone in the more southerly of the two bedrooms, but grateful that because of that, she had more space in which to work. By the time she'd put two lightweight coats of paint on, the room was already looking much more cheerful. And although she knew she now needed to stop, because Bernie would need to come in tomorrow and put at least one more coat on the ceiling before she finished off the walls, she couldn't help but want to see how it looked with the wardrobe uncovered.

Before she'd really thought about what she was doing, she'd whipped off the plastic sheet, and was tugging off the cotton one as well. Even as she was gasping, "Oh! That looks *so* good!" she made the mistake of putting her hand on the wardrobe. Instantly she felt as if she was stumbling forwards straight into the wardrobe, despite the other part of her knowing that she was only leaning on it in reality.

For a few brief moments everything seemed to move in a giddying swirl, and then as her vision stabilised, she realised that she was looking into the bedroom of a much earlier era. The wardrobe was back in its alcove, and she was looking across towards the door onto the landing – in reality several feet away from where she was actually standing now. The man she now knew was William was sitting on the edge of a moderately large bed, but looking much older than when she had seen him last, even though for her it had been only a couple of days. He had a letter in his hands, and whatever it said had reduced him to tears – and somehow Fliss knew that William wasn't the kind of man who cried much about anything normally.

"Why won't you come home, Cuthbert?" he suddenly sobbed, the words almost being torn out of him. "I need you here. I can't look after this house on my own anymore."

In despair he flung the letter away from him, and the lone sheet fluttered across the room towards the wardrobe. As it settled and slid to a halt, Fliss saw a date, or at least she saw a year, 1758. Wasn't that the year before Cuthbert married? And how old would William be then? She struggled to keep her thoughts steady enough to work it out, but came to the conclusion that he must by now be about fifty-eight, helped enormously by the recollection that he had probably been born at the turn of the century, since he'd been twenty-four at the time of his marriage in 1724. It shocked her that William looked a very old man now. Had she had to guess, she would have thought him well into his seventies by his appearance.

"Time hasn't been kind to you," she said aloud without realising she was doing so, and at her words William's head flung upwards.

"You!" he cried in horror. "I thought you gone for good!"

"Oh thanks," Fliss replied sarcastically. "Nice to see you, too. So what have you been up to, William, that your own son doesn't want to see you, eh? Did Flora ever come back?"

"Flora is dead, taken in childbed," he said so softly and hoarsely that Fliss barely heard him.

"Oh no, I'm so sorry to hear that! She seemed like such a lively young woman. How very sad."

"It was sad, but little you care. You brought a hex upon this family when you appeared, one we have never recovered from."

"Me?" Fliss was shocked. "I brought nothing on you! If you've been unfortunate, going on the last time I saw you, you've brought it on yourself. Daughters don't just turn on their fathers for no reason, you know. I speak from bitter experience here! You must have been pretty rotten to her to have got her as upset as she was when I saw her. Why did she blame you for her brother's death, eh? Where did you send him to that was so bad? Where?"

Looking up with bloodshot eyes, under-hung with bags of loose skin that would have done a bloodhound proud, William replied,

"In case you are one of God's own, I will answer you truthfully, and if you are one of the Devil's then it matters not, for I am condemned anyway. I thought to keep in with both sides who wanted the crown. So I sent Cuthbert to my cousin Phineas, who had, and still does have, a good position at the court in London under King George. I make no apology for that. I did what I could for the boy, and he has benefitted from it, though you would not think so from his lack of gratitude."

Fliss snorted. "Maybe that's because, as a small child of eight, what he wanted more than a career with the king was his mother! Did you ever think of that? And he never saw her again, did he? So what sort of memory does he have of this house? A home he probably feels he was thrown out of as unwanted, and with the one person he really loved dead and buried long ago."

She saw her words hit home and rolled her eyes in exasperation. Really? Had William never once thought what it must have been like for that little boy? How scary it must have been to be uprooted and sent to people he could scarcely have known, and then worse, to know that the one person he'd have been sure loved him had died, and would never again come to sing him to sleep or comfort him when he cried. Upper-class mothers of the day hadn't been as hands-on as ordinary women, she knew that, but even so, there was a special bond with your mother that it took some real betrayal to break – and that was something else she knew of from first-hand experience.

"What of Nathaniel, then?" she demanded. "Where did you send him?"

William's expression flashed to one as if she had physically stabbed him. "Marjorie's cousin, Angus Macintosh, sent word that he was with the Stuart prince's army at Derby. He was so full of the belief that a Stuart king would once again sit on the throne of England." The tears were now flowing down William's parchment-like cheeks. "I believed him, even though Marjorie kept telling me that Angus was always a dreamer. And so I sent Nathaniel with a manservant to ride with speed northwards. If they did not meet with Angus at Derby, I knew that Angus would try to visit his sister in Melrose, so I sent them onwards to there, for Marjorie had told us that he had tried to persuade his brother-in-law – her husband – to join him, just as he had her brothers. Well they did find him, but only as the army fled north again."

"Oh dear." What else could Fliss say? The Jacobite cause by then was already doomed.

"Hmph!" William snorted. "You immortals might have known the way things would go, but I did not!" and Fliss hadn't the heart to say that if he'd opened his eyes and read the broadsheets a bit more widely, then it would have been clear even then that the promised help from France had never materialised, and without that there had never been much chance of Bonnie Prince Charlie winning – or at least that was how she understood things to have been.

Nor could she plausibly explain that she wasn't what he called an 'immortal'. What else would he call her when she seemed to him not to have aged at all since he'd last seen her? He would never understand that for her only a couple of days had passed, so of course she wouldn't have aged.

William was now glowering at her. "If bloody Angus was still alive, I'd have gone and slit his treacherous throat myself!" he hissed, and yet Fliss saw straight through that. William was nobody's idea of a man of action. Indeed, if he had gone and challenged this soldier cousin of his wife's, it was more likely that it would have been him with his throat slit. "He was supposed to take my boy to the Stuart court in Edinburgh, not drag him into the far north and a massacre!"

God, you're another one who always shifts the blame onto someone else! *Fliss thought bitterly.* It's never your fault, oh no, not you! *And that left all the nastier taste in her mouth, because she knew that if her father had been in William's shoes, he would have behaved exactly the same. It had never been his fault that he got passed over for promotion at work. Never his fault that the client wasn't happy with what they got. Never his fault, full stop.*

"The Stuart court in Edinburgh?" she found herself flinging back at William. "There never was *a Stuart court in Edinburgh in 1745 or '6! Prince Charlie hardly set foot in the place apart from going there to try and raise more troops. Even I know that! If you'd stopped and thought about it properly for even a few minutes, you'd have realised that you'd be better sending your son to France, where others of the prince's court were waiting for the word to come and join him. That would have been a better place for a little boy of ten, not being dragged the length and breadth of Scotland in a dying army! But then you didn't think of what it would be like for him any more than you thought about Cuthbert. For you they weren't sons to be loved, they were like expendable pieces on a chess board."*

"No!" roared William, staggering to his feet with his fists clenched but still by his sides. "No, you evil thing! I loved my boys!"

"Not enough to go and fetch them home when you saw how their loss was tearing Marjorie apart," Fliss snapped back. "Or was poor little Nathaniel already dead by then? …But even so, you could have gone to your cousin in London and explained that Marjorie was dying for want of having one last child at home with her. Or is your cousin another like you, too worried about what everyone else will think to show an ounce of compassion?"

"You know nothing!" William sobbed.

"I know everything!" riposted Fliss. "I know just what it's like to have a father like you, because my own is another one cut from the same cloth as you. I know only too well what your children have been through, because I've been through that heartache myself, and it hurts …it bloody hurts!"

"I banish you in the name of Jesus Christ, Our Lord!" screamed William. "Be gone, She Devil!"

In a voice dripping with scorn, Fliss hit back with, "I'm no devil, 'she' or otherwise. And the devils which you think plague you, William Spink, are those of your own guilty conscience. Well, I wouldn't hold your breath on Cuthbert coming home before they nail your coffin lid shut. From what I can gather, you ceased to be any sort of father to him before he'd even reached the age of ten, so why would he bother with you now?"

And this time it was her own willpower which brought her back to the present, not a severing of the connection in the past.

Later on, she would wonder whether that was why she was then able to connect so much better through time with some of the pieces touched by those in the past as well. The ones where the connection was broken by those in the past became one-off events. But when she herself pulled back, it was almost like a telephone call where the caller was able to stay on the line after the receiver had cut the call at their end. For now, though, she was only too glad to throw the two lots of protection back over the wardrobe, and go and find Bernie to go home.

In the past, however, William was left shivering and shaking, staring wild-eyed at the wardrobe as his manservant came hurrying up the stairs as fast as his aging legs would carry him, having heard his master's cries of distress. The young footman following close behind him, wondered whose heart was likely to give out first – old Robert's in front of him or the master's. When they got into the bedroom, they were shocked at their master's wild state.

"Best go for Doctor Jones," the older man decided, and then added, "and after that, better go for Rector Portman. He might know more what to do than the doctor."

As he tried to calm his distraught master, old Robert was thankful that Rector Underhill had died five years ago. He knew it was wrong to think such a thing of a man of God, but a more malevolent cleric he had rarely come across. He'd certainly done nothing to ease the mistress' suffering all those years ago, and though he would never admit it to anyone now, old Robert had long held a flame in his heart for Mistress Marjorie. She had deserved better than the master had given her, and he had originally only stayed on with William Spink because he'd hoped that young Miss Flora would one day come home with a husband and children, and fill the house with light and laughter again.

By the time Flora had died he was too old to be looking for another post, and so Robert had hung on, just hoping that when Master Cuthbert finally showed up, that he would be more of his mother's boy than his father's. Having seen the cold and distant letters which had come of late, though, he knew now that it was a false hope. If Cuthbert came home, old Robert would be thrown onto the parish's mercy as being of no further use, and that and that alone made him go and fetch a quilted coverlet to put around his master's quaking shoulders. Sir William dying would be no good for anyone else in the household, yet he couldn't help reflecting bitterly, *Whatever it was that you think you saw, I'm glad it's finally making you pay for everything that you've put us all through.*

Cuthbert

1758

When Cuthbert arrived at the house a month after his father's funeral, he was greeted by old Robert and Martha, the housekeeper, who was also well into middle age.

"Welcome home Master Cuthbert," Robert said, trying to put some warmth into his voice for this sneering young man who stood before him.

"Who are you?" Cuthbert demanded, barely bothering to look at someone he had already mentally half dismissed.

"I'm Robert, sir. Your father's manservant, and the person who taught you how to ride when you were a boy."

That made Cuthbert blink and look at Robert properly. Good God, how old was this man now? Surely he was far too old to be of any use?

"You're dismissed," he said with an indifferent wave of his hand. "Pack your bags and be out of here by nightfall. I have no use for you."

"Sir!" Martha protested. "You cannot do that! Robert has nowhere else to go!"

"And for questioning my orders, you can pack your bags and go too," was the response she got. "In fact, all of you can go. I will be fetching my own servants from London."

Yet it was Martha's bitter aside to Robert of, "Then I hopes he pays them more to put up with his bad moods than the pittance his father paid us. They'm going to earn every penny, I reckon!" which made Cuthbert reconsider.

He'd managed to ensure that no word had come back to here of Uncle Phineas' bankruptcy, having always had to call him 'uncle' even though he now knew that Phineas had been merely a cousin. And Phineas was now somewhere on the Continent with his long-suffering wife, with Cuthbert having had to arrange to collect what little post came his way from an inn, now that the house overlooking the smart little square in London had had to be sold. That was the main reason why he'd not been back for the funeral – the letter just hadn't reached him in time – but he wasn't about to let on to that here. Worse, far from having the glittering career at court that his father had erroneously presumed he had, thanks to the lying letters Phineas had made him write, Cuthbert had barely been making ends meet in London, and so it had come as an almighty relief to know that he had finally inherited Sytchampton House and the small farming estate and factory which went with it.

Even so, he'd been intending to bring in just as many new servants as he absolutely had to have to run the house, until he knew how much income he might have. There were no servants retained in London, and he certainly wouldn't employ any of Phineas' when they knew too much of the truth – Cuthbert wasn't going to risk gossip here such as he'd endured in the capital. But Martha's words instantly gave him another idea. If his father had been paying them so little, would new servants come and work for only that? Even bearing in mind that the main recompense for most servants was that they had a better roof over their heads than they could ever afford themselves, and food on the table regularly, too, most still wanted a bit of actual money for their labours. Yet this sounded as though his father hadn't given any increase in pay in years, and that was music to Cuthbert's ears.

"What was my father paying you?" he called after them, and when the seven of them turned and trudged back, sullenly telling him what each of them got, it was all he could do not to laugh out loud. That wasn't even half of what he'd had to pay servants in London – or at least back when he'd still been able to afford them.

"*Hmph*!" he managed to snort imperiously without letting his glee show. "Then you may continue to work for me at those rates. Do not expect any more, mind you, and you will have to earn it as well. I do not pay shirkers."

Muttered, 'yes sirs', came back, and it was almost more than he could believe that they all agreed to his terms. He'd been expecting at least the gardener and his lad to have spat at his feet and walked off. God in Heaven, he might just pull this off! He might be able to live as a gentleman again! And if he was really lucky, there might even be enough for him to invest a little in Robert Clive's new ventures in India, where – if the newspapers were to be believed – he had successfully taken over Bengal, and a man like him might make enough to truly become a gentleman of means.

What he didn't hear were Robert's quiet words to Martha once they got through into the kitchen.

"Something is not right," Robert declared. "Why change his mind like that? It was the money, of that I am sure."

Martha nodded, agreeing with, "And did you look at his clothes? His coat needs mending and those boots of his have seen better days. Where is all the money the master said young Master Cuthbert has? It has surely not gone on himself."

"Aye, and he be as thin as my rake," Walter the gardener added, as he accepted a mug of small beer off Fanny, the cook. "That young man have had less to eat of late than us, I tell you."

The servants clustered together as Robert, as their leader, said, "So we all agree, we stay on and say nothing. It's hard enough to find work for younger men, what with folks leaving the farms for the towns these days. The Good Lord knows, we do not live like princes here, but this is better by far than being paupers living in some hovel. So none of us give him cause to dismiss us, agreed? We need time to find out what is going on with this young master of ours."

"Robert is right," Martha said firmly, then looking to Sarah the young housemaid. "If he looks like giving you any trouble, we shall just have to make sure that you are never alone in a room with him without Robert or Henry present. It will hardly be difficult in a house of this size when there is only one of him to five of us indoors."

"Thank you," said Sarah, although she hoped that her frizz of red hair, face full of freckles, and bony build, would deter any amorous advances, for she was sure she would compare badly to the fashionable women the young master must be used to. For once she would be kneeling in church and instead of praying that Will, the blacksmith's lad, would look her way at least once, she'd be begging God to make sure that her master's gaze went straight past her.

Everyone knew what had happened to Mary, the maid from another big house down the road. Thrown out when her belly began to swell, even though everyone also knew that the poor girl had been beside herself fending off the young master of the family. It hadn't saved her reputation, nor the burden of a new mouth to feed for her parents, and Mary now had to work in the fields at whatever bits of jobs she could get. Sarah didn't want that, she really didn't. Yet mercifully the first week went by, and then the second, and young Master Cuthbert seemed content to let things tick along as they had for years – for which all of the servants gave thanks on Sunday.

They might not have been quite so glad had they known how relieved Cuthbert was to discover that he had access to his father's money as soon as he'd signed some papers. Praise the Lord there was enough to pay the bills for a few months, and having sat at his father's desk and gone through the estate accounts, he could see that what had drained the money recently had been the elaborate funeral that his father's lawyers had taken it upon themselves to arrange for the old man in his absence. Give it another few months for the rents from the farm and the smallholding to start building things back up again, and for the next lot of orders to be fulfilled at the glove factory and be paid for, and Cuthbert would be comfortable if not rich. And with there being sufficient in the bank for now to pay the servants with, and a few tradesmen like the grocer, he might just get away with nobody ever knowing how impoverished he'd been when he arrived.

It took a month or two for him to start receiving visitors, in no small measure due to the fact that his father had long since ceased to entertain at the house, and so their neighbours had almost forgotten about the Spink family when it came to sending out invitations. Summer passed into autumn, and Cuthbert gradually relaxed as it was born in on him that his father's dying had been the best thing to ever happen to him. He was master of his own household, the money from this year's harvest had come in, and if he was really careful with his money, he could maintain the pretence of being a gentleman of substance.

So much so, that as the celebrations for the foiling of Guy Fawkes' attempt to blow up the Houses of Parliament back in 1605 on November the fifth came around, Cuthbert decided that he might dare hold a party. There could be the traditional bonfire out in the garden, which would mean that people would spend less time in the house to find fault with it, and if Fanny the cook was hardly capable of laying on elaborate feasts, she could certainly acquit herself well enough to provide an array of passable dainties for people to nibble upon as they enjoyed the festivities. Invitations were sent, and replies came back, and only one asked if they might stay the night on account of the old lady being too frail to travel back again in one day.

The house was scrubbed and primped, and decorated with fresh floral arrangements, and if the old part was hardly fashionable, that did not matter since none of the visitors – not even the old lady's maid and her husband's valet – would need to sleep there. Cuthbert's own servants shared the two rooms over the kitchen and scullery, with Martha, Fanny and Sarah in one room, and Robert and Henry in the other. So, if the two visiting servants had the top floor rooms at the front, that should keep them nicely detached from his own and away from gossip.

What Cuthbert hadn't been expecting was for the old lady's maid to be so well-endowed. He was practically breaking out in a sweat just at the sight of her dress straining over her bosom, and it painfully reminded him that he hadn't enjoyed a woman in a very long time. So much so that the evening itself went by in a blur, Cuthbert having only part of his mind on the general small talk, and the rest of it on how he was going to get that girl alone.

His chance came shortly after breakfast. Both guests, who were of his father's age, declared that they would not return to their bedrooms for the stairs would be too much for them, and so the valet and the maid were sent up to pack. Cuthbert hardly needed to excuse himself from speaking to his guests, since both of them were nodding off again in the armchairs in the morning room, which left him free to stalk his prey. The moment appeared when the valet had taken his own small bag downstairs, and was busy in the room beneath, packing his master's. The maid, however, was still up in her room, which was above Cuthbert's own, thereby ensuring that nobody beneath would hear a thing.

Slipping silently into the room, Cuthbert closed the door and made his way around the bed to where the maid was bending over a bag on a chair. Reaching around her, he grasped her breasts with both hands, panting,

"There you are, my little dove! What a glorious handful you are!"

"Sir!" squealed the poor girl, shocked and frightened.

'What are you doing' wasn't a question she

needed to ask – it was horribly clear what he was going to do, and that was confirmed as he spun her around and pressed her face first up against the wardrobe with him at her back. He let go of her one breast now that his weight was crushing her against the doors, and instead reached down to start hauling up her skirt. Struggle though she might, she couldn't get free of him, for Cuthbert was tall even if he wasn't heavily built, and he was strong, especially now that he was better fed.

As she felt his hands reach what he'd been after, she began to weep, especially as it dawned on her that he must have had his breeches held up by only the top button in readiness. Otherwise how was he thrusting himself at her so soon?

In the future it was Monday, and Fliss was back in the bedroom collecting her paint tray and roller. Bernie was downstairs, but would be up to put a coat of paint on the landing before coming back into here, so she was about to go and put the first coats of paint on the walls in the other rooms. Therefore at first she didn't query what the rhythmical bump, bump, bumps were, assuming that it was Bernie carrying his steps up or something.

But then she heard Bernie's voice downstairs, and looked out to see him chatting to the postman in the drive, and at that point she woke up to just what those bump, bump, bumps were!

"What the hell?" she exclaimed. She might not have a husband in tow, but she'd not lived that reclusive a life as to not know what the sounds were of someone having sex, and fairly vigorous sex at that. But who on earth would be doing that up here? Then she realised that the sounds were coming from the wardrobe, and her first thoughts were that William was at some poor girl.

Before she'd thought about what she was doing, she'd thrown the covers up, and slapped her hands against the mirrored doors.

"Oye! What the hell do you think you're doing?" she growled, getting the now familiar swirling, sinking feeling as the way opened up between times.

As it opened up fully, Fliss found herself face to face with a weeping young girl, and a different man's face behind her.

"Leave her be, you filthy animal" Fliss screamed, and the girl fainted while the man went white and staggered away, visibly wilting. "She's just a kid! Leave her alone!"

The man collapsed onto the bed, still staring at her bug-eyed, mouth working soundlessly.

"Can you get up? ...Sweetheart, can you hear me?" Fliss called. "Sweetheart, get up and get out of here!"

There came a groan from the floor, and then Fliss saw the girl roll over onto her side, retch, and then at first on all fours, begin to crawl away. By the time she had got past the bed, the girl had managed to haul herself to her feet using the bed's footboard, and then risked the dash for the door. Turning her attention back to the man, Fliss demanded,

"Who the hell are you?"

She half expected him to make the same demand back, but then realised that what she could see of his shirt, and the breeches around his ankles, looked very similar in design to William's. So maybe she wasn't far off the same era again?

"Where's William? And why are you in his house raping his maid?"

"F…F…Father's dead," Cuthbert finally managed to splutter, scared witless by this apparition dressed like nobody he'd ever seen before, and clearly furious with him. And where was that behind her? He was facing no mirror, so how could he see a reflection of the room but not himself? (For the mirrors on the doors were a later addition beyond his time, and Cuthbert had never seen a mirrored door to compare it to.) It looked like this room, but where was all the furniture? Why did it look so barren and deserted? Was this some warning of the future, some dread reminder to mend his ways?

For Fliss, his calling of William 'Father' mean that this could only be one person – Cuthbert – because who else was there left of William and Marjorie's children? He certainly looked as though he was a chip off William's block! If he'd inherited any of Marjorie's softer qualities, his time away from here had evidently killed those stone dead. But the way his face had fallen into what she could only describe as a petulant pout pressed all of the wrong buttons with her yet again. Ben did that. Ben, her bloody brother who'd had everything handed to him on a plate, and yet who couldn't even be bothered to answer her phone calls, much less help.

And so in a cathartic rush, the words came pouring out of Fliss.

"Ah, Cuthbert, is it? What a bloody disgrace to the family you are! What would your mother say, eh? Or your sister Flora? What do you think their ghosts are thinking of you right now, hmm?"

"M…M…Mother? F…F…Fa…"

"Never mind your fucking father! He's in enough trouble in the hereafter if there's any justice. Anyway, he's a bit beyond redemption now, isn't he? But you,

you're still here, and you need to think about changing your ways, sunshine! Look at you! You're a grown man now, not the baby boy of the household who throws tantrums and gets just what he wants because nobody wants to upset you."

That was really her memories of Ben flooding in, not what she was seeing, but Fliss was past caring at this point.

"For God's sake, wake up and think of others for a change! What's that poor girl to do now, eh? She's probably scarred for life after having your bony body banging away at her. God knows, you're hardly anyone's idea of an oil painting, are you? Not exactly the devilishly handsome lover you might give in to on a whim. More like being shagged by a skeleton! Well the next time you get the urge, use your right hand instead, not some poor kid who just happens to be there at the time."

In her fury, she banged her hands on the mirrors again, and suddenly the wardrobe rocked on the uneven floorboards which were not yet fully screwed back down after Phil's work. As it wobbled, it broke the connection and Fliss found herself panting in fury but back in the modern world

Meanwhile, Cuthbert had no idea of what even half of what she was saying meant, but he was getting the gist of it – mend your ways or you will burn in Hell, and his father was most likely there before him. Terrified, as she winked out of existence and the wardrobe doors returned to normal wood, he fumbled with his breeches, and then staggered out onto the landing. Down below he could hear Robert saying softly,

"Get her out of here before he comes down," and the valet saying,

"I'll go before I bloody kill him! I'll not have my intended ruined by a man such as him."

Oh God, what have I done? Cuthbert thought, rapidly waking up to what his blind lust had done, and that in one fell swoop, he might have ruined his reputation around here for good. *What can I do? What can I say?*

He heard the measured tread of old Robert plodding up the stairs, and the sprightlier footsteps of Henry with him. No hope of fooling both of them. Henry alone he might have persuaded that the girl had led him on, but not with Robert muttering and glowering in disbelief beside him. And he might have physically threatened old Robert into silence, but not when Henry was such a hulking young man. What to say? What to say?

"Now then Master Cuthbert, what have you been up to?" Robert asked, as he reached the top of the servants' stairs and looked up the last few landing steps at Cuthbert, still weakly hanging onto the hand rail around the void which threw light down the stairwell. And just for one awful moment, Robert wondered whether he was about the throw himself over it.

"Woman …in the wardrobe. Ghost!" Cuthbert blurted out, mentally wincing at how feeble that sounded. But then was even more shocked when Robert turned to Henry and said,

"Oh Lord have mercy, looks like the white lady is back again. Better go and send for Rector Portman. Either his prayers didn't work the first time, or something has brought the ghost back."

And at the thought that his bedrooms might be haunted by a very angry ghost, this time it was Cuthbert's turn to faint.

Chapter 14

Monday

Feeling outraged at what she'd witnessed, it took Fliss several minutes to get her breathing back to normal. But then it occurred to her to wonder why it had happened twice with this particular wardrobe? She went across the landing to the other bedroom and placed both hands very firmly on the painted wardrobe. Nothing happened.

"How odd," she muttered. "This was the one I saw the boys with, but there's nothing there now." She gently tapped on it in various places and opened the door, sticking her head right inside, but all there was was a perfectly normal old wardrobe.

She walked over to the other old wardrobe and inspected that too. Nothing.

Really puzzled now, she went back into the other room and properly uncovered the wardrobe. Looking at it harder, she could see what Bernie meant about the mirrors on the doors not being original – they sat just that bit too proud of the decorative beading. And if that was the case, then without them this wardrobe looked much heavier and, for want of a better word, chunkier than the French ones. So was this an altogether earlier piece and English, too? They'd thought this one had been made for this room, so if it had, there was nothing odd in it being older than the two in the other room.

She opened the top drawer and looked in there, not really knowing why, but then caught sight of the hatpin she had put down there for safe keeping, and then forgotten about it. Picking it up, she could still see her own blood still dried on it, and that made her wonder. Had she actually bled *onto* this wardrobe? It would only have been a few drops and on that top shelf inside, but was that enough to have made a stronger connection?

Sitting down cross-legged on the floor in front of the wardrobe she studied it, trying to remember if she'd had something of the boys' in her hand when the other wardrobe had linked to the past, and if that was significant too. Ah! The parchment! Yes, she'd been holding those pieces, hadn't she.

She was still sitting there when Bernie came upstairs and stuck his head around the door.

"Something wrong with it, Fliss, or are you just shirking?" he asked teasingly.

She turned and grinned at him. "No, not shirking, just thinking. You're beginning to train me, you know, Bernie. When you first said that the mirrors didn't belong on those doors, I couldn't see it. But I've just had a closer look and I can now see that they stand proud of the decorative moulding. Well surely someone who was enough of a craftsman to make those lovely curved-fronted drawers at the bottom wouldn't have been so ham-fisted as to leave mirrors poking out, would he?"

Bernie's face lit up in pleasure, making Fliss wonder how many times he had tried to hammer such information into his sons without success.

"Yes!" he exclaimed in delight, coming to give her a hug as she got to her feet. "That's exactly it! You see, Fliss? You have got an eye for this."

"So could this be older? For instance, *early*-eighteenth century and English, rather than *late*-eighteenth century and French?"

"Absolutely, yes it could. Let's face it, fashions changed a lot slower without modern social media, or media of any sort apart from newspapers. And what was the latest thing in London might take a decade to work its way out to the provinces. I think things like ladies' fashions changed a lot faster, for instance, but when it came to furniture, you had to allow for the time it would take for the local cabinet makers to learn how to make something in the new style – and they couldn't just Google a manual on how to, they had to wait until printed patterns became available in their area, or they saw an actual piece to copy. So yes, this has been made by someone who really knew what they were doing, but it's also been interfered with over the centuries, and we're not seeing it as it was originally intended to be. About the one thing we can say for certain is that the original commission probably picked out this lovely burr walnut for its glorious pattern in the grain; and you're right, it looks very English from that point of view, because there's been no attempt to gild or inlay anything in the rococo style at all."

Fliss took a deep breath, crossed her fingers where Bernie wouldn't see, and asked,

"Then could this date from something like… oh, I don't know… say the 1740s or 1750s?"

Luckily Bernie took any hint totally the wrong way. "Still searching for your own Highland hero, your own Jamie Fraser and the Jacobites, Fliss?" he teased gently, but adding, "In truth, I can't see why not. You're talking a mere thirty or forty years before the dates of the other furniture, which I think is pretty definitely French and late eighteenth-century. So if that was when this house was in its heyday, then yes, I think this might be a slightly earlier and more local piece from that era."

"Interesting," was what Fliss said, "Let's get painting," but thinking to herself, S*o there's nothing anachronistic in this piece being here in William's day, even if the French bits and pieces weren't here then. But who was it who brought the French stuff in? I'm now certain it couldn't have been William, so was it Cuthbert?*

He doesn't seem like the sort to have fought in France, and anyway, wouldn't he have been a bit old for that by the late 1780s or early 1790s? When did the family tree say that William died? …Hmm, 1758 I think, and by the Michaelmas Daisies which were in the vase I saw over on the table in the window behind him, it was that autumn or maybe the year after when I saw Cuthbert. And he looked like a man in his thirties, but then he was what I'd call gaunt, so maybe he looked older than his years? When was he born? Somewhere in the mid seventeen-thirties, I think …so, oh my goodness, if I'm right, when I saw him, he was only in his early twenties!

That still had to mean that when the French Revolution began, Cuthbert would have been a relatively old man for the time, in his fifties, and Fliss couldn't see him being the ardent wooer of some minor French countess who, however bizarrely, had crossed paths with him. *It has to be one of his sons who made the French connection,* she decided. *But which one? Was it Nenius or Aquillia?*

Shaking her head at these useless musings, Fliss made herself get moving, pouring the paint into the tray and loading up her roller. For the rest of the morning, she happily put the first couple of coats onto the northern one of the two top floor bedrooms, relieved to see that the soft yellow worked as well in this room as the peachier colour had in the other. In both cases they were making these rooms with their tiny windows, relative to the size of the rooms, look a lot brighter and more welcoming.

Nice choice, Fliss, she congratulated herself, as she stood back and surveyed her work. The simple satisfaction of seeing this job turning out well was doing more for her than all of the prescription pills, and she once again offered up silent prayers of thanks that Bernie had come and rescued her. Even if an estate agent came and photographed these rooms empty, they would look inviting, not dull and gloomy, and that was the object of the exercise, wasn't it? And this was her success, not one which the company graphics designer could claim as their own, even when it wasn't. *Job well done!* she thought with a burst of enthusiasm. *But I would love this room as my own bedroom,* she couldn't help thinking.

"All yours in the peachy bedroom, Fliss," Bernie declared as they stopped for a shared lunch with Phil down in the old kitchen, a room Fliss was also falling in love with. "Surprisingly, two coats was all that ceiling needed. I think the landing is going to need at least three all over, though, but hopefully the bedroom you were working on this morning will be good with just two on the ceiling as well."

"When's Josh coming to help you install the new bathroom and the new stuff in the existing ones?" Phil asked.

"Next Monday with a bit of luck," Bernie replied in between mouthfuls of ham sandwich. "That's why I don't want to put the final coat on the landing just yet. We've a lot of stuff to take upstairs still, and I don't want it to get scratched and have to redo it. It's well prep'd now, so it can wait. While Fliss finishes off the walls in the two top bedrooms, I'll crack on with the ceilings in the first-floor bedrooms now that you've got the ceiling roses in, because tomorrow Kev and Sean will be back, and we'll have a go at relaying that parquet flooring."

"Did you ever decide what the stains on that were?" Phil asked.

Bernie shook his head, "Not for definite, but I think Sean is probably right and it is very old blood."

"That's not going to cause you problems, is it?" Phil wondered. "You don't need to contact the police or anything?"

"And say what?" Bernie pointed out. "As with the house Sean worked on, it could be a perfectly simple accident or a natural death. And it's sunk so deeply into the wood that we couldn't even get a stain to come off on a cloth, so it's probably been there for centuries rather than even decades. With no body and no hint of foul play, I can't imagine that the police have time to fret over a case where the possible perpetrator has been in his grave for nearly as long as his supposed victim. No, Phil, this won't slow us down. We'll just try not to use those blocks unless we have to."

Thank goodness for that! Fliss thought, burying her nose in her large tea mug to avoid looking at Bernie. *I don't need any further creepy connections through blood. If a prick from a hatpin can launch me back to see the past, heaven only knows what a whole chunk of floor could do! Just go back into the bedroom, put the last coat of paint on the walls, and don't touch that bloody wardrobe!*

That was something she managed to do without incident and with no small amount of relief. They would decide what to do with the floor in terms of sanding and waxing, or covering, before they shoved the wardrobe back into its place, and for now Bernie wanted to shift the furniture out of the would-be bathroom before they painted the doors up on this floor, again because of the danger of chipping the new paint. Phil would also be working on the electrics for most of this week, the job complicated by having to work around the ancient beams in the black and white half of the house, but in order to allow Bernie and Fliss some lights to work by, he'd electrically split the house into its two halves, and so at the end of the day they had a ceremonial switching on of the lights in the Queen Anne half.

Even with only bare bulbs, this part of the house suddenly sprang into life, and Fliss couldn't refrain from running up to the top floor to see what her efforts looked like.

"Oh my goodness!" she called back down to Bernie. "I can't believe it! I managed to do both rooms and not miss a patch!" She felt ridiculously pleased about that. Her first efforts and she hadn't made a total mess of them. And that also reinforced something that Bernie had said, that her confidence had taken a terrible hammering in the loss of her old job, and then with the constant chipping away at her that her parents had subjected her to. *I can do this,* she thought happily, *bloody hell, I can actually do this!*

And so the next morning, as Kevin and Sean came back, providing much banter and laughter, Fliss went up to the first floor and began work on the bedrooms there and with a lot more confidence in what she was doing. Even better, there was no furniture in these rooms at all yet, so nothing to poke at her imagination – because that was what she was convincing herself her experiences had to be. *It's the bloody pills combined with you being so stressed,* she told herself firmly. *No wonder you're all over the place. Maybe you could start cutting down on them a bit? Just half a pill at a time?* Now that really would feel like a major step in the right direction. It wouldn't be a fast process she knew, but the fact that she could even contemplate doing it was a sign that she was in a much better place than she had been a bit over a month ago when Bernie had rescued her. *Little steps, Fliss,* she reminder herself, *don't try to overdo it, just keep taking these little steps. Life is getting better!*

And small steps were also the case with the decorating itself. With these rooms being taller and having full height walls all the way around, Fliss' arms were aching by the time she'd put the first coat on just one of the rooms, for she'd had to use a long-handled roller for the first time. It might not have felt much heavier when she started, but by the time she'd finished, her strokes of paint were more than a little wobbly, and she was glad to move over to the brush to deal with the corners and around the door and window. So after lunch she was glad to extend her break a little by going and seeing what the men were up to.

Bernie's plumbing skills had been more than up to capping off the water supply in the Chandlers' former kitchen, and she now realised that Kevin and Sean must have ripped out the old units last week, because the room was completely empty aside from Sean and the parquet blocks.

"What do you think, Fliss?" Sean asked, sitting

back on his heels and waving a hand at his handiwork.

"It looks great!" Fliss enthused. "Love that herringbone pattern you're making."

"Yes, I think it always looks a bit better than just going for the brick pattern."

"Is it just you working on this now?" Fliss was surprised, having expected to see all three of them in here.

"Only room for me," Sean explained, "and if you're going to get the blocks to interlock properly, it needs to be a continuous process, not different patches trying to be matched up."

"Gosh, it's all far more complicated that I thought," Fliss confessed, but then wondered, "Where are the others, then?"

"Well Phil is finishing off the main ring for this half in the old lounge across the hall, and then he's going to put some sockets in down in the cellar. When he's done and can give me power, I can sand this floor down and wax it properly. Bernie and Kev are having a go at the plaster in the old house. Most of it only needs cleaning off and then a new skim going on, so I think Kev's carrying on from where Bernie left off with the cleaning, and Bernie's probably mixing up some foul lime plaster outside. Be careful with that stuff if you go and have a look, Fliss, it's not nice stuff, so don't touch it with your bare hands."

"How ever did they manage in the past?" Fliss wondered, to which Sean answered cynically,

"Probably died young!"

"Thanks for that cheery thought," she laughed. "I'll leave you to your parquet if you're going to say morbid things like that."

Yet, when she got back out into the hall, she could hear tapping noises. They hadn't opened up the way through on the ground floor as yet, and so the fastest way for Fliss to reach the orange hall was to go up and through the bedroom above it and down the old kitchen stairs, even if she ran through the bit that gave her the creeps. It meant she came into the orange hall from the kitchen hallway to see Bernie and Kevin rapping away at the wall in the corner.

"What on earth are you doing?" she asked.

"Trying to find the extent of the original doorway," Bernie explained. "When I was taking the pipes out of where Sean's working, I thought that the obvious way someone had got the water supply into that newer kitchen was to just drop the pipes down from the bathroom up above it. But to my surprise they didn't go up, they went down and through – that's why we haven't put a replacement skirting board in there yet, the last two pipes need to come out of the plaster at the bottom.

"They ought to have come through here under the quarry tiles …except that they didn't. When we got the floor up there wasn't a single pipe." He shook his head, puzzled. "We need to find them, Fliss, because I don't want to leave old pipes just capped off with the risk of one of them then bursting and ruining all our hard work."

"So where do you think they are, then?" she asked, coming to stand beside them.

Kevin brandished something in his hand. "Pipe and wire detector," he explained. "An absolute boon to workers like Bernie and me. Saves you a lot of grief drilling into a wall and then finding you've just taken out all the electrics." He grimaced. "Except it's not working that well here. Or rather, I'm getting a faint signal, but that probably means that it's buried somewhere in this ridiculously thick wall."

Bernie nodded. "So that's why we're trying to find the original doorway through into the hall of the Queen Anne bit. That will save us trying to knock our way through, and to be honest, I'd be seriously unwilling to take a hammer to these old walls except in the direst emergency – like the place started flooding."

"And have you found it?"

Kevin knocked with his knuckles on the plaster. "Can you hear that? Now listen to this," and he went and knocked on the wall to his left.

"Ooh!" Fliss gasped. "That sounds hollow!"

"Exactly," Bernie said with a smile. "We were just trying to decide the extent of the hollow bit, and then we'll have a go at getting to it."

"Can I stay and watch?"

"Of course you can."

As Bernie began the first careful chipping away at the old plaster, Kevin explained. "What's got us foxed is that everything to the right of here ought to sound solid, but it doesn't. It's like there are hollow bits behind here, but only in places, and there's no obvious reason why."

He waved an expansive hand at the hall. "Like Bernie's probably explained to you, this is the next phase on from the full black-and-white parts of the house, so they'd got the knack of actually plastering whole walls by the time this got built. You've still got the heavy beams in the ceilings, and they're undoubtedly behind the plaster too. And whoever this local chap was who did the work wasn't confident of plastering a ceiling at that time, but he did a decent job on the walls. But our hollow bits don't match up with where we think the gaps between the oak beams ought to be."

He stood back and pointed upwards. "See? You can see where the main beams in the ceiling are. They must be sitting on equally big beams in the walls…"

"…or there'd be nothing to support them!" Fliss caught on. "Oh, I see! But the gaps between don't match up with your hollow-sounding bits?"

"Not entirely. Listen. This bit ought to be hollow, right? And this bit up here does, but," and he bent down and knocked lower down, "this doesn't, does it? This bit sounds as though it's solid behind there."

"Could something have crumbled over the years?" Fliss wondered.

"That's exactly why we've got to get in and find out," Bernie declared. "If it's something crumbling, we've got to make absolutely certain it's nothing structural. And please God it isn't, because the Davenports will have forty fits if they have to foot the bill for restoring even a minorly listed building on that scale."

A few more taps with his hammer and chisel and suddenly Bernie was through, although to what was still unclear. Fliss moved back out of the way to allow Kevin to work alongside Bernie, and slowly the outline of the doorway began to emerge. Sure enough, there was a deep cavity behind what they were taking out, and when Kevin shone a torch through into the gloom, on the far side they saw wood.

"Great! That looks like it might be the original door," Bernie enthused. "Oh, that is a find, because you can bet it's better wood than anything we could replace it with nowadays."

There was further cause for relief when Bernie pronounced that, on closer inspection, the plaster they had chipped out was of a sort probably used in the nineteen-thirties, which was presumably when the house had first been subdivided. A bit more probing and they came to the original doorjamb and then the original plaster infill on the far side of it, the nineteen-thirties layer at this point being little more than a thin skim.

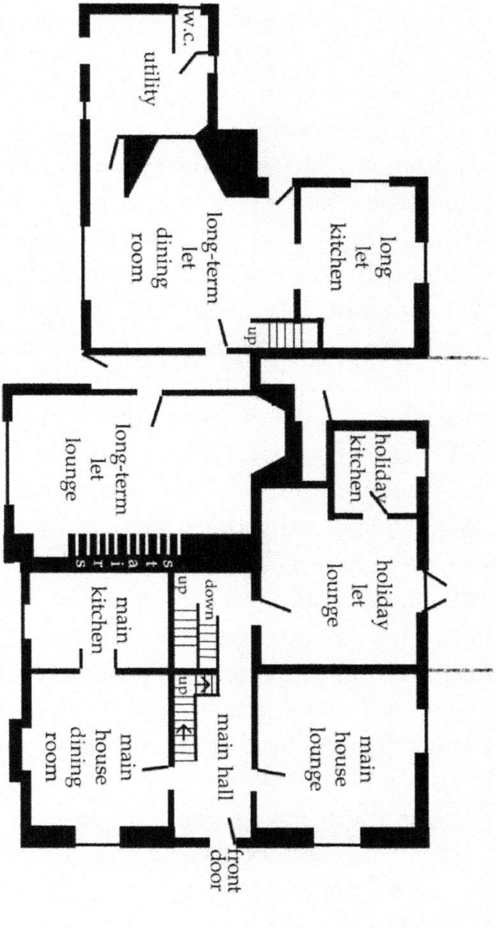

The ground floor with the old stairs exposed

"And that's probably why this wall looks worse than the rest," Bernie declared, "because they've just flung this other stuff on over the lime plaster and it's lifting off now. That's going to be a bit fiddly, but I can certainly get that off and then do a nice finish in a plaster that will bond properly the original."

He stepped through into the cavity, shining the powerful torch over it. "And the other good news is that I can't see any sign of woodworm on this wooden ceiling, or on this left wall. Hmm, but something's not right on this other side. It looks as though somebody's just wrenched the wood panelling out and rammed it back in. I wonder if that was our crazy plumber?"

Kevin handed him a floorboard-lifter, and it only took Bernie gently easing the clawed end into a gap for a whole section to topple out towards him. Luckily Kevin was standing close enough to help him catch it as it fell, because it was a heavy piece of panel. But as they eased it fully out, they found themselves looking at the underside of a cramped and narrow staircase.

"Well here's the other staircase to the old house," Bernie said with satisfaction. "Mystery solved there, and it also explains why the wall seemed so thick. Looking at the rake of those stairs, I would have thought that there ought to be another doorway at the other end of this wall to give access to it. It certainly doesn't give out on the other side into the Chandler's former kitchen. I know that because I checked every part of the adjoining wall in there looking for the pipes."

He shone the torch upwards in the new cavity. "Ah! And here are the pipes! What a cockeyed way to put them in. Why go through the wall at the bottom from the kitchen, and then run them up the underside of these stairs to the bathroom? Why not go straight up? *Tsk*! Anyway, that's a relief. I can get these old pipes out and seal them off up in the bathroom, now that I know where to look without getting the entire floor up. Thank God they took the drains straight outside and I haven't got to ferret around finding them!"

"What about this other missing door, then?" Fliss wondered. "The one to these stairs? If the sealing up has been done with modern stuff, doesn't that mean that you aren't so worried about uncovering it to find out why you've got those odd pockets behind the wall?"

"Well part of it is going to be this," Bernie said, playing the torch's beam over what looked like very fine soil or grit, which lay in random lumps on the floor. "The thing is, Fliss, we've got to find out where this has come from – or at least why these fine bits have fallen through the boards of the old stairs. We can't just leave it now that we've found it, because there's no good reason why it should be on the top side of the steps to trickle through, either. I just hope that nothing's falling down from the adjoining wall of the Queen Anne bit."

Therefore after a tea break, and letting Sean come and have a look at what they'd discovered, Kevin went around to the other side of the hidden door on the hallway side, stripping the wallpaper off that patch of wall to find the door they now knew had to be behind it, and open it up. It would certainly make life a lot easier if they could just walk through on the ground floor as well as the first.

Fliss was still wary of that space in between. She'd only stepped in briefly to look at what Bernie was showing her, and even then, it was as if a whole army of ants were crawling over her skin, and she hadn't forgotten that the first time she had seen William was leaning back against the continuation of one of these upright beams upstairs, and it was where she still got the shudders walking through the doorway upstairs. But she didn't mind helping Bernie try to find the lost door to the stairs from safely within the orange hall.

At first that involved nothing more technical than holding a measuring tape for him as he calculated where the stairs must end from what was visible of their underneath. But then after that it was a case of very gently scraping at the surface of the plaster to try and find some sort of edge.

"We've got to be careful," Bernie cautioned, "because they might have sealed it up because of the need to put some extra bracing pieces in between the two big uprights."

"Like the iron brackets you sometimes see in old pubs and places?" Fliss wondered.

"Sort of, but I don't think they'll be metal, if only because the detector didn't pick up anything like that. And a big chunk of metal brace would surely have had it pinging like mad. It's more likely to be wood, and possibly just knocked into place, not nailed or anything."

They carried on, picking away at the wall more like archaeologists than builders, wary of digging into something unseen but vital, until Fliss suddenly exclaimed,

"I think I've found a keyhole!"

Sure enough, when they cleared around it and went a little deeper, it was a small hole, not for a key but probably for the spindle of a now lost doorknob. With that giving them a good idea of where at least one edge was, they chased out to that edge and then began following it around. Although the day was now getting on, and in theory the others had finished for the day, everyone was so curious that they were all standing watching Bernie work by both of the generator's lights when he announced,

"That's it, that's the edges of the door found!"

"Let's get it open, then, since we don't need to find a key," Sean enthused, coming to help Bernie, as Phil crossed his fingers and said,

"I just hope that there's no errant wiring in there like your random pipes underneath the stairs. I've disconnected everything I could find, and there shouldn't be anything carrying any current, but I always worry in old places like this in case some twit put an extra fuse board in somewhere before the main fuse board that I don't know about."

But it wasn't a shock of the electrical kind that they got. As the door swung creakily open on old rusty hinges, it was Fliss, standing to one side, who got the first view and screamed,

"Oh my God! There's a body in there!"

But the door had already creaked open wide enough for the men to now see it as well.

"Oh bugger," Sean sighed. "I think we might have found who bled out on the parquet."

Chapter 15

Monday – Tuesday

"Sod, sod, sod," Bernie muttered. "There's no getting around this. We'll have to inform the police now. Christ, in all of my years on the job, this is a first."

"Hang on, Bernie, though," Sean said calmly. "Look at what he's wearing. Isn't that a uniform? And it's old. In fact, it's bloody ancient. Surely this is a job for an archaeologist, not the murder squad?"

Bernie sighed but shook his head. "The police still have to be informed and an assessment carried out." Then peered a bit closer at the grinning skull and then at what was holding the other bones together. "Bloody hell! I think that's a French army uniform, and Napoleonic at that. What the hell is he doing here?"

"Could he be the owner of the French furniture?" Fliss suggested, wishing that her pulse would stop pounding, because she was starting to feel distinctly wobbly again.

"I suppose he could be," Bernie said dubiously, "but he'd have to have been a bit of an idiot to parade around in his old army uniform. People around here wouldn't have been any more enamoured of seeing someone who fought against the British on their own patch than their descendants would have been of, say, a German soldier in uniform after either of the world wars."

"Perhaps that's why he was killed?" Phil suggested. "And looking at that great big crack in his skull, it certainly looks as though somebody tried to brain him. You don't need to be a forensic scientist to tell that he didn't do that to himself."

Still muttering darkly under his breath, Bernie went outside to get a clear phone signal and call the police, and when he came back announced that they'd all have to wait with him until someone had come and at least pronounced the scene of no further interest in terms of an investigation. Not that the others were objecting. Phil, Kevin and Sean had all nipped out to ring those at home to warn them that they'd be late back, but more in excitement than anything. Clearly the thrill of this once in a lifetime experience was something they weren't going to miss out on, and Fliss could in part understand that for them it wasn't as gruesome. This man had been dead for the best part of two centuries at the very least, and after all this time, he was just so many bones. There were no smelly, oozy bits to turn anyone's stomach, indeed not so much as a single maggot in sight, so he was more desiccated than anything.

For Fliss herself, though, the creeping ants had just got a lot worse, and she was glad to get out of the room and across into the sanctuary of the flagstone-floored kitchen. She'd make as many mugs of tea for the coming police as they wanted as long as she didn't have to go back in there and look that skull in the face. And that wasn't helped by the voice in her head which kept insisting that he was very much a victim. While the four men stood nursing their fresh mugs of tea, and speculating on who this soldier might have crossed, and whether he might have come seeking vengeance, with the scenarios getting ever more dramatic, Fliss' gut feeling was that something far sadder had happened to him. That he'd not expected this for a moment when he'd come here.

Luckily the police didn't take long to arrive, and the sound of a powerful car pulling into the drive had Bernie going and opening the back door. A tall, heavily-built man, with close-cropped hair just starting to grey at the temples, got out of a large Subaru, with a very svelte lady getting out of the other side.

"DI Bill Scathlock," the detective said affably. "I hear you've got an old body for us, so I decided to shorten the process and bring Dr Sylvia Warrener along with me. She's a forensic anthropologist and osteo-archaeologist, and this," waving hand at another lady getting out of the back, "is Dr Carol Whitmore, our pathologist. Between the two of them they should be able to pronounce judgement on your body fairly swiftly, and if it's as old as you say, then it will just be a case of getting it properly removed, and that's very much Sylvia's department."

"Wow, you were very quick off the mark," Bernie said faintly, having not expected to have such a quick resolution.

The detective smiled. "Ah, well it did help that we were all having a Chinese together when I got the call, so since Carol and Sylvia were willing to come with me, I was able to save my colleague having to make the calls to whoever was on call at the pathology department."

"Great," Bernie said weakly, "well you'd better come and have a look at him, then."

Even Sean and Kevin were a bit taken aback by Dr Warrener's exclamation of, "Oh I say, he's a rather splendid specimen!" as she walked in and saw the body illuminated by Bernie's lights.

She and the pathologist stepped forwards to take a better look, but it wasn't long before the pathologist turned away saying, "He's all yours, Slyv', he's long past needing my attentions."

"Nothing for me then, either," the detective said with obvious relief, then explained as he caught the surprised looks. "There's always the off-chance that it's some re-enactor who's come to grief a couple of decades ago, and that would definitely be my case. But it's always twice as hard when you're working with what people can remember from that many years ago, because the trail is already stone cold, you see."

"Ah," Bernie sympathised as he grasped what he meant. "Yes, I can see that that would complicate matters."

"This is a lovely old place," the detective said appreciatively. "Did you say that you're restoring it?"

"Yes," said Bernie, "would you like the guided tour while your friends are working?"

"Love to!" Bill Scathlock said with enthusiasm, and so Bernie and Fliss gratefully escaped from the macabre scene of the body being examined on the stairs, and led the way out.

Having insisted that they call him Bill now that there was nothing here for him to officially investigate, the detective was all enthusiasm for the house. With the first stop being the old kitchen, he was soon delighting in the old beams and chimney, and then the exposed ceiling beams in the bedrooms upstairs.

"What a fabulous old place," Bill said appreciatively, as they made their way into the bedroom above the hall. "What a terrible shame that someone daubed all that awful orange paint around downstairs."

"It is pretty disgusting," Bernie agreed, and then led Bill across to the doorway into the newer half. "This is why we knew there was such a depth of wall down below," he explained, showing Bill how thick the wall was even up here. He lifted one of the boards where Phil had been working and shone the torch down under the floorboards. "You can see the big old oak beams supporting the floor on this side."

Yet because he was already bent down, he didn't see the big detective's shudder as he crossed the threshold in front of Fliss, who'd really only trailed along to get out of the hall. As Bill turned to look back, he saw Fliss shivering too, and said softly, "Weird atmosphere just there, isn't there? Just don't tell my colleagues that, please."

"I'm just glad I'm not the only one to feel it," Fliss agreed with substantial gratitude. "I was beginning to think I was losing the plot."

"No, you're definitely not," Bill assured her, "And I don't think it's just because of your dead chap downstairs, either."

He didn't say any more, because Bernie was carrying on talking about the house and how he had come to be working on it. "I suppose I'll have to inform the owners," he said miserably, "but God knows what they're going to say about this. Will it hold the work up much, do you think?"

"I wouldn't have thought so," Bill said confidently. "But your owners sound like they might kick up a fuss from what you've said. Would it come better from me if I rang them and informed them?"

"God! Would you?" Bernie's relief was visible.

"One phone call is hardly going to disrupt my entire day tomorrow," Bill said affably, "and it's amazing how people who would argue the toss suddenly calm down when they realise they're taking to a DI. If it saves you a world of grief, I really don't mind. You've been quick off the mark to inform us, so we can get this one off the books at speed. It seems only fair to return the favour."

So it was a very relieved Bernie who led the way onwards and upwards through the Queen Anne half of the house, and this time Fliss was prepared and watching when Bill crossed over the threshold on the top landing.

"Blimey, another one," Bill said *sotto voce* to her, as ahead of them Bernie switched the first bedroom light on. "This house has a troubled past, I'm sure of that," and he gave another shudder. Then he astonished Fliss even more by saying to Bernie,

"Lovely choice of colours up here, they really warm the rooms up," while looking at the wardrobe with the hatpin in it with a troubled frown.

My God, he feels it too! Fliss thought, finding it an unexpected relief to discover that someone as down to earth as a detective would nonetheless pick up on the same vibes as she had. *Oh thank heavens it's not just me!*

By the time they returned downstairs, everyone else was ready to leave. Dr Warrener said that she would be back first thing with help to get the body out and taken away, since he seemed to be partially stuck at the moment, and everyone went their separate ways.

"That's a relief," Fliss said to Bernie when they got home and gratefully kicked off their work boots, carrying the fish and chips they'd picked up on the way back through to Bernie's kitchen. "For a bit there I thought we'd be tied up in a murder hunt, and I'm not sure I'm recovered enough to cope with that just yet."

"Not just you, kiddo," Bernie said, subsiding on the chair with a huff of relief. "Gave me a right nasty turn that did, seeing him all scrunched up on the stairs like that. Though at least that explains the soil we found. Somebody must have chucked it down the stairs to try and at least cover up the smell of him rotting away down there, and then boarded up the top of the stairs afterwards. Bloody silly thing to do, though, it was just inviting them to start having trouble with damp. Knowing that now, it's a miracle that the damp in that hall isn't worse, but thankfully we can dismiss any further structural troubles creeping up on us from there at least.

"Oh, and Sean says he told Dr Warrener about the parquet floor, and gave her some of the bloodstained blocks to take away to her lab. But she seemed to think that it was perfectly possible that the body and the stains are connected. So that's one mystery solved."

Yet although they both flaked out in front of the TV afterwards, Fliss' mind was still churning, and she wasn't anything like as convinced as Bernie that the mystery was solved. For a start off, it just didn't ring true to her that the soldier would have been wandering around Worcester in his uniform. That seemed to her to be little short of suicidal, because back then he'd have stood out like a sore thumb. And why on earth had he come to the house in the first place? Was he an old enemy of somebody like Cuthbert? Or maybe a former friend from before whichever war he'd taken part in, and had come to visit, only to find that his reception wasn't as warm as he'd expected? Whichever way she looked at it, Fliss was certain that the unknown soldier hadn't been there long before he died, and her gut instinct was saying that one of the resident family members had turned killer.

Tuesday morning came around after a disturbed night of fleetingly remembered dreams for Fliss, and she was rather glad that she and Bernie could only go and open the house up for Dr Warrener and her team, because she hadn't the energy to do a lot today. Bernie hadn't needed much convincing to stop off on the way to pick up a large bag of sticky jam doughnuts, and so having made the obligatory tea for Dr Warrener's team and offered them doughnuts, she and Bernie thankfully escaped through to where Sean was once again laying the unstained parquet, taking him tea and doughnuts too.

"Phew, that was all a bit grisly, last night," Fliss said, biting happily into a doughnut, and sinking down to sit cross-legged on the bit that Sean had already laid yesterday, so as to be out of his way while he worked. "Did you tell them where we found the stained wood?"

"Certainly did," Sean said, sitting back to take a swig of his tea. "That detective and Dr Warrener both agreed with us that the Chandler's lounge, where the stained blocks came from, was probably where the murder took place."

"He was very knowledgeable about houses," Bernie said appreciatively. "He agreed with me that

that room would have originally been the morning room, on account of it being the only time it would have got any sunshine. He said he'd like to come and see the house when we've finished it. Nice of him to say that, wasn't it?"

And Fliss and Sean shared conspiratorial smiles of affection for Bernie, knowing that he'd been relieved beyond belief not to have to make the call to the Davenports. Just for that alone, the DI would be in Bernie's good books for a very long time even had he loathed the sight of the house. For him to show enthusiasm for the project had really made Bernie's week.

They stayed there until Dr Warrener herself came through to tell them that the anonymous soldier was now safely tucked up in a body bag in the back of her van.

"His uniform is interesting, though," she said with professional curiosity. "You were nearly right, Bernie, when you said Napoleonic, but looking at his insignia more closely, I'd say that he's from just before then. My guess is that he's wearing the uniform of a soldier in the very first fighting in France, just before Napoleon came to power, and possibly in the couple of years between the execution of Louis XVI at the beginning of 1793, and the rise of Napoleon to become the national leader in the autumn of 1795."

Bernie's natural curiosity was piqued, making him say, "That's very specific. How can you tell?"

Sylvia Warrener smiled. "Oh, I was part of a dig in France years ago, and we came upon some bodies of soldiers of the era. But they weren't anywhere where we knew of fighting with the British or Austrians, for instance, so it was fair to assume that it was where there was still some internal fighting going on. But then we were in the Loire valley, where the Wars of the Vendée took place, so that made sense."

"That's what you were telling me about, Bernie," Fliss said. "That was the counter-revolutionary fighting, wasn't it?"

Sylvia looked at Bernie with surprise. "You know about that? Oh how nice to meet someone so well informed. Then I'll do my best to identify where he comes from and let you know. My old dig was near Le Mans where the counter-revolutionaries were finally defeated in December '93, and those bodies' uniforms are what this body's remind me of. So I see nothing anachronistic in having someone escaping the fighting in that region, making it to the coast, and coming across to England, which would most likely make his year of death something like 1794. And because he would have been fighting on the royalist side – even though both Louis and Maria Antoinette were dead by then – I'd have expected him to be welcome over here. But then maybe in a rural backwater, as this must have been back then, they didn't know one Frenchman from another? Maybe they thought they were getting rid of some treacherous revolutionary? Terribly sad for our chap if they did, though."

"What an awful twist of fate," Bernie agreed, but that awful voice in Fliss' head chose that moment to yell at her,

That's not what happened! He didn't die because of that!

Luckily Bernie and Sylvia hadn't noticed her wincing, and Bernie was asking,

"Was it that blow on his head that killed him?"

"Not just one blow," Sylvia pronounced. "Several, though to more or less the same spot. And delivered with some force, too. Carol and I were talking about it on the way home, and we both agreed that if that appeared on a modern body, we'd be describing it as a frenzied attack. Practically all of the back of his head was bashed in, and by something large and heavy."

"Not a sword, then?" Bernie wondered.

"No, not at all. Much broader than that. My money would be on something like a heavy vase or a weighty old decanter. Something thick enough to withstand repeatedly bludgeoning away at someone with it – because it looks like all of the fractures were made with the same shaped object – but not anything with a sharp edge. That's the cut down by his ribs, but to me that looks like someone else then made sure that he really was dead by stabbing him, and it was probably made when he was already dead, or so close it made little difference."

"Poor bloke," Fliss sympathised, wondering what possible motive Cuthbert or his sons could have had to be doing something like that to a random visitor. Cuthbert had struck her as too much of a coward to do something so violent. Attack a defenceless girl, yes, but not a soldier who would have been able to stand up to him.

As the team's vehicles emptied out of the driveway, Sean looked at Bernie and Fliss.

"You two go on home," he said kindly. "It's a bit late in the day for you to be starting anything now. I'll carry on with the floor in here and lock up after myself. Take Fliss home, Bernie, she looks like she could do with a quiet afternoon," but Fliss knew from the way that he covertly winked at her that it was Bernie who he thought needed the afternoon off, and so she didn't protest.

"I'll ring Kev and Phil, and let them know we can start again tomorrow," Bernie announced as they got into the truck, but there was no mistaking the fact that he was glad to have the afternoon off. And the longer it went without screeching phone-calls from Mrs Davenport, the more he was breathing sighs of relief that DI Scathlock must have got them off their backs for a while.

For Fliss, though, the question which kept going around in her head was: *If you killed a trained soldier in the seventeen-nineties, are you the same man who was so cruel to little Nilmani and Ishwar? Because if you could kill so brutally, I can't imagine you bothering much about the feelings of two small children. And if you are one and the same, which man were you? One of Cuthbert's sons, Nenius or Aquillia? Because I reckon it has to be one of you two. Did he come thinking he was coming to friends, only to have his trust betrayed and his head caved in? And if you did betray him, what possible motive could you have had, or were you just plain evil through and through?*

Chapter 16

Wednesday – Friday

With everyone back and working the next morning, it was easier for Fliss to keep her mind off the murdered man. Once more up in the first-floor bedroom, she found it physically less strenuous today too, having finally got the hang of using the long-handled roller. And she was glad to be up here, because Bernie and Sean were inspecting the woodwork of the discovered staircase, and she knew that she would have terrible jitters seeing Bernie stepping into that space, because in her head it was somewhere in some strange, weird way between worlds. Already Bernie was saying that being able to now see the back of the plaster adjoining the hall, he thought that the hall would originally have been open to the stairs, not a solid wall, and that if they were careful removing the lath and plaster, there was a rather nice carved banister and rails still lurking in the gloom. However, although Fliss had made vague murmurings about how nice it would look as a place to display vases of flowers or photographs, the truth was that nothing would persuade her to set foot on even the first step.

You'll be lost if you go up there, the odd voice inside warned her, and somehow, she couldn't shake the feeling that this was a dire warning.

Therefore, she resolutely stayed out of the hall, except for using the quicker way to now get to the kitchen for their tea breaks and lunch, and instead worked hard to get both a second coat of paint on the room she'd already begun, and the first on the other main bedroom. That still left her at the end of the day with time on her hands, though. Bernie and the others were still audibly beavering away, making Fliss feel guilty for not doing something, at which point she remembered that the storeroom still needed emptying of some pieces. Ones which there hadn't been room for in the bedrooms when Phil still needed to get into them and be able to lift the floor boards, as well as getting to the skirting boards in various spots, but which now had to come out so that the new bathroom suite could go in. *I can't move the big stuff,* she decided, *but I'm sure we saw some smaller pieces in there. If I can shift those, that will be a help.*

And so she went upstairs and switched the bright new lights on in the storeroom, which allowed her to see more of the pieces at the back clearly. Sure enough, there were a couple of small cabinets, which although rather solid and probably made of mahogany, were pieces that with care she could move by herself. Taking it steadily, she got those up and into the bedroom where she'd had her encounter with Cuthbert, relieved that even when she'd got them up there, she didn't feel so much as a tingle from them.

Fired on by that, she managed to move a couple of ornamental tables, too, and then a rather battered but very fine free-standing mirror. She was so confident having moved that and not felt a thing, that she was rummaging around in the storeroom wondering which others of the few remaining pieces she might try and move, when without thinking about it, she put her hand on the desk. Immediately there was that creeping feeling over her skin and a buzzing in her ears.

Look in the desk! the inner voice commanded.

"I don't want to," Fliss whispered back to the air.

You have to! It's important! the voice replied.

"No, please, not another body. I'm doing so well at the moment, but I won't be if I keeping coming across things like that."

It's not a body, that damned insistent, internal voice persisted. *It's clues. Clues you need to read.*

"But how do you know that?" Fliss whimpered, but this time the voice didn't reply, leaving her feeling frustrated and scared.

Taking a deep breath, she turned and looked properly at the desk. In some ways it looked more like an ornate old harmonium that Fliss had once seen, complete with decorated music stand and candle holders. Here the top pigeon holes, which must once have held blank letter-paper and envelopes, and ink and sealing wax, also had small ornamental shelves to the side, which Fliss guessed might have been for the all too necessary candles. Even in the downstairs rooms, on a dark winter's day, you would be hard-pressed to see what you were writing without them. But however ornamental the whole top piece was, there wasn't a single place where anything could be hidden.

Below it was a sloping front which would drop down to make the writing part of the desk, and grasping the two small knobs at the top, Fliss gave a tug and the front swung smoothly down to sit securely anchored on two metal sliders, which looked like they might be more modern replacements. Now that it was open, Fliss could see more compartments at the back of the desk in the section beneath the top piece, but once again, these were obviously empty. Even a careful exploration with her fingertips – remembering getting stabbed by the hatpin – revealed nothing, not even a single slip of paper, and so Fliss closed that back up again.

Under the desk section was a long drawer which ran the full width of the desk, but that also was completely empty, even when she pulled it right out and looked in the cavity it sat in. All of which had Fliss feeling annoyed with herself. What had she expected when that voice was just the product of her overwrought imagination? Of course, there wasn't anything here, because how would she – how *could* she – know such a thing?

Getting down on her hands and knees for one last look, she checked the back of the desk, which was a solid enough panel of wood, and probably there to keep any draughts off the feet of the person sitting at it. But this had no compartments in it, and with a huff of disgust, Fliss was just hauling herself to her feet once more when she realised that there were three very slim drawers just beneath the top piece, but above the drop-down part. She had initially assumed that they were merely decorative woodwork, because they all had ornate carving on them. And that carving disguised the fact that there were tiny ring-pull handles on each of them, all three of which lay flat within the carvings so that they were barely visible.

"Why am I bothering?" Fliss asked rhetorically, and with a sigh of resignation that she wouldn't be finding anything here either.

The first one she tried was one of the side drawers, which wasn't the easiest thing to get open by virtue of the little ring-pull not wanting to lift very far anymore. And when that proved to be just as empty as the rest of the desk, she very nearly gave up. But as much to prove to herself that this was all in her mind and should be ignored, she went to the other side and fiddled with the pull until she could get that one open too. When it did open, this one came free with such a jerk that the whole drawer came out in her hands, but as she came to try and work it back in, she realised that she could see something paler in the centre of the desk's casing. That centre drawer had something in it which was poking out over the top of the drawer itself.

"It's probably just a bundle of old bills," she told herself sternly, but having realised that this time nothing was going to get the drawer to come out from the front, she managed to wriggle her hand inside the casing and poke at the drawer from the back. It was a good thing that she had slim hands, because someone like Bernie would never have managed it. Either that or he would have got stuck, and Fliss had a brief giggle at the thought of the fire brigade being summoned to extract Bernie from the desk in the manner of the best comic farces.

Yet when she had managed to poke and prod the slim drawer sufficiently forwards from the back to have something to get hold of at the front, it was clear straightaway that these weren't bills. Someone with cramped and tiny handwriting had written the bundle of top letters at least, and going by the pretty seal on the uppermost letter, possibly a woman. Once she had worked the top few of these out, Fliss was able to tug the drawer a bit harder, and suddenly the whole thing came free, though not as much as the previous one. It was still a bit stuck, but Fliss thought that this time it was probably because there was a letter wedged at the back of the drawer between it and the case.

As she carefully emptied the drawer out, she realised that there were at least two correspondents here. One at least was probably another woman, while the other had a much bolder and more masculine handwriting. And once she had got all of the loose stuff out, she could wriggle her fingers in and extract the last two letters, which had been what had jammed the drawer.

With them all out on the top, Fliss was just wondering what to do with them when Bernie's voice came up the stairs,

"We're finishing up down here, Fliss. Are you nearly ready to go home?"

"Won't be a moment," she called back and felt a surge of relief at having an excuse – if only to herself – not to start reading the letters right away. Instead, she scooped them up and tucked them into the bib of her overalls. *You can come home with me and I'll tackle you when I feel able to …and possibly with a stiff gin and tonic to hand!* she decided. There, she had done her bit and done what the nagging inner voice had wanted. She'd found the bloody letters, and anything more could wait until the weekend.

On the way home she told Bernie about starting to empty the remainder of the old storeroom, and he agreed that he and the others would come and move the rest tomorrow.

"If Josh is coming on Monday, we need to get it emptied by Friday anyway," he declared, "So we might as well do it in plenty of time now that we've done working on the bedrooms for now."

That seemed as good and practical a reason for Fliss to leave it at that, and although she was careful to get the bundles out of her overalls before putting them for the wash, she drew the line at taking the letters up to her bedroom. It was one thing having the boys' things up there, but she didn't want anyone else haunting her dreams, thank you very much. Whoever this was, they could stay downstairs in her laptop bag.

It turned out that it was Kevin and Sean who came to move the remaining furniture with her the next morning, and upon going to find Bernie when they were done, Fliss found out what he'd been doing. In the first-floor floorboards there was now a large hole, exposing where the hidden stairs had come out.

"I think it might be nice to put a toughened glass panel in here to give it some light," Bernie said, sitting with his legs dangling down into the hole, and giving Fliss all sorts of palpitations.

"That's not such a good idea!" Fliss instantly exclaimed, only then realising that she would need to give some kind of sane reason. "This is going to stay as a bathroom, isn't it?" she managed to dredge up. "Would you want to be getting undressed and having someone in the lounge looking up when you're in your next to nothing? I don't think so!"

"Blimey! I hadn't thought of that!" Bernie admitted, recalling that the room was empty because he'd removed the suite already, and that's why he'd forgotten its function in his enthusiasm for the floor, but also realising that he'd been thinking of a wall separating the stairs from the room. Yet if they put one back there'd be no light to take advantage of. "I was just thinking of some of the conversions I've seen in the trade magazines with glass floors," he confessed. "But you're right Fliss, most of them were on landings or upstairs studies. I can't think of one where it was a bedroom, let alone a bathroom. Oh well, it was a nice thought while it lasted." Then cheered up to add, "But I'll ask Phil to put a row of little spotlights in along here so that it can be lit up. That would look very posh."

"Lovely!" Fliss agreed, glad that Bernie wasn't close enough to her to see how her pulse was racing at the moment, especially after the thought came of: *I really, really don't want to walk up or down those stairs.*

Glad to be taking the normal stairs down, even though Kevin and Sean were like a couple of kids in wanting to try the new ones, Fliss thought that she'd avoided disaster for the day. Certainly, she was able to spend the rest of the day doing the preparation on the walls of the first-floor landing, and even removing cobwebs and other bits from the walls of the main stairs and the servants' stairs. So when they went home she didn't feel like disrupting her return to normality by tackling the letters, which she still hadn't mentioned to Bernie.

Her second Friday at the house came around, and once again Fliss' mind was on the weekend. Could she persuade Bernie to go out for a meal, she was wondering? Nothing fancy, but maybe for a curry or a Chinese? The mentioning of a Chinese by the detective had her thinking that she'd once upon a time enjoyed doing that back in the days when she'd had friends, so it might be nice to do it again. *Yuk sung*, she thought, practically able to taste her favourite starter, *Oooh yes! Yuk sung and vegetable won tons – I haven't had those in ages! And duck in black bean sauce with special rice …good grief, my tummy's rumbling just at the thought of them!*

She was so lost in memories of happy meals with fellow students that she never gave a moment's thought to going back up to the top bedroom last thing, to make sure that all of the windows were shut before they left the house to its secrets over the weekend. Now that the paint had thoroughly dried in these rooms, she also thought that they probably did need that one extra coat of emulsion, especially when compared to the ceiling. And it was as she was leaning back to inspect the ceiling and the walls where they butted up to it that she leaned back against the one wardrobe she'd vowed not to touch again if possible.

It was only as she felt herself suddenly going giddy, and turned to grasp the edge to steady herself that she realised what she had done. *Oh crap, no! Not again. Not now!* she groaned as the room swirled dramatically once more. *Please don't let me be late getting downstairs and they come and find me flaked out up here. Bloody hell, Fliss, why must you barge around like a bumblebee in a bottle? Haven't you learned to be more careful yet?*

The room shifted, and this time she saw not the guest bedroom she had been in before, but a room laid out as a nursery. A wooden crib was in the room alongside a small bed, plus a basic wooden rocking chair, and a washstand with basin and pitcher, on the rail of which there looked to be cloth nappies hanging to dry. In front of the fireplace, more of the cotton nappies were hanging on a clotheshorse, along with tiny pieces of clothing which had to be for a small baby.

She heard heavy footsteps coming up the last few stairs and then the door creaked open. A pale young woman led the way in, followed by a much older man.

"Here she is, your third little great-niece," the young woman said, lovingly scooping up a tiny bundle from the crib

and bringing it forwards to the man, who was standing right in front of where Fliss was looking out from.

"Och, she's a bonny wee lassie," he instantly replied in a broad Scottish accent, and with a beaming smile. "What a lovely wee girl. You must be very proud."

The young woman's faced fell. "I am, Uncle John, but another girl is not what Cuthbert wants."

The older man straightened up and gave a very Scottish, "Hmph!" of disgust. "My nephew should be grateful for having the children he has. Two bonnie lasses and two strapping lads is more than his mother managed, despite her best efforts." He leaned back over the bundle swathed in blankets and stroked it under the chin with a loving smile. "Oh, your grandma Marjorie would have loved you, little one. What are you going to call her, Alice?"

Oh! This is Cuthbert's wife! Fliss realised, but then forced herself to listen more to what was being said.

"Cuthbert would not wait to see her born before going back to France," Alice said, unable to stop tears from now trickling down her cheeks. "He said to only bother letting him know if it was another boy."

"Ach, for the love of God, what is the matter with the boy!" the man called John, who Fliss guessed must be Marjorie's brother, snorted in disgust. "What is so important that he had to return and not be here for this? Dear me, he really is his father's son. I thought, or rather I hoped, that with my sister's blood running through his veins that he would grow into a different sort of man. But that clearly was not to be. Oh dear.

"Well never mind, dear heart, you have at least one man of the household here now, and I shall insist that we have this precious little soul baptised before I return to Edinburgh. Indeed, if you are well enough, I think you and the wee ones should come for a long visit with the family you have scarcely had chance to get to know. Especially now that your own father and mother are gone and you have nobody in the way of family

nearby. There's plenty of room in my house now that my own dear ones are all away and married themselves. It may be a bit of a squash for you all at Sunday dinner, but I am sure my lovely wife will manage – she has had plenty of practice with her own brothers and sisters and their families, so you will just be carrying on the family tradition. …Now then, what names did you have in mind for this sweet girl, eh?"

Yet Alice could only shake her head and shrug.

"Oh, come now," John said affably, "I have yet to meet the mother who did not have at least one or two favourite names in mind."

But Alice now had to resort to her handkerchief, John taking the little bundle off her with the practiced ease of a man who had cuddled his own children and grandchildren, so that she could blow her streaming nose.

"Cuthbert insisted on naming the other children, even though I did not and do not like the names Ingram and Nenius, so I felt there was little point in picking a name when I would never get to use it."

Fliss thought it was a good job that Alice had her head buried in the handkerchief at that point, and didn't see the silent words that John was swearing angrily as he rolled his eyes in frustration.

"What about Catriona?" John suggested cheerfully. "That's the name of our cousin who William sent poor Nathaniel to. She lives with my brother Iain these days since his own beloved wife died, and is a kind, sweet soul. The best thing her fool of a husband did was to die at Culloden with Angus, her brother, but I wish that he had not dragged wee Nathaniel there with them. If he had lived, he would have been master of this house, and you might have had a better life."

Alice gave a wet sniff. "Cuthbert says that his brother was a fool, or at least that's what his cousin Nenius says."

"Cousin Nenius? Who in the name of creation is he?" John demanded, baffled.

Alice gave a watery smile. "When Nathaniel was sent to your side of the family, their father sent Cuthbert to his cousin Phineas."

"Aye, I recall that."

"Nenius is Cousin Phineas' son. Cuthbert does not tell me much, he says it not for women to know such things," and again Fliss caught John covertly rolling his eyes at that. "But it seems that Cousin Phineas suffered a financial disappointment some time before Cuthbert inherited this house."

"The daft old coot went bankrupt, you mean."

"Bankrupt?"

"Oh aye, I do do trade across the water from time to time, ye' know."

"Goodness, I had no idea Cousin Phineas was that famous."

John snorted. "Infamous, more like! Any poor unfortunate can fall foul of fate and go bankrupt once, but it fair takes talent to do it twice – and in both England and France! And if my dear wife had had to abase herself as his did by …well what she had to do is not for the ears of well brought up ladies like yourself. Let's just say that if my dear one had had to do that for us to survive, I would have taken down my father's old sword, blunt though it is, and fallen upon it in shame. …So was it Phineas who got in touch with Cuthbert this time, and that now has him scurrying over to France all the time? Or was it this son of his? Because I cannot believe that either is good news."

"Oh, it was Nenius. I believe that Cousin Phineas died a few years ago."

John sighed. "I do not know whether to think that good or bad news. Dear me, and your blind fool of a husband has decided to fall in with them again, has he? I can see that I must have a word with your husband's man of legal affairs while I am down here. There must be something we can do to put things into place so that if history should repeat itself, and Nenius' financial recklessness takes Cuthbert down with him, you and the children will have something to fall back upon. Yes indeed, we must."

He took Alice by the arm, leading her to the door saying, "Come, bring the little one downstairs with us. She will not disturb me, and I have something in my flask which will bring a bit of colour to your cheeks."

I bet you do, Fliss thought with a giggle as she pulled back from the scene. *It's likely your homemade whisky, which is probably like fire-water, but I must say, I do like the sound of you and Marjorie's family. You sound a far more sensible bunch than William and Cuthbert. In fact, you remind me a lot of Bernie, coming and rescuing Alice like that. Maybe I might read those letters after all if they're from you?*

Chapter 17

The weekend – Monday

Perhaps because she had removed the letters from the house, over the weekend and despite what she'd thought, Fliss quite successfully forgot about them. There was no nagging inner voice poking her to deal with them, and they were rather overtaken by Bernie thinking that she was now strong enough to have a look at the bundle of children's drawings he had rescued. Far from depressing Fliss, she found herself delighting in the clumsy attempts to draw elephants and tigers, but also what had to be the boys' home village.

"Do you think this is some kind of fortress in the background?" she asked Bernie as they singled out a handful.

"I think it's pretty reasonable to assume that," he agreed. "Whether their father was with the army over there, or in some sort of trading capacity, in that period it would be normal to assume that Europeans would live within spitting distance of a fortress – somewhere they could safely retreat to in times of unrest."

"Was there a lot of unrest? I know next to nothing about India's history apart from what I've started reading here."

"I'm no historian, but yes, I think that as British and French troops in particular moved deeper into India, the local rulers didn't just lie down and give up. Some of them fought long and hard against these incomers, and were a real thorn in the side of The East India Company in particular. You can't blame them. They were being crushed by a foreign power with a totally different set of beliefs."

Fliss sighed. "I'd love to know what their father was doing there, because it might explain why he brought the boys back here. Was he so callous as to think he had his own two readymade servants? A couple of pliant kids he could mould as he wanted, and wheel out to show off to his neighbours when they came around as the exotic entertainment? I hope he's rotting in hell if he did."

Bernie winced at the harshness in Fliss' tone. Was this something else lingering from Fliss' own past that made her so bitter, he wondered, having to respond with,

"Not every parent of children of mixed race in India or Britain back then was that cruel and calculating, Fliss." Then was quietly horrified as she replied too swiftly with,

"Doesn't have to be because they were of mixed race! Some parents over here favour one child and make the other the bloody skivvy!"

"Fliss, you can tell me to sod off if you want, but what the hell makes you say that? Is that something else your mum and dad did to you?"

She gave a heavy sigh. "I won't say that they treated me like the domestic skivvy …but only because whatever I did was never good enough for mum for me to be let loose on any rooms a visitor *might* see. But upstairs it was my job to clean Ben's room as well as mine. Or rather, it was always me who had to do our shared room, never him, and then once he got his own room that just carried on – and believe me, he delighted in messing his room up even more, just so that I'd have a harder time cleaning it to Mum's standards. You can see why we're not close. And once I was old enough to be trusted with things like bleach, it was my job every Saturday to scrub the bathroom from top to bottom while Ben got to go out and play football. Mum said it was good training for when I got married – much good that's done me!"

"Holy crap on a cracker!" Bernie gasped, too stunned to be able to say anything else.

Fliss just shrugged. "Can't undo the past, can you? But I was so conditioned that when I went away to uni', I automatically took over the scrubbing of our shared house until my flatmates sat me down and told me to stop it. When it all came out about what mum had made me do, Laura said I was in danger of becoming one of those mothers who does everything for their kid, because they don't want them to have the same experienced. Much chance there is of *that* happening now!" she concluded bitterly.

Wishing he had never opened up that can of worms, and angry as hell at his brother- and sister-in-law for their callousness and indifference, Bernie consequently agreed only too willingly to them going out that evening for a meal. Anything to give Fliss a taste of what normal life was like, was how he thought of it, and privately wished that of all the jobs he'd taken on over the years, that it hadn't turned out to be this one that had such strong connections to children, and abandoned ones at that. It was clear just from the way she was putting on a bit of weight, and getting a healthier glow in her cheeks, that in most respects he'd been dead right, this job was just what Fliss needed. He just wished that it hadn't come with this weird connection. And she perked up so much after being out for the evening, that he insisted that they go out for a drive in the country the next day, and have Sunday lunch out at a pub.

So it was with Fliss in a much brighter frame of mind that they went into work on Monday, and he introduced her to another of his former workers, Josh. Fliss didn't take to Josh as much as she had to the others, and so she was glad to stay out of his way as he laid new pipes and installed the new suites. At Bernie's request he began with the straightforward job of removing the dreadful en-suite in the room above the hall – not a job Bernie had wanted to tackle himself because it was technically awkward – after which Bernie pulled down the plasterboard walls, and spent time showing Fliss how to mix up a special lime plaster to repair the original wall.

It reassured her that by the time they were taking off the loose stuff, she was getting no more strange vibes off this wall. This, after all, was the very room where she'd first seen William, and so she hoped that – if this wasn't all a product of her stressed imagination as she feared – removing the soldier's body had cleared the air, so to speak. Just at the moment, Bernie wasn't letting her loose with a trowel in her hand, but she was watching his every move intently, determined to learn as much as she could. And maybe because of concentrating so much, she was resolutely blocking anything else that was trying to come through.

Having repaired that wall, they moved on to minor repairs on what had been the upstairs of the holiday let, because of all the shower rooms, this one had been the most recently upgraded, and didn't need replacing beyond a new shower and taps. And with Fliss never having felt a thing in this part of the house, all was good. They also did repairs in the two other bedrooms of the oldest part, with Bernie explaining that the prime reason why he wasn't working on the main bathroom where the oldest stair came up, was because he wanted to make sure that the police had no further questions to ask about it.

"It has made me think, though," he said as they took a break, and went to inspect what Josh was installing in what would be the main bathroom on the top floor. "I always thought it was a bit odd that they put the servant's stairs in back-to-back with the main flight, and as you said Fliss, that the only stairs up to the top floor were the servants', even if the old skylight void was left alone. But now I'm wondering whether originally there was just a nice big landing on this first floor, and the stairs up to the top floor ran off it in full view, not boxed in like they are now."

"How do you mean?" Fliss asked, having trouble visualising this.

Bernie gestured to the main stairs with his tea mug. "Well you've got that nice void over the main stairs, haven't you, partly lit from the skylight. And the more I thought about it, the more I wondered why you wouldn't have just gone around another couple of turns up to the top floor? I mean, that would be the obvious thing to do, wouldn't it?"

He strolled over to the void now, with Fliss following him, both of them looking up and down it. "But then when you stand here where the main stairs come out on the landing, it's clear that taking another turn of the main stairs from here would unfortunately have blocked this landing off. There just wouldn't have been the space to get through without getting on your hands and knees because of the sweep of such stairs. So I wonder whether the local builder who did this extension was, at that point, not very used to

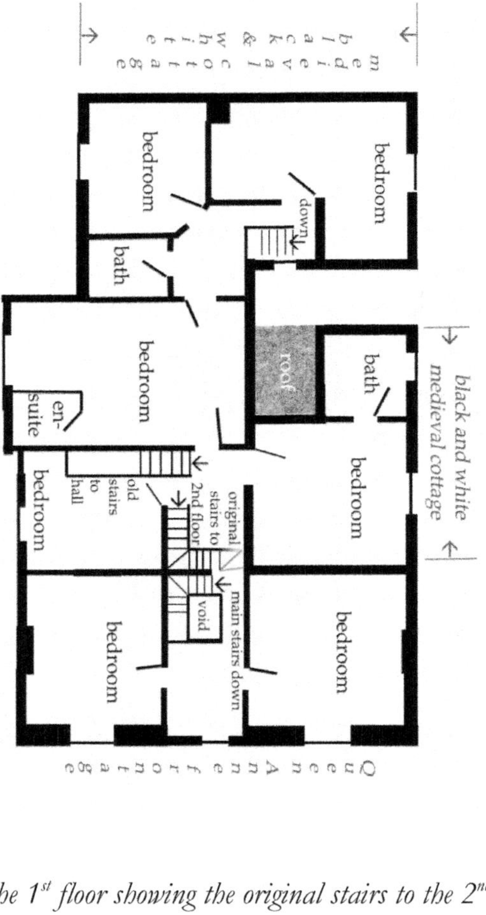

The 1st floor showing the original stairs to the 2nd

adding on frontages like this? I mean, they're common enough when you get fully into the Georgian era, but this is earlier, and might well have been the first one that bloke had ever done."

"Oh, I see what you mean. So you think he got up to this level and then thought, 'oh bugger, I've messed this up, the stairs don't fit!'"

"Something like that, yes. And possibly all the more so if the main build was already higher, and the rough basics of the top rooms already in. It could mean he put in a separate staircase of some sort up to the top floor – sort of back-to-back with the main ones, and creating an archway on the landing – which those odd three steps up on the top landing are the remains of. A main stair to the second floor roughly in the same place as the surviving servants' stairs, but which didn't block any doorways. Certainly, if you look at the floorboards upstairs, they've been lifted and cut and generally mucked about with quite a lot in the past.

"So it occurred to me that far from being built at the same time as the main stairs and front, maybe *these* servants' stairs were a much later addition? And initially the stairs we rediscovered last week simply got downgraded to being the servants' stairs when the new front and stairs went in, and it was only when they needed to seal the body into them that they had no choice but to make a new servant's staircase."

"Wow! They built a whole new staircase to cover up a murder?" Fliss gasped. "I wonder what excuse they gave the builders?"

"A large backhander to not ask any questions, I suspect," Bernie said dryly. "No doubt money talked back then just as much as it does now."

"Hang on a moment," said Fliss, dumping her empty mug on the floor and going back to look at the doorway into the current bathroom area, which the old stairs had once come up into. "If the old stairs we uncovered always came up into here, then surely there must have been a wall on this side of them? There must have to make the remaining room private, even if back then it was just another bedroom …unless it was some sort of landing that later on got boxed in?

"…No, that doesn't make sense. No, surely there had to once have been an outside wall to that old staircase on the far side to the hall? The outside wall which perhaps had its upper section taken away when the stairs had to connect not just to the old first floor, but the new front as well?"

"And what about this?" She waved a hand at the doorway into the bathroom from the landing. "Look at it, Bernie! It virtually opens *over* those old stairs now that we know they're there. Well you wouldn't have a door swinging open *towards* the stairs, would you? Because you can't reach the door handle until you're on the top step, and then you wouldn't be able to pull to open it without going back down.

"This specific doorway couldn't have been in this spot. Even if they were creating little more than a box-room, its doorway couldn't possibly have been *this* one. Looking from where we are on the landing, it *must* originally have been to the left of where it is now, in a spot currently hidden behind the surviving servants' stairs. Surely that proves your case? And what's more, once they built those new stairs to the second floor – the ones we've been using – they'd have *had* to move that first doorway across to where it is now, because otherwise it would have been totally blocked in by the newer staircase.

"Do you see what I mean? Until they blocked in the hall's stairs, there'd have been no need for two full flights of servants' stairs going up to both upper floors. Whatever happened, though, this doorway had to be moved, and maybe it was easier to move a door than do something more complicated with stairs?"

"My God, you're right!" Bernie exclaimed enthusiastically, and hurried into the deserted bathroom. Luckily this had never been tiled, and they had avoided stripping the wallpaper off until the shifting of the old porcelain had been done, simply as some additional protection for the old walls. But now Bernie had the ends of the lengths of paper in his hands, and was hauling off the sheets almost in one go, the glue having long since ceased to stick it down in anything but the most superficial manner.

"Ah ha!" he declared triumphantly a few moments later. "Well done, Fliss! See this line in the plaster? That has to be where the original door jamb was." He gave an experimental rap with his knuckles over the spot and was as surprised as Fliss when a wedge of plaster promptly fell off. "Blimey! Looks like we're going to have to do a fair bit of repairing on this wall, too. Somebody just roughly plastered over the wooden frame to try and make it match the rest of the wall."

As Fliss began picking away at the loose bits of plaster, most of which came away in her hands the moment she touched them, Bernie went and got one of the stepladders. Getting up to above the door frame, he poked at the plaster up there and also found it crumbling, almost showering Fliss below him as it came away in large flakes.

"Good grief, there's something written up here," he said, fishing his torch out of his pocket and shining it at the back of the plaster on the other side. Coming down he handed the torch to Fliss. "You go up and see if you can read it – your eyes are younger than mine. Somebody made a lath and plaster infill up there, but didn't put a few laths in just there so that what they wrote could be found, I reckon. It's why the plaster was so loose, but you see what you think."

Climbing up, Fliss could immediately see what Bernie meant. This was intended to be found, and given the lack of light in here, whoever had done it had possible relied on these walls being papered over so that his botched plastering wouldn't be spotted at the time. And peering at it, she found that if she angled the torch a bit to the side, its harsh light didn't burn out the letters quite as much.

"I think this might have been done in something like charcoal," she relayed down to Bernie, "but perhaps done when the plaster wasn't totally dry so that it's sort of bonded with the plaster. It says… 'I did this because the master bade me.' …or at least I think the word is 'bade' and not 'made', but either makes sense. On the next bit it says, 'I know my work covers an evil deed. I swear unto God that I did this out of fear. If they do this to their own what would they do to my family.' Oh my lord, Bernie, we have to let Dr Warrener see this!"

"I'll give her a call," Bernie decided. "Can you write what it says down in this notebook so that I can repeat it back to her?"

It was the end of the day when Sylvia Warrener turned up, along with Carol Whitmore, and it was at that point that Bernie and Fliss realised that they must be at least partners or possibly married.

"Don't worry, this won't make it any more of an official investigation," Carol told them cheerfully.

"This is just Sylv' indulging her professional curiosity."

"What a find!" Sylvia was already exclaiming from the top of Bernie's steps, and taking multiple photographs of the words. "I don't think I've ever seen a confession like this to being complicit in a murder before, or at least certainly not for this era. How fascinating! I don't suppose you know who this 'master' is who he's talking about, do you?"

"Best guess," Fliss replied, "is that it's Cuthbert Spink or one of his sons, Nenius or Aquillia. They're the ones who fit the general period, but one of them must have gone out to India, so it's hard to tell who was here when."

That prompted questions by the two about the other finds, and so Bernie ended up inviting them back to his house to see them. The shoebox in which they'd put the children's sandals, the prayer sheets, and the cloth was brought out, and along with the carved toys, were pored over in delight by Sylvia.

"These are amazing," she declared. "It's so rare to find examples of folk art."

"She means the stuff ordinary people used," Carol explained with an affectionate grin to her partner.

Sylvia peered over her glasses with a smile. "Alright, I know I'm getting over excited. But seriously, these ought to go to a museum somewhere. There are a lot of Asian kids out there nowadays who never get to see stuff from their own cultural heritage. This could be really meaningful to them."

"In that case, you'd better have these too," Fliss said, and went and found the children's drawings.

"Good grief, you've given her Christmas and

birthday all in one," Carol laughed at Sylvia's gasps of delight.

"We kept them but had no idea what to do with them," Fliss admitted, silently glad that she could hand all of this stuff over to someone else. Maybe then it would stop plaguing her?

However, Carol added, "For my part, I'm more curious as to the sequence of events. I know it's long before my remit to look into, but I can't help how my brain works any more than Sylv' can hers, and I always want to know why and how. I think you've done a remarkable detective job with the uncovering of that staircase, and then working out how it must have been sealed up. I can't wait to tell Bill about this. He'll love it!

"But what has me puzzled is this: if they killed the soldier in the morning room – and I think you are right, the stains on the parquet do confirm that – then what was going on that they couldn't just pass him off as an intruder? Let's face it, in those days a gentleman of that kind of status wouldn't be queried for defending himself against someone unknown being in his house. They weren't worried about things like excessive force back then. And of course, you've now got that rather splendid confession from the builder who did the work."

"I wouldn't go as far as to call him a builder," Bernie interrupted. "Compared to the work in the rest of the house, that moved doorway is a right botched job. And incidentally, it also explains some rather clumsy patched up work in the wall opposite too. I thought the damage had been done when the spiral staircase was put in, but maybe that was allowed by the planners because that facing wall had already been damaged long ago when the doorway was shifted?

Whoever did it, I'm sure it couldn't have been the original builders of the new frontage – it's just not good enough."

"Could he simply have been the man who could do the approximate job, who was perhaps a tenant on the estate?" Carol wondered. "He sounds as if he knows that his own family are within reach, so to speak, of this master. Maybe he was worried about reprisals if he spoke out? Potentially even taking the blame for it all? I've lived with Sylvia for long enough now to know that once you get back into the nineteenth century and beyond, that an ordinary man's word against one of the gentry's was never going to stand up."

Sylvia looked up briefly from the drawings. "Oh yes, that's absolutely right. In theory the workman ought to have been able to get a fair hearing from the law, but the reality was very different, especially out somewhere like here, where the case would have been heard in court by men of standing who might be friends with the gentleman in question."

"But why does he refer to 'one of their own'?" Carol persisted. "That sounds like the dead man was known to the family, and even more, as though people in the district might have known of him too."

"I see what you mean," Fliss agreed, wishing that her stomach hadn't turned flips and somersaults at Carol's last words. "Our dead soldier wasn't a stranger to them, was he? Or at least, if not well-known, at least someone they knew *about*, maybe someone who had had to ask for directions to the place from locals just to get here?"

And even after the two women had left, Sylvia carrying the shoebox as if it carried diamonds, not letters and toys, Fliss' mind wouldn't let go of that idea. Who had killed whom in that house? What was their relationship to one another? And why had they gone to such lengths to cover it up?

Chapter 18

Tuesday - Friday

Back at the house, Bernie suddenly had the idea of investigating the wall underneath the discovered staircase, because as he explained to Fliss, that was where the bulk of the original outside wall still survived. If there was going to be rot which he'd need to deal with, that would be where it might have taken a hold. And sure enough, now that the loose soil had been cleared away and they could stand inside the space, Fliss could see the huge oak timbers which would once have framed the outside wall of the hall, though elsewhere hidden behind Georgian brickwork. The ones Bernie had revealed on the hall side, by taking the later infill out, were now obviously too lightweight to have supported the upstairs floor by themselves; whereas the ones they saw now were huge and matching those seen in the wall of the rear hallway where Fliss had first walked into the house.

"This big Jacobean hall is almost a separate building, isn't it?" she said in awe, as she and Bernie compared the measurements of the timbers. "It might be sandwiched between the oldest part and the Queen Anne frontage now, but when it first went in it must have been pretty much a complete build all of its own, just butting up to the oldest part and displayed in all its glory before the front went on."

Bernie nodded. "And if you got the render off the outside walls, I suspect that you'd find that the Queen Anne part isn't exactly keyed in, either. The frontage probably just butts up to what was the holiday let, and it's only where they hit the staircase that they actually took the floor of the new part right across into the old bit."

He walked outside and looked up at the first floor. "Mind you, it does look as though the roof is cut a bit short on the front side. If we were to investigate under that lead flashing, who knows what we might find."

"Well can we leave that until we've bought the place, please?" Fliss said firmly. "I don't think we dare uncover something else that's going to raise the Davenport's bill." She didn't want to add that she herself couldn't bear the thought of any new mysteries coming to light, or at least not for a year or two.

Luckily the mention of the Davenports successfully squashed Bernie's curiosity, since there was no good reason for him to go poking around up on the roof, and they went back inside. Nor was it as if they hadn't got enough still to do. Phil had vanished, promising to return to install the spotlights Bernie wanted over the old stairs, and to wire in the new grand kitchen Bernie had planned for the space which had been the Davenport's dining room. The old long-let kitchen, which had previous been a scullery, would become one again with a washing machine, tumble dryer, and dishwasher plumbed into it; but Bernie was now really showing how sympathetic he was to old buildings with the free-standing units he had planned for what would return to being the main kitchen. The huge chimney breast was to become the focal point, with a modern range cooker installed into it, Bernie declaring that if ever there was a kitchen crying out for an Aga, this was it. And so Fliss spent an enjoyable few days helping him get the whole of that ground-floor part of the house up to the point where they could start putting things back into it.

But then that mean that by the Thursday there was little Fliss could realistically do to help Bernie, and when he suggested that she start cleaning down the walls in the old hall, she felt she could hardly decline.

"Clean them as best you can without soaking them," he instructed her, "And then providing that orange paint isn't something we have to physically take off by sanding it away, I'll come in and put a skim over them. I suspect that's the only way we'll ever fully cover that bloody awful orange! Make sure you get anything flaking off, though," and having become used to Bernie's standards by now, Fliss at least felt that she knew what she was doing with preparation work.

Being on her own in the hall, however, was not something she was happy about. Kevin and Sean had also departed for other jobs, and even the annoyingly cocky Josh had finished yesterday until such time as anything else needed to be plumbed in. And so, although she could hear Bernie cheerfully whistling along to the radio across the hallway, she still felt very much alone.

Determined not to start shying at shadows again, she resolutely began tackling the wall between the door and the fireplace. That was the one farthest from any natural light, and so needed to be done in while she still had plenty of daylight. The days were getting lighter, and although last weekend the clocks had shifted to summertime, by the end of the afternoons there still wasn't that good a light in this old part.

"You can do this, Fliss," she whispered to herself, scrubbing away at something which looked as though it ought to start flaking off at any moment, being determined to do a good job for Bernie to start repairing on. "Come on, nothing spooky in here, nothing at all."

And as she made her way along the wall up to the fireplace, nothing made her even so much as twitch. The fireplace itself was a glorious thing, with a huge stone mantel, and when she stuck her head into it to see if she could see right up it, she discovered that it still had the old hooks in it which once would have held legs of pork curing in the smoke of the fire. There was even the old hook which would once have swung out to bring a kettle out over the fire, and Fliss lovingly scrubbed that free of the soot of ages before carrying on.

It meant she was utterly unprepared when she came back, with a bucket of clean water and more sugar-soap to start on the other side of the fireplace, to find that this was far crumblier. "What the heck?" she muttered as another piece of surface plaster came off in her hands. "What's going on here?" And then another piece came away and she found herself looking at wood, or to be more precise, a length of wood which looked worryingly like the frame to the under-stair doorway that they had uncovered along with the body.

"*Bernieee!*" she wailed, wishing she didn't sound quite such a wimp, and yet having that awful sinking feeling that the house had just given up another of its secrets.

He came running through. "What's wrong? Have you hurt yourself?"

"No. Look!"

"Bloody hell, another doorway! Well I never. I always presumed they must have accessed that other part of the old house from a continuation of the back corridor, but this must lead straight through into the holiday let's lounge." He stood back and scratched his chin thoughtfully for a moment. "Hmm, doesn't look as though we'd be disrupting any Jacobean wattle and daub by going through, so maybe that means this was originally a doorway to the outside in that first building? Maybe even the main doorway? I always thought the door from the original kitchen to the hallway that still exists looks a bit narrow to be the first front door. That would explain it if it was never meant to be one. Or maybe it only went in when the Jacobean hall stopped this from being the outside door?"

"Are the Davenports going to object to us opening up another doorway?" Fliss wondered.

"I don't know. I'll try and give them a ring when we get home tonight, but I think that we need to get this opened up. If needs be, I can always put a lockable double door on either side of the thickness of this wall, so that they can leave it closed if they want and with it still being warmer than a single door, or open it up later on. But I think I can sell it to them as us exposing more original features – which is great if they want to sell it on as we suspect – because this is a lovely bit of wooden framework you've found here, Fliss."

This time it didn't take as long to get back to the original doorway, and immediately Fliss could see that it was the same black oak beams as the structural

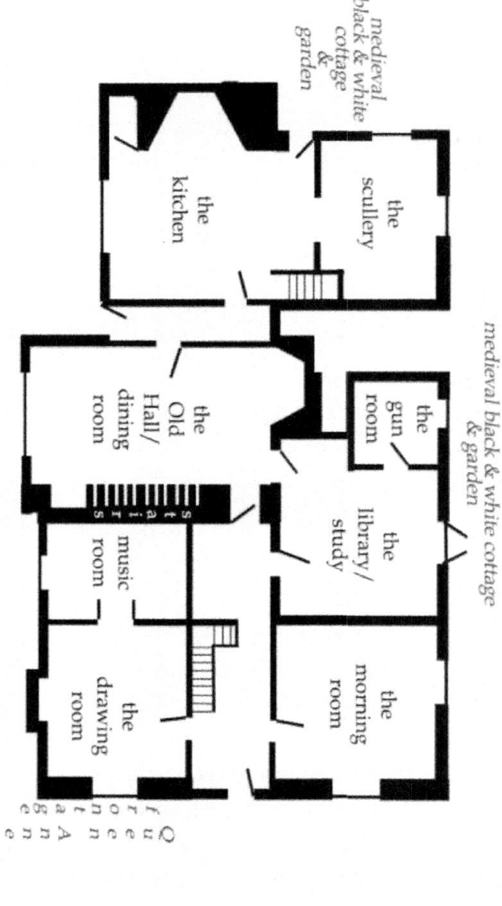

The ground floor with original doors and stairs

timbers. There was no doubting that this had been meant to be like this both on the oldest part and then here in the hall. And although the hinges on the old door they discovered still hanging on the holiday let's side of the gap needed to be well-oiled in order to work again, Bernie was confident that he could get the door moving again.

"Just you wait and see," he declared, as he squirted WD40 onto the hinges. "Give this time to do its stuff and we'll have a working door here."

He then went back to working on the kitchen, and Fliss tried to get back to her cleaning, but that doorway kept itching away at her senses. Every so often she could swear that she heard a strange kind of humming coming from that corner of the room, not helped by the fact that she was now washing down the woodwork of the newly exposed banister to the old stairs, and that all by itself was sending shivers down her spine. When she got to where the doorway to the stairs was, the door itself having been taken down once Bernie realised that it was not original to the space, she took one look at the lower steps where the body had been slumped, and knew that she had reached her limit.

"Nope, not happening," she said with a shudder. "If I'm a wimp to Bernie for not wanting to touch this, then I'll just have to be a wimp, but I can't, I really can't."

She peeled the rubber gloves off in order to rub her nose, which was also itching furiously right now, and as she draped them over the banister rather than over the side of her bucket – not wanting them to fall in and leave her with soggy gloves – she felt a sudden stab in her finger.

"Ouch!" She looked down and saw that there was a slightly pointed bit of wood lying proud of the banister. Not a full splinter, but with enough of a point to scratch her with. "You little bugger," she swore, and without thinking about it reflexively put her finger to her mouth to suck at the tiny bubble of blood. In that instant the humming got louder, and as she belatedly whipped her finger away and retreated from the banister, in the process turning towards the doorway.

Suddenly it was as if the door was wide open, and she could see through into what she knew of as the holiday let's lounge, but looked to be more of a library. There, as clear as if he was standing next to her in her own time, was a gaunt figure whom she recognised as Cuthbert. A much older, balding, and greying Cuthbert, and now with a pot belly, making him look in profile like a matchstick whose end blob had slipped to halfway down.

"You will *go!" he was saying, and to emphasise his point, jabbed a bony finger towards an unseen person who was further into the room.* "You *will go to France," and the finger moved sideways, "and* you *will go to with him."*

"But Father, I don't want to," the voice of a young male came, which by the way it was cracking possibly meant that his voice had not fully broken. That made him young indeed to be sent to either place.

"You'll go where I send you, my lad, and there is an end to it! I have had enough of your rebellious ideas, no doubt put into your head by that damned Scottish uncle of mine, who has insisted on interfering in our family business. Well, no more! Your mother, God rest her soul, is long gone, and though I was glad to send you into Uncle John's care so that I did not have to concern myself with the care of a squalling babe, you are a babe no longer, and will behave as a young man of this family now."

Cuthbert swung his gaze back to the other person. "Well? Have you nothing to say for yourself? …No? That makes a change."

Which one was going where, Fliss wondered? Was it the younger to France and the older to India, or the other way

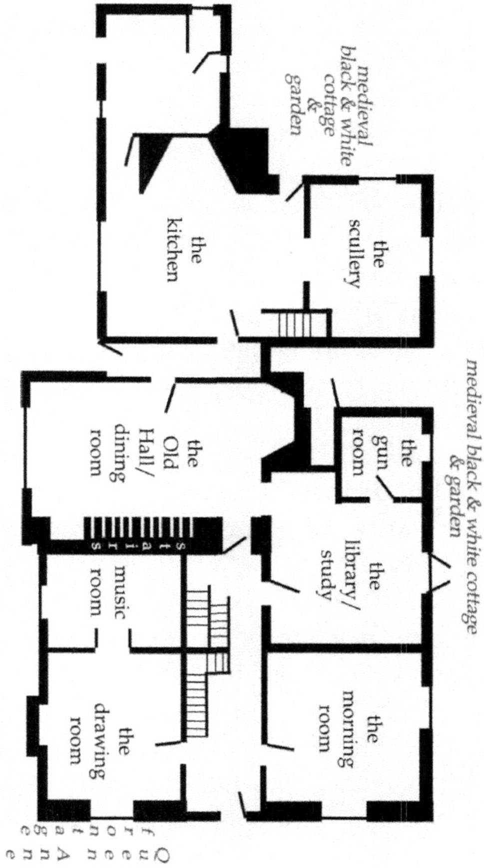

The house as Fliss sees it with revealed stairs and doors

around? Did they both go to both places? Any which way, it wasn't good. If Cuthbert was into his late middle-age, then France could be on the brink of the Revolution, and India would still be unsettled. And as Cuthbert moved out of sight, his pecking walk making him look like an arthritic stork, she heard a door slam – presumably the other one which led into the newer main hallway – and felt compelled to call out,

"Be careful! France is dangerous right now!" And then thinking of the dead soldier, "Someone is going to come to you from there, but they aren't a danger to you. You need to protect them from the revolutionaries!"

But before she could see what affect her words had, Bernie's voice echoed from the kitchen as he came towards the door.

"You okay in there, Fliss?"

As soon as he spoke the scene vanished, and by the time Bernie came through the door there was nothing to see.

"You okay? You look a bit pale."

"I'm sorry, Bernie," Fliss said, waving a hand at the steps. "I just can't clean those. Not where that body was. I can't."

"Hey, don't stress about it," Bernie replied, coming to give her one of his wonderful hugs. "A couple of steps aren't worth getting upset about. I'll do them in the morning. Anyway, I was just about to come and say why don't we pack it in for today? There's footie on the TV tonight, so it'd be nice if we can get home and have something to eat, and still leave time for me to call the Davenports before it starts."

"Great idea," Fliss said with relief, and gladly cleared her things away.

Yet the day wasn't done with odd occurrences. They had a quickly made meal, and then Bernie sat in his chair and tried to ring Eric Davenport.

"That's odd," he said after the third attempt. "I keep getting a 'this mobile is not switched on' message, and there's no option to go to voicemail."

"No voicemail?" Fliss repeated in surprise. "That's not normal, is it? Most people have it even if they don't use it. That sounds worryingly as though it's been deliberately switched off. Have you tried Mrs D?"

"No, but I'm about to."

However, although this time there was the chance to leave a voicemail message, Mrs Davenport was equally not picking up the phone, and had not called back by the time they went to bed. Therefore, over breakfast Bernie decided that he would ring DI Scathlock and see who he had managed to get in touch with. When the detective answered, Bernie was quick to apologise for disturbing him, but explained the situation.

"Has Mrs Davenport not been in touch with you?" Bill Scathlock's voice responded in surprise. "I told her that she needed to get back to you as soon as possible after what she told me."

"We've not heard a thing," Bernie told him. "And I must admit that after finding the body, I was expecting a screaming match. I was just counting my blessings up until now that we'd heard nothing, but now you've got me worried. What's happened?"

"I'm sorry to have to tell you this," Bill said, sounding genuinely apologetic, "and if I'd thought she wasn't going to come clean with you, I'd have rung you sooner. The thing is, Eric Davenport's done a runner."

"What?" Fliss and Bernie both exclaimed together, Fliss having heard since Bernie had his phone on speaker.

"Far from going to his old army mate's," Bill expanded, "that trip into Worcester on the day when you last saw Mrs Davenport turns out to be when he went and drained their joint accounts. To say that Mrs Davenport was hysterical when she spoke to me is putting it mildly. Luckily, she had a substantial savings account in her own name, although I'm not feeling too sorry for her because I think you were right, she was intending to sting him for everything he had, and had been salting lumps of money away over the last few months with the intention of getting them out of his hands.

"I don't know if he found out about that, and that's why he did what he did, or if he's as bad as her. But Eric Davenport has left his wife with that house you're working on and not a lot else. Even that flash car you saw was apparently a leased car, and has had to go back."

"Blimey!" Bernie gasped, completely taken aback. "So there's no money in the bank to pay us with?"

"Not a *sou*," Bill said regretfully. "That's why I told her that she legally needed to inform you of the situation. At that point you could have decided whether you wanted to carry on and finish the place so that you can get the best price for it. Or call it a day, have it go on the market in the state it's in, and hope that you've covered your costs. But she was very clear on that – the house is going up for sale because she's got no other option."

Bernie grimaced and it must have sounded in his voice as he said, "We're a bit past just sticking it on the market by now."

"Oh dear."

"Oh dear is about bloody right. It's not much better than a building site right now, and I've got subcontractors who'll need to be paid, for a start off.

Between you and me, I can afford to pay them myself, but that's not really the point, is it?"

"No, it's not. She's getting perilously close to fraud if she's planning on sticking that house on the market once it's done, and then skipping town once it's sold before she's paid you. And I have to say, I felt there was something very off about her, even just talking to her down the phone. If I hadn't got tangled up in a serious case the next day and it slipped my mind, I was intending to call you this week just to check up on her, so I'm very glad you called me."

"No, I'm grateful to you," Bernie assured him. "If you hadn't caught her before she went silent, I don't know what I'd have done. Probably carried on as we're going to have to do anyway, but at least now we're forewarned. That's undoubtedly why Mrs D didn't ring me back yesterday. She's not going to want to talk to me if she's planning to pull a swift one on me."

"There is one good thing, though," Fliss interrupted them with. "If she wants to sell the house, she'll have to use an agent, and we've not seen hide nor hair of anyone coming around to take photos. So doesn't that rather imply that she wants us to finish the house so that it fetches the best price?"

"There is that," Bill Scathlock agreed. "But she was right upset at the mention of the body. Houses where there have been violent deaths can be awfully hard to shift, and usually end up going for far less than the normal asking price would have been, which I suspect is why she was begging me not to let anything of this discovery get into the papers. Not that either Sylvia or Carol is unprofessional enough to let something be leaked. Sylvia would probably like to make an announcement about those things you gave her, which by the way she's still thrilled to bits with, but she wouldn't do it without the owner's permission – though I did tell her about this, and suggest that legal ownership might have passed into a very grey area if they've played silly buggers with the previous owners too."

"That's all good to know," Bernie agreed, and thanking Bill once again ended the conversation.

On the way over to the house, though, he was obviously brooding on the matter, which finally decided Fliss on suggesting something.

"Didn't you say that the locks on the doors were pretty feeble by modern standards?" she began.

"Yes, so what of it?"

"Well maybe we should upgrade them," she suggested with a sly wink when Bernie turned to look at her. "If we're the only ones with the current keys to the place, then Mrs bloody Davenport can't mail her keys to some agent, who can then come poking around when we're not there. It would give us some advanced notice of what her intentions are and when, wouldn't it? No more nasty surprises, such as us driving in one day to find a big 'For Sale' sign up; or worse, having someone turn up to view the place when we didn't even know it was on the market yet. DI Scathlock's right, Bernie, that damned woman is almost certainly trying to wriggle her way out of paying you, so at least if you know which agent and when, you could always get your solicitor to write and tell them that you need paying out of the proceeds. That way it's all on record, isn't it?"

As it sank in what she was suggesting, Bernie perked up. "By heck, Fliss, that's a bloody good idea. Do you know, I was still feeling a bit guilty about cancelling those house clearers and letting them charge her without doing the job. Not my style, you see, just not me. But if she was always intending to diddle us out of money, it makes me feel a whole heap better about that! My goodness it does.

"So yes, we'll do that. In fact, let's detour and go and get those locks right now. We can fit them today and have the place secure before the weekend. Last week she was probably too knocked sideways by hearing about Eric, and then the body, to do much – well most people would be, wouldn't they? But I've been worrying over whether she would try and get the place sold before news of the dead soldier came out, especially if it's going to make the place harder to sell. And that might mean that after me calling her last night, she's on to an agent today. If she sends the keys via a courier, she could have them to an agent by tomorrow, and if they think the commission is big enough, what's the betting that they'd come out to at least have a look on a Saturday?"

"Then we get in first," Fliss said firmly, while thinking to herself, *would it be too bad if it was me who leaked the news of the body to the local press? Because if that drops the price of the place, and Bernie can get a court order on the sale so that he gets paid out of it, we might not have to find as much as we thought to buy it. And even with its ghosts and strange visions, I still desperately want to live there, even if I can't quite work out why.*

Cuthbert, Nenius & Aquillia

1790

With his fifteenth birthday coming up in a few weeks' time, like most young boys, Quill couldn't wait to grow up. And like most normal lads, he wanted to leave home, but not because of any wild dreams of adventures – he just wanted to get out of this god-awful house. His oldest two sisters, Elizabeth and Marjorie, were married and living not that far away, but with them having been fifteen and thirteen even when he was born, and with neither of them wanting to be a substitute mother to him when their mother, Alice, had died when he was only three, he scarcely knew them. His oldest brother, Ingram, had died along with baby Caroline the year after he was born, and so he had never known them either. That left his remaining sister, Catriona, who had just turned twenty-one this year, and was resolutely remaining in Scotland with the intention of marrying the man she loved there, regardless of all of their father's threats to disinherit her. And then there was Nenius.

Bloody Nenius, as Quill always thought of him as. Eight years older than him, and a nasty bully, just like their father. It had been a perverse blessing that Quill had been so young when his mother had died, because Cuthbert had no intention of paying for a nurse to come and look after him, whereas Nenius at eleven was just about old enough to cope with a tutor and the housekeeper's attentions. And because Cuthbert had for some peculiar reason developed a perennial dislike for Catriona as the remaining girl left at home, she was immediately sent north, since at only nine years old she was too young to be shoved out into service, and Quill had been sent with her. That had led to a blessedly happy childhood for Quill in the company of his distant cousins, and so it had been something of a shock for him to be abruptly recalled to the family home three years ago. And although Great-uncle John had by then passed away, nonetheless his son – another John – had pleaded in many letters for Quill to be allowed to stay with them, but Cuthbert had been immovable. Quill was the spare heir, and Quill must come home now that he needed no women to fuss over him.

It was only when Quill had got here that he realised that his father's panic had been caused by Nenius falling seriously ill that winter. If Bloody Nenius had not spent months coughing his lungs up, there had been a good chance that Cuthbert would have forgotten about Quill until he was old enough to be able to refuse to return as an adult himself. But his luck had run out. With Cuthbert now into his fifties, he was no longer up to travelling back and forth to France, and what was worse, things had become very unstable over there in the last few years.

Yet what Quill had also swiftly realised was that his father was an arrant coward when it came to saving his own skin. If his life was going to be even vaguely imperilled by crossing the water, then he wasn't going, but he had no such qualms about sending one of his sons – contradictory though that was to his equal panic over preserving an heir for the place. But then his father was a mass of contradictions, Quill discovered. On the one hand, more than conservative in his religion, he was also superstitious beyond anyone else Quill had known, and that included Cousin John's dotty old maternal great-aunt, who had whole reams of rituals, fetches, and tokens, covering almost every eventuality. Worse, he was prim and proper and judgemental in the extreme, but seemed to have no conscience about his own actions, which included self-indulgence and self-preservation above all else.

Nor did it help that Cuthbert had discovered that Quill spoke better French by far than either he or Nenius did, thanks to Cousin John's oldest son having married a French lady, something Quill repeatedly kicked himself for having let slip. Why, oh why, he wondered, had he been such a fool as to correct Nenius at the dinner table when he got that common phrase so horribly wrong? But then he'd only been home a couple of days, and hadn't really grasped just how bad things were here. He'd come from a loving family home, and walked into a living nightmare of a kind he had scarce believed existed.

For a start off, these days he was fairly sure that his father was bedding the housekeeper, Bessie, a buxom woman who certainly wasn't being kept on for her efficient running of the household. The old staff Great-uncle John had talked of as being so loyal to his sister, Quill's grandmother Marjorie, were all long dead, and in their place had come a few individuals whose morals were – to Quill's eyes, having been used to his cousin's devout household – loose, to say the least. About the best of the bunch was old Henry, the gardener, but he and his boy kept well away from the house unless summoned there. But Kenric, the so-called butler, seemed to know very little of what he ought, and an awful lot about things which any law-abiding man should not. And Quill was pretty sure that although Bessie claimed to be a widow, that she was no such thing, and that the parlour maid, Tess, was actually her illegitimate daughter. She certainly seemed to share her mother's appetite for men, because Quill knew beyond any doubt that she was keeping Nenius' bed warm.

Indeed, this lust for their kept women on the part of his father and his brother was proving downright embarrassing. Quill had learned very fast to stop and listen at the door before entering any room, because he had fled, scarlet-faced, after walking into the dining room in all innocence, only to be greeted by the sight of his father, breeches around his ankles and pumping away at Bessie, who was leaning on the dining table. Her uproarious laughter at the sight of him, eyes wide and jaw dropped, had only made things worse. And to top it all, he had been unable to forget the sight of his father's skinny white legs, wobbling away like some already-plucked old rooster, as his shirt tails flapped like redundant wings.

Nenius had hooted with laughter when Quill had confided in hushed and horrified tones at what he had seen, and had then implied that it was probably time Quill became a man, and would he like Tess to teach him the ways of the world? Even more horrified at that, let alone that he'd be sharing her with his brother, Quill had declined; but had poured his heart out in a letter back to Cousin John, a man who was far more of a father figure to him than this rake of a man he was forced into the company of. Yet although Cousin John had shared his dismay, he had also confessed that there was little he could do to extract Quill from the house. At the end of the day, Cuthbert was Quill's natural and legal father, and if he wanted his son to live with him until he came of age, then live with him Quill must until that day which right now seemed way too far in the future. All John could exhort Quill to do was to remember the morals he had been brought up with within his own household, and to remain steadfast to those in this time of adversity.

That hadn't been much consolation to a homesick twelve-year-old, and three years later it still wasn't to a thoroughly fed up and disgusted fifteen-year-old. And so Quill couldn't wait to leave home. What he hadn't bargained on was that it would come in the form of being sent to France with Nenius. At twenty-three, Nenius had already been away on his father's behalf several times since Quill had been back, affording Quill some blessed respite from tripping over him and Tess, if nothing else. And although he had come back the last time half scared out of his wits, nonetheless Cuthbert had decreed that it was time that he should take Quill with him and introduced him to their business contacts over there.

"But Father," Nenius had protested, "it is dangerous over there. We may not have a trade there by the time we return! You have not seen it. They are descending into war. There are no noble ladies buying our gloves at the moment. They have other things to worry about – like keeping their heads on their necks!"

And Quill could believe that, because the so-called noble ladies Nenius and his father sold to were not the owners of the great chateaux, the ones who could afford armed guards at their gates. They were the lowest ranks of nobles, and those merchants who had managed to claw and climb their way into the bourgeoisie, with maybe a fancy house in the local large town, and somewhere more modest in the countryside. All of whom were only too aware of how dangerous things might get after the king had dissolved the National Assembly last summer, and had sent troops to disband it. Even worse for these people, had been the storming of the Bastille a few weeks later in July, which had been a sure sign of worse to come.

"Those in control have taken over the Church lands and are selling them off," Nenius had tried to explain, "and most of our customers spent heavily on that when it seemed like a chance to get rich quickly in land if nothing else. But now people are trying to use those bonds they bought the lands with as currency, and the whole thing is falling apart. We have no trade left over there, Father, can you not grasp that?"

But Cuthbert couldn't or wouldn't, and having heard by now of the number of times the family fortunes had taken dips because of his father being tied to his own cousin's misfortunes and financial follies, Quill suspected it was wilful blindness by this stage. And so he stood in the library as his father broke the news to his brother and himself, feeling his heart sinking into his boots at the prospect …and then that woman's voice had come through. Where, by all that was holy, had that come from? Because of one thing Quill was sure, that had been none of the women he knew in this house. Nobody around here spoke like that, in that accent.

And as she faded away, Quill saw his father sink to his knees, his hands clasped before him, weeping, "The White Lady! She has come again!"

The door banged open and Nenius came back in.

"What was all that about? …Father?"

"There was a voice," Quill managed to say, just about managing to stop it from cracking in dismay this time. "A voice from over there," and he pointed to the door through to the old hall.

"She spoke again. The White Lady," Cuthbert announced reverently.

"What? That damned ghost you say came to you and your father?" Nenius said with a snort of disbelief. "Don't tell me you saw it too, Quill?"

"I saw nothing," Quill admitted, "but I did hear her, Nenius. I heard her as clearly as I hear you now. And whoever she is, she speaks like nobody from around here." Then he thought that maybe this would be his chance to get out of the dreadful trip. "She said that France will be dangerous now. She said that there is a revolution coming."

Nenius snorted. "We hardly needed a ghost to tell us that! Not with King Louis seeming to be powerless to stop anything."

Cuthbert was struggling to his feet, wagging an angry finger at his oldest son.

"Ah! But she said," and his face took on a rapturous appearance, "'Someone is going to come to you from there, but they aren't a danger to you. You need to protect them from the revolutionaries!' …What do you say to that, eh? Not so quick to explain that away, are you?"

But what Quill didn't like was the sudden sly smile which spread across Nenius' face. Their father was too caught up in the moment to spot it, but Quill had a nasty sinking feeling that Nenius had seen some way to work this to his advantage.

"Protect them from the revolutionaries, you say?" Nenius checked.

"Yes, yes, yes!" their father spluttered. "And if the White Lady says that, then we must do it! I failed to heed her warnings before, and that was when your namesake got his hooks into me, Nenius. Well, I won't risk that again!"

"Quite right, Father," Nenius said in a placating tone. "Quill and I must go to France with all speed in order to return with this precious person in time, must we not?"

"Yes, yes, yes!" Cuthbert jabbered again, but as Quill left the room, going out by the door into the hall, just in case he could spot some unexpected visitor who might explain all of this away, he felt desperately uneasy. Why had he had such a shiver when he walked through that door this time? As if some ghost was walking over his grave?

He'd heard of this apparition when his father had been drunk enough not to realise how weak and foolish he sounded, or that he was confessing to raping a visiting servant. So he wasn't that surprised that his father would believe that voice now, regardless of where or how it had appeared. Indeed, for all Quill knew, it really might be the same voice, and his father genuinely recognised it. But what worried him far more was why Nenius had suddenly changed his tune. What was he walking into over in France that his brother knew about, and his father didn't? Why had that mention of a person who presumably needed rescuing so pleased Nenius, and who was it? Because Quill was certain that Nenius knew this person already, even if he'd been keeping quiet about it up until now.

Chapter 19

Friday

The fitting of the new locks didn't take as long as Fliss had thought, and though it wasn't a cheap outlay, by the time they had got good high-security locks on every possible external door, and the downstairs windows all locked too, both she and Bernie admitted to feeling a lot better. Not happier. That would only come when they knew what Mrs Davenport was planning. But at least they felt that they had regained control of the situation.

"She was so damned insistent about you setting the alarm, back when she left," Fliss reminded Bernie, "so she can hardly complain if you've upgraded the locks. You have your perfect excuse right there. No point in having that alarm system – even if it is so old as to be barely worth it – when they had door locks that even I could have broken into."

Bernie gave a satisfied nod. "Exactly! And I must admit I feel a lot better about this generally now that we have the place properly secured. It was a job I always had one eye on doing, and would certainly have done by the time we started moving the expensive electrical equipment in. The French windows in the old holiday let desperately needed those sturdy bolts top and bottom. As they stood, you could have just leaned on them and they'd have sprung the latch.

"I have to confess that every day I was keeping an eye on the lanes as we drove in, in case we suddenly had an influx of travellers in the area. I have the greatest of respect for the true Romany gypsies, but so many who like to claim that name are just mobile crooks. They'll nick anything that's not nailed down, and even some that is. It's a shame, because they give the decent ones a terrible name. I've given some of the proper ones work in the past, and they do what you ask them to do and do it well, even if they do want paying in cash, but the other type you don't want anywhere near a building site." He looked around as if seeing beyond the walls of the kitchen where they were at the moment. "They'd strip the copper pipe out of here in no time, and never worry about the damage flooding would do to an old place like this."

"You've really fallen in love with this house, haven't you," Fliss observed, "but then I have too. I can't bear the idea of it being sold off to someone who just sees it as an investment." Now, she thought, was the time to give Bernie the good news she'd got this morning by email. "By the way, my flat in London is sold. I've got a completion date in just a week, because the buyers aren't in a chain, and neither am I."

Bernie's eyes lit up. "That's great, Fliss! And I don't just mean because it would give you money to buy into this if you wanted to. I think it's a very good thing that you've severed your last tie with London. You were never truly happy there, were you?"

"Not really, but I think it was in the last five years or so that I was really miserable. The worst of it for me is that I can't believe that I didn't realise it sooner.

You know, woken up back when I was well enough to have just changed jobs and moved to another city. Only after I got back to mum and dad's – and you know what a mess I was then – did it dawn on me how bad my life had got. The tough part then was that I couldn't see how to get out of the hole I'd dug for myself." She reached out and hugged him tightly. "Honestly, Bernie, I can't even begin to tell you how grateful I am to you for doing what you did. Without you, I don't think I could have gone on much longer."

"Oh, now, now," Bernie protested, blushing furiously. "I'm your godfather and uncle, what else would I have done?"

Fliss stood back and gave him a wry smile. "You could have done what my parents and my brother have done, which is nothing"

"Not my style, Fliss, *so* not my style."

"No, I know it's not, but that doesn't mean I'm taking it for granted, either." Then knew that she had to lighten the mood a little, or they'd both end up sniffling sentimentally into their tissues. "But in the spirit of getting me out of things I don't want to do …would you scrub those stairs today? The ones I wimped out of doing yesterday?"

Bernie laughed. "Crafty sod! You get me all sentimental and then drop that one me. *Tut!*" But he cheerfully went and got one of the buckets and tackled the stairs, while Fliss did the other half of the long wall she had started on.

It was much more convivial working alongside Bernie, and not for one moment did she feel anything at all from the old doorway. Nonetheless, it didn't make her any the less apprehensive when Bernie went to see if the door would open, having found the frame on the other side and cleared it too. Part of her expected to see Bernie vanish in a puff of smoke, even though her sensible part knew that that was ridiculous. It still took some easing with more oil on the hinges and latch, but eventually, with dramatic creaking which would have done a horror movie proud, the door jerkily opened.

"Oh wow!" Fliss gasped. "Look how much lighter that makes this room! The French windows let so much light into that other room, but I hadn't thought how that would affect here. It wasn't like…" she just about managed to stop herself from saying, 'when I saw Cuthbert in there.' Bernie would soon change his mind about her sanity if she had. As it was, he turned and quirked an eyebrow at her, but she managed to cover it with a shake of her head and a smile, before saying, "…I imagined it might be. I doubt Mrs D could object to us opening it up when it makes this room so much brighter." It was a pretty bland statement, but Bernie wasn't pressing her further, so she let it lie.

"What colour do you think we should do the hall in now?" Bernie asked instead. "Does this change your ideas of colour schemes? Is it a good job we haven't bought the paint yet?" He'd been wondering whether a creamy-white might be the best solution here, but wanted to give Fliss another chance to prove to herself what she could do.

"Not exactly. I must admit this room was giving me trouble. Unlike the bedrooms, I didn't want to go too much into the pastel, feminine colours. I mean, it's not a very feminine room, is it? But with all this dark oak, I think it's crying out for something that bounces the light around a bit, regardless of what we do with the floor in the end. Did I remember rightly when you said you'd prefer to use a modern distemper on these walls?"

Bernie nodded. "Thank God whoever painted this at least used a water-based paint. I was dreading it being oil-based when we came to clean it off. But yes, I would prefer to put something on that will breathe on these old walls."

"So that narrows it back down in terms of brands," Fliss mused, frowning in concentration. She stepped backwards until she was right up by the fireplace, or rather she thought she was. It was only as she put her hand behind her, intending only to make sure she didn't trip up over the hearth's edge, that she found she was touching the doorjamb instead, and the inside of it at that.

Oh crap! she thought. *No! Don't anticipate it, Fliss, don't call the bloody thing to you. Focus! Paint, that's what you're talking about, paint!* And with an anxious cough to cover her inner quivering, she managed to say, "I think there were some very pale greenish shades on that colour chart. One I'm fairly sure was called Acorn, which is that sort of palest green with the faintest hint of brown in it that you get from the fresh acorns out of their shells. That's neutral enough to cope with almost any coloured furnishings going in here."

"How very fitting," Bernie chuckled, and impressed with her choice. "Acorn in an oak-beamed room."

"That's why I remembered the name," admitted Fliss, hanging on to the doorjamb as she began to feel more and more light-headed. "There was …there was also a washed-out aquamarine …and …and a pinkish st… a pinkish stone…"

"Fliss!" she heard Bernie's voice calling urgently, but he seemed to be so far away, far away and fading fast. "Fliss!"

She was standing at the edge of the lounge of the holiday let, but it was as she had seen it when she'd watched Cuthbert, with large, heavy bookcases around the walls. The door to its modern kitchen, where she had scrubbed the parquet blocks, was standing open and now she could see thorough into it, and it was nothing remotely kitchen related in this era. Indeed, it seemed altogether larger, as if it took in what was now the alleyway in between there and the old kitchen. Up on its far wall hung what looked like muskets, not that Fliss was anything like sure about precisely what they were. Did they have actual gunrooms back then, or was it just that this was the place where they happened to keep stuff like that? Cuthbert hadn't seemed the military type, so were those from William's time or even his father's? And were there swords or daggers in there which might relate to the stabbing of the soldier? Was she even remotely in the right era for that? There was no way of knowing just by looking at the room, and she was too woozy to think straight about that right now.

'Don't let go of the doorjamb!' *Her inner voice screamed at her.* 'Whatever you do, don't let go! If you do, you'll come fully through into this time.'

Getting a death-like grip on the wood, Fliss risked turning around to look into the hall.

No orange paint!

"Woah-aagh!" she heard herself calling out as the room spun alarmingly, and she grabbed the wood with her other hand again, having had to loose it with one to complete the turn.

No Bernie! …Oh God, no Bernie? …Why couldn't she even see him? If she had seen Cuthbert through this hole – or whatever it was – in time, why couldn't she look back and see Bernie?

"Aaagh!" she groaned again, making the mistake of leaning her forehead against the wood. Oh no! That made everything worse! And she hurriedly opened her eyes back up, and pushed herself away from the wood until she was just hanging on to it with her hands.

"Deep breaths, Fliss, deep breaths," she gasped, sucking in air like a drowning woman. "For the love of God, don't faint! If you do and you let go…aaagh!" as the world did another lurch.

For the briefest instant she saw a woman. That woman wasn't really fully there in the way that Cuthbert and William had been before, but Fliss got the impression of someone who was walking with a very seductive sway across the room. She was dressed in a style which Fliss vaguely thought was of the French Revolution period, but then what she knew of the costumes of the day came almost entirely from films and TV, and she knew that that was hardly a reliable source. It looked a bit Scarlet Pimpernel-like, with a wide collar that flared open on the silk over-dress thing, and lots of ruffles showing within it. And the waist nipped in dramatically, with the skirt of the top part then cut right back to expose a large amount of petticoat. It certainly wasn't the kind of empire-line dress that Fliss associated with Jane Austen costume dramas, but was she even remotely right to think that this style she was seeing came right before then? Damn it, why hadn't she bothered to check on that earlier, especially after seeing Cuthbert?

And although the figure wasn't a particularly voluptuous woman, there was an awful lot of her bosom on display – more than even the pushed-up bosoms that went with the empire style. That might have been because whoever she was happened to be indoors, and didn't have a top layer or scarf-like infill on, but Fliss thought it was more because she was deliberately trying to entice someone. Not that Fliss was prudish, but she had seen that swaying hipped walk enough times to know that this was a woman in full manhunt mode. A few girls at university had been like that – absolutely predatory when it came to men – and Fliss had liked none of them, mainly because they didn't care who they hurt once they'd set their sights on someone. No matter if this was someone's much-loved boyfriend, those girls had gone for the conquest, not caring about the hurt and guilt they left in their wake.

And so Fliss loathed this woman upon sight. You are trouble! *she immediately thought.* Heaven help any man you set your sights on. You'll tie him in knots and then leave him when you're bored with him.

But there was nobody to call any warning to, or at least not that she could see. And then the view did another of those stomach clenching lurches, and she was looking at a teenage boy walking across the same hall. He, too, was much fuzzier than Cuthbert had been, yet was sharper than the woman was.

"Don't…" she croaked, struggling to clear her throat and make herself heard. "Don't trust her!"

But the young lad was gone.

Then almost as if she was being wrenched forcefully back to her own time, the room reeled again, and as she lost her grip on the doorjamb, she was aware of two things. Firstly, of Bernie now holding her tightly, and the second of that bloody awful orange paint everywhere, which she'd never been so glad to see.

"Fliss! Fliss?" Bernie was saying urgently to her. "Can you hear me, Fliss?"

"*Gnphff*," she half snorted, half choked. "Yes, I can hear you."

"Oh, thank God!" and she became aware that Bernie was holding her very tightly, and because of that she could feel his heart pounding. "You faded… fainted! …You fainted."

But Fliss was sure he'd been more accurate the first time. She *had* faded. She'd faded into that other time, but the reality of that was so bizarre for Bernie that he couldn't bring himself to accept it. Or maybe it was a bit of that, and a bit of him not wanting to frighten her silly by admitting to her what had really happened? Either way, Bernie was resolutely refusing to confront what his eyes had told him was going on.

"Come and sit down and put your head between your knees," he said, fussing over her. "Good heavens, love, you gave me quite a fright there."

You and me both! Fliss thought, but wouldn't say aloud. "Cup of tea," was what she did manage to croak out, and heard Bernie say with relief,

"What a good idea, come on, I'll help you through to the kitchen and put the kettle on."

Clearly, he wasn't about to leave her in the hall in case he came back to find her gone, vanished into wherever it was that he'd seen her fading to. And Fliss desperately wanted to ask him what *he'd* seen. Had he looked through the doorway and seen the old library that she'd watched Cuthbert through? Or had he seen something else? Had he seen the version of the old hall that woman had walked through, for instance? Fliss knew the words her much-missed grandmother would have used to describe someone like that, and they included 'floozie' and 'tart'!

But instinctively Fliss knew that she couldn't ask him. It wouldn't be fair. Bernie was already scared to death by what he'd seen, even if he wouldn't admit to that to anyone. He'd spent too many years in the macho culture of the building trade to be able to confess to being scared silly by something he couldn't even see right now, let alone have ever touched. *No, I mustn't do that to him,* Fliss thought. *I know in my heart what happened, but it would be selfish and cruel to ram it back down Bernie's throat, even if I think I really need to know.*

Heaven only knew how many teabags Bernie must have put in the pot, because the tea was so strong that for once Fliss requested some milk and sugar, and even then it was the colour of mahogany. But then looking at the way he was swigging his mug-full back, she thought that the strength was as much for his benefit as hers.

"It's okay, Bernie, I'm okay," she reassured him. "I just cut my pills back to one a day a few days ago, that's probably why I'm a bit lightheaded. Nothing to worry about."

"No working alone for you, my girl, not for a week or so anyway," Bernie declared firmly, and Fliss wasn't going to argue with that. The more she thought about it, the more convinced she was that it had been Bernie's solid presence, and him running to grab her, that had stopped her from slipping through into the other time. And if she'd gone through, would she ever have been able to come back?

But would it be so awful if you did go through? she found herself wondering. *If you* could *go through? What the hell have you got here that's worth staying for? Can you honestly see yourself still living with Bernie in, say, five years' time? Wouldn't that have become claustrophobic by then for both of you? And Bernie's not old, he'll only be sixty next year, so there's still time for him to find someone to share his proper retirement with who isn't an utter nightmare like Aunt Margot was. So is it fair to him to have his goddaughter-niece endlessly hanging around in the background?*

No, she decided, it wasn't. Moreover, for all that she was enjoying the restoration of this house far more than she would ever have believed, of late she couldn't see herself doing this for the next twenty or thirty years until she could afford to retire. It was this specific house which had the strong attraction, not so much the job, however gratifying it was to find the right colour schemes for rooms. Indeed, she wasn't sure that the compulsion surrounding this house was even what she could call pleasant, but more of a demand on her subconscious that she must pay attention to.

As she sipped the overly strong tea, it dawned on her that the plight of the boys had almost been the gateway to getting her to look into the past, and that now that that had happened, she wasn't feeling that dreadful urgent pull to them which had quietly worried her with its intensity. Yes, she still yearned for a child to love, but it was for a child in the here and now, and she was managing to get a bit of perspective on the boys now that the archaeologist had all their things. Meaning this pulling her in was far more to do with this weird house, and even the decorating of it was starting to feel secondary to uncovering the mysteries it was hiding.

Forcing the mystery aside, she made herself focus on her own future. If not this, then what on earth was she going to do? Because once she'd sunk her money into this house – if she did buy into it, which right now she suddenly wasn't so sure she wanted to do – then she was still going to have to have something to live on. And so although that evening she sat down, and worked out whether being part owner of a prestige property would then let her get a mortgage on a much smaller place without much of a deposit, it still then came back to having enough regular income to make the monthly payments whatever that mortgage was.

God knows how anyone on minimum wage ever lives independently, she thought as she went to bed, having realised that currently her work options were dire.

And decided that those people probably didn't – either needing help from family, or house-shared, or lived in social housing where the rent was more linked to what they could afford to pay. *And you don't fit into any of those boxes, Fliss. Bernie's the only family who wants to help; the only one you could ever trust to help long-term. So if you're going to house-share with anyone, it might as well be him, and with a share in this house. Because once you have what you get for your London place, you aren't remotely in the running for social housing, regardless of if you can't afford anywhere else. They'd demand you live off that money until you had nothing left, when you could only pray that you could get a foot on the social housing ladder – and that's too precarious a chance to take!*

All of which brought her back to square one: what was she going to do instead of being the albatross around Bernie's neck for the rest of her life? Living with him was one thing. On the other hand, handing him her life and expecting him to find all the solutions for her was utterly unacceptable. He'd done so much already she couldn't ask for more.

What was she going to *do* with her life? Because she felt a powerful need to start taking control of it. She'd gone to university as much because her parents had shoved her so hard out of the door, and she'd drifted into advertising because it was the job she could get which would at least pay the bills. But now Fliss realised that she'd been unintentionally drifting. She'd gone with the flow. Yet 'the flow' wasn't what she wanted and was what had landed her in this mess. So if she was going to sort her life out, she absolutely had to make conscious decisions, even if as yet she hadn't any to make.

Chapter 20

The weekend

After the fright of Friday, Fliss was determined to have a normal weekend, and yet although she left Bernie watching a major league match, telling him that she was going to treat herself to some new clothes, once she got into Worcester, she couldn't put her heart into it. For no reason she could explain, there just didn't seem to be any point in buying a smart new sweater for a job she irrationally knew she would never have. With cold, hard reason, she was well aware that she wouldn't get another career post like she'd had even if she could have coped with the stress, yet she knew she was equally far from unemployable. Yes, she needed to get properly back on her feet, but she had skills and experience which she could translate to other jobs. And granted there weren't that many choices around here, but Birmingham wasn't an impossible commute from here, so why could she not see herself doing that?

Getting more and more tetchy with herself, in the end she gave the shopping up as a waste of time. Yet getting back to Bernie's, the match was still in full swing, and so rather than disturb him, she suddenly remembered all the letters she had found and not looked at yet. It was a nice day, spring was well and truly in the air, and Bernie had a rather pleasant summerhouse in the garden, which it was warm enough to use for the first time now that April had come around.

And so, making herself a cup of coffee, having realised that while she'd missed her morning coffees that also, tea today would remind her too much of what had nearly happened yesterday, she picked up the laptop bag and her mug and went outside. The almond tree in the garden was full of blossom, the birds were chirruping their hearts out, and it was all so lovely and peaceful that for a while Fliss just sat and chilled out. So it was only when the errant thought crept into her mind of, *isn't this lovely without hearing any traffic*, followed by, *you wouldn't ever have to hear traffic again if you went through to the past*, that she recalled what she was intending to do.

Stop romanticising! she told herself sternly. *Remember how you felt – feel – about Nilmani and Ishwar? Well that man is probably around in the time you were looking at. And do you want to meet him? Not bloody likely! And if you could go back, what if you end up in a time when bloody awful Cuthbert or one of his sons is around, eh? That's a scary thought if ever there was one! It's one thing to be the ghost who puts the fear of God into them, it would be quite another to be a flesh and blood woman in their own time and at their mercy. The life of real women in the past was nothing like as sanitised as the dramas make out, and you'd be lucky not to find yourself destitute since you wouldn't fit any of their preconceptions of what a 'nice' woman ought to be.*

So there you are, then, stop being woolly-headed. Read these and wake up to what the real past was like. Tell that annoying voice to clear off – wherever it's come from – and make your own mind up like the sensible modern woman that you are!

As she unwrapped the bundles of letters, it quickly became clear that while the ones in the bolder writing were all from the same man, albeit addressed to two women, the letters going to him were in at least two, possibly three different hands. And the letters to the man were all addressed to Mr Aquillia Spink, although at various different locations within Bengal – modern day Pakistan.

"Oh, so it was you who went to India!" gasped Fliss. "*Hmph!* I don't like you already then, Mr Aquillia Spink, because that means you're the boys' father."

However, the first letter to him threw her completely as she read,

Dearest Quill,

We are all distraught here that you felt you had no option but to go as far as India to escape Father and Nenius. Cousin John appreciated that you believed that they would come and cause trouble up here for us had they believed that we were sheltering you, but he says to tell you that we would have found a way for you to stay.

However my dear Dougal says that he fully understands why you felt you had no option but to run. Oh how I hate Nenius for bringing That Woman into the house. She has been nothing but trouble from the start. But we are shocked beyond belief at what you have since told us of Father's behaviour. I had thought him many things, but not that. And Dougal also says that your fears about the law may not be unfounded. If That Woman is as good an actress as you say – and we do not doubt you – then if she stands in court alongside

Father and swears to his versions of events, it may be very hard to dispute their crooked testimonies.

Therefore we beg you to take every care in that distant land, and to come home safe again to us when it becomes possible,

Your loving sister,
Catriona

That didn't read anything like what she had expected. In fact, it sounded as though Aquillia, or Quill as his family seemed to call him, was more the victim than the villain. And who was 'That Woman'? Clearly Catriona deeply disliked her, but was she just a visitor or someone living in the house?

The next handful of letters went on in much the same vein, all of them very loving, and beseeching Quill to take care. Yet when Fliss looked at the envelopes, going by the return address all of them had come from Scotland, and were dated from 1795 onwards. Looking at the man's letters, which she now saw were from Quill himself, these were much later, and addressed to his older sisters, Elizabeth and Marjorie, so presumably whatever he had written to Catriona had stayed up in the north, and were now long since lost.

If Dougal was Catriona's husband, as seemed likely, then from the address he was Dougal Gunn, a merchant of Edinburgh, and might even be traceable. On the other hand, Elizabeth was Mrs E. Williams and living near Hay-on-Wye, so with such a Welsh surname and being right on the border, Fliss thought that it would take a more expert researcher than her to track down the right woman. Similarly, according to the addresses, Marjorie was Mrs M. Smith, an even worse surname to try and trace, and Fliss immediately resigned herself to knowing nothing more of these other two than that Marjorie lived a little closer, near Ledbury but on the Much Marcle side.

The next letter she looked at of that bundle to Quill gave her a real clue and was startling indeed.

Dearest Quill,

I do not know how to tell you of the news we have had from Sytchampton House. Certainly it has all of us appalled. A letter came from Father proclaiming with delight that Nenius has a daughter. As you may imagine, since no mention has been made of That Woman since the year when you left, we all presumed that she too had departed. Surely, we thought, she must be so notorious in Worcestershire for it to be impossible for her to stay, for we only have Nenius' word that they are truly married. She may more likely be his mistress, and should have been thrown out the moment she brought such misery to you all. Sadly, it transpires that that has not been so.

And upon reading this, you also must be wondering as we did how Nenius, as a permanent invalid, could have fathered a child onto her? For it <u>is</u> her. It is Marie-Janneton because Father mentioned her by name, and there cannot be two women with that cursed name living so close to the house. There can only be one answer to that, which is that our father in his old age is still not beyond siring a child upon his son's so-called wife, repulsive though that is to us.

Dougal begs me to tell you that, since our father cannot possibly claim this child as his own without such dire scandal as to ruin even one as conniving as him, you must still be the next in line to inherit the estate. The idea that Nenius will live long enough to come into it in his own right upon Father's passing worries all of us, for we know that helpless as he is, he would not live for long after that. We do not wish him dead, of course, but rather we want his passing to be a peaceful one when God calls him, not when he is just in the way. That Woman is ruthless, as we know only too well, and may be plotting to secure the house for herself in the name of her children, which cannot happen while our father still lives. God be praised that this first child is a girl and therefore would not inherit over you. That Woman must be furious to not have had a son, and we must give thanks that if our father proves capable of further children, that these too will be daughters.

However, Dougal and I beseech you not to come home and confront them over this, or if you do, to come to us first. Dougal will then employ strong men to accompany you both south for your own safety. I would not wish either of you to be alone in the house with That Woman for I fear you would not live long.

Your loving sister,
Catriona

"Bloody hell!" Fliss swore. "Marie-Janneton? And Nenius' wife? I wonder if she's the French connection? And is that the woman I saw? It sounds as though she's got a strong enough stomach to let Cuthbert at her if it got her what she wanted, so was that her I saw all wriggly-hipped, attempting to seduce old Cuthbert? Blimey! He must have been a randy old goat, or she had one heck of a way with her if she could keep him going until she got pregnant. One quick tumble between the sheets is one thing, but this is two years after Quill left, so if he knew her, she'd been there a while. And presumably Cuthbert must have believed she was his proper daughter-in-law to let her stay, and not some passing fancy of his son's?"

This was certainly starting to put things into a different light, but Fliss reminded herself not to get too carried away with this alternate version of Quill to the one she imagined. Just because he wasn't as bad a person as his father and brother, it didn't automatically make him a good one either. And yet in the very next letter from Catriona there came information which confused Fliss even more.

> *Dearest Quill,*
>
> *Please do not think that we disapprove of you finding love with a native woman. Dougal and I are only glad that you have found someone who cares for you as we care for one another. If you have no intention of ever setting foot back in England, then what becomes of Sytchampton House is of little interest to you anymore. I am sure that Lizzie – or Elizabeth as she now insists on being called – and Marjorie will be horrified that you would walk away from the estate, but Dougal thinks you have made a very sensible decision to leave things in the hands of the lawyers when the time comes,*

> *rather than coming home. He assures me that you have a very good job with the Company, and will be living in some comfort, so I must not worry. I am only sorry that when your child is born that we will never see him or her, and that breaks my heart, for you are a much-loved uncle to my children still. I hope that Aaryaa knows how lucky she is to have you, and what a loving father you will be to this child.*
>
> *Your most affectionate sister,*
> *Catriona*

"Damn!" muttered Fliss. "Affectionate father? Loving uncle? That doesn't sound like the man Nilmani talked of. What on earth happened to change him that much?"

And yet it wasn't Nilmani who was the child Aaryaa was carrying, because Catriona was effusive in her congratulations upon the birth of Quill's own daughter, Debjani, which came in early 1800. But what was also interesting was the news that Quill was best out of the way now that there was outright war with France – and not just in danger from this woman of Nenius'. Catriona spoke of pressgangs for the navy marauding about the coast, and the danger of Quill being caught by them as soon as he landed should he return, because it seemed they were no respecters of persons. Respectable clerks and merchants had found themselves being hit over the head and dragged off to the ships, waking up to see England disappearing over the stern of the ship, she reported, and with no way to get off and return to their homes.

It was also interesting that Quill must have written glowingly of the Governor of Mysore – one Arthur Wellesley, the younger brother of Earl

Mornington of Ireland – and it took a moment before Fliss realised that of course this was the future Duke of Wellington, still only the younger son of an Anglo-Irish lord at this point.

"Wow! You really did witness history in the making, even if you didn't know it at the time."

The family letters continued between Catriona and Quill for another couple of years with the announcement of another child coming for Quill and Aaryaa, which turned out to be another little girl, called Lotika. It was really puzzling Fliss now, because everything she was hearing back from Catriona's side suggested that Quill had no intention of marrying any of the European women he was meeting out there at various parties, even to the extent of being amused by various friends who tried to match-make. And by the time she had read through to 1807, Fliss was struggling to see what could have made Quill leave his beloved wife and family and India, because if what she was getting via Catriona was even halfway right, Quill loved it there.

Then all of a sudden, there it was. A letter with black edging to the paper, signalling that it bore news of a death, in 1808 and it was in a different hand.

Dear Brother Quill,

this new hand wrote,

I fear that by the time this reaches you, we will be no more. My beloved Catriona died yesterday, and I write with such haste because I too am sickening of this fever which has ripped through our community. I have not the strength to write more, and only pray that our son John and his family are spared, along with our daughter Mairie and hers.

Do not weep for us. We have been happy together all these years, and I could not imagine life without my dearest wife, so it is best it happens this way.
Dougal

"Oh no!" Fliss gulped, feeling terribly sad at the knowledge that the sister who had written so affectionately to Quill was gone. Certainly, there were no more letters from Edinburgh anymore aside from one from a lawyer, informing Quill that he was one of the trustees for the sum of money Dougal had left for his grandchildren when they came of age. And again, that jarred with what Fliss thought she knew of Quill. If he could be that trustworthy, why had he not been so with his own children?

There was now a gap in the letters, but it wasn't that much, given that Quill and Catriona had probably only exchanged about four letters a year, not least because of the time it had taken each one to get to its recipient. Even so it wasn't until 1812 that the first letters started to arrive from the older sisters, and the first was far more formal and less loving.

Dear Aquillia,
I write to urge you most strongly to return home at once,

the first one began, this being the cramped and spidery hand Fliss had seen on the top letter when she had pulled the letters out of the drawer.

for our father appears to have taken leave of his senses. Our brother Nenius has at last succumbed and gone to meet his Maker, though whether he finds that to be the welcome into the hereafter he believed, I shall not comment upon.

"Blimey, love, don't you hold back!" Fliss giggled. "You sound like a right old besom to me. No weeping and wailing over your brother's death from you, is there?"

> *However, it is not his fate which bothers your sister and me now. You should know that Father is utterly in the clutches of That Woman, even to the extent that he is claiming that he must not leave her destitute, but will marry her himself if needs be to save her from the wrath of Napoleon.*
>
> *Our Father in Heaven alone knows what perverse fate he imagines this to be, for I cannot believe that the fate of one French widow is of the slightest interest to the Corsican General. Furthermore, you should know that Marjorie and I believe that all of her talk about her chateau in Brittany is naught but fancy. She – or to be truthful I have no doubt, her late first husband – may well have had a substantial farmhouse of the kind that Marjorie now lives in, but the thought that one with such loose morals would be a true lady is laughable. I believe That Woman knows full well that we cannot send anyone to France to check her story, not even to the extent of finding her husband's grave, much less a house which may have changed owners several times in the chaos there.*
>
> *Yet Father is utterly convinced by her, and whenever we have tried to get him to see sense, all he does is repeat endlessly the warning he heard from the White Lady. Whether this apparition ever appeared is*

more for the rector to decide, but the exhortation to save this person from the Revolution is one which Father will not let go of. And Nenius then appearing with That Woman in tow within months, claiming that she was in great peril, was all that Father needed to believe that she must be the one he had to protect. That she has behaved with such immorality since then has no bearing upon the matter for him, but it does for us!

Since you are not married and without heirs, it is my sons who stand to inherit after you are gone, and as your oldest sister, I demand that you come home and preserve the estate for them. You may be able to afford a cavalier attitude towards your inheritance, but as a widow with little means to further my children's prospects, I cannot. Therefore I expect to hear by your return of letter that you are on your way.

Elizabeth

"Holy crap on a cracker!" Fliss gasped. "You hard-faced old baggage! Did Catriona not tell you about Quill's family in India? Or was her being a native Indian and the children half-caste such a slur as to render them invisible and unimportant to you? Blimey, you had a nerve! Not one letter up until then, and then you as good as tell him that just because it suits you, he has to put his whole life on hold and come home. It would have bloody-well served you right if he'd stuck two fingers up to you and decided to stay."

And that seemed to be what happened. Quill's letter back was the first she had read of his, and his bold sweeping handwriting appeared to mirror an equally decisive personality. It was dated in the October of 1812 and began,

> *Dear Elizabeth,*
>
> *I find it remarkable that in all of the time that I have been in India, serving my country through trade if not war, that this is the first time you have seen fit to contact me, and at a time when your only reason is for your family's advancement. Therefore let me set the record straight. I have no intention of leaving India. I have a very good post here with the East India Company, which you must surely know means nowadays that I am as good as working for the government, since they took over the Company some years ago. I also have a family here, whom I have no intention of abandoning just so that I can come home and expire in short order to your convenience.*

"You go, Quill!" Fliss chortled. "You tell her! The bloody cheek of the woman!" Yet her inner voice was also laughing at her. *And you thought you'd hate his guts*, it prodded her. *Soon changed your tune over that, didn't you! So what about Nilmani and Ishwar, eh? Don't you care about them anymore? And what about those other children of his? Was he quick to leave them behind in India, because as girls they were of no use to him in establishing his line to inherit? Who can you trust in these letters to be telling the truth, and how will you ever find out who was right and who wrong?*

Chapter 21

The weekend

The next letter in the sequence, going by the dates, was from the other sister, Marjorie and came from January 1813. She was nothing like so bullying in tone, but also seemed to be genuinely more anxious. She began,

> *Dear Aquillia,*
>
> *I realise that you have little reason to love either Elizabeth or myself. We allowed you to be sent off into the far north as a child and never thought to ask how you were. I now look back and feel deeply ashamed of that. However, as an adult you must by now have realised how intolerable it had become for us to live under the same roof as Father. Once dear Mamma had gone it was soon obvious that he could not live without a woman's attentions, and if initially he did not bring such women actually into the house, Lizzie and I had some mortifying encounters with him and his paramours in the gardens. You were too little to understand, even had we told you, and I confess that as young girls we felt that we would not be believed if we had written to Uncle John or Cousin John*

and told them. If you believe nothing else, please believe me now when I say that it was this, and not you, that had us refusing to look after you. Had we done so, we knew that we would most likely never get to leave for another ten years or so, and that would have been beyond bearing.

Good grief! What were you up to, Cuthbert? Fliss found herself wondering. *In the garden? Holy-moly, did they catch you having a quick shag in the shrubbery? I know you couldn't live out in the countryside and not be aware of sex and what it involved – certainly not by the ages Elizabeth and Marjorie were by then. But I don't think any kid is prepared for seeing their father doing something like that.*

She thought back to their mother, Alice, and went back into the records she'd saved on her laptop. Yes, Alice had died somewhere in the first quarter of the year, so it had probably been during that first summer that the sisters had come across Cuthbert doing God-knows-what. But of course, all of that would have started to change as the weather got colder, and surely the teenage girls, as they'd been by then, had been sharp enough to know that too? Sooner or later Cuthbert would have been bringing his assignations indoors.

Further clarification came in the next paragraph.

Lizzie was lucky enough to already have Ernest interested in her, and so she managed to persuade his family to take her on for a while as his aunt's companion until she was old enough for them to marry. I was not so fortunate, and had to go into service to escape Father's clutches. I cannot bring myself to write of what I went through at that place, but let me just say that I counted myself as blessed to have not got with child at that point.

"Oh no! You poor girl!" Fliss didn't need any further infilling to know that young Marjorie had caught the eye of some man in that family, and that he had raped her, possibly many times. No wonder she had detached herself from the family. To her they'd have seemed like the cause of all of her miseries. And if she was going through all of that, then she would've had scant time or chance to worry about a little brother who had at least been sent to people who cared. But she could also see that to the child Quill had been, it must have looked as though his sisters hadn't given a damn about him. What a mess Cuthbert had caused.

I cannot say that I loved my husband Matthew while he lived, but he was a good and respectable man. He never once complained of my inability to provide him with heirs, but later on in life I was able to confide in him about the brutal treatment I had suffered, and we both agreed that what I endured was most probably the source of me being barren. It has been the greatest sadness of my life that I have not had children, and I want you to know that I do not share Lizzie's disregard of the family you have in India. If they have brought you the happiness that was denied me, then I do not begrudge you that for a moment.

However, I must beg you to consider at least making a visit back home. We need a man of the family to take some form of legal stand against Father and his wild plans. For my part I would not expect you to stay, but when I have told you of what may yet happen, I pray you will be moved to come and help.

"That all sounds a bit dramatic," Fliss said to the little robin, who had come hopping around the summerhouse's door, no doubt hoping for crumbs. "But what do you think, little robin? Sounds like Marjorie was someone I could have got on with – if nothing else we'd have understood one another when it came to kids."

She turned the letter over to the next paragraph.

You may know better than I what went on when Nenius brought Marie-Janneton home from France. Were you with him then? I do not know and neither does Lizzie. Was she really Nenius' wife, married to him properly in a church? Lizzie and I do not think so, if only because Father is so very worried that now Nenius has died that she might get sent back to France.

That may sound foolish, but I have to tell you that she has a talent for making enemies, and there are many women amongst the neighbourhood who would gladly do her a disservice. I think having met her you may guess what she may have done, for that one knows no restraint where men are concerned, and wives are not the fools she takes them for. Therefore there may be one of them who knows of a very legitimate reason why she may fall foul of the law.

Certainly she has some hold over Father which he will not confide to either Lizzie or me – and it cannot be of his rakish behaviour, since he laughed in our faces on several occasions when we remonstrated with him over that. We argued that he brought us into disrepute as his daughters by his lewd behaviour, but he cared nothing for that. Therefore it must be something far worse, and something which for once has him in genuine fear for his own miserable skin.

"Blimey! I wonder whether he killed the soldier?" Fliss took a swig of her now cold coffee, but was too caught up in the tale to go and warm it up or make a fresh mug. But what cause would Cuthbert have to kill a French soldier? As Sylvia and Carol had said, as an English gentleman – albeit a singularly unpleasant one – Cuthbert would still have had the ascendancy over the foreign man in an English court of law, so why had he not called the police, or whatever they had had back then? Fliss wasn't sure when the first actual police service had come into being out in the shires, but she did know that before then there was some form of law enforcement because of the magistrates' court in Worcester, which was very old. And why had the soldier come to the very house where a French woman happened to be staying? Had she been closer to the truth when she had guessed that one or the other of them had been a revolutionary, and the other their opponent from the counter-revolutionary camp?

Then a truly dreadful thought occurred to her. Who was this White Lady? She frantically picked up Elizabeth's letter again. Oh no! It was someone who had appeared to Cuthbert and his father, William.

Well she had seen both of them, hadn't she? God help her, was *she* the White Woman?

"Oh no! No, no, no! What have I done?" she gasped, clasping her hands to her mouth in horror. "I meant you to protect the soldier, but did I inadvertently incite you to kill him instead? Did you take what I said totally the wrong way? On no, I'll never forgive myself if I did!" and she snatch Marjorie's letter back up, desperate to find out.

Whatever it was in the past, it means that Father is in a terrible state. Lizzie does not see it in the way that I do, but for once I believe he is truly frightened for his life over something. Lizzie believes that he fears Marie-Janneton will actually kill him if he does not do as she says, but for my part I think that it is something else, possibly something to do with the law. Maybe it is something which has him fearing he will end his days in a prison? Do you know what it is?

Father says that if she does for him then we will all suffer. Our reputations, according to him, will never recover. Therefore it must be something which would affect you too as our remaining sibling, and it is for that reason that I beg you to come home and try and put this to rest. Whatever it is, if it that bad I would not have you suffer for your father's sins when you have endured so much, as have Lizzie and I. Please come home for just a while, Quill, for all of our sakes, including your children's.

With my very best wishes,
Marjorie

That was quite a turn up for the books and no mistake, and it seemed as though her more conciliatory letter had a very different effect on Quill, because his language in his reply of April 1813 was couched in much more civil tones.

Dear Marjorie,
I received your letter which has made me view Elizabeth's summons in a different light. Sadly I know only too well of what went on and just what hold Marie-Janneton has over our father, and unfortunately over me too. If she were to reveal what she knows it might go well for her, but as the men of the household we would be regarded as the guiltier ones, even though hers was the greater sin. She was the cause, the incitement, and the instigator, but I will say no more of the matter in a letter for fear of it going astray.

"Bloody hell!" Fliss swore. Surely this had to be about the French soldier's death? So had this Marie-Janneton more or less forced either Cuthbert, Nenius, or Quill – as she found herself thinking of him now – to defend her in some way? It didn't sound as though Quill had been the one to bludgeon the poor man to death, but had he witnessed it? Or as bad, had he been forced to help in the cover up?

He certainly wasn't giving anything away in the rest of his letter.

Moreover, Father is right – the stain upon our family's reputation would linger for a generation and more. Out here my family would be immune to such things, but it might impact upon my standing within the East India Company, and therefore I must take the threat seriously. However, I have to tell you that I cannot drop everything and come home immediately, not least because if I hope to have my family cared for during my absence, and a job to return to when I get back, I must arrange things with my superiors, and I cannot guarantee when they might see fit to release me for such a long spell. Nor dare I tell them of the real reason as to why I must attend to my father, for that would be as damaging as if Marie-Janneton did her worst.

I will endeavour to let you know how soon I might return to England, but I feel it is best to warn you that it may not be this year by the time I have made the long journey,

Yours,
Quill

That was frustrating for Fliss, because she really wanted to know now what had gone on. This side of Quill sounded as though he had always intended to return to India once his business in England had been concluded. So what had happened to make him stay and leave his family behind? Maybe he was being blackmailed by this Marie-Janneton? That would certainly explain why, after getting here, he would feel that he had no choice to stay. It still didn't explain why he hadn't engaged some family already going to India to take little Nilmani and Ishwar back home with them, though. Surely there couldn't have been any reason to force them to stay with him?

With a puzzled shake of her head, Fliss turned to the next letter out to Quill, which was another of Elizabeth's.

> *Dear Aquillia,*
>
> *Why are you not home yet? Surely you understood the urgency with which I wrote to you? Have no doubts that had it not been a need of the greatest severity, I would not be placing my children's future into the hand of a brother I scarcely know.*

"God! You really are an evil old witch, aren't you?" Fliss exclaimed in disgust. "You're pretty much calling him worthless in your eyes, and yet you still expect him to turn up on demand!"

Was it only Marjorie who saw the wider danger to all members of the family, maybe even to the surviving distant relatives up in Scotland, she wondered? Because the way Marjorie had written of things, this was a scandal that would cause such a stink as to make the national papers. Then she wondered whether there were such things as national newspapers back then. A swift Google search revealed that *The Times* had come into existence in the January of 1785, so yes, presumably by the beginning of the next century it had reached the wider distribution of the rest of the country outside of London.

And there must have been other newspapers which in those days had as great a reach, even if they hadn't survived into her own time, so it was feasible that a great scandal in Worcester would get reported far and wide. At which point Fliss recalled the visit by Quill's great-uncle, John Macintosh, and him inviting Alice and the children to his home, so presumably there had been enough visits in the following years that his own neighbours and friends would know of the English family? So the Scottish family could not be considered immune to the scandal either.

"I bet when Quill came back it was more because of what Marjorie wrote than you," Fliss declared, scowling at Elizabeth's letter, which continued with,

> *Father is still insisting that if needs be, to save the situation he will marry That Woman himself. Are you really prepared for Her to become your step-mother and to have that hold over you? There is no way for us to prove that her daughters are <u>not</u> Nenius', and in truth may not be Father's either, despite what he may think. Indeed, given that all three look more like Her than anyone, should she become Father's second wife, we would have to drag an awful lot of skeletons out of the closet to even come close to insinuating that. Worse, in the process we would have to drag the names of a lot of influential men in the neighbourhood through the dirt with us, and they might not be forgiving towards us in those circumstances, even to the extent of denying their liaisons with Her.*
>
> *That means we are on our own to prevent this disaster! I understand that Marjorie has written to you too. I hope you have not been persuaded to dither over this matter because she has less to lose than I do? Such a thing coming to light might*

damage one even as distant as you are at the moment, therefore even if it only to save yourself, you must come home now.
Yours,
Elizabeth

Fliss was aghast at Elizabeth's callousness. Less to lose? To her mind Marjorie had already lost more than Elizabeth by far, because even if all of Elizabeth's children had not lived to adulthood – something she would have to look into – then she came across as so thoroughly hardened as to brush their deaths off, whereas Fliss recognised in Marjorie another woman who had desperately wanted children and not had them.

To her surprise Quill seemed to have thought the same.

Dear Elizabeth,
I am appalled by your lack of feeling towards our sister. Just because Marjorie does not have children of her own who have a vested interest in the house, it does not mean that she is not alert to the problems which face all of us. I too recognise what a disaster it would be for everyone in the family if Marie-Janneton should feel that she has nothing left to lose by revealing the worst.

"But what is the worst?" Fliss growled in frustration. "Who was it who struck that soldier down? Which one of you was the actual murderer?"

However, Quill had another point to make, and one which harked back to Catriona's letters.

Do not forget, sister, that while you as a woman would not be personally imperilled by this, I would. Should I return at the wrong time, there is the greatest of dangers that I might get press-ganged into the navy, or swept up into the army. It is only this year with Napoleon finally in retreat that there is the hope of peace, and even you must allow that it would be an even greater disaster if I should return and then end up on some ship bound for who knows where, unable to leave it for years, and not able to as much as write letters. That would be even worse than me being where I am now and a free man.

Therefore I urge to you to a little patience. I have already written to the family solicitors, taking the approach that my brother's widow is taking advantage of our father in his dotage. We both know that this will not be taken as seriously as it ought, but it sows the seeds of doubt should Marie-Janneton try to press Father harder, and he does something foolish such as trying to get the banns read. I am endeavouring to arrange things with the Company for an extended absence, but these things take time.

Yours,
Quill

However, Elizabeth was clearly not possessed of a shred of patience, and there were six more letters from her at monthly intervals, each one getting shriller and more insistent than the last. In response, Quill's letters became terser and more waspish, with him not replying to any of the last three as far as Fliss could tell. In contrast Marjorie only wrote twice more, each time apologising for being the bearer of more news of their father's rising panic. In the last one she wrote,

> *He says that he will have no choice soon but to make Marie-Janneton's girls the heirs to Sytchampton House. I managed to see him last week when I knew that She would be out of the way, and he told me that he has already spoken to his own man of law, who was horrified at him wanting to change his will in favour of Lucretia, Drusilla and little Selina. (Such names! Surely they are not French but reveal Her grandiose ideas of herself?) He told Father to go away and think very hard about what he was about to do, but going by Father's state, he will do it before the end of the year unless we can prevent it. I fear it is only the fact that despite having lived here for years, Marie-Janneton has very little idea of how things are run in England, and so for now she is placated that his will can be changed, and is going to be, albeit not with speed.*
>
> *I hope you approve, but I went to see the rector while I was in the area. Obviously, I could not say much, but conveyed my worry that my brother's widow had 'Catholic' ideas that it would be acceptable for her to marry Father. Given that Rector Arnold has hardly been beyond the next shires, he has no idea of what a French Catholic might or might not believe, and so he swallowed my story without*

question. And as it was a weekend, I stayed over in an inn and went to our old Church, suitably obscured by my widow's hat and veil so that Father would not recognise me. I may therefore report that the rector took Father on one side after the service and seemed to be remonstrating with him most vigorously. Since She was not with him, the rector had no opposition, and I believe this may have brought us more time. Nonetheless I am so glad that you think you may re-join us in a few months' time.

Your affectionate sister,
Marjorie

But it was what she had hurriedly tacked onto the bottom which had Fliss once again gasping in dismay.

PS. I received your latest letter as this was about to go to the post. My dearest Quill, I cannot believe it and my heart bleeds for you and the two boys. To lose your beloved Aaryaa and your three oldest in one fell swoop is just beyond tragic. Smallpox is such a cruel affliction, and I do understand why you would consider returning home permanently now. Such a loss will be harder for you to bear if you are forever surrounded by reminders. I will pray for you and for them, and for you to have a trouble-free journey.

May God bless you,
Marjorie

Smallpox? Fliss sat back in horror. So that's why the boys' mother never wrote back – she was dead!

Quill hadn't separated them from their mother at all. She had got it about as wrong as it was possible to get.

Quill

1814

Quill stood at the side of ship and watched the coastline of India fading over the horizon.

Oh Lord, what have I done? he found himself praying. *Have I done the right thing?* and his gaze turned to the figures of the two small boys who were lying asleep on the deck, worn out from crying.

In truth, Quill himself felt far from done with crying, though as an Englishman returning home, he would in future have to contain his tears until he could shed them alone. *Oh Aaryaa, why did you have to leave me alone?* his silent wailing thoughts came again. *And our three lovely oldest too? Why did I not take you all with me to the hills instead of leaving you in Kolkata?*

It felt all the worse for not having got back to see his beloved family before they had been cremated. He understood why it had been done so fast, and that it hadn't been just because of the normal Hindu rituals. Smallpox went through settlements like wildfire. And there was a part of him that was glad he hadn't seen Aaryaa's lovely face disfigured and ruined, let alone his pretty daughters and his oldest son. But it was also proving impossible to explain to Nilmani and Ishwar that there was no home to go back to. The simple house they had lived in had been burned to ensure the disease hadn't lingered, which again was a sensible enough precaution on the part of the soldiers who had been at the East India Company's base of Fort William in Kolkata. Yet the fact that most of his English things had remained at the Fort meant that he was not left with just the few clothes he and the boys had travelled with, whereas they had had to be bought clothes even to have sufficient to travel in.

He turned and looked at Nilmani clutching the carved wooden elephant tightly, even in his sleep. That had been made for him by a grandfather he would never see again either, and the little boy just couldn't grasp that. Why, he'd kept asking, couldn't they go and see their mother first before they left? Why not his grandparents? Why could he not go and fetch his beloved pet lizard?

And Ishwar? What on earth was going through Ishwar's head was beyond Quill to find out, because his youngest hadn't said a word after they'd been taken inside Fort William. Nilmani had taken on the role of speaking for both of them, but Quill had the dreadful feeling that Ishwar thought his mother was still waiting for him as well.

"Amma is not there," Quill had found himself saying over and over, using the Bengali word for mother. "She became very sick. Debjani, Lotika and Devesh, too. They all got very sick and died while we were away."

"But they were well when we left," Nilmani had protested with a child's logic.

"Yes they were," Quill had agreed, feeling his own tears welling up all over again at the thought of how everyone had been so excited about the two youngest going with him for the first time. After all, it was only intended to be a short trip. What could possibly go wrong? And once they got there the boys would be staying with Aaryaa's aunt while Quill attended to business, so all would be well.

Yet all hadn't been well. The aunt had become a very frail old lady since his last visit, and the boys had run wild during the day when Quill wasn't there. And so when the message had come about the smallpox outbreak, and his family's sickness, there had been no question of Quill leaving those two with her and rushing home by himself. Not that he could have done anything. Not a damned thing! Even if he had ridden hard straight back, he would still have been too late to hold his loved ones one last time. And if he had, he undoubtedly wouldn't be here now, and Nilmani and Ishwar would be orphans and on the streets. But that was a blessing Quill found it dreadfully hard to thank God for right now.

And he was far from sure that finally giving in to his sisters' badgering letters and returning home was right, either. Yet in the four months since his family's deaths, he had come to realise that India had lost all of its charm for him now. Worse, it had become almost a daily occurrence to return to his lodgings to find his houseboy in a panic having lost the two boys, who resolutely tried to find a way back home to the house they could not believe wasn't there anymore. All of which meant that he'd decided to take up a post which had been offered to him back in England by his kindly superior.

"It is not of the rank you have out here," he'd been told. "But I gather that you have a home to go to, and this will not require you to be in Bristol all of the time. It is not even with the Company, but local government. I only know of it because my brother-in-law will be your superior, and wrote to me of the trouble he has had getting a suitable man for the job.

Even then I would not have suggested it to you had you not spoken of your family entreating you to return, and then your own tragedy. Go home, Quill, and heal your wounds there."

Except that it wasn't home, or at least not what others thought of as home. That had been the house up in Edinburgh which his distant cousin now needed for his own growing family, and he hardly had room for Quill and two small boys. And so Quill was bracing himself for the encounter with a father he had no love for, and a sister-in-law whom he actively despised – a sister-in-law with a very dark secret.

Chapter 22

The weekend

The last letter which had been preserved was little more than a note from Quill to Marjorie, saying that he had landed at Portsmouth and was making arrangements to travel firstly to Bristol, to report to his new employer, after which he would travel to Worcester. But that was the point when the trail ended. No more letters had survived, and Fliss realised that there might not have needed to be any. By then Quill could have at least met Marjorie in person, even though Fliss had her doubts as to whether he would have welcomed Elizabeth's presence.

She sat back and thought about everything. How soon after they had come to England had Nilmani started trying to write to his mother? If it was almost as soon as they had got to Sytchampton, then his grief would still have been very raw. And smallpox? That probably meant that they had never so much as attended a funeral for her and their older siblings, because even back then, surely people had known to get rid of the bodies at speed? So had Nilmani and Ishwar been in complete denial of those deaths, unable to process them in any meaningful way, and then in the misery of being forced into English society, had taken refuge in the sincere belief that all they had to do was get back and all would be well? If that was so, then her heart broke for them in a whole new way.

And Quill. Had he tried over and over to explain to the children what had happened? From the little Fliss knew of society at the time, once back here he may have found it much harder to spend time with them, because it would have been expected that the servants would take care of them, not him. That surely was why Fliss had seen a local woman coming to put the boys to bed. But was there more to it than that?

The more she thought about it, the more Fliss began to wonder whether Quill had walked into more of a trap than he could have anticipated? Had he decided he mustn't show too much affection for the boys, because if he did so, then he was just asking for his father or this Marie-Janneton woman to threaten them simply to get a hold over him? Rather odder, why had she herself not picked up on the other children in the household? If she had sensed the boys, why not the three girls? It was almost as if the house was picking and choosing what it showed her, but that was such a freakish thought as to leave her shivering in spite of the spring sunshine. If it had just been her maternal instinct going into overdrive and making her pick up on a child, then surely, she should have been yearning for those girls too? Because Fliss had never just wanted a son, any child would have been welcome. So why had she only ever been shown the boys?

She had a look at the letters again. The Nenius who was Cuthbert's son had died in 1812, so if there had been any hope of Selina (the youngest) being his, she couldn't have been born many months after that. But realising that since Quill had left England probably somewhere like 1797, for Catriona to have been so horrified at Lucretia's birth a few years later, she must have been born somewhere around 1800. That meant three girls born between 1800 and the end of 1812. Lucretia, as the c.1800 child, would have been a teenager by the time her supposed father Nenius had died, and therefore Drusilla (the middle girl) was probably ten or eleven by then. It therefore made sense to think of Selina as more like eight or nine years old when Quill had arrived home. Therefore they would hardly have been playmates with his much younger sons. Even so, Selina wasn't so old as to not need the love of a mum, and even if she hadn't connected to Nilmani and Ishwar, it didn't explain why she hadn't come through to Fliss.

Then a really nasty thought came to her. Nilmani had said in his letters that Ishwar had sickened. Could Marie-Janneton or Lucretia have poisoned him? The house would always have passed to a male back in those days, so had they been trying to remove what they saw as obstacles to inheriting, or at least to them staying there for life? Marjorie had written that Marie-Janneton had little grasp of law, so had she thought that if there were no male heirs her girls could inherit? Was it the death threat to the boys which had made the house show them to Fliss? Nilmani might not have been so very far from the truth, and Fliss realised that he might have seen people in India who had died of things like snake bites, so he could well have had some idea of what poison might do in a way that a modern western child wouldn't.

Heaven help you, Fliss thought, *but did you live up to your name, Lucretia? Did your mother have a fascination with the Borgias? She certainly had a leaning to the dark side, given that Drusilla is the name of the sister to mad, bad Roman emperor, Caligula. As Catriona said, what names to give the girls! Even Selina means the moon, so did Marie-Janneton have a love affair with all things dark? She comes across as more than a little crazy to me.*

What she really found herself wanting to do now, though, was to talk to Quill. She desperately wanted to hear his side of the story. Was it his prompting which kept coming through to her? Had she finally got it right, and he truly was a victim in all of this? Or was she deluding herself still? And that deeply mattered to her right now, because it seemed to her that it would be a barometer of her own mental health, of her capability to determine with some accuracy who she should trust, and who she ought to avoid, if she could sort these folk out.

Once upon a time she'd believed that she was a pretty shrewd judge of people, back in the days when she'd been capable of weighing up clients, and knowing almost from the start who would be trouble and who would be easy to work with. Therefore if she'd now got Quill summed up correctly, that could be a sign that she was coming back to something like normal. If, on the other hand, she had made a right mess of sorting this all out, and he was a right obnoxious sod, acting against Cuthbert because he was cut from the same cloth and only looking out for himself in a competitive way, then she must take a hard look at herself too. Would it be time to seek out some professional therapy then, for instance? It wasn't a path she wanted to go down, because somewhere deep inside herself that felt like an admission of failure. But then was that something lingering of the criticism from her parents which she ought to let go of as well?

"Oh heck, I don't know," she muttered irritably, and went to make herself another coffee.

Once she got back, however, she resolved to work at this from another angle. If she wanted to talk to Quill, how would she go about it? The painted wardrobe had given her an insight into the years when Nilmani and Ishwar had lived in the house, and they had actually managed something like a conversation, which in theory meant that it ought to also connect to Quill at that point. The doorway through between the old hall and what had then been the library had connected to possibly twenty years before that. And the older wardrobe even further back to before Quill had been born – so that one was really no use at all if she assumed each place or piece had its own separate connection to the past. But was there somewhere else, or some*thing* else, in the house which would take her more directly to Quill?

She thought about the other, unpainted wardrobe, but also the desk. Had Quill himself ever used those, aside from him keeping the letters in the desk? Somehow, she had the gut feeling that if he and she could communicate via the desk, then that would have already become apparent, or at least more so beyond the urgent mental prodding to find the letters. Where that had come from, she still wasn't sure. Who had done that prodding? Was it a person – maybe Quill's spirit – or was it the house itself? The thought of the house communicating with her gave her the shivers far more than Quill's ghost, because it hinted at sentience where there shouldn't be any.

Maybe finding out if she could control contact might set all that straight in her mind, she mused, because if she could establish an element of control over what appeared to her and when, she wouldn't be finding the house suddenly feeling a lot darker and less appealing as a place to live in. The carved French wardrobe, hadn't been tested in any way and might be the ideal test subject, and it was at that point that she remembered that the hatpin was still in the oldest wardrobe's drawer. *It's only a pin prick*, she told herself. *It's not like you've got to carve a slice out of yourself, and it's a lot safer than stabbing your finger on that damned banister in the hall! You'll have a bit more control over that, and if you feel woozy and flake out, then you're only going to totter back into the present – just don't open the bloody wardrobe doors in case you fall in!*

However, when to try this was a whole other problem. She didn't want to upset Bernie by doing it when he was likely to walk in on her. That would be asking for all of his protective instincts to kick in and to stop her from going to the house at all. It might even be the one thing which would convince him that it was better to sell the house, get his money for the work, and move on, and she definitely didn't want that …or at least not yet. It might come to it, but there was a way to go yet. And so although she didn't want to lie to him, she knew she was going to have to find a way to do it when he wasn't there, or at least while he was very definitely tied up with working with someone else.

You don't even know whether it will work, she reminded herself as she wandered back into the bungalow to start preparing their meal. *It might be a total failure. Time travel or even just time conversations? Who's ever done that in reality?*

Yet fate took a hand that very evening. The phone went, and when Fliss heard Bernie saying,

"No, Jonas, it wasn't like that, it wasn't like it at all," she guessed that Mrs Davenport had had a screaming fit at one or both of Bernie's sons. By the time Bernie managed to get off the phone, he looked harassed and angry.

"I'm going over there to have this out with them," he announced, taking a large mouthful of the hefty scotch he'd immediately poured himself. "This is ridiculous. They have to understand that I can't just knock the price down because they made unrealistic promises. And they also need to get a grip on the fact that regardless of what I charge, I might yet have to go to court even to get what I'm owed."

Trying to soothe him, Fliss said, "I'm sure we can get them to see sense," but Bernie immediately shook his head.

"Oh no! There's no 'we' in this! I'm not having you caught in the crossfire. You have enough trouble with your own parents; I'm not having my boys slinging mud at you as well. No, Fliss, you can stay here, or go out for a drive if you fancy it, but please don't come to Jonas'." He sighed and sank into the big armchair. "This is a row that's been brewing for a long time, and some things got said just now which shouldn't have, so it's long past due that we either clear the air or break contact for a while. Like I said to you when you first came here, I'd never turn either of them away if they were in real trouble, but this is another matter altogether; and it comes down to trust and respect, neither of which they're showing me right now, and for no good reason other than their own avarice. If I'd behaved towards them as your dad did to you, then it would be somewhat understandable, but I never have.

"So it's time for me to pull rank as their father, and remind them just who gave them this almighty leg up in the first place – who handed them a successful business on a plate. I don't like the thought of doing it, and I don't *want* to do it, but if I don't, they're going to keep on trying to walk all over me until I'm too old, and too weak and feeble, to put up a fight anymore. Well I'm not having that. I still have my self-respect. And if skilled craftsmen like Phil and Sean can respect my decisions, then I think it's the least my sons can do. I'm not asking them to like it – they're entitled to their own opinions too – but I won't have them berating me like that over the phone like I'm some five-year-old having a tantrum," and he took another hearty swig of the whisky.

What could Fliss say beyond, "I'm so sorry. It shouldn't have come to this." But then she thought to add, "Just please make sure that my father hasn't been stirring things and making them think that they're about to be shoved aside for me. Because he's just about petty enough to have done that. Do you know, he actually rang my old boss up and apologised for me letting him down?"

Bernie sat bolt upright. "You are fucking kidding me?" It was an indicator of his current stress and shock that he swore that strongly, because Fliss had never heard him use the 'f' word in her company before – Bernie had old-fashioned standards in that respect, which Fliss thought very endearing.

"I wish I was," she sighed, "but no, he did. So I wouldn't put it past him to have stirred things with your sons. And that's why I'm going to agree not to go with you. Because if he has, heaven forbid, then my turning up with you could be like throwing petrol on a fire. But I just want you to know that, Bernie, and that's it's not that I wouldn't come with you for moral support otherwise."

"I know you would, kiddo," Bernie said affectionately, reaching out and squeezing her hand. "Bloody families, eh? Who'd have 'em!"

However, in the morning it gave Fliss the perfect opportunity to drive over to the house alone. Bernie had set out before her, grim determination written all over his face, and just in case the row went worse than expected and he came home far sooner than Fliss anticipated, she only waited until she was sure he wouldn't come back for something he'd forgotten before setting out herself. At least Jonas lived the other side of Evesham, and Edmund beyond that outside of Broadway, so it was a good hour's run each way from Bernie's, if not more. Therefore Fliss reckoned she had at least three hours clear, even if it descended into a shouting match and Bernie walked out soon after arrival. The one thing she was keeping her fingers crossed over was that if that happened, Bernie would leave and then stop somewhere to cool down, not make the drive back angry and distracted.

There was nothing she could do to influence that, though, besides having her mobile phone on her, and so she drove over to Sytchampton House, let herself in, and then made sure she locked the door after herself. She had enough sense to know that it would be folly to leave the door so that anyone could walk in on her when she was in that strange state between worlds. And had Mrs Davenport rung Jonas because her chosen estate agent had tried to access the house yesterday and not been able to get in? That was something else to consider, because if Jonas in his arrogance had promised that there would be someone there to let whoever in, even on a Sunday like today, or at least there being no problem with gaining access with a key, then she might have genuine reason to be concerned about that interruption.

With that in mind, she also made sure that she pulled Bernie's little Renault Clio right around to the far side of the garage area which had the rougher furniture in it. Behind all of that stuff, it wouldn't be visible from the drive if someone else pulled in, so if an agent did turn up while she was inside, they hopefully wouldn't be any the wiser that someone was there who could let them in. She also locked the door and reset the alarm after herself once she was inside to keep the illusion of the place being deserted – she didn't want some salesman wandering in while she was in a dream world!

And feeling more than a bit foolish for doing it, nonetheless Fliss wrote a note for Bernie about what she was going to do and put it on the landing outside the bedroom. She had every expectation of coming back out and then throwing the note in the skip, or even burning it, but despite her excitement at what she was about to try, she was still trying to be sensible about things. The last thing she wanted was for Bernie to be worried sick, thinking she'd wrapped the car around a tree somewhere and was lying undiscovered, or possibly worse, had had a complete mental relapse and just gone driving off into the sunset without knowing what on earth she was doing.

Once she was organised, she went and retrieved the ornate hatpin from the drawer of the other wardrobe, and took it through into what she thought of as the boys' room. Remembering how wickedly sharp that point was, she was very careful to keep it well away from herself until she was right by the carved wardrobe. The last thing she wanted to do was to accidentally poke herself with it, drop some blood elsewhere, and have a totally unpredictable experience that she couldn't get herself out of. And in the same train of thought, she went and got her kneeler pad and put it on the floor so that she could sit down in front of the wardrobe. Sitting would be better than standing if she did actually faint, she reasoned. She was just hoping that her view into the other time wouldn't be reliant on what she could see in this one, or she might yet have to stand up. Either that or sit on the wardrobe floor, which was another good reason to have the modern plastic pad which she could put between her and the old wood as some kind of barrier. Therefore she had the wardrobe doors just a little ajar in order to be able to open them without much effort, but also because she reasoned that the inside of the wardrobe might be less smothered in generations of polish, and therefore more receptive.

When she felt she was as prepared as it was possible to be, she took a deep breath and then poked her thumb hard with the hatpin.

"Bloody hell!" she gasped in pain, as a bubble of blood welled up on her thumb. Her eyes were watering as her thumb's nerves protested at this abuse, but she made herself lean over and smear the blood along the inside bit of the wardrobe's floor that she could reach without leaning too far in.

For a moment nothing happened at all.

She was just thinking, *oh well, it was worth trying*, when she heard a sob. Or rather it wasn't an out and out sob, but more as though someone was trying to stifle one. Putting the hand she had stabbed back down onto the wardrobe's floor, she felt the room doing its by now familiar lurch, and held on tight. The swirling sensation always made her screw her eyes shut, and so it was only when she could bear to open them again that she almost whooped with relief. It had worked! Her delicate yellow on the walls had gone, and in its place was the more mustard-like version she had seen with the boys.

Carefully looking around, she realised that the painted wardrobe was where she had replaced it in the one chimney alcove, and this wardrobe was opposite it behind the door, which was also where she had placed it in the future. But now the larger bed which the two boys had shared was gone, and there was a small single bed tucked into the other chimney alcove. And on that bed sat a man, a man who had his hands over his face and whose shoulders were shaking. Here was the source of the sobs.

What do I do? Fliss wondered. *Do I speak? Is he going to be horribly embarrassed if he realises some random woman is watching him?* This wasn't something she'd expected and so was utterly unprepared for.

For several minutes she just knelt there, feeling more and more uncomfortable at witnessing this man's grief, and she was fairly sure by now that this must be Quill. As best she could tell, he was fairly tall, but much better built than his father, being slim yet broad-shouldered. In the poor light he looked to be fair-haired, though that could have been permanently bleached by the hot Indian sun, and his skin still bore the remnants of the dark tan he must have had in India, so that at least indicated that she had hit around the right time. But that probably meant that he was still grieving for his lost wife, or perhaps it was not that much later on and grief for Ishwar, especially if he'd been outside a lot and kept his tan topped up, and the shifting of the beds implied that this might be the case. Whichever it was, this wasn't the introduction she had hoped for at all. A few times she heard smothered words which might have been names, but she wasn't close enough to hear properly.

Then she heard vague noises coming from somewhere else in the house of that time, and whatever they were, they were enough to have him sitting up and fishing his handkerchief out to wipe his eyes and blow his nose. What neither of them was expecting was for him to stand up to leave, and them both see one another at the same time.

As Fliss began with, "Hello, Quill…" his face darkened with anger and he snarled,

"You! You have the nerve to show yourself here again? How dare you? Haven't you caused enough damage already?"

"Me?" Fliss spluttered, completely taken aback.

"Yes, you, you foul sprite! Go on! Be off with you to whichever underworld you sprang from and never come back!"

"But…!"

"No! I'm not my father! You can't toy with me and twist me with your honeyed words. Go on! Get out of here!"

Fliss was so shocked that far from letting go of the wardrobe, even as she reflexively stumbled to her feet, she instead held on even tighter, and so she was still connected when the swishing of material announced the arrival of a woman. And what a woman! Almost instantly Fliss recognised her from the younger version of herself that she had seen in the old hall, and now it was her turn to exclaim,

"You!"

Yet the sexy woman she had seen back then was now a wreck. Oh, she looked well fed enough, and was wearing good quality clothes. In fact, Fliss was fairly sure that her dress was made of silk, not just cotton or linen. But her face! She was ravaged! What on earth had caused that?

And now the woman turned and saw her and went deathly pale.

"She is real," she gulped, and even in those three words Fliss could hear the French inflection.

Quill's anger now turned on this woman. "What? Did you think my father such a feeble-witted fool as to be scared by anything less? She predicted you coming. She's the reason why my brother had such an easy time of it persuading Father to let you stay. And because of that, she's now the reason why I had to marry you to protect the family name, may God have mercy upon me! Because I swear that one day you will push me too far, and you will go to join your real husband in the staircase!"

Chapter 23

The weekend

"Her real husband?" Fliss echoed in shock. "You mean the soldier from the staircase was her *husband*?"

Quill turned piercing blue eyes on her and snapped, "Little you care!"

"But I did, I do!" protested Fliss. "It was *him* I was trying to tell you to protect, not her!"

That stopped Quill in his tracks. "What?"

"I promise you, I was," Fliss pleaded. "I'm not a ghost or a spirit, and I'm certainly not some powerful witch or anything. I'm in the future, and in the future – over two hundred years in the future – we, that's to say my uncle and I, are trying to repair this house, and in the process, we discovered the old staircase and the body of the soldier. Please don't ask me how I'm talking to you, because I can't explain it any more than you can. But one thing I can tell you is that for me it's only been a couple of weeks since I saw your father in the library, and heard him telling you and your brother to go to France. We'd only discovered the body days before, and so I thought I might be able to warn you to look out for him."

"Why would you do that?" the woman asked with a sneer. "He was nothing to you …unless you lie, of course, and you were a mistress I knew nothing of."

"Mistress?" Fliss gasped. "I never even saw him until he was just a skeleton in a dusty uniform!"

And something of her genuine shock must have got through to Quill, because he turned on the woman, saying,

"Do not drag everyone else down to your disgustingly low level, Marie. Not every woman whores herself around the neighbourhood and ends up a poxed wreck like you."

So that was what was wrong with her, syphilis! Or might it be gonorrhoea? Not that Fliss had ever knowingly seen anyone with either, much less at such an advanced stage, and neither was good from the little she knew. But then if this was Marie-Janneton, and she had done even half of what Quill's sisters thought she had, then it wasn't really surprising that she'd become syphilitic – if that was what poxed meant in that era. But more importantly, right now Fliss needed to convince Quill that she hadn't deliberately set this bloody awful train-wreck of events into motion, and antagonising Marie wasn't going to help with that at all.

"Please, Quill, just hear me out," Fliss begged him. "I know that all that I'm going to tell you is going to sound strange beyond belief to you, but I promise you, it was never my intention to make a bad situation worse. I promise you I wasn't."

"I promise you," Marie-Janneton mimicked cruelly, giving a very French, "*Phfaa*!" after it. Then giving Quill a look of such disdain and revulsion that it fair took Fliss' breath away, she announced, "I will not stay to hear some ridiculous ghost's story. But then you were always a fool, Quill. A fool then, and a fool now!" and swept out.

Fliss gulped and looked back at Quill in horror. “Good God, she’s awful!”

“She’s a murdering bitch,” he snarled back. “But unfortunately, she’s got a hold over every magistrate in the immediate area, and she won’t hesitate to use it to get me hanged for her French husband’s murder if I don’t do as she says.”

“I know I’m no medical expert – I mean, no doctor – but I have to say that looking at the state of her, I don’t think she can have long to live. Such diseases are treatable in my time, so I’ve never seen anyone that ill with it, but the way it’s eating away at her, she really must have only months to live, if that long. I hope that gives you some consolation.”

Quill moved closer to the wardrobe and said much more softly, “I have thought that too. And unlike you, I have seen men in that state out in India – mostly soldiers, but some others also – and you are correct to think that she will not live long now.”

“Is that why you agreed to marry her?” Fliss now wondered. “Because you knew at that time, even if she didn’t, that it wouldn’t have to be for long?”

For the first time she saw a glimmer of a smile from Quill. However rather than pursuing that, he asked,” If you can know that, how did you not know what to say to my father?”

“Because like I said, I’m not some all-knowing being, I’m just a normal woman, and all of this is as strange to me as it is to you. Venereal diseases I only know of from newspaper reports in my own time, not because I’m all-knowing. And at the points when I spoke to your father and grandfather, at each time I had no idea of what was going to happen in their personal futures. I was just trying to do my best.”

“Oh!” That seemed to genuinely surprise him.

And ploughing resolutely on, Fliss continued to explain, "You have to understand that while years passed between firstly your grandfather seeing me, and then your father, it was honestly only days for me, so I didn't have time to think about it, or go and dig for clues. And worse, this is the first time I've found a way to control when I appeared to you. All of the other times, it was purely by accident. I had no idea that these windows, or whatever they are, were about to open up until they actually did. So I was more than a bit shocked myself to find that I was looking into the past. That's not normal in my world any more than it is in yours. In fact, I've never ever heard of it happening to anyone else, so I was totally unprepared for it."

"When was the first time?" Quill asked, and Fliss could see that his anger had slowly evaporated, and that he was actually listening to her now.

However, it occurred to Fliss that this was fraught with danger. Mentioning his children might come across to Quill as her trying to manipulate him, and so she decided she had to give him a bit of context for it.

"Okay, so I need to tell you something first," she began. "We were clearing out the old furniture from the cellar where it had been dumped – I mean abandoned – and I was just moving the one base of a dresser when I found some letters. Well, 'letters' is a bit grand for what they were. They'd been written by a little boy. A little boy who was missing his mother desperately."

She saw Quill stiffen and hurriedly added. "I haven't been able to have the children I want so badly, Quill, and once I started reading them, I couldn't stop." She didn't have to fake the tears that welled up at the memory. "I thought you must be the most evil bastard walking to have taken them away from their mother."

"I didn't take them! She died!" Quill protested angrily.

"I know that *now*. Since then, I've found some more old letters which you must have brought home that were written to you from your sisters, and it was then that I learned what had really happened. In fact, that's why I deliberately tried to come through to you today, because I desperately wanted to know more. But that first time I was just cleaning the wall by that wardrobe that's behind you, and my uncle and I found where the boys had hidden some things of theirs. And then when I was alone, all of sudden everything started going strange, and I saw them. I saw Nilmani and Ishwar."

Quill was looking furious by now.

"Please, Quill, I'm not saying this to upset you! I know now how much you loved all of your family, and I already know from what Nilmani wrote that your lovely little Ishwar died. …Oh God, has he died yet or am I too soon for that? Oh please, please let that not be news to you!" And she got one terse shake of his head. "Then I'm begging you to tell me, Quill, have you found Nilmani? The last letter I discovered that he had written to his mother said he was going to run away, and I may not know a lot about your time, but I do know that it's no safer for a little boy to be out on his own in the world than it is now. Is he safe? Is he alright?"

Something of the raw emotion in her pleas must have got through to Quill, and she saw him taking a couple of deep breaths before saying. "Yes, he was found by a carter some miles away. They are bringing him home tomorrow."

"Oh, thank God for that!" and Fliss didn't have to fake the relief in her voice over that. "I know that…" Oh lord, how to phrase this properly? "…that none of you could possible still be living two *centuries* further on into my time," that really made Quill start as he took in for the first time just how distant she was, "but I couldn't find out anything more about him, and even though my uncle told me I was being foolish, I was so worried about him."

"Luckily the carter had already met him when he delivers to us," Quill said gruffly, obviously trying to hide the depth of his relief from Fliss. "Nilmani always likes to give the horse an apple."

Fliss' instant reaction of, "Oh bless him! That's so sweet!" brought a twitch of a smile to Quill's severe expression, which further relaxed as she added, "You must have been worried sick when you found he'd gone. I know in your place I would have been …well, I was anyway, even if I couldn't help find him."

His response was just an '*hmph*', but Fliss could tell that he had been worried out of his mind and pressed home her advantage.

"The thing is, Quill, I've gradually begun to put together a picture of what's gone on in this house. And although I didn't know that the dead soldier we found was Marie-Janneton's husband, just from your sister's letters it was clear that she's been an evil influence. But then that had me wondering what sort of mother she can have been to her own daughters? Has she tried to make them into younger versions of herself? Did she set things into motion long before you got back?

"Because as I've tried to work out their ages, it's occurred to me that the oldest must be twelve or thirteen by the time I'm speaking to you now? And then thinking back to what Nilmani wrote, and his belief that Ishwar was poisoned by living in England, it had me wondering whether he wasn't partly right. I don't mean that England just by itself was so bad for Ishwar, but maybe that either Marie-Janneton or Lucretia had decided to get rid of the boys who stood in their way of inheriting everything?"

Quill went white. A whole range of emotions flickered across his face, and then he staggered back to sit down heavily on the bed.

"Quill? Quill? Are you alright? Please, speak to me!"

"I never saw it," he croaked. "I never saw it when Lucretia said she would help with the boys. They've never quite been able to understand the servants with their broad local accents, and though I threw the worst of those out when I came home, I've never dared to bring a governess in for my boys. Not with Marie the way she is." He had to stop and resort to the handkerchief again, but then looked back up at Fliss. "Maybe you aren't as bad as I thought after all. At least you've given me that warning."

"I wish my other warnings had been clearer," Fliss apologised. "I desperately wish that I'd worked all of this out in time to save Ishwar, I truly do, because I cried my eyes out when I realised that he'd died. I would have given anything to keep him safe, I honestly would.

"It didn't help that from my point of view, I went from seeing your sons then backwards in time to seeing your grandfather, then forwards to your father. So at my end it all got very jumbled up for a while. I hope you don't mind me saying this, but your father was a nasty piece of work."

Quill gave a bitter snort. "That's the least of what I've called him down the years."

"I'm sure," Fliss sympathised. "I've probably said similar about my own father. …Oh he's not a rapist," she added hurriedly, seeing Quill's startled expression, "And as far as I know, he's never murdered anyone, but that's about as far as I can go defending him. He's a troublemaker, and he's certainly never given a damn about me, so I do understand something of what you must have gone through as a child."

"Really?" He was still sceptical.

Fliss gave a bitter laugh. "People aren't any different in my time, Quill, and that goes for parents. Most of them at least *try* to do their best for their kids, but others… well you have to wonder why they ever bothered having a family, because they never seem to want them beyond what they can do for them – the children for their parents, I mean."

"Oh!" Quill was quite lost for words at this revelation for a moment, then added, "My father wasn't actually the murderer. Or at least if he played a part, it was only when poor Henri was past saving."

Now it was Fliss' turn to say, "Oh?" but then thought to ask, "Was Henri the husband? …Yes? …Who did kill him, then?"

Quill sighed deeply. "Not that it matters now with both of them in their graves, but I think it was my brother who struck the first blow. The first blow, mind you, not the killing ones." He got to his feet and walked slowly over to the wardrobe, coming to stand right by it and leaning on the side, his hand almost by Fliss'.

"Not the killing one?" she asked, but feeling more than a little distracted as she realised that she could feel the warmth of him through the portal now that he was only a foot or so away, and also smell the faint lemon cologne he must be wearing. Of all the things to happen, she hadn't expected him to make her heart flutter.

"No, not the killing one," Quill was answering sadly. "Poor Henri Dubois, he had only come to try and find his wife. He thought, you see, that she had had to flee when the fighting came close to their home. She called it a chateau, but he called it a *manoir*, so something a bit more than a large farmhouse, but not much grander. He heard from his neighbours that the English glove-seller had been in the area at the time when things had become very dangerous, and then that his wife had gone. Worse, the poor man arrived home to find his entire house had been stripped of every decent piece of furniture; but until he arrived here, he thought that once his wife had left, that others had come in and robbed the place. He was so shocked when he saw *his* family's furniture here in England! But not knowing that my brother had already been her lover for some time, he – poor fool – initially thought that the nice English merchant had merely brought her to England for safety."

His expression became sour. "He had no idea that Marie had become fed up with him and his high ideals about supporting the nobility. She'd heard about Sytchampton House, and must have presumed from Nenius' bragging that it was better than what she had already got." A deep sigh forewarned Fliss of what was coming next. "And then, of course, you played right into Nenius' hands. He had already been trying to find a way to bring Marie to England as his wife, because she – conniving viper that she is – had told him she was a widow, and therefore free to marry. Her husband had always been absent when Nenius had been invited to her bed, you see, and the presence of men's things at the farmhouse were passed off as an absent brother's possessions – a brother which in truth she never had."

"Didn't your brother learn differently from the other people in the area?" Fliss wondered.

Quill rolled his eyes. "You would have thought so, would you not, but Nenius' French was never that good, and he always thought himself so much better than everyone else; a trait he got from our father, unfortunately. So even if the other locals had warned him about Marie – and personally I cannot imagine that they did not – he chose to ignore them. I was just a lad of fifteen when I went over there with him on his last visit, which was when we brought her back; and to be honest with you, I was scared to death the whole time we were in France. Dangerous does not come close to describing the situation as it was that year. And since I was the one who spoke by far the better French, I was the one who went and bought food, and arranged for rooms in inns and the like. I hardly had chance to stop and draw breath, much less wonder about the woman we were taking back home with us.

"And then my fool of a brother told me that she was actually his wife. That they had married in secret over a year ago." Quill shook his head, still baffled. "I believed him then, though not so much now. To this day I do not know whether she tricked him into some ceremony with a fake priest, or whether he knew that they could never wed, but wanted her nonetheless. In truth, Nenius was not the brightest of men, and he was always led by lust. Once he had his sights set on a woman, he saw nothing else, not even if it was right before him. But he certainly snared me in his trap to gull Father. I came back to this house quite convinced that they were man and wife, and so when Father questioned me, I answered wholly honestly, and in the belief that what I told him was the truth."

"Quill, that wasn't your fault. You were only a boy. Your father shouldn't have relied just on you to prove or disprove your brother's story."

"I know that now."

"So how long was it before Henri turned up here?"

"Ah… I need to tell you that Father was near apoplectic at the news that Nenius and Marie were married. Furious does not come near to describing it, because he had had grand ideas of marrying Nenius to someone with money – oh not nobility, but at least some much grander merchant's daughter over here, which would have given him access to a whole other social world. He was going to throw them out, he declared. He was going to report her to the magistrates, he vowed. And then suddenly one morning it was all, 'dearest Marie, would you pass the bacon,' and 'dearest Marie, could you bear to try and sort out the cook so that we have something edible to eat tonight?' I spent half of that breakfast with my mouth hanging open like some village idiot."

Fliss was already feeling sick. "Oh yuk, she seduced him, didn't she?"

Quill quirked an amused eyebrow. "I do not know what 'yuk' means, but I think you understand me. Yes, Bessie, the housekeeper, who to be frank was never much use, walked out that day, declaring that she would not share with a 'Frenchie'. It was strange to me, because I had not thought Bessie possessed a single moral bone in her body, but I actually felt considerable sympathy towards her at our last meeting. She said that she had her standards, and sharing a man's bed with another woman went far beyond that. And given that she must have put up with quite a lot from my father during the years she served as servant and bed-warmer, even I thought she did not deserve to be supplanted so derisively, and by a much younger woman who normally would have been repulsed by such an old man."

"How old was she then? Marie, I mean."

Quill shrugged. "Twenty-three or twenty-four, I would guess. She has never told me just how old she is, and I know that she lied at our marriage when she told them her age. I would have added easily ten years onto that by then, but clearly she had no fear for her immortal soul by lying in an English church. To be frank, I doubt she would have worried any more in a Catholic cathedral!"

"Charming!" and Quill smiled at Fliss' sarcasm.

"Not a word I would ever use for her," he admitted with a wry smile, then his face fell. "Those early couple of years I spent in this house with her and my brother and father were the worst of my life. I never knew what I was walking in upon, and I could not possibly repeat to a decent woman what I saw. Let me just say that those three sank to depths of depravity I had never dreamed existed, sometimes alone, sometimes together."

Just the thought of a threesome between scrawny Cuthbert, poxed Marie and Nenius, had Fliss' stomach turning over. "Vile!" was the only word she could come up with that went anywhere near to expressing what she was thinking.

"Vile, indeed. And it was not two full years – though it felt like far longer – when Dubois came looking for her. I had ridden out the morning after he arrived, only wanting to be well out of the way when the accusations started to be thrown. In my naivety, I believed that my father would be horrified that he had been so deceived by his son, and would at the very least throw Nenius out, and send Marie packing with the man who was her rightful husband. I could not have been more wrong.

"I heard more from the servants later. Or rather the only two we had left, for none of the others had been able to stand it after the first few months that Marie was here. There was a terrible fight, with Marie screaming, and Nenius claiming that he thought that she was his – and if he had known different at the start, by then I think he had convinced himself that it was true that she was his wife. But worst of all, Father kept on shouting that he could not and would not live without his dear Marie.

"As near as I have ever been able to piece it together, Dubois walked out of the drawing room, where the shouting was taking place, and retreated to the morning room to collect his thoughts. Heaven knows what the poor man thought by that stage, but I fear he was scarcely able to think straight at all by then. Certainly, Marie followed him, and then Nenius followed her, perhaps fearful that Sytchampton House had not proved to be the palace she had thought it would be, and that Dubois might yet win her back."

He shook his head sadly, "The nearest I got to the truth of that dreadful day after that was two nights later, when Nenius got roaring drunk. Marie was somewhere with Father, and neither of us wanted to know doing what, and I had felt obliged to go and keep Nenius company as he lay in his bed in agony. And so Nenius began drinking brandy like it was wine, as he'd begun to do all too frequently already to lull his spiritual pain, though now it was to ease the physical one too, and after a few glasses it loosened his tongue. Drunk as a lord he may have been, and not a little delirious on the morphine he'd been given, meaning much was slurred and barely comprehensible.

"What I gathered was that he followed Dubois into the morning room and punched him, believing him to be a liar and a scoundrel, and that Dubois went flying over the end of a chaise and cracked his head upon the club foot of the card table. But then Marie followed him in and picked up the brandy decanter, and began hitting Dubois over the head with it. Even Nenius was appalled by that, and he was pulling Marie off Dubois when he spun her around so that his back was to Dubois. At that point, with some dying surge of strength, Dubois pulled himself upright and stabbed upwards with the long knife he had at his belt, but instead of getting Marie, he hit Nenius."

Chapter 24

The weekend

As Fliss gasped in dismay, Quill continued,

"I truly believe that Henri Dubois saw her for the evil woman that she is in his dying moments, and was trying to rid the world of her. But in his frailty, he plunged the knife into the wrong person. It took Nenius in the back, and it must have been as keen as a razor, because even with Dubois' failing strength it cut right to his spine. Ever after that, Nenius could feel nothing from his waist down, or rather he got worse and worse until the pain descended into total numbness."

"Oh! So that's why you and your sisters knew that the girls couldn't be his!" Fliss gasped. Nenius had been paralysed!

Quill nodded. "Just not possible, you see. But then when I returned home that day, it was to find that the servants had carried Nenius up to bed and were tending to him, but there was still the body of Dubois lying on the morning room floor. He must have been there for hours."

"We thought that by the amount of blood which had soaked into the parquet," Fliss agreed.

"Did you? That was very astute of you."

"Well not me personally, or not all of it. We had some help from someone who looks into suspicious deaths who confirmed what we suspected. And you're right, he must have lain there for hours, because he could hardly have had much blood left in him by the time you got there."

Quill inhaled deeply. "Yes… when I got there. Hmmm… Father must have gone mad, because he had taken the knife which had done for Nenius and plunged it into Dubois. Right through his belly! The damned thing was still sticking up out of him, and how Father had the strength to do that I still do not know, aside from a moment of complete insane fury, but Dubois was actually pinned to the floor. It took me all of my strength to pull the knife out, at which point I wanted to ride for the magistrates.

"I think it was at that point I finally realised that my father was no longer fully sane, and neither was Marie. They would not have it. No magistrates, no inquest into Dubois' death, not even on the grounds of Nenius defending himself. It must be covered up, they told me, and threatened to swear that it was me who had struck the killing blow if I dared to go against them. And may God forgive me if I am wrong in this, but I believe they likewise delayed in sending for a doctor for Nenius for the same reason, worrying more about whether they would be accused of the killing."

"Oh my God, that's callous!"

"Beyond callous. And again, in the years since then, I have often wondered whether my brother might have walked again if he had not been bumped and banged all the way upstairs to his bed by Kenric and the gardener, and had a doctor been called to treat him right away. Moreover, in the first few years, although I was in India by then, I do know that Nenius could move about a little if he was supported by someone and used a crutch on the other side, because I had the occasional letter from him. Poor fool, his was a gradual deterioration, and for all that he brought it upon himself, I still would not have wished that hell upon him." He sighed. "And you must think me a miserable specimen to think this of my father, but I do believe that he was glad that Nenius became bedridden so that he had Marie all to himself."

"I don't think you that at all. In fact, I think you're probably only too right in your suspicions."

"Do you, Miss…? Oh… I don't even know your name."

"I'm Fliss. Felicity, that is. But everyone who knows me calls me Fliss."

"Do you not like being called Felicity? I always thought it a rather lovely name."

Fliss wrinkled her nose in disgust. "I don't! It always reeked to me of the kind of meek girl who did exactly what she was told all the time, regardless of whether it was right or not. I suppose it didn't help that my mother always made so much of calling me by my full name because she thought it sounded more upper class."

Another flicker of a smile passed over Quill's face. "Hmm, very much as I loathe being called Aquillia, then. I would have given much to have been one of the many Johns, Toms, or Harrys, I met out in India. They always said they wished they had a more distinctive name, but they could have had mine with pleasure."

Fliss laughed. "So just as you find Quill less obnoxious, I find Fliss less so, as well. Fliss is me, and while that's nothing special, at least it's not pretentious – I am who I am."

Quill looked faintly surprised. "Nothing special? Dear me, you can say that, just after telling me that nobody around you can do what you have done, and come to speak to me? I think you underestimate yourself, Miss Fliss."

"Oh please, not *Miss* Fliss! Heaven's, that makes me sound like some school mistress. No, just Fliss is actually fine, thank you, and it's not me who did this coming through thing – that's just something I found by accident." She did find it endearing that he would be so respectful, though. *The better manners of a different generation*, she thought wistfully. *You never got that at work, did you?*

"Fliss, then."

"So when did you leave for India? Was it before or after Henri Dubois was walled up in the staircase?"

"After. That is why Marie has such a hold over me." His expression became pained. "I will never forget that night for as long as I live. With Bessie and Tess gone already, there was just the strange man named Kenric left in the house, with a rough woman he brought in, called Maud, to do the cooking. Where Father got Kenric from I do not know, but he was there by the time I was forced to return here from Scotland. It would not surprise me to learn that he had served time in the county gaol, and that Father took him on in an outward show of piety brought on by one of the rare times he attended church, and in order to impress the rector; but in reality, because he knew that this was someone else whom he could have a hold over, and could therefore ask almost anything of."

"If your father was as promiscuous as you've said, and as I gathered from the letters, do you think that by the subsequent time we've been talking about, that maybe Kenric had as much of a hold over him? That he didn't want Kenric going somewhere else and telling people what he'd seen your father doing?"

"I think that is entirely possible. Certainly, Kenric had a smugness about him when Father summoned him, and told him to help me carry Dubois' body to the old staircase. 'We shall tell people that part of the old wall has collapsed,' my father told us. 'We shall seal up the stair with Dubois inside.' The boy I was could not see how that was going to work, but in truth, the longer it went on without us reporting the killing, the more frightened I became."

"Who did the sealing up and the building of the new servant's staircase, then?" Fliss asked curiously. "Only my uncle and I found a confession written in the plaster of a wall, which implied that whoever that builder of the new stair was, he had been forced to do it under some considerable duress."

"Did you?" Quill seemed astonished by this. "Good heavens!"

"We did. And my uncle is quite an expert plasterer, and he said it looked to him as though the man who did it had deliberately left some laths out so that the plaster facing it would crumble and his words would be found. We thought that he hoped by the time his confession was found, that both your father and Marie would be dead – or rather, with what we knew at the time, that he'd hoped that the murderers would be dead by then."

"Whatever did he say?"

Fliss racked her brains. "If I remember rightly, he said, 'master bade me do this.' And then he wrote, 'I know my work covers an evil deed. I swear unto God that I did this out of fear. If they do this to their own, what would they do to my family?' Or at least that's what I remember reading, but I think I've got it right. It was such a shock to find it, you see, because that was the first time that we thought that the dead man might have a personal connection to your family."

Quill was aghast. "Poor old Sidney," he gasped, then realised that Fliss had no idea who he was talking about. "Sidney Lloyd is the brother of one of our two farmers who lease their farms from us. He was a passable carpenter, though not a master craftsman by any means, and he's very old and frail nowadays. Mostly he worked for the local farmers and other families of that station, not in the bigger houses."

"Well, we're pretty sure that he must have got blackmailed into building the new servants' staircase after your father had the other one filled in. I presume he would be the one who did do that? That there wouldn't be another man in the area your father could have had such a hold over?"

"I believe I heard from Catriona that a new staircase had been put in for the servants after the collapse of the old one. She, of course, knew nothing of what had really happened, and it came as a substantial shock to her and her husband when I wrote and told them what little I dared to put in a letter. I was so worried that they might be persuaded to travel back to see Father, you see. So I felt I had to warn them never to accept such an invitation for fear of their lives, because at that stage I honestly believed that my father and Marie were so insane as to be a danger to anyone who questioned them of almost anything."

Fliss thought hard for a second. "So you're sure in your own mind that this Sidney Lloyd was the man who built the staircase, even though you weren't at home at the time?"

"Oh yes, if only because, many years later, I saw the bill for the work when I came home and went through the accounts – rather my forte, you see, are accounts. And I was astonished that he did the job for so little. When I questioned Father, he was so addled by then that he was simply smug at having got the job done at a bargain price, but if Sidney was threatened with being blamed for the killing, that is a wholly different matter. Dear me, I must make an effort to go and visit him, and set his mind at rest that nobody from the family will ever persecute him like that again."

"Would your father have gone through with it? The threat of blaming it all onto someone else who would have had a harder time defending themselves, I mean."

"Oh yes, and that was the hold Father had over me. I was the one who had to bring in the earth from the garden to throw over Dubois to stop the stench from pervading the house, and having done that much, I was a prime candidate for him to put the rest onto me." Quill looked grim even at the memory. "I did not want to do it, not the shovelling of earth over him, nor the lying about where he had gone. In fact, I was most sickened by doing it. But I had little choice."

"Heavens! Did your father and Marie continue to threaten you even then? Even after you'd helped them cover up the body?"

Quill nodded. "That was why I ran away. They said that Nenius was too ill to speak to anyone, and that they would swear that it was I, and not him, who had struck the first blow. Why I would have done such a thing, I later realised, would not have withstood questioning, and any magistrate with an ounce of common sense would have worked that out, because given that it was Nenius who had been wounded, it was more likely that it was him who had started the fight. But of course, if he had been wounded, who had battered Dubois' skull in? That was what worried me more. That it might be thought that I had attacked Dubois in a frenzy upon seeing my supposedly beloved brother wounded."

"Wow, they really had you trapped, didn't they?"

"They did indeed. And Father had come at me with his cane when I tried to refuse to lift the body. He struck me about the head with the heavy ebony knob on it, and I was terrified that I would join Dubois in the wall if I did not do as they said." He shuddered. "To this day I have never seen a head so bashed in as his was, not even in war. Blown off, yes, but not that kind of battering. That was and is something horribly unique for me, the act of the truly insane, and I feared back then that they might do the same for me one night as I lay in my bed. And on that night, when I raised my hand to my father in self-defence, it was Kenric who grabbed me from behind and held me tight."

"Oh Quill, I'm so sorry! From what I gather, you had quite a normal childhood up in Scotland with your family up there. You must have been hopelessly unprepared for what you walked into here, and wouldn't have had a clue how to deal with it."

He looked startled. "You are the first person apart from my late wife who has understood that. Nowadays, having lived a lot more, I was not so easily twisted by those two when I returned, and they did not like it when I came home and they found that out. Moreover, by then my father was a feeble old man, and even Marie did not have the strength to wield something as heavy as that decanter anymore, not even in the worst of her fury and despite not being that old either. But back then, as a young lad who had lived in a decent, Christian family for so long, I was wholly out of my depth. I believed I had no choice but to go along with them if I wished to live to see another day, and even now I think I was probably not wrong in my fear at that time. Both my father and Marie were most dreadfully dangerous in their terror of being found out, and might have done almost anything in the heat of the moment."

"Then I'm glad that you got away from them. How did you get to India, Quill?"

For the first time he smiled. "I remembered that Cousin John had entertained a business associate of his on several occasions at his house, and that this man was stopping with Cousin John because he actually lived in Bristol, and was only in Edinburgh on business. He had always seemed a kindly gentleman and very respectable, and so I decided to throw myself upon his mercy."

He gave a wry laugh. "At least having travelled all the way from Edinburgh to Worcester five years before, the distance between Worcester and Bristol did not feel as though I was going to the ends of the earth, which it might well have to many a young local lad."

"How did you get there? I can't imagine that your father let you have much in the way of money."

"He didn't, but for once his poor local reputation worked against him. I met a farmer heading for market on that first early morning, and I did not have to say much to have him offering me a lift on his cart. Just the fact that I told him that I could not stay another night under my father's roof was enough. Of course, back then I did not have much idea of how gossip runs through a small community, but Bessie had not been silent in her anger. And though she had only spoken to other servants while seeking another post, it had not taken long for those servants to take the news of Master Spink and his carrying on with his son's wife to their masters and mistresses."

He shook his head in disbelief. "My father rarely went to church by that point, you see, so he was able to fool himself that nobody in the area knew a thing. The truth was far from that. Indeed, it was only when I returned here and began my own regular attendance that people gradually began telling me bits and pieces. Suffice it to say that by the time the lad I was ran, a week after Henri's murder, there had long been substantial sympathy for my plight amongst the decent families of the area. So when I told the farmer of my plan to reach my cousin's contact in Bristol, when we got to Worcester, he took me to the wharves and found a collier's barge that would take me down the River Severn to there, as long as I would work my passage.

"I have never been afraid of work, and even if I had, my fear at that point was so great that I would have rolled my sleeves up and done my best. But years of helping Cousin John as best I could as a young lad, by fetching and carrying heavy reams of paper, and delivering packages, had translated into me doing most of the cutting of the firewood for this house once I was here – because heaven forefend that Kenric should sully his hands by then, and Nenius would not either, even when he was still able. So if nothing else I had some strength in my arms and a strong back, and I was certainly motivated to work hard. Anything was better than ending up in some prison, I believed."

"Oh, Quill," Fliss gasped, "that's so sad. You weren't much more than a lad and to be that frightened is just awful."

He took her sympathy graciously. "Fear is an awfully good motivator, and I did find the man in Bristol. I confess that by that stage I was only too glad to pour my heart out to him, and being a Christian man, he was suitably appalled at what had gone on. But he was also sensible and practical enough to realise that one lad's testimony, if contradicted by two or three adults, was not going to save me. The discovery of the body was the least of it, you see. It would come down to who struck the killing blows, and if my father turned on me to save his and Marie's lives, I would be for the gallows, of that there was little doubt."

Fliss scowled. "I know it's not what a lady is supposed to say in your time, but I truly hope the old goat rots in Hell for that. That's a really evil thing to do to your own son."

"Hmmm …he didn't actually do it, of course."

"I know, but the fact that this business man knew of his infamy enough to believe that you were in real danger says a lot for your father's wicked reputation."

Quill blinked in surprise. "I had not thought of it in quite that way, but you are right, Miss Fliss. Even if my father's reputation had not made it to Bristol, he had to have heard enough from Cousin John to find it credible that my father would do such a thing."

Even though she found it amusing that he still called her 'Miss Fliss', Fliss didn't let that show, instead asking, "So was it this man who helped you get to India?"

"It was. He was in a position to make enquiries, and within the week I found myself heading out to sea as the clerk to someone working for the Company. We were only in India for a handful of months before he succumbed to a fever, poor man, and since I had been doing his work for those last few weeks, I was given his job. It was only a lowly position, but I was more than grateful for the chance to show what I could do, and I worked hard at it."

"You must have done a good job. I read in your letter that you sent to Marjorie that you had a good position by the time you left."

"I did, and it was all my own doing."

Fliss smiled sadly. "Oh, I hear you, Quill. I'm here doing this because I had a very stressful job in London, and it damn near killed me. I got there through sheer hard work, grit, and determination, but to hear my father talking, all I did was sit back and it all fell into my lap. He didn't even contribute to my keep while I was at university. I had to work a part-time job the whole time I was there, not just in the holidays like my friends did, but he's never once given me any praise for doing that. Instead, I'm just a burden he now feels he never ought to have had to bear."

Belatedly she realised that he was looking at her in astonishment. "University? Do mean that you actually have a degree?"

"Yes, I do, and from a good university too. You won't have heard of it, because in your time there's only Oxford and Cambridge. But in way less than a hundred years of when you are now, there'll be a lot of universities founded in other cities, including Bristol, and it was one of those that I went to and studied English literature."

"Good Lord! So you're quite the educated lady?"

"Yes, much good that it's done me." Then she thought that sounded way too self-pitying. She hadn't lost a partner she dearly loved to a killer disease that nobody of the time knew how to cure, and for all that her father was a miserable old sod, he hadn't got the pure evil streak in him to kill someone outright. He'd come dreadfully close to doing it to her by omission, given her memories of thinking that it would be better to just not be here anymore, but to do it by his own hand? No, he hadn't got the nerve for that. And so she qualified what she'd said by adding. "It's still not easy for women to become leaders in business, I'm afraid, and you take a lot of grief along the way. If I'd been a man, I'd have been several steps up the ladder from where I was when I became ill from over-working."

Bemused by this insight into an alien world, Quill asked, "But what of your husband? Did he not mind you doing this?"

"Husband? Chance would have been a fine thing! I was so busy working I never had time to go and meet men. That's why I haven't had children, you see, and it was the realisation that I'm getting too old to ever have them now that caused me to get ill. I'd given up the chances of everything for a job that's thrown me aside like I was yesterday's newspaper, fit for nothing."

"Oh Miss Fliss, that's truly awful!" Quill said and without thinking reached for her hand.

Chapter 25

The weekend

"You are not a ghost!" Quill gasped, as Fliss squeaked in surprise, but found herself still holding on to his hand.

"And neither are you," she said shakily, but also feeling a thrill at this contact that wasn't wholly to do with being able to reach through time. *Bloody hell,* she thought in frustration, *why is it that the first man I've been truly, deeply attracted to in too many years is someone who's already dead?*

"I wish you were here in my time," Quill said echoing her own thoughts. "I feel I would have an ally here then." He sighed. "I thought to send Nilmani away to school for his own safety, you see."

"To get him out of this house and away from Marie? Oh, I can quite see why you'd do that now. Even before you heard my suspicions about Ishwar, you must have been thinking that this wasn't the healthiest of atmospheres for him to be growing up in."

"You have it exactly. I have gradually managed to get some halfway respectable servants to come and work here, and to impress upon them that I am the master here, and what I says goes, not anything Marie might decide."

Fliss knew she had to ask the awkward question, just in case she never managed to speak to Quill again. "But why on earth did you marry her? That I don't understand."

Quill leaned his head against the wardrobe's wood and groaned. "Sheer desperation, Miss Fliss, sheer desperation and nothing more. You see when I got back here my father was not a well man. It took me no time at all to realise that he was as poxed as Marie …oh I do beg your pardon!" and he blushed in embarrassment at having mentioned such a thing to someone he now thought of as a respectable woman.

Fliss smiled wanly at him. "No need to apologise. In my time we know about it, not least because of announcements about treatments." She wasn't about to try and explain the degree of sexual freedom in the twenty-first century, or the rise in sexually transmitted diseases. Life in a shared office with a lot of very sexually active young people, many of whom had shared houses and beds with one another, had left her knowing more than she'd ever wanted to know about that! "So yes, I perfectly understand that if your father had been her regular partner for many years, there was an inevitability that he would catch it from her."

"Goodness me, you are very matter of fact about this!"

"Quill, I lived on my own in London for over ten years, and if I didn't indulge in that kind of life myself, I still couldn't be blind to it going on around me. I've not been cosseted like a lot of the nicer ladies you know."

"What a terrible shame, you ought to have been cosseted more than a little by the sound of things," he replied without hesitation, making Fliss blush now.

"Your father," she said hurriedly. "You said he was ill when you returned?"

"In body not well, but even more so in mind, I am afraid to say. He was prone to strange delusions, and one of those was that he would be persecuted by demons as he slept the endless sleep of the dead if Marie was not fully taken care of. Despite dear Marjorie's best efforts, by the time I got home, Father was well on the way to marrying her himself."

"Would that have been so bad?"

"Actually it would. Because you see as his wife, he could leave Sytchampton House and everything in it to her, and my sisters and I would have had a hard time contesting it – especially if he had done it in Nenius' name as well, since his oldest son was the father of the girls who were the only ones of the next generation who could inherit via a direct male line. Elizabeth's children would have had a claim, of course, but nothing like as good as Nenius' or mine, and the chances of a court upholding any claim of half-Indian boys like Nilmani and Ishwar in the face of what Elizabeth would be claiming was scant. Father had even begun making enquiries about getting married outside of this parish to avoid the reluctance of our own rector."

"Good grief, he really was serious about this, wasn't he?"

"Deadly so, I am afraid. And at the time I was still very deeply in mourning for my own dear wife. I could not conceive of a time when I might find somebody else whom I would actually want to marry. So I talked it over with Marjorie in private, and we agreed that it would be best if I were to marry Marie. That way, when Father died, I, as his son, would automatically inherit, and not her as his daughter-in-law and nothing more. And although Marjorie does not have your worldly understanding of what ails them both, even she had grasped by then that neither of them could last that many more years; whereas I was and am in good health."

"And long may you be," Fliss said fervently. "Don't forget what I told you about poisons! What goes for Ishwar and Nilmani could also apply to you."

"Yes and no," Quill said knowingly. "You see I have always insisted that she and her oldest two eat with me in the dining room, and from the same meals that we share with the staff. Our food may be served on better plates, but for everyday meals we are not such a high household that we can afford for Cook to produce two sets of meals. And though I have used economy as the reason for it to Marie, I had already thought that my eating alone would be asking for trouble.

"And of course, she had no reason to kill me while Father lived, because that would have taken her straight back to the place where she was when Nenius died. It would be much harder for Father to dispose of everything to a daughter-in-law, whereas as my wife – and potentially then my widow – she was cunning enough to realise that she would be in a much stronger position."

Fliss could see that but still thought, "You were taking an awful chance on her being patient, though, weren't you?"

"Not really. Marie is not that intelligent, and her current state has not helped her ability to reason. She is a creature driven by her physical desires, and so as long as she can live in a good house like this, wear silk dresses, and eat well, she is mostly satisfied." He went pink again as he added, "I cannot believe I am telling a lady this, but …I came to an arrangement with Father and Marie. I said that I would take Marie out of Worcestershire to marry, so that nobody we encounter here would be any the wiser, and that she must never mention to anyone that she was my wife. Not that they have socialised much to have many people to talk to, and Marie is now quite the pariah in the district because of her loose behaviour and has been for many years, so she has no friends.

"As far as everyone in the neighbourhood would be concerned, I would continue to be a grieving widower returned from India, and she was my late brother's widow. In return, the marriage document would be lodged with our family man of law so as to be proof of our marrying should anything happen to me – which of course satisfied her immediately. But I also said that I cared not if she and my father continued to do what they had been doing for years. The one thing I would not do – would not *ever* do – was consummate that marriage."

"I should think not!" Fliss exclaimed. "Good grief, one night with her and heaven alone knows what you would have come away with!"

Quill laughed awkwardly. "My, you do understand, don't you! But yes, that was why. Moreover, since this house has always been in two parts, I determined that I, as the master, would have the more prestigious front half with my boys, at least in terms of bedrooms. My father had always preferred the older master bedroom, and that was the one thing Marie had never been able to convince him to move out of – despite our grandfather being nervous of the room, as Nenius told me, though I do not know why. So they stayed there, and her girls had the two back bedrooms either side of the servants' stairs. It has meant that as far as our servants have been concerned, Marie and I have little contact."

Fliss felt a twinge of guilt again. "I think your grandfather's fear might have been because he saw me

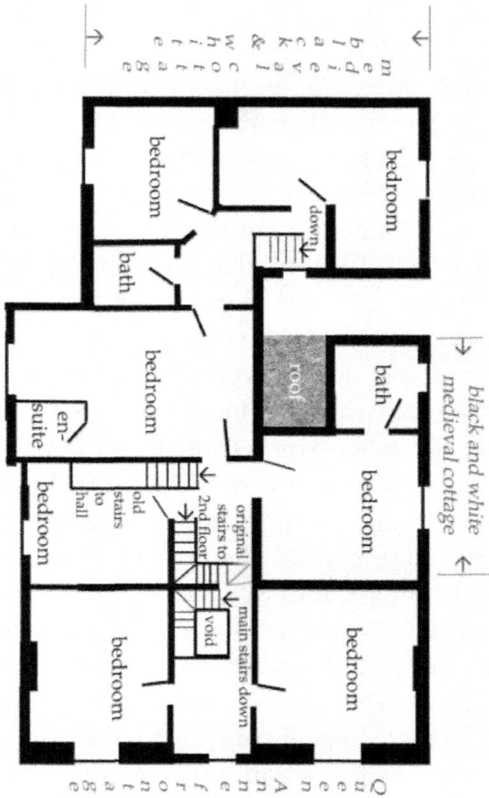

The modern 1st floor but showing the original stairways

in that old part of the house," she confessed.

"Whereas your father mainly saw me in the front part. But was the vile Kenric still here when you returned? And where did he sleep?"

"Ah, Kenric," Quill grunted, but managing to raise a smile. "He at least had gone to meet his Maker some years previous to my return – before my poor brother, praise be, and so they had to get a proper care for Nenius, which is undoubtedly why he lived as long as he did. And as for the dreadful cook and maid-servant my father had by then, I soon got rid of. My current few servants live out except for the cook, who uses the room where you found the inscription on the rare occasions she needs to work late and stop overnight. Otherwise even she lives in a cottage just down the drive. It's safer that way."

"So was the new servants' staircase already commissioned to be built when you ran for your life, or was it wholly new to you when you came back? I know you said that the local man, Lloyd, did the building, but when you left, had you father already said that a new staircase would have to be made? I only ask because my uncle and I presume that a wall must once have divided the upstairs room from the original servants' staircase, which no longer existed in our time, either – or at least not until we uncovered it – and I wondered if you remembered it like that?"

"I ran a week after we filled Dubois' body into the old staircase," Quill confessed. "I was so terrified and shocked by them both by then – and frightened out of my wits in case Nenius died and I got the blame for that too – that all I could think of was getting out of the house. I think I would have slept under hedges and in ditches and felt safer than I did those nights after the murder. I am sure I kept moving on pure fear all the way to Bristol, and then slept for two days without a break. But in response to your question, the room at the top of the old stairs was just a separate storeroom when I left. I was quite surprised to find it had been made into a bedroom once I returned – not that any of us would sleep in it, knowing what was beneath!"

Fliss suddenly remembered something else she wanted to ask Quill as well. "And why was Henri Dubois in uniform? That's really puzzled us. We couldn't think why on earth he would have risked walking around the English countryside as a French soldier when the two countries were at war – I presume they were at war?"

Quill frowned in concentration. "After all of this time, I cannot recall whether we were actually at war with France at the time when Dubois died. What I can tell you is that he was not a revolutionary, of course, because he had been on the other side. As for why he wore his uniform that day …during dinner the previous night when he had just arrived, he had been telling us all of the rank he had risen to. Poor man, I think he thought that Marie would be impressed with him, and how bravely he had fought. She was anything but! All she wanted to know was how much pension he would be paid."

"Given that his side lost and the French Revolution carried on, I'm guessing that was none?"

"Sadly, you are right, and that did not please Marie. She had no intention of returning to France, and the chaos, unless there was a lot of money involved. And of course, when I showed Dubois up to this room for the night, he nearly fell over when he saw his own furniture up here. So he got up the next morning and put his full uniform on to try and impress Marie."

"Or maybe he knew that, in spite of having survived on the battlefield, he'd be lucky to get out of the house alive, and wanted to die as a soldier?" Fliss wondered.

Quill was taken aback. "My goodness! Do you think so? It certainly makes more sense. I never have been able to understand why he thought Marie would be impressed by the uniform."

"And maybe he got up feeling unwell?" Fliss dared to suggest. "Did he start to feel unwell during the night, and fear that Marie had already started to slip him poison? Lucretia isn't likely to have learned how to do that from any books in your library, is she? Somebody taught her, and that pretty much has to have been Marie. And that makes me wonder who she had practised on to even know that something – whatever potion she used – worked? It's one thing putting down poisoned bait for rats, it's quite another to know how much to use to kill a grown person."

Quill clapped his free hand to his forehead. "How did I not see that? Of course! I have never understood why Dubois did not fight back harder, but if he was already weakened, then that makes it a wholly different matter."

"It does rather, doesn't it? So do you think that that might have added to Marie and your father's fears? I'm thinking that even in your time, someone who knew their stuff would be able to tell if somebody had been fed something like arsenic or cyanide?"

"I have no idea," Quill said in astonishment, "but you make a very persuasive argument. Yes, indeed you do. And it explains why they would have thought that they might *both* be in trouble, because Father was always parsimonious with the portions at dinner, and insisted on serving up the soup and meat himself. Dear me, if he had had to admit to that in court, it would have been hard to say who gave Dubois the fatal dose – him or Marie – because she kept pressing wine on him throughout the meal, as Nenius, the servants, and I could testify to."

"It would explain a lot about their paranoia, wouldn't it?"

"Certainly, it would, and now that I think back to those days, Marie had asked for more arsenic to deal with the rats in the barn when Kenric went to fetch other supplies only the day before Dubois died."

"That would mean that if whoever he bought the stuff off testified to a court to that effect, and Kenric said he was only getting it because Marie had told him to – because from what you've said, he'd save his own skin first, with little loyalty to them – she could have looked very guilty indeed! …So moving forwards again, when did your father eventually die?" Of course, she knew the year from the internet, but in the light of what they'd just said, she wanted to hear whether it was quietly in his bed, or from some odd misfortune or ailment as Marie grew impatient. "Am I right in thinking that you came home in 1814?"

"Yes, you are. It was Easter before we got here, having had to stop in Bristol first. Right away I was thrown into the family arguments, because Elizabeth was certainly not quiet either, and so I married Marie in Bristol the next time I had to go there, which was in the May. For the rest of that year things were as quiet as I dared hope they could be. Everyone was at least content with the arrangements, although

Elizabeth is as much of a cross-patch as our father was, and will never be satisfied."

His gaze became distant and sad. "My poor boys. I had very little time to spend with them at that point, and while it swiftly became clear that working in Bristol was not going to be practical, now that I was back in England changing my work was not as complicated. And so by the autumn I was here almost permanently, which I was glad of for the boys' sake, because they were not adapting to life here at all."

"No, I got that impression. Did Ishwar ever get any better at English?"

She could see Quill' eyes starting to fill at the memory as he shook his head. "No, I do not think he did. However much I tried to speak to them only in English, it was only when I spoke to him in his mother's tongue that he showed any signs of understanding. Schooling with a local parson was torture for him, yet I feared leaving him alone with Marie for too long during the days while I was at work."

A rebellious tear broke loose and trickled down his cheek. "Nilmani coped better even if he was far from happy, and it was only into the next year that I realised that with a steadier hand managing this estate and the factory, that I need not work at anything other than that. I had saved and saved while I was in India, you see, needing very little of what I was eventually earning to live on out there. I never gambled, as so many of my colleagues did, nor drank heavily nor womanised – I think the ghastly example my father set was sufficient for me to see that that way lay ruin."

Fliss squeezed his hand. "I think that would have put anyone off," she said gently. "I suspect you were either going to be just like him or the exact opposite.

There wasn't much room for in between after your upbringing. And in your case the good examples you got from your family in Scotland were so well ingrained into you, that you saw your father for what he was, and were repelled by it."

"I do believe you are right." He cuffed the tear away with his free hand. "It was a good thing that I was on hand daily by the time summer last year came around."

"What year was that?"

"Oh? …Oh, 1815."

That made Fliss blink as she realised that the letters that Nilmani had written had been done in a much shorter span of time than she'd thought. Obviously, the schooling he'd had here had done much to improve his handwriting, however much he hated it, and had also made him grow up very fast. But Quill was continuing,

"All the news of Napoleon breaking free from Elba had my father in a frightful state. Heaven alone knows what was going on in his addled head by then, but he became terribly hard to manage. We had to resort to locking him into his room sometimes, having found him wandering in the lanes a couple of times, ranting about how we should all be killed in our beds when Napoleon came for his revenge. Even Marie realised that it would only take him to start talking about her late husband and it could be fatal."

"Oh, good grief! Yes, I can imagine that. If he was that off with the fairies, he might not've had a clue as to who he was talking to anymore."

"Off with the fairies?" It made Quill laugh. "An odd expression, but one which fits very well. And our locking the door on him did not have to go on for long. He went through a sudden deterioration, and he died at the beginning of January this year – that's 1816, Miss Fliss."

"I'm not trying to upset you, but when did Ishwar die? Before or after your father?"

"After," Quill replied shakily. "We had Father's funeral after Epiphany and Ishwar was buried the first week in Lent. That bloody woman wanted him put in the same grave as Father and Nenius to save on the cost of a new grave!"

"No! That's awful!"

"That's what I said, but in stronger language. I was not a gentleman that day, I am ashamed to say. I swore at her most vilely, and I think at last she began to see that I would not be manipulated as my father and brother had been. We have fought almost daily since then, and I do believe that she might have realised that I will now outlive her, for she is weakening too, and Father's death has served as a most dreadful warning of what her end could be like."

A sudden idea came to Fliss. "Quill, if you say that only your father, Marie, you, and your lawyer know that she's your wife, could you not put her into an asylum? Her name must be mud around here by now, so I can't imagine that your nicer neighbours would think badly of you for getting rid of a notorious woman like that. Especially if they see the state she's in now. They don't need to know that she's a murderess to have precious little sympathy with her if she's been blackmailing them." Then wondered whether people called it blackmailing back in his time, but he clearly understood what she meant, so it must have been a word he knew.

"And the ladies might not know what's caused her illness, but I bet a fair number of the men would, and they wouldn't be slow in telling the others." She saw him flinch. "It might sound harsh …well it does sound harsh, I'll admit, but think of it this way – if you want to keep Nilmani safe, you've got to get Marie and her girls out. It's him or them."

Quill straightened as if suddenly becoming resolved. "May God forgive me, but you have only said what I have begun to think, albeit muddled by my grief for Ishwar, but I had not added on the perception of her within the wider area, nor of a solution." He looked her squarely in the eyes for the first time, making her realise that they were a true blue, and right now they were flashing angrily. "I will not lose my last child for her!" he declared forcefully, making Fliss tentatively suggest,

"And you could seem to be magnanimous if you send her daughters away to school. If that's what you were planning for Nilmani, surely it can work in reverse? If Lucretia, Drusilla, and Selina are away at separate schools, then they can't collude either with each other or with their mother. You'll be giving them enough of an education that they'll be able to look after themselves when they're older, so you're hardly leaving them destitute."

The relief washing over Quill was visible, making Fliss feel quite gratified. "An excellent suggestion!" he agreed warmly. "My goodness, that's a most practical solution. Yes, Lucretia is now sixteen, nearly seventeen, so a little old for school, but Drusilla can go away for the new school year. There is time for me to make arrangements by then. Lucretia I might find some respectable work for. Indeed, I believe that a milliner in Worcester is looking for a girl to bring on, and that is as respectable as a girl from such a tarnished family could expect to get. I have been so worried about what will happen when I am left with their care, for those oldest two are very much their mother's daughters."

"Well you never know, at least one of them might not be so very like her if they're given the chance to get away from her influence?"

"They might indeed."

"And what of Selina? You said the older two, but why not her?"

Quill sighed. "Ah, Selina …she, poor child, is sickly, no doubt on account of her mother hardly being clean when she was carrying her."

"Heavens! You mean Marie got pregnant while she was syphilitic? God, the poor kid hasn't got it too, has she?"

"Erm… Not as far as I know. She has always been frail, though. That's why she has the bedroom across the stairs from the old stairs you found to be near her mother, while the other two have the rooms over the kitchen. She was not the next in line after Drusilla, you see. Marie had two boys in between, but both were stillborn. So Selina was only born in 1809."

"Oh! So much more of Nilmani and Ishwar's age, then? I thought she'd be older."

"No, but she has never been well enough to play with them. And of course, she could not understand Ishwar, and he could not understand her."

"I think kids have ways around that if they're given the chance," Fliss told him gently. "Play is play, it often doesn't need words. I think you might find that with Marie out of the way, that Selina and Nilmani find a way to be more like brother and sister than you think they can at the moment. And not wanting to throw oil on the fire or anything, but if there's that much of a gap between Lucretia and Selina, is there a lot of jealousy there? I'm just thinking that if it was Lucretia rather than Marie who fed Ishwar poison, she was awfully good at it for a first attempt. Has she been trying to get rid of a little sister who takes up too much of her mother's attention?"

Quill looked at Fliss in dismay. "I had not even remotely considered that," he gulped. "Dear me, Miss Fliss, you do make a very persuasive argument for separating them all out. And if what you have suspected is anything like true, then it is almost my duty to ensure that the sisters do not meet again until Selina is old enough to stand up to them. She may not be my brother's daughter – indeed I do not know whose she is, given that she looks and behaves like nobody that I know – but I am not without compassion for a child in those circumstances. I was beyond grateful that my grandmother's family stepped in and took care of me, so I cannot in any conscience fail to do the same for her."

"There you go," Fliss said cheerfully. "Sorted!"

There was a sudden bang of a door being slammed downstairs.

"Oh Lord, that sounds like trouble," Quill sighed. "I had better go and take care of it."

"I'll try and do this again," Fliss promised hurriedly. "I don't know how long will have elapsed for you, but I'll try either tomorrow or the day after in my time. So it might be a week or so for you …that's if you'd like me to?"

"I would love you to," was Quill's response. "Just to have someone sane to talk to has been such a balm to my soul, and you have a way of coming up with some very practical solutions."

"Okay, 'til then…" she never got to finish the sentence. A loud scream came from below, not of anger but of shock, followed by the shrieked,

"Master! Master! Come quick!" and Quill released her hand and dived for the door, the connection severing as his footsteps rang on the stairs.

Lucretia 1813

Lucretia dreaded being sent to Ombersley to collect things for the family. The last few years had been a living hell for her and Drusilla, with both of them agreeing in private that neither their mother or grandfather were fully sane anymore. Things had been bad while their poor invalid of a father had been living at home, but when he'd become too ill for anyone to look after without paying more than grandfather wanted for a nurse, the only thing left had been to send him to the hospital in Worcester. The scandal that had created in the neighbourhood, though, had rebounded worst on Lucretia and Drusilla as the only members of the family who ever went out in public anymore.

Grandfather could not be trusted to find his way home if let out alone, and even together, Drusilla and Lucretia had been unable to steer him down the right lanes the last time their mother had sent them with him to pay a bill at the provisioner's. Then Marie-Janneton had gone herself, declaring them all useless and incompetent, but that trip had ended even worse, with her being pelted with handfuls of mud and horse-shit and chased out of the village. Even in her addled state, she had been mortified by the cries of 'whore!' and 'witch!', and worst of all, 'murderess!'.

Her daughters hadn't understood why that last of all should have had both Mamma and Grandfather weeping and shaking for a week afterwards. Yes, they could see that people might think that shoving poor Father off into what amounted to the workhouse could be seen as killing him off, but he'd actually rallied and seemed a bit better once there and was being properly cared for. He certainly hadn't died. So why were they so shaken by *that* accusation when normally they didn't give a fig for what people said?

One morning, she and Drusilla had set off at dawn and walked into Worcester to see Father. The family no longer owned a horse, and couldn't have afford someone to look after it either, so it was walk or nothing, but they had made it there and been allowed in to see him. They had been very aware of the dark looks the wardens and nurses gave them, but some of those had softened as they heard both girls weeping at their father's bedside and saying how much they wished he was still at home.

"Mamma listens to nobody now you're gone," Drusilla had sniffed. "She goes around saying that things will be different now that she is in charge, but oh, Papa, it's only getting worse!"

"I have to cross things off the list she sends for when I take it into the shops," Lucretia wept, "because even I can see that we couldn't pay for half of what she's asked for with the money she's given me. Please, Papa, can you not write to someone in the family to come and take charge of things? Surely there must be someone?"

Yet the someone who had turned up was a sour-faced aunt they'd never met called Elizabeth, who had done nothing but argue violently with Grandfather and Mamma, and then left in high dudgeon, declaring she would never set foot in the place again. And so it had been left to Lucretia and Drusilla to make the best of things.

Yet the first time Lucretia had gone into the village on her own, the jeers and catcalls from the local youths, and some others old enough to know better, had been enough to have her vowing that her younger sister should not have to endure that. If it was wet, she had to scrape the thrown mud off her cloak, yet if it was too dry for mud it was worse, because her persecutors thought it worth their while getting their hands filthy with dung or rotten fruit for the sport of baiting her. And she very swiftly learned never to respond. That only made things ten times worse.

Lucretia had learned to dread the twice weekly walk into the village, but this time things turned ugly beyond even her wildest fears. The butcher had a new delivery boy, a great hulking lad of little brain but great brawn, who was just about capable of lugging heavy deliveries around the village, or taking the trap out to those customers wealthy enough to pay for deliveries. Known as Gorm, though whether that was his proper name Lucretia never knew, he instantly picked on her in the way that all bullies scent a ripe target. But Gorm didn't want just the usual sport. No, Gorm had other plans for Lucretia, as she discovered when he pounced on her from the bushes half a mile out of the village.

Dragging her back out of sight into the field, she had been totally overpowered by him, and unable to stop him as he hauled up her skirts and had his way with her. As he stood up and hoisted his grubby trousers back on, he sneered down at her,

"Told 'em you was a whore like your mam! Your type are always ready for it, ain't yer?" He dragged his cuff across his nose, leaving a trail of snot on it. "I ain't gonna rob yer. Not 'cause I can't, but so as you ain't got nothin' you can pin on me, see? Just your word against mine that this happened! And who's gonna believe you, eh? Me? I'm a respectable 'prentice. You? You's your mam's 'prentice whore! Nobody ain't gonna believe you! So you be ready to keep me sweet when I sees you again, or I'll be tellin' folks just what you'm like."

He stalked off then like the cat who'd stolen the cream and got away with it, leaving Lucretia sobbing on the ground. Eventually she'd managed to drag her sore and battered body upright and the parcels back into the string bags. But walking back had taken forever, and she had barely got inside the gates when her legs had given way.

How long she would have sat there in the dirt she didn't know had not Meg, the gardener's wife not walked past. The gardener of Kenric's day had mercifully moved on, and now Meg's husband Tom came three times a week just to tend the vegetable beds which kept the family fed. They didn't live at the house but in a tiny cottage further down the lane, and mercifully, Meg was a kind and caring soul, who had long pitied the girls of the house. Now Meg took one look at Lucretia's shattered expression and guessed what had happened.

Running for Tom, for by now it was the end of the day and he'd returned home, between them they got Lucretia up to the big house. Yet their calls for help brought nobody but Drusilla. Where old Master Spink or that mad Frenchwoman were was anyone's guess, and apparently it was the cook's night off. So between them they got Lucretia up to her room over the kitchen, and Meg managed to kick the range into life enough to heat the water sufficiently for it not to be cold. Then she and Drusilla helped Lucretia into the tin bath and did their best to scrub the evil of the day off her.

Bit by bit, Lucretia managed through chattering teeth to tell them what had happened, and though Meg believed her – and so did Tom once he was told – they both agreed that Gorm had been correct, nobody was going to believe Lucretia's word over his.

"It's evil, that's what it is!" Meg declared with disgust. "Nasty bully of a boy!"

Tom sighed. "Aye, he is, but his master's cut from the same cloth. No point in going and complaining to him. Or at least not the likes of us. He might take notice of some customer who he values, but the master here ain't one of those."

"I'll come up and do a bit of cleaning," Meg volunteered with a sigh. "God knows That Woman has been pestering us for me to for ages, but I let my dislike of her rule my decision. That and knowing that she'll only pay coppers for a week's work, not the going rate. But now I think we need to keep an eye on these girls for their sakes."

What she only said later to Tom as they walked home was,

"What if the poor girl gets with child from this? Or if not this time, another, because that bloody boy sounds like he's not going to leave her alone. Dear God, she's only fourteen! Still a child herself in so many ways, but it's still possible she could catch, and how will she cope then?"

"I'll go and get the groceries next week," Tom said with a sigh. "Madam up there will have to wait until Thursday when I'm going in to work at Master Oldbury's, but I'd rather the inconvenience than see the poor lass go through that again."

For the most part, Marie-Janneton complained loudly but accepted the change. Not that she was overly concerned at the way Lucretia had become a pale shadow of herself, or the obvious loathing that both girls now displayed for her. The only one of her children she ever bothered about was Selina, and that was only because Selina had the same fascinations as she did, for even as a small child of five, she delighted in watching the rats writhe and die from the arsenic they laid down for them.

For Lucretia, her worst nightmares were coming true. As the months went on, she realised her courses had stopped and she was beginning to thicken around the middle.

"What am I going to do?" she sobbed on Meg's shoulder, as they sat with Drusilla in one of the top bedrooms of the new wing, which was one of the few places they could guarantee that Marie-Janneton wouldn't interrupt them, on account of her refusing to climb the extra flight of stairs. "How can I take care of this baby? We can't even protect ourselves? And what if it's a boy? You know how Mamma has wanted an heir for Grandfather? They'll take him from me and make him into one of theirs, and there won't be a thing I can do about it. They'll take him into Ombersley and have him baptised as her son, and who would argue if she swears he's hers? Nobody's seen her to know she hasn't been with child. And if she says it's mine, then what little reputation I've got left is gone forever and I'll never be able to leave here."

Meg, whose greatest sorrow had been that she and Tom had never managed to have a babe live beyond a few weeks, knew immediately what the solution was. "I'll take it," she said. "Boy or girl, I'll take it, and Tom and I will love it as if it was our own. You can see it and know it's safe, and never have to worry about what your evil Mamma will do or say. All we have to do is hide how you are for another few months, and with the way she never looks at you, that won't be hard. Drusilla can come and fetch me when your time comes, and we'll get this room ready for your lying in. Closer to the time, we'll find some excuse as to why you're going to sleep up here for a while, though I doubt they'll question it."

As the winter drew on, Lucretia was easily able to hide what little bump she had under the extra layers of clothing needed against the cold of a house which was never heated, except for the old hall where Grandfather and Marie-Janneton spent their days. And since Drusilla and Lucretia had preferred to waddle around swathed in extra layers rather than spend time in there, Lucretia's pregnancy remained hidden. Even as she screamed her way through the baby's birth, Cuthbert and Marie-Janneton were too soused in brandy to wonder about the cries from above, and Meg helped her deliver a healthy baby girl only days after Lucretia's fifteenth birthday.

"What are you going to call her?" Meg asked, wanting so badly to name the baby herself, but knowing that if Lucretia had nothing else to give her child, then at least it could be a name.

"I… I don't know," Lucretia said hoarsely. "I've not dared dream she would even live."

"She's a blessing for Meg and Tom, and a joy to you," Drusilla said, looking at the tiny bundle in its blankets with tears of happiness in her eyes, "so why don't you call her Felicity?"

"Oh, that's a lovely name!" Lucretia said through her exhaustion, and Meg agreed.

"Welcome to the world Felicity Spink," Drusilla started to say then stopped herself. "No! Thanks to you Meg, she'll never have our cursed surname."

Meg's smile couldn't have got any wider. "We'll have her baptised as Felicity Miles, and we'll do it over at my folks' church in Rochford. That way she'll never be connected back to here."

Chapter 26

The weekend

Happy and easier in mind after her conversation with Quill, Fliss was even more relieved to discover that she still had loads of time to get back to Bernie's before he was likely to appear. But what she wasn't anticipating was a deep compulsion to go back and make that connection with Quill again. Actually touching him had made a connection of a whole new kind – had made everything more real, especially him. Whatever it was, it was way more than just satisfying her curiosity now. It was Quill himself that was calling to her.

Or was it? Fliss wondered whether it was him or something to do with the house, because once she was back at Bernie's the dreadful urgency to dive back into the past receded to a deep yearning. Of course, that was certainly helped by the man she now knew Quill to be. If he'd been a less personable man, and less deeply concerned for Nilmani, then she would be finding this hankering to join him a lot easier to resist.

On the other hand, what possible reason could she give him for thrusting herself upon him? Because Fliss was clued up enough to realise that once in that past world, she would be utterly reliant upon his good will to keep her. If things didn't work out between them – and at this point she had to be honest with herself and admit that she dearly hoped that this attraction would turn into something more romantic and lasting – then she would be in a worse position than she was now, because there were even fewer opportunities for women of her age to work in the early nineteenth century than now.

A governess, she mused. *You've already said that you have a good education, so why not offer to come through and teach little Nilmani and that poor kid, Selina?* If nothing else, it would give her some element of security, though not a lot. Good governesses were always in demand, so she wouldn't be destitute, but it wasn't a life she would seek out if it meant moving houses every few years.

However, there wouldn't be much that her own general education couldn't provide for a child of that time, because there was only so much that they would be expected to know. She might have to do some swift brushing up on her history, but that would probably be better done back then. If she read up too much now, she might be relying on discoveries made in the intervening years, which would sound false and ridiculous to people of Quill's time. And there was a limit to what anyone would expect a child to know in that era, with Fliss' own general education being far in excess of what young girls in particular of the late Georgian period, or the following brief reign of Queen Victoria's uncle – the often-forgotten King William IV – would need to know. The only part she would fall down badly on was her lack of any musical skill, because she could paint things like watercolours with a modicum of skill if no great talent.

Literature, on the other hand, she could deal with easily. No modern novels, of course, but even in her Modern English degree, she had needed a basic knowledge of Shakespeare and Chaucer, and with a bit of thought she guessed she could probably work with some of the major poets too. Weren't Byron, Keats and Shelley working around that time? She might come across as a bit progressive if she brought them to the children's attention, but that wouldn't necessarily be a bad thing. And John Donne and John Milton could be included, because they earlier and major poems such as *Paradise Lost* been written by then.

Homework! she told herself firmly. *If you're seriously considering doing this, then it's time to stop messing about and do some serious reading! You don't have to go through the portal tomorrow, but equally you can't leave it too long if a day here is more like a week on the other side, or heaven forbid a month, even when you're tapping into the same portal.*

Yet that also brought with it a shiver of concern, because when had she so suddenly and fully committed to going back in time? She wasn't given to making snap decisions like this. Damn it, the very reason why she was in this position of being Bernie's houseguest was because she hadn't been quick enough, or decisive enough, to shift jobs before she had crashed and burned. So why now? Where had all this impulsiveness come from? It had to be something more than a dread of becoming the proverbial albatross around Bernie's neck.

And lovely though it would be to have what amounted to the sole care of a child, at the end of the day if Quill decided he would rather send Nilmani away to school after all, then there would be precious little she could do about it. He wasn't her child to make decisions for. Moreover, if Selina was already seven, how many years would it be normal to tutor her for? As a governess, Fiss might only have half a dozen years where she was useful to Quill if he never got to see her as more than a useful aide. In which case, could she hope to come back to now if he dispensed with her? It was all very disconcerting and not a little troubling.

However, by the time Bernie got back, she had the dinner already prepared and the meat roasting in the oven even if she was no closer to solving her dilemma.

One look at his face was enough to know that the meeting had been traumatic.

"Come and sit down," she said soothingly, going and pouring him a whisky while he struggled with his boot laces. "Was it bad?"

"It wasn't bloody good," he growled. "Admittedly they were shocked when I told them that a detective from the West Mercia force told me that Mrs Davenport was trying to defraud me – well okay, I know he didn't quite say *that*, but he came pretty close. So I'm grateful to him for ringing Mrs D, because without that I don't think I'd have convinced Jonas and Edmund that she's lying through her teeth."

"They were both there?"

"Oh yes. Neither of them has the backbone to face me alone. They're still wary of the old dog's teeth."

"Bernie, you're far from an old dog. And anyway, isn't loyalty supposed to be a dog's greatest virtue? Well, you've certainly been a loyal father to them. I wish I could say they'd been the same. I trust you far more than I do my own parents, so why can't they?"

"Thanks for that, Fliss," he sighed wearily, but with a smile for her. "But as for my sons, I've told them straight – I want no more recommendations from them, nor will I rubberstamp any projects of theirs. If they want to get into the restoration business, then from now onwards they are going to have to either get that accreditation themselves, or properly employ someone who does. I'm withdrawing any reference to that from the company, and if they persist in using it, then they'll be hearing from my solicitor, because I'm not going through this again."

"Oh Bernie, I'm so sorry."

"Don't be. It's not your fault. Do you know that Jonas told me that I should cut corners on this house, if that's what it took to bring it in at a price that the Davenports wanted?"

"No!"

"Oh, he did! I told him straight, 'I'm not ruining my reputation for your foolish promises. You should have costed the job out better *before* you told the Davenports what it could be done for.' It was water off a duck's back to him, though. Reputation is something neither of them have ever had to worry about yet, so of course they don't value it. But I've said that first thing on Monday morning, I'm ringing my solicitor and getting the name of the company changed – whatever it takes. The way they're going on, sooner rather than later, somebody is going to be suing the arse off them for shoddy work, and I'm not getting dragged through the muck with them."

He paused and took a few grateful large sips of the malt. "Oh, and by the way, I wouldn't have expected it if you hadn't warned me, but your father *had* gone to the boys." Fliss groaned and buried her head in her hands. She'd so wanted to be wrong about that. "I do not understand Graham Allcock, I truly don't. Whatever possessed the man to do such a thing? There was no need to involve my boys, none whatsoever."

"Sheer spite," Fliss sighed. "My father never could stand to think that someone might point the finger of blame at him. While I was still there with them, he could berate me as much as he wanted, but once you swooped in and rescued me, he was left with too much time on his hands to reflect on how he'd behaved. And my father can never bear to as much as consider that he was – or is – in the wrong, much less fully admit to it. So in his warped view of the world, it has to be you and me who are wrong. It's the only way he can excuse himself, you see? But it's never enough for him alone to know that. He has to make sure that everyone else knows it too. He has to make sure he's very much *seen* to be in the right, even if he has to twist the truth to do it. That's why he went to your sons, damn him, and I bloody knew he would!"

"No use crying over spilt milk now," Bernie sighed, "but I won't lie, I could have done without that being thrown into the mix."

"I'm sure you could," she sympathised. "It also makes me feel that I really don't want to ever see either parent again." As she saw Bernie about to protest, she waved a warning finger. "No, Bernie, that's not a kid's knee-jerk reaction. It's not me saying I don't want them just to spite them back. It's actually me recognising that it honestly won't matter to them whether they ever see me again. Have they tried to ring me even once since I've been here? No. And it's been weeks now. Even if they were in a huff at first, by now they ought to have started wondering if I was okay or not, and it can hardly be because they don't know your phone numbers. So if they haven't tried to make contact it's because they don't want to."

He grimaced. "I see your point. And I can assure you that neither of them has rung on the quiet and only spoken to me."

"I never thought that they had. I trust you enough to know that you would have told me if they had. …But that makes my point, doesn't it? What would be the point in me ringing them up, or going to visit them? They're never going to think any better of me. That's become blindingly obvious. And do I honestly need their approval that much anymore? No, I don't. Once upon a time I craved that as much as any normal kid does, but try as I might, I could never get it, not one little bit. Not one word to the effect of 'you did well', nor my mum slipping me a little treat behind Dad's back, if he was the instigator. So she picked which side she was on a very long time ago, and seems to have no conscience about what all of that did to me.

"All of which means that if I can't repair our relationship, why do I need to see them? Even if something awful happened to them, like one of them having a stroke or a heart attack, I honestly don't think that they'd *let* me go and stay with them to help. Whichever one was left coping, they'd rather pay for a nurse than have me for free, because at least that way they could brag about how much they were paying for the service, and they'd have something to moan about because I wasn't there. Me doing things for them would deprive them of both, and I'd sure as hell pay for that in terms of the misery they'd inflict on me."

"God, what a bloody awful way to go through life, looking at the world like that."

"I won't argue with you there. I think so too, and it's one of the ways I never, ever want to be like them.

But it means that unlike you and the boys, we will never just be taking time out from one another to let things calm down. When Jonas and Edmund were little, I can remember visiting with mum, and you chasing the boys around the garden and them howling with delight. You gave them normality, Bernie, even if Aunt Margot did her best to stifle it. But there's never been 'normal' in our house. I sometimes wonder if there's something wrong with my mum because of the way she's so detached. You know, something which if she was a kid now would be diagnosable."

"What, you mean like autism or something?"

"Not exactly. More like a personality disorder like narcissism, though she doesn't care enough about herself and too much about what my father thinks for it to be that. It's more that there's something dreadfully missing in her. But then once you acknowledge that, you can see that there's nothing I can ever do to make things right with her, any more than I can with my dad. I can't, because they don't even see that there's anything wrong, much less that it needs to be changed. In their eyes, they have no incentive to change since nothing is wrong. And if I try, all I do is end up making myself ill. There are so many scars now, I've got weak spots left, right, and centre when it comes to them. So for my own sake, if I'm ever going to have normal relationships again – even just regular, normal friends – then I need to *not* have them in my life at all."

Belatedly Fliss realised that this was half of the speech she'd rehearsed for telling Bernie why she wanted to go through the portal to Quill, but now wasn't the time to tell him that. *You've got to give him a plausible reason why you suddenly went off down that verbal rabbit-hole!* she thought furiously, coming up with,

"So don't you dare think that your argument with my cousins has also put the tin hat on my relationship with my parents when I then don't go and see them again. Because it's not. That was dead and buried long before I came home this time, let alone coming here – I just didn't recognise it. Nor is your relationship with Jonas and Edmund anything like as bad. Yes, you're going through a rough patch, and they're idiots for not seeing what they're losing in you, but I'd put good money on a bet that they'll come around. It might not be for a while. They're both as stubborn as Aunt Margot was. But permanently estranged? No, I don't believe that, not at all."

Bernie smiled wanly. "Thanks for that, Fliss, I needed to hear somebody say it because it felt bloody final this afternoon."

The only response Fliss could make to that was to go and give him a big hug. However, when the phone rang later that evening and Fliss answered it, she was astonished to hear a familiar voice on the other end say,

"Hello, Fliss, is Dad there?"

"Edmund? Oh!"

"Don't hang up, Fliss, please. I want to apologise to Dad."

"Oh?" That was a turn up for the books, but Fliss was feeling more than a bit protective of Bernie at the moment, not least because she was sure things wouldn't have been half as bad if her father hadn't shoved his nose in where it didn't belong.

"Oh God, Fliss, this is a mess. Jonas and I have been arguing for months now, I just didn't want to tell Dad." She heard his huff of breath down the phone. "Bloody silly, really. I suppose I just wanted to prove to myself that I could handle things without having to come to him for help."

"What sort of help?" Fliss asked warily. "You do know your dad may have to go to court to get paid for this job, don't you? I don't think he has spare cash to hand out."

"Bloody hell, I wasn't going to ask him for money," Edmund said in disgust, making Fliss retort,

"Well one of you has for your latest venture!"

"Oh you have got to be kidding," Edmund groaned. "Shit! No wonder he was so angry today. Fliss, I didn't know that, honestly, I didn't, that's why I let Jonas rant on at him."

Realising that so far, she'd only heard what Bernie knew of the situation, Fliss crept out to sit in the kitchen to talk, feeling she needed to get a grasp of what was going on, if only to back Bernie up.

"So come on then, tell me, what have you and Jonas been arguing about?"

"This new bloody contract we're bidding on, for a start off," Edmund said bitterly. "I didn't want to go for it in the first place. I think Dad's right, it's too big for our firm to handle alone, and I'm not happy about the number of subcontractors we'd need to have on board. We're just not set up to keep an eye on things with that many people, it's asking for trouble. …And the other reason why I haven't talked to Dad much of late is because …well, Sally and I are getting divorced."

"Oh, Edmund, I'm so sorry!"

"I know. I'm gutted about it. But I've gradually come to see that Sally's right about one thing – we got married far too young. As we've grown up, we've grown apart, although that's not all of it by a long chalk. At least the kids are old enough to understand, though they're both miserable, as you can imagine. And the thing is, the more Jonas dragged us into these bigger and bigger contracts, the more hours I was working, and Sal's just had enough. She's sick of me coming home exhausted and grumpy, and with no time for her and the kids. When she asked for the divorce, she told me I was hardly ever there, so I might just as well write her a monthly cheque, because she's taking care of everything else on her own.

"That was such a wake-up call, Fliss. But worse, it was just around then that Jonas started saying that we ought to put our houses in as security, so that we could get a bigger advance from the bank. I was furious!"

"I bet you were," Fliss sympathised. "Blimey, of all the times for him to ask! I know we're not close, and you don't have to answer me, but would I be right to think that you will be moving out, and Sally keeps the house because the kids are both at school still, albeit not for much longer?"

"You get it," Edmund sighed, seeming more relieved than angry. "I wish Jonas had. I said that it just wasn't possible, and the more I stuck to that, the angrier he got. Jeez, he's just like Mum for that! Can't bear to think that he can't get you to do what he wants by sheer will power. That eventually, you'll cave in for a quiet life."

"But you genuinely *can't* this time, can you?"

"No, I can't."

"So what's going to happen, Edmund?"

"Well after Dad left this afternoon, we then had the biggest row ever. We were both wound up, and so once we got started, we pretty much didn't stop until an awful lot had been said that I think we'd both been keeping bottled up. In typical Jonas fashion, he immediately started blaming me for not backing him up enough with Dad. For not pulling my weight; for never having his vision for the company; and for not appreciating that as my big brother, he was trying to take me with him to the top."

There was another of those heavy sighs. "That might have worked when we were kids, Fliss, but not now. I've brought my own skills to the company, because I'm the one with the practical knowhow. Oh, he's the money man. He relishes that far more than he ever did learning bricklaying or plastering – and Dad insisted that we got taught that properly at college. I think he knew that as teenagers we wouldn't take as much notice of him. When Jonas came to doing the accountancy courses later on, he put far more effort into those, but tonight he made it sound as though he *had* to do them for my sake, which was a long way from how it was at the time."

"That was your mum's and mine's trait, heaven help us both," Fliss sympathised, "making it sound as though they'd suffered god-knows-what all because of you."

"God, I'd forgotten that! Oh, and by the way, Fliss, I never believed what your dad said about you, not for a moment. Why on earth you'd want to take over a building company just didn't make sense to me. Work with us, yes, but not take over. But Jonas is nothing if not paranoid, especially if he thinks he's going to miss out on something. He took it all in, hook, line, and sinker."

"And my father can be bloody convincing when he gets all righteous," Fliss sighed.

"Well he didn't convince me," Edmund said with genuine sympathy in his voice.

"So what's happening now?"

"Oh God, we're splitting up. Jonas and me, I mean, not harking back to Sally. I told him tonight that I want out of the company. There's been an offer, you see. If we can't come up with the money to do this big contract on our own, then we can go in as a subcontractor to this big firm. I won't bother you with the names because they won't mean a thing to you, but they will to Dad. And the thing is, Fliss, they have a reputation for throwing up cheap houses that end up having to have loads of things put right on them. The first time Dad refused to bankroll us – not what you were talking about, but a couple of years ago – Jonas was furious, and so this time he was like a dog with two tails when we got made this offer. He saw it as us being worth taken on board by one of the big guys. I saw it as us sticking our reputations on the line, and risking getting taken over when we got into a financial mess. So I think that's why Jonas went off on one at Dad today. He thought that if he could get Dad on board, then I'd follow, because if Dad believed in it then it must be okay."

"But your dad didn't and stuck to his guns."

"And rightly so. But now I've had it with Jonas. It took me losing my wife, my kids, and my house to see it, but it's finally sunk in that I'll never be able to do enough for him. It's so bloody ironic – I'm the one who looks more like Mum, but the older I get, the more like Dad I realise I'm becoming as a person. Whereas Jonas looks like Dad, but with every passing year he's acting more and more like Mum in personality, and I've reached a point where I can actually look back and wonder how the hell Dad stood her for so long. I may have wrecked my own marriage by being absent, but at least Sally and I still speak to one another like civilised adults most of the time. But remembering how Mum used to speak to Dad when we were in our late teens… *Hmph*! I think Sally and I would have hit the skids a lot sooner if she'd spoken to me like that."

"So what are you going to do? Can you just walk away from the company? Is that possible? Or does Jonas have to buy you out?"

"That's actually what I wanted Dad's advice on. My feeling is that I'm prepared to let Jonas get on with it with this contract as long as I'm removed as an official owner. I can't afford to be financially tied up in it if it all goes pear-shaped, you see. If he makes the money he thinks he's going to on this deal, then he can pay me for my share. But I told him that if Dad's removing his name, then we can take my name off the register at Company's House at the same time."

"But where will you live?"

"Don't know, if I'm honest. Somewhere bloody cheap, that's for sure. I'm going to have a very lean couple of years in between finding work and paying alimony."

"I'll take the phone to your dad, then, but I think he might have a solution."

Even as Fliss walked through to the lounge, smiling broadly at Bernie and saying, "It's Edmund on the phone. You're going to want to take this," she was feeling lighter in spirits herself. This couldn't be better, because the other big thing that she'd been worried about with regard to her leaving, was what it would do to Bernie if he became fully estranged from his sons at the same time. Now, though, the obvious thing was for Edmund to step back into working with Bernie. If Jonas had always been the friction point – and it sounded very much as though he had – then without him there, Bernie and Edmund should be able to repair their relationship no problem.

Better than that, as long as they could afford to buy it with their pooled money, where else would Edmund live but at Sytchampton House when it had so many rooms? *You can have the other half to your dad,* Fliss thought happily, *and I can go to where I'm needed and wanted, and where I feel I belong.* Because despite the short time of being at the house, and the even briefer conversation with Quill, Fliss still had that overwhelming compulsion to be with him and his children.

Lucretia 1814

Sitting on the sill of the top floor bedroom window, Lucretia wondered if there was any point in living any longer? She missed little Felicity with an intensity she had never expected, and it was all the worse because Meg and Tom had left last month, taking Felicity with them. That hadn't been done maliciously. It was simply that Tom had been offered the permanent position of under-gardener at a great house over in Herefordshire, with a much sounder cottage to live in than the ramshackle place they rented from Cuthbert Spink for more than it was worth. So Lucretia understood why Meg had tearfully told her that they simply couldn't afford to turn the chance down. And knowing that little Felicity would have a much better life over there had softened the blow.

Or so she had thought.

The reality was something entirely different.

The first week had been bad. The second beyond difficult. But by the end of the month, she was in complete torment. She'd even thought of writing to Meg to see if there was a place for her working at the house, except that Meg couldn't read or write, and neither could Tom, so there wasn't any point in doing that.

How could that tiny person have burrowed her way so totally into Lucretia's soul that life without her could seem pointless, she wondered? She knew that Drusilla was beside herself with worry for her, to the extent that she had now taken on the hellish job of going to Ombersley, the only plus to that being that the obnoxious Gorm – spurred on by getting away with raping Lucretia – had done it to a much more respectable lady's maid in the autumn, and was now locked up in Worcester gaol. And since he had initially bragged to his cronies about what he had done, his subsequent incarceration had quelled any ideas of theirs of following suit, even to the extent that the mud and dung throwing at the Spink girls had stopped.

Yet the time on her hands only made Lucretia's torment worse.

She would come upstairs and tried to fold the linen away in the big chest on the landing in the way that Meg had shown her. But for her there was no cheery humming along at her task as Meg had always done. Somehow, when Meg had been here, she had managed to brush away the doom and gloom which pervaded the house, and made the rooms she took care of feel almost homely. Now that was all gone.

Just do it, Lucretia thought, opening the sash window and leaning out. *All you have to do is just lean a bit further and then it will all be over. No more missing your baby. No more having to spend your days trying to avoid Mamma and Grandfather and whatever foul things they're up to*, because by now Lucretia was fully aware of what her mother and grandfather did together, and was sickened by it. Granted her one and only experience of sex had been sufficient to convince her that she never wanted to do it again, but she could also see that their example was hardly one of demonstrating a loving and caring relationship. Many was the time when she had walked in on them and wished she could wash her memory like dirty laundry, and erase forever what she had seen. But it wasn't to be, either for her or Drusilla, who was as equally revolted. That Selina seemed perversely fascinated by the same things, they had once put down to her not knowing in her childishness what she was seeing, but of late they had come to wonder whether there wasn't something very wrong with their youngest sister.

Go on, lean a bit further. Just open your arms and fly to heaven, the treacherous voice in her mind said, and she was quite ready to do it until she saw the ghost.

It was a woman, but dressed like nobody Lucretia had ever seen. And she seemed sad. The way she walked over to the wardrobe and touched the paintings with her fingertips, tracing the figures, and then having to stop and wipe her eyes with a strange looking handkerchief, made her seem less alien to Lucretia.

Then she heard the woman saying, "You poor little kids. Where was your mum when you needed her, eh? I wouldn't have let you go so easily."

The language might be strange, but Lucretia knew in that instant that this woman would understand her. She would empathise with her longing to have baby Felicity back. Nobody else here did, not even Drusilla, though her sister tried so very hard to. But this stranger, she might just be the one to grasp how dreadful Lucretia's spiritual pain was. Where she had come from, and where she went to, Lucretia didn't know, but across that strange divide she suddenly felt a very strong connection.

From down below she heard the strong voice of her Uncle Quill, and instantly the woman disappeared, but that brought up a whole flurry of other emotions for Lucretia. He had appeared only weeks ago with his strange little boys, and since then the household had been in turmoil. When he'd first appeared, Grandfather had been positively ecstatic in his welcome, but within days that had changed to ranting and raving as he realised that his youngest son was now not a man to be bullied. As for her mother, she alternately hissed and spat at him like an angry cat, or flirted with him outrageously. Some days it amazed Lucretia and Drusilla that her bosom didn't fall out while they were sat around the dinner table, she wore her bodices laced so low, yet his obvious disgust had had an unexpected effect on Lucretia.

For herself, there had been initial terror that he might discover that she was making visits to the gardener's cottage and ask her why. But then Tom and Meg had left within a fortnight of his arrival and that fear had vanished, even if it had left a gaping hole in her soul. Yet stranger, and out of nowhere, she found herself with the most almighty crush on her uncle, had she known what a crush was. Unfailingly polite, never drunk, and displaying a sense of morals that Lucretia had only ever read about in books, he was everything every other member of their family was not. He was hardly rakishly handsome, but for a fifteen-year-old girl who had only ever been exposed to the worst kind of men, he was like a Greek god descended from the heavens.

Maybe, she sometimes wondered, it was because she desperately wanted someone to love her and to love in return? If she couldn't have Felicity, could she find someone to partly fill that vast empty space? Yet that roused in her only further sorrow and pain. What would such a man think of her if he knew she'd had a baby only months ago, and out of wedlock at that?

Would he look at her with complete disgust? Or worse, would he throw her out at a moral degenerate?

Such things she debated long and hard at night with Drusilla in the sanctuary of one or other's bedrooms. And Drusilla had seen her point.

"Uncle is a very proper man, isn't he?" Drusilla sympathised. "You can see it in the way he looks as though Grandfather and Mama almost put him off his dinner with the way they behave. And he never goes and sits with them during the days, does he? He's always off working. And isn't that what real gentlemen do? I know that right now he has a job. But don't even fine gentlemen have to look after their estates? Grandfather has never done that here, but then maybe that's why we never have any money?"

"I think we should offer to help look after his boys," Drusilla had added after a moment's thought. "If we do that, maybe he'll see that we're not like Mamma?"

And so they had tried to help the two very lost and confused little boys to settle in. But it had been harder than they expected, not least because neither boy could seem to understand that their family in India was dead. Quill tried. Lucretia and Drusilla tried. Yet all they got was Nilmani writing letter after letter to a mother who wasn't there anymore. And in the end, rather than tell him that there was no point in taking them to the post when she went into Ombersley, Drusilla had taken to hiding them in the back of the old dresser.

But for Lucretia, the worst stab to the heart had come only days ago. For some strange reason, Uncle Quill had taken Mamma with him when he went to Bristol. At first, both girls had dared to hope that he might be taking her to some asylum, and that they would never have to see the woman who sometimes turned on them, ranting and raving, and accusing them of crimes only she could conceive of, let alone do.

Then they had returned, Mamma initially looking triumphant until the massive row between Uncle Quill, her, and Grandfather had erupted at the dinner table on the first night they were back.

"I will never consummate my marriage to you," Uncle Quill had told Mamma in the frostiest of voices. "You may continue your filthy practices with Father for as long as you like. But know this: if you breathe one word of this marriage to anyone, I will deny it. I've done this only to keep this family safe from prosecution by the law, which includes me and my sisters. It was not done out of any love for either of you two!"

Lucretia had choked on her soup. Uncle Quill had *married* Mamma? Why? Why would he do that when she was the one who loved him? Why would he take a mad old woman like her when he could have someone who would be faithful and honour him as she would? Someone young enough to give him more children. Children who might fill the awful gaping void in her life that Felicity had left. The only reason she could think of as she tried not to cry her way through the meal was that, somehow, he had learned of her bastard, and like everyone else, had condemned her for something that wasn't her fault. And if so, was there really any point in trying to live on?

Chapter 27

Monday

The phone conversation between Edmund and Bernie was a long one, and Fliss stayed out of the lounge to give Bernie some privacy, going and clearing up in the kitchen and preparing what they might need tomorrow night. When Bernie eventually came through to her he looked as though he might have shed a few tears, but he was smiling broadly.

"You two good, now?" Fliss asked with a grin, coming to give him a hug.

"Oh God, yes!" He almost took her breath away with the strength of his hug back.

"I'm so glad that Edmund rang back tonight. I think the longer it went on, the harder it was going to be for either of you two to let your guards down with one another."

"You're probably right about that, but right now I'm just glad that maybe losing my rag with them brought one of my boys to his senses."

"To be fair, Bernie, I think Edmund was three-quarters the way there already. He sounded absolutely gutted over his divorce."

"Yes, he did, didn't he? I always liked Sally, not like Jonas' stuck-up Chantal, who always seems to have one eye on what affect her words have on people. That one likes to stir things up, of that I'm sure, and I'm not wholly convinced that she hasn't had someone else on the side – but then I'm not sure that Jonas hasn't either."

"Sounds like they're two for a pair."

"Oh, they are, but Edmund and Sally I thought would be together for keeps. Just goes to show what I know, doesn't it?"

Fliss put the kettle on to make a tea for him and a decaf for herself, saying, "Don't beat yourself up over that, Bernie. It's tough out there these days. And at least Edmund knows what he did wrong and can admit it. It didn't sound as though either of them have someone else in the picture, did it? So you never know, after a break, they might yet get back together. Some people do manage to do that when the stress point gets taken away. I think the most encouraging thing is Edmund leaving Jonas, because then there'll be far fewer pressures on him from that direction. Was he right with his suspicions about that company Jonas wants to hook up with?"

"Oh, totally! Utterly disreputable shower, they are! I wouldn't touch them with a barge pole."

"So what's Edmund going to do for work, then?"

Bernie's face broke into a smile. "Well at some point he's going to come over to the house to see what we're doing. I've told him, if nothing else, he can come and do some of the work with me. I can only pay him the same as any other bloke I'd take on, but it's better than nothing. And nothing is what he'd get out in the wider world, I'm afraid. He's been away from the physical side of the job a bit too long, you see. He's not up to speed with all of the regulations, or at least his qualifications for them. So it's either go it alone – with all of the financial pitfalls that that could bring, especially with the economy in the state it's in – or try and change careers completely, unless he does come back to me. I can't see anyone taking him on as a subcontractor, not least because you don't want someone who's been used to being the boss telling your workers what to do behind your back."

"No, I could see that causing a lot of trouble. But I'm so glad you've asked Edmund over. I've been feeling for a week or so that I'm not as much use to you as I ought to be. …No, you don't have to sugar the pill for me, Bernie, honestly you don't. I'm not that fragile that I can't see that this particular job has turned into something far bigger than you were expecting – the floor in the old hall being a prime example. So while I can put paint on with the best of them, I'm absolutely no help when it comes to working on things like sanding and sealing the parquet, or repairing the plaster. But Edmund will be, and he ought to be given the chance. If he mucks it up this time, well then more fool him, but I don't think he will for a moment. Honestly, Bernie, I'm well happy to stand back and watch and learn. I'm not feeling shoved aside, truly I'm not."

What neither of them was expecting, was to hear the rumbling engine of another big utility vehicle pulling into the driveway only an hour or so after they'd arrived at Sytchampton House the next morning. They'd set off later than before to allow Bernie to make his various phone calls, but with as much in place as possible at this stage, they had come to carry on with the house. Bernie was working on a tricky bit of walling in what had been the holiday let, repairing where the now removed spiral staircase had damaged the wall, and so Fliss went out to see who it was. To her surprise a tall, rather haggard man got out of the cab, and it took her a moment to realise that it must be Edmund.

"Hello, Fliss," he said coming over and giving her a kiss on the cheek. "Looks like you've had as rough a time of it as I have."

She looked at the shadows under his eyes and the crows' feet at their corners and gave a wan smile. "Tell me about it! We're neither of us the kids we were the last time we met." She didn't want to say, 'I'd never have recognised you if I'd met you in the street', but then he was probably thinking the same about her.

Back then it had been Jonas who was the taller one of the two boys, but of course neither of them had hit twenty by then, and unlike girls, lads could still put on a growth spurt at that age. Certainly, Bernie was somewhere around five feet ten or eleven, but broad shouldered and chunkily built, whereas Margot had always been tall for a woman at nearly the same height, so it shouldn't have surprised her that Edmund was well over six feet. And it was hard to tell just how much he looked like Margot, not because of him, but because as a young woman Margot had been one of those women who wouldn't be seen dead without full make-up on. Later on, Fliss had only seen her a handful of times, and firstly Margot had piled on the weight as she'd started drinking heavily, then had become gaunt with sagging skin as she'd stopped eating but carried on drinking. So Fliss had no clear memory of what Margot should have been like if she'd been normally healthy as she got older to compare Edmund to.

The smile she got, however, was pure Bernie, and she immediately warmed to her younger cousin.

"Come on in," she said, linking her arms through his. "Let me introduce you to Sytchampton House."

As she walked him around the place, she could see the light coming back into his eyes. *This is going to be far more of the rescue package for you than it ever was for me,* she thought happily, as he admired the way that Bernie had repaired the plaster in the kitchen.

"That chimney breast is a beaut'," Edmund enthused. "I can see why Dad said it was crying out for an Aga. It'll fit perfectly. And I love that he's stripped it back to the bare bricks and just sealed them. They're lovely."

"Thanks, son," Bernie said gruffly as he wandered in behind them, but Fliss could see that he was as proud as punch over Edmund's praise.

"Tea or coffee, Edmund?" she asked, to give Bernie chance to recover from the surprise that Edmund would have come this soon.

"Oh, tea, please, and for heaven's sake, call me Ed. Everyone else does. Edmund sounds so bloody pretentious."

I must stop thinking that he and Jonas are two of a kind, Fliss thought as she dumped the teabags into the pot. She had been mentally going back to a point when she'd visited on what might have been something like Edmund's fifteenth birthday, and she had called Jonas 'Joe', assuming that was what all of his mates would call him. So she'd been utterly unprepared for the furious response of, "I'm Jo-*nas*! And he's Ed-*mund*! We're not some common kids from the local comp' you know!" And Fliss, who had been only too glad to have her name shortened, had been genuinely shocked by the teenage tantrum which had followed. But clearly that had been Jonas' take on the world, spurred on by his mother, and since then Edmund had tried to come out from his shadow.

"Ed it is, then," she replied, turning back to him with a brimming mug. "I hope you like it strong. Your dad takes it so strong you could stand the spoon up in it!"

"Love it," Ed declared, taking a sip of it and grinning at her. "You make a good cuppa, Fliss."

And so they took him around the house, but most interestingly for Fliss, as they passed through the recently opened doorway under the old stairs out of the original hall, Ed gave a shiver.

Bernie was enthusiastically saying, "And I think that when the front was first built the cellars were accessed by steps from the outside, not up ahead like now," so he didn't notice, but Fliss did.

"Bit of a creepy atmosphere there, isn't there?" Ed said to her, as she led the way with him right behind her.

"Isn't there just," she replied. "The detective who came out when we found the body thought the same thing, but oddly your dad doesn't feel a thing."

"What's that?" Bernie asked, coming into the hallway of the Queen Anne part behind them.

"Oh, I was just telling Ed about the detective liking the house," Fliss said with a covert wink to Ed, who took the hint and said no more on the subject.

Or at least he didn't until they got up to the top floor. Like Fliss he clearly felt something as he went up the last three steps to get to both the view down through the void of the main stairs, and the two topmost bedrooms. Right on cue he shivered, and he and Fliss again exchanged glances. Yes, like her, Ed obviously sensed the portals, so what remained to be seen was whether he saw anything. While she was in the bedroom where she had contacted Quill, Fliss was very careful not to touch either of the wardrobes.

There was only so much she could expect Ed to deal with all in one go, particularly as he'd been under so much stress already, but he too was drawn to the painted wardrobe, and as he lovingly touched the wood, for one brief moment Fliss could have sworn she felt the tell-tale start of the room spinning. For him it didn't last, but she saw him looking hard at his fingers as he moved away, having clearly felt the same kind of tingling that she got. But for her that was encouraging, because even if the pull wasn't as strong for him, it meant that potentially he could connect with her once she was on the other side.

However, Ed was now complimenting them on the colours they had chosen for the bedrooms, and was enthusiastic about coming to help.

"When can you start?" Bernie asked cautiously, and was as surprised as Fliss when he answered,

"Right away!" Then seeing their shock, explained, "I went into the office really early this morning and emptied my desk out. I had this gut feeling that me and Jonas in the same space wasn't going to work anymore given what got said yesterday, and after all these years I know what a spiteful shit he can be when he feels someone's against him. It was a good job I did too, because he was in earlier than normal, and the face on him when he saw I was there…!" Ed grimaced. "Jeez! It was like he'd barely paused for breath from last night! He just went for me. And when he picked up a paperweight and threw the bloody thing at me, I just walked out."

He winced again. "The bloody yard was full of the blokes getting ready to start work, and they all heard him, so I told them, 'He's the boss from now on. Sorry lads, but I've had enough.' How many of them will still be working for him by tonight is something else, because I've done an awful lot of soothing ruffled feathers over the years."

But then his face broke into a grin and he waved a hand in the direction of the truck. "I've got all my gear in the pick-up. Even dug my old overalls out last night, though I must have been a fat little piggy the last time I wore them, because they hang off me now. Just tell me where you want me to start, Dad, and I'll roll my sleeves up and get stuck in. It's not like there's anything else I can do right now. I've made all the phone calls, and heard that you'd been there only minutes before with the same requests, so our solicitors have decided that since two of the three original owners are singing the same song, they'll represent us, and Jonas will have to find someone else."

"Can they do that?" Fliss wondered.

"Seems so," Ed said with a shrug. "I don't think they'd have offered if they couldn't. And by the time I'd told them my sorry tale, they advised that it would probably be best if I stayed well away from the yard now, because that averts Jonas being able to make any claims that I've been undermining him with the lads, or ruining his reputation by talking to our customers when they ring up. So if I'm not there, I sure as hell don't want to be sitting in my cubbyhole of an office back at the house, with Sal walking round with a face like thunder, because just when she says I'm never there, she's suddenly tripping over me. Rather undermines her case, you see, and I want us to still be friends, not have her thinking that I've been absent because I wanted to be, and then coming around when I think I'm going to be losing everything."

Fliss could sympathise with what he was saying. "I've had enough colleagues go through divorces to know you're not wrong in thinking that, Ed. Better to let things cool down there as well, not rub the metaphorical salt into the wound."

They could both see that Bernie was thinking that it was a strange world out there these days, but he didn't question their comments, instead asking Ed what he thought of the tiles he'd picked for the new bathroom up on the top floor.

"Love 'em, Dad!" was Ed's response. "When are they going on?"

"After the new Velux windows go in, which with a bit of luck should be at the end of this week. After that I can tidy up the plaster on the ceiling and skim the walls at the same time," showing Ed the elegant new light fittings which would be on the wall, and where Phil had had to chase out the old plaster to wire them in, "and then once that's properly dry, they can go on."

"Dad, this place is going to look amazing!"

"And we have a bit of a cunning plan about that, too," Fliss confessed, and told him about their thoughts on buying Mrs Davenport out, minus what she owed them for the work if she couldn't pay – which was almost a certainty by now. But then adding, "So with this much space, I think there'll be plenty of room for you here. I was never going to need that much room, so it makes so much more sense for you to come here too, not be living in some bloody awful bedsit."

The word 'bedsit' made Bernie start. He'd looked shocked at Fliss making the offer so fast, but she instantly saw that he'd not really understood just how bad it could get for Ed once he had to start paying alimony, and how little there'd be left for him. Ed himself came and drew her into a tight hug, too choked for words, but seeing his reaction confirmed to Bernie that that was exactly what had been about to happen.

"You're not going into some bloody *bedsit*!" he declared gruffly. "Bloody hell, Ed! You never said things were that bad!"

"Didn't want to worry you," Ed confessed. "Bad enough that I've balls-ed up my marriage because I didn't stand up to my brother sooner. But I've still got some shreds of my self-respect left to not want to come running to you, and expecting you to put things right like when we were little."

It was the right thing to say to Bernie, that Fliss could see, but although he nodded in approval of his son wanting to be enough of a man to stand on his own two feet, she could see that he was also enough of a proper father to want to have spared Ed that.

"You can go and get your stuff and come back to mine," he announced. "It's got three double bedrooms, for heaven's sake! And Fliss' stuff is in the little cupboard room that used to be the third bedroom before I extended the place, but there's not that much of hers that we won't be able to fit yours in too."

"Just don't expect miracles in the kitchen department," Fliss said with a grin. "I seem to remember Sally being a very good cook, but I'm not."

"Anything that makes a change from cold shoulder and tongue pie is good with me," Ed quipped back, and so it was in jovial mood that they made their way back down the stairs, this time stopping at the other bathroom and showing Ed the confession in the old plaster.

Before Fliss could protest, Bernie had the floorboards back up and was showing Ed the top of the old stairs, and she could only be grateful that like her, Ed was far from eager to set foot on them. However, the bigger problem for Fliss now was not revealing what she knew of the body from her conversation with Quill. She had just been about to launch into telling Ed that the man's name had been Henri Dupont, and that he'd come here to find his wife, when she had to fake a coughing fit to cover her half spoken first words. How the hell could she explain how she knew?

"Dust in my throat," she spluttered as Ed turned to look at her enquiringly, hoping that her pleading looks would be understood, and that he'd not question her further. Thankfully she saw him give another shiver, and then he said,

"It's probably a good thing that the top of those stairs will be hidden by whatever floor covering you put in in here."

"Really?" Bernie said, but too busy putting the boards back to look up at Ed, who now had to cover his own discomfort by saying,

"Well, they're awfully narrow, aren't they? The treads, I mean. Given modern shoe sizes, they aren't very deep, are they? Not like for folks from when it was built, so not the safest of stairs to use nowadays. Better to keep them as a decoration in the hall like you said," then pulled a face at Fliss that said, 'I hope I got away with that'.

"I suppose so," Bernie admitted, "but the oak is a lovely colour, and I'm sure they're still sound, despite all that earth some twit chucked down on them."

And again, Fliss had to bite her lip not to contradict him, because Quill had been far from a 'twit', and under serious coercion.

"I'd love to see how you mend that wall," Ed said, gesturing at the top of the doorway where the confession was, and steering the conversation away from dangerous ground and back to the restoration. "I don't suppose that's historically important enough to warrant putting a perspex screen over it, like they do in some of the National Trust places when they've found something interesting underneath?"

"I doubt it," Bernie said, standing up and squinting up at the plaster over the doorway. "I can always ring that archaeologist lady, though, and check."

As he led the way out and through to the older part of the house, Ed said softly to Fliss, "There are some weird atmospheres in this house, aren't there? And even odder that it's only in specific patches. I've been in some old places in my time, and if they have a creepy atmosphere, it's usually all-pervasive, or at least only a bit stronger in patches. I've never come across a place like this, where it's all warm and welcoming, and then suddenly you get such a sharp cold spot."

"Oh, Ed," Fliss sighed, "when you're a bit more settled I've got so much more to tell you, and even so, I'm not sure that you'll believe me. But if you've picked up on the odd bits yourself, that's more than your dad ever has, so hopefully you might not think me ready for the straightjacket yet."

Lucretia 1815-16

Over the course of the year, Lucretia saw the ghostly woman a handful of times. Most of the time she was dressed in the strange blue outfit that had trousers and a bib front, but twice she was in more colourful clothes, though equally as strange. By Lucretia's standards she was scarcely dressed, yet at the same time Lucretia never got the sense that she was improperly clothed. If she was trying to seduce someone, as Mamma eternally did, then she must be failing miserably, because there was no bosom on display at all. The only bare part of her was her arms, and twice those seemed to be liberally splattered with what looked like distemper. No, whoever this ghostly woman was, Lucretia had the strong sense that she was working, not courting, and that made her like her all the more.

"Look at me!" she pleaded, as she sat by the window of the top floor room on a chilly but bright spring day. "Please, come and talk to me. Come and join me. I want to be your friend!"

But the ghost never spoke to her.

The most recent time she saw her, Lucretia thought that the ghost was talking to someone else in the room. Certainly, she seemed quite animated compared to previous times, and her lips were moving even if Lucretia couldn't make out the words.

And then only days later she overheard Uncle Quill telling Martha to come and fetch him instantly if she felt something peculiar up in what Lucretia thought of as her sanctuary, even though Quill had made it into Nilmani's bedroom after Ishwar had died. Indeed it had been coming up here to tidy this room, which had been used as the boy's play room when poor little Ishwar had still been alive, that had resulted in Lucretia seeing the ghost on the second time. And now she wanted to talk to the ghost as much about Ishwar as she did about little Felicity.

The way Ishwar had sickened and died had frightened Lucretia and Drusilla. They had tried bringing him in wild strawberries and raspberries from the hedgerows as treats during the summer, hoping to cheer him up and find something that he liked to eat. But although he ate them, there was no joy in it. All he did was cling longingly to his carved toys and speak to his brother in that strange language of theirs.

He doesn't want to be here any more than I do, Lucretia had often thought sadly. *He would rather die and be with his mamma and sisters than be here with us, and I can't blame him. Who would want to live in this mad house?*

She could not console him, she realised, but it did prompt her to be as kind to him as she could be. There was little money to spare, and she got none of what there was, so she could hardly buy him treats from the village, even if she had dared venture there. Yet things had improved late in the autumn of 1814, for Uncle Quill gave up the job in Bristol and came home to stay. Proper servants had arrived, though they did not sleep in, and a kind of order had established itself over the household.

That had increased the arguments between Uncle Quill and Mamma, though, especially as Grandfather had begun to fail as another autumn had come around. Neither Lucretia or Drusilla shed a single tear when the old man finally died, but both confessed to a terrible fear that his ghost would be haunting them now.

"He won't let go," Drusilla had said, as they both sat by little Ishwar's bed, trying to coax him into eating a little rice pudding to settle his stomach. "That evil old man will be with us for as long as we live here. Why doesn't Uncle Quill sell this cursed place now, and take us to live somewhere else?"

"Who would want this place?" was Lucretia's response. "With the reputation it's got, would you risk buying it and moving in? Anyone respectable would be scared stiff they might be tarnished just by the address. No, 'Silla, he won't get anyone to buy this heap. Certainly not at a price that would allow him to buy something similar, anyway. All we can hope is that he gets the rector in to cleanse the place of the old villain's spirit."

"I have incense," Nilmani had confessed. "Only a tiny bit. I found it in one of the trunks Papa brought back with us. We could light it just in here. That might keep the *chhaaya* away."

"Is a *chhaaya* a ghost?" Drusilla asked.

Nilmani wrinkled his nose in thought and tried to explain, "*Kaalee chhaaya* is a …a spectre, I think you call it? A bad ghost. Not quite a *raakshas* …a demon, a devil, but still very bad. I remember my family lighting the incense to keep the *chhaaya* away …I think."

He didn't sound overly sure, but Lucretia and Drusilla thought it worth a try anyway.

"We'd best do it in the fireplace," Drusilla had decided once it had become clear that they would need to burn something to get the incense to work. It had taken a bit of questioning before they realised that what they needed was charcoal, and then finding some of that had proven harder than expected, so in the end they made do with some half-burned coal from the hall fireplace. It had smoked badly when Nilmani first put the incense on, but both girls decided that once you got used to it, the smell wasn't unpleasant. Certainly, the smell of it did more to cheer Ishwar up than anything else they had done, and though Uncle Quill had come storming up the stairs demanding to know what on earth was going on, when Lucretia pointed to Ishwar's smile, Uncle Quill had choked up and gone silent.

Whether the incense had worked or Cuthbert Spink had been taken to his maker never to return, there was no hint of him haunting the house over the following months. Much sadder was Ishwar's sudden decline and death only weeks later. Nilmani was inconsolable, and while Drusilla did all she could to comfort him, for Lucretia it was all too much. This endless cycle of people sickening, or going mad, and dying in this house was crushing her spirit. Some days she felt as if they were sealed in their own private bubble of Hell on earth. Other people in the outside world went on with their daily lives never knowing what went on here, or that there were three young people caged in this terrible place.

And that feeling of being trapped had changed Lucretia's feelings about Uncle Quill. From hero he had gone to seeming like her gaoler. He never took her or Drusilla anywhere, even though sometimes he took Nilmani in the recently acquire horse and trap which he drove expertly. That he would not want Mamma seen abroad with him she quite understood, for these days Mamma was a terrible sight to behold, even when she was silent and not raving. But she and Drusilla had done nothing to be so confined.

"Does he blame us for Ishwar's death, do you think?" Drusilla asked her one day, as they shivered up on the top floor, not wanting to go downstairs when Mamma was home alone down there with Selina.

"I don't know," Lucretia answered, so downcast that these days she worried Drusilla almost as much as Nilmani did.

"I think we need to run away," Drusilla decided. "You'll be seventeen at the end of the year, and I'll be fifteen in the summer. We're old enough to get some kind of work, surely? Not everyone must get an apprenticeship or a job in a big house. I think I'd rather pick peas in the field than live like this for the rest of my life. I want to have friends. I want to run in the sunshine and laugh with other people. Not be stuck here. Could we find our way to Tom and Meg, and ask them for help? We know the name of the big house they work for. It can't be that hard to ask the way. And that way you could see Felicity again. You couldn't say she's yours, but I'm sure Meg would let you cuddle her for a bit."

Yet Lucretia shook her head. "I think that would be worse than never seeing her again. It's so hard, 'Silla. Right now, although I know she must have grown, she's still the little baby I held for such a short while. But if I see her, she becomes a real little girl again for me. A proper person like you! And that means I'd miss her even worse when I had to walk away."

Drusilla sighed, reluctantly understanding what her sister meant. "Then could we ask the ghost for her help?" she suddenly wondered. "That's who Uncle Quill was talking to, you know. I heard him telling Martha about it, and her telling him that many years ago Grandfather was visited by a ghost who warned him to change his ways or it would all go bad. Well he didn't and it did, didn't it? So she must know stuff. Maybe she's even powerful enough to change things? Why don't we leave her a message?"

"But where? I tried calling out to her when I saw her, but she can't seem to hear me."

"Uncle Quill told Martha that it's something to do with the carved wardrobe."

"Not the painted one?"

"No. I thought it would be that one too. All those strange people on it. You'd think that ghost would like that, wouldn't you? But no, Uncle Quill was very clear – it's the carved wardrobe you have to watch out for, and he said to be careful not to prick your finger on a splinter and get blood on it, because the ghost said that's how the window, or whatever it is, between her world and ours gets opened.

"So why don't you and I write her a letter, and then go and put it in the wardrobe and jab our fingers with a hatpin or something? If we both do it, that ought to be double the power, shouldn't it? And if we tell the ghost about Felicity, maybe she can go and find her for you."

Lucretia smiled at her sister's enthusiasm, but asked. "And what good will that do? The ghost can't whisk my baby back here, can she? And I wouldn't want her to."

"No," Drusilla admitted, "but she might have some magic way to let you see her. Through another one of those special magic windows, perhaps? Or even if she can go and see her and come back and tell you she'd alright, that would cheer you up, wouldn't it? And maybe she could even help us find a way out of here? A ghost that clever ought to be able to come up with something, surely?"

"Alright," Lucretia agreed. "We write the ghost a letter and we tell her everything. But we're going to have to be very careful. I think Uncle Quill hates us enough to try and stop us if he finds out. He's like all the other men at heart," she added bitterly, "he only cares about what he can own and control, and we're not his so he doesn't care. He'd rather we were gone."

"Then if the ghost can help us," Drusilla said firmly, "he might just get his wish in a way he doesn't expect!"

Chapter 28

Monday

Mercifully, once they'd passed through to the old house again, there were no more awkward moments, and the three of them got into a discussion about the possibility of putting wallpaper onto one wall of each of the three oldest bedrooms. The two which were over the big old kitchen, where Lucretia and Drusilla had once slept, had partially sloping ceilings on the house end-walls, and those would stay as they were to show off the lovely old beams and in-fills. But the wall between them was plain plaster beyond the tiny chimney breasts, as were the ones to the hallway, and now Ed suggested,

"They're only small areas, so you could put a really nice paper onto them. The company you're getting the distemper from for in here also does wallpaper based on original period papers. It's hideously expensive if you were thinking of papering one of the big, tall-ceilinged front rooms, for instance – especially when you've got to keep an eye on the cost now that Mrs D has done the dirty on you – but in here it would only take a roll or two. I think it would really set the character of these rooms off a treat."

"Ooh! Those are the ones I saw and liked!" Fliss exclaimed. "Oh yes, they would look so good in here!"

And so by the time they were heading back into the kitchen for some lunch they were well into discussing the house in this era, for which Fliss was relieved. However, at the back of her mind was always how she was going to try and get to talk to Quill later on. Was there some way she could leave Ed and Bernie talking and slip away? Maybe if she dropped the hint to Ed that there was something she needed to do on her own, which she would explain later on, he might keep Bernie distracted? Going on the previous times, she wouldn't need long in the here and now to have quite a long conversation with Quill, so she could reasonably say she'd only be gone for ten minutes or so.

Her chance came later on that afternoon. Bernie had created one of his special mixes of plaster, and was about to show Ed how he was going to patch over the confession in the wall without destroying it, and it gave Fliss the chance to say,

"Bernie, much as I love learning from you, this is more of a master class for Ed than for a beginner like me, so I'm going to leave you two to it. I'll be back in a bit to see how you're getting on."

And so with Ed already asking intelligent questions of his dad of the kind that were way over Fliss' head, Bernie just vaguely nodded and got back to answering Ed. *This is so good for both of you*, Fliss thought happily. *This time around you want to learn, Ed, and this is what you always hoped your future would be like, Bernie. I'm so pleased for both of you. You don't need me here, but there's someone who does*, because once again there was that overwhelming feeling that she had to go back. And so with that, she jabbed the hatpin into her thumb, squeaked in pain, but still smeared the blood onto the wardrobe.

"Quill?" she called urgently the moment the room started its now familiar swirling. "Quill? Can you hear me?"

Oh God, what was she going to do if he wasn't there? What if it was longer than she'd thought between speaking? Or maybe it was the wrong time of day? She hadn't thought of that. It was considerably later right now than when she'd spoken to him yesterday, so was it night time for him? Or was it the early morning when he was up, and out and about, busy with the stuff he must need to do to keep the estate running? *Oh Fliss, why must you be such a fluff-head?* she chastised herself. *Why didn't you ask him what the time was when you were talking to him? It might have given you a better idea of when he'd be around.*

She couldn't hang around here all day either, or Bernie would come looking, wondering whether she'd tripped and broken her neck somewhere, because God alone knew, she'd given him enough reasons to think that over the last week or so. Compared to Ed, she was a one-woman disaster zone! And just when she was about to give up and go away, berating herself for being a total idiot, she heard someone coming pounding up the stairs with someone further down below calling,

"I done feel it, master, like as you said, like ants crawlin' on my skin. I come as soon as I felt it, just like you sez."

"Miss Fliss?" she heard Quill calling her name. "Is that you?"

"It's me, Quill, it's me!" she called back as loud as she dared, and more than a little frightened at the way her pulse began to race at the sound of his voice. Was she being a complete and utter fool? Totally delusional? Fooling herself that this man some two centuries in the past might feel anything like the turmoil of feelings towards her that she felt for him?

That was soon answered as Quill came into sight, and far from stopping, hurried forward to plant his hand firmly on the wardrobe door. Putting her own hand up to his, Fliss felt the warmth of him again, but was totally unprepared for what happened next. As their hands met palm to palm, it was Quill who curled his fingers forward to interlace with hers, both of them jumping slightly as once again they realised how very solid they each felt to one another. His face broke into a startled grin, and Fliss knew that she was grinning like an idiot too.

Ever so gently, he drew her hand towards him, and suddenly Fliss felt a draft on it that had nothing to do with her own time.

"Oh my God!" she gasped softly, feeling the thrill of both his touch, and of knowing that it looked as though she really would be able to step into his world. Her whole arm up to the elbow was now in Quill's time, not just the hand holding his. Then sanity crept in, and as they shifted to releasing one another's hands, she asked urgently, "What time is it for you?"

"I beg your pardon?"

"What time of day is it? I never thought to ask you what the time was when I was talking to you before, and then when I came to try and contact you again, I had no idea whether it would be in the middle of the day or the night for you. No idea whether I ought to expect you to be around, you see?"

"Oh! …It's around three in the afternoon, I believe."

"Really? That's great, because it's about that for me too! *Phew!* I was having a right panic for a moment there!"

He laughed. "I would not like to think I had reduced you to panic, Miss Fliss."

"Oh, not *you*! I was blaming myself for not thinking clearer. And how long has it been since you saw me last? For me it was only yesterday."

"Really? Oh, then I must tell you that it has been five days for me."

"Right, so we really need to try and keep a track of this difference between us. I should tell you that there's very little chance of me appearing to you after about seven in the evening, or before around nine in the morning. That's because we aren't actually sleeping here at the house, and have to travel to get here every day. So please don't sit up expecting me in the middle of the night, for instance, because I don't think that will happen even if we're an hour or two adrift."

"Ah, that is good to know. I was most worried that you might try to speak to me when I was not here."

"Me, too! …Oh, and what was the crisis that called you away the last time?"

Quill winced. "Ah …that was Marie."

"Oh, no! What did she do?"

His eyes closed and he inhaled sharply. "She has what you might call a taste for brandy."

"Oh, Lord, pissed as a rat, eh?"

His eyes flew open, and then he guffawed. "Good heavens, Miss Fliss, that is a little explicit …but in essence, yes. Rather more worryingly, Martha found her in the morning room on her hands and knees, with the chair pushed to one side and trying to lift the rug. She was raving about needing to get the stains out."

"Oh, heck!"

"Indeed. You and I know what stains she was referring to, but luckily Martha has only come to the house within my time as master, and so she has no idea what it was about. She took it as a slight on her housekeeping, but equally knows that Marie is frequently not sober by the afternoon, and so thought that was all it was."

"You really need to get her out of the house before she gives more away," Fliss said firmly. "It's gone beyond where you could hope to brush off anything she might let slip if she gives someone chapter and verse on what happened."

"I thought the very same," Quill agreed, "and so a couple of days after we spoke, I went and met with the master of the hospital." Fliss knew that 'hospital' in his time probably meant an add-on to the workhouse, not the kind of facility that she would associate with the name. "I explained the situation in terms of my late brother having brought a most inappropriate woman into our household. I had already spoken to the master of the Hallow workhouse, and he was most reluctant to have her, but then he does have a large number of poor folk to find places for. So it had to be the largest one in Worcester.

"My goodness, Miss Fliss, you were so very right to tell me that her reputation had gone before her. Even at that distance, the man knew exactly who I was talking about. Moreover, he was most sympathetic to my plight when I said that I did not want her shocking influence abroad in the house with my young son there. Even though he no doubt thinks Nilmani some quite exotic creature, and not quite as an English boy, he still saw Marie's influence as potentially toxic, and not only to my son but to the servants too."

"That has to be a relief, surely?"

"In a strange way, yes, it is. We packed her bags and I took her there yesterday. There was much screaming and clawing from Selina. She called me many foul names, but then Marie turned on Lucretia, who along with Drusilla was far quieter than I'd expected. In her madness she thought her almost grown-up daughter another woman vying for my attentions, you see, and it was all we could do to hold her back. I truly believe that in some strange way, the two oldest girls will be glad their mother is gone."

"I know Lucretia can't be a pleasant girl to have about the place, but I can't help but feel sorry for her in that instance. It must have been a nasty shock."

"It was, and I think for the first time it sank in just how deranged their mother has become. Certainly, the place has been much calmer since Marie has been gone. I spoke to both her and Drusilla when I returned from taking Marie away, and put it to them that I was making arrangements for them to leave as well, but that in their cases I wanted them to be able to have a fresh start without the taint of their mother's insanity following them around."

"And how did they take that?"

"Rather better than I expected, to be honest. I didn't tell them that they would be going to separate places. That is a conversation for later on, and much will depend on how they behave in the coming days. Under the pretext of spring cleaning the place, I ordered Martha and Mary to move both girls into the empty top bedroom at the front. Neither girl was happy about it, but I told them that it was only for a night or so until their rooms could be properly washed and aired. It gave me time to go through all of their things, you see."

His expression became grave again. "I prayed that you would come soon, because this morning I found arsenic in paper wrappers in Lucretia's bedroom. There is no possible reason for her to have such a thing if your suspicions about her were not correct. We send for it when needed to deal with any rats or mice which find their ways inside, and of course they tend to make for the pantry and the kitchen, where there is plenty to eat, not up in the girls' rooms." His eyes filled as he sighed, "My poor Ishwar."

Fliss wished she dared step through to his time and hug him. "You couldn't have possibly known, Quill, it's not your fault."

"I'm his father – surely I should have been able to protect him?"

"I think you'd be hard pressed to find another man who had to deal with both a murderous sister-in-law and her murdering daughter or daughters!" She wouldn't call Marie-Janneton Quill's wife, not under any circumstances. That had been the woman he had loved and lost in India, not the one who had blackmailed him. "Can you seriously tell me that any of the many men you must have known down the years would think to check for one child trying to kill another under the same roof?"

Quill sucked in a deep, steadying breath. "No, that is very true. Even if I had woken up to what was wrong with Ishwar in time, I would have still laid the blame at Marie's feet."

"And for once her protestations of innocence would have been perfectly true."

He blinked in surprise. "I had not thought of it quite like that, but you make a good point. I would have been thrown by her insistence of innocence, for by now I know when she is being sly and trying to throw me off the scent."

"There you are, then," Fliss said soothingly, "stop blaming yourself. The only way you could have anticipated any of this would have been if you'd been as warped in your thinking as they were – and you're not! I've had the benefit of a considerable distance in time to look at it from, not being caught up in it myself, and that made all the difference as to how I saw things. You're far from mad, and so there was never going to be a way that you would think things through in the same sequence that even they did. …Do you have any ideas as yet where you're going to send the girls?"

"Doctor Fishlock is going to get some recommendations for me."

"Would I be right in guessing that Doctor Fishlock is the man in charge of where you left Marie?"

"Oh, of course, his name would mean nothing to you. Yes, Doctor Fishlock is in charge of the hospital side of the workhouse, and his interests lean towards possible cures for insanity." Quill winced. "However, I think he is enough of a man of the world to know exactly what the source of Marie's insanity is, particularly as he was most tactful, but insistent on knowing whether she had thrust herself upon me as she has done with other men of the area. When I assured him that nothing in this world would persuade me into her bed, he was most relieved. He did not name names, but it seems that more than one or two gentlemen are showing signs of having the same complaint, and with Marie as the common suspect."

"I just hope they haven't given it to their poor unsuspecting wives."

Quill thought for a moment, but then shook his head. "If they are the men I think they may be, then I suspect that the very reason they were such easy catches for Marie was because their wives have made it clear that, having supplied them with heirs many a long year ago, that they have no desire to be intimate in any way with them."

"Hmm. Ladies we would describe as 'old dragons', maybe?"

Quill snorted with laughter. "Oh, most definitely 'old dragons' in a couple of cases!" he chuckled. "Though not so much in others, who are just weary of being with a husband they never wanted to marry in the first place, but had to because their parents arranged it. Before I went to India, I would have accepted such arrangements without question. But having had my own dear wife… Let's just say I have a different perspective on things now. But in answer to your earlier question, he hopes to have a few names of places for the girls for me by the time we meet again at church."

That made Fliss ask another question. "Is it Monday for you, too?"

"No, Friday."

"Oh!" That might complicate things. "I'll start making a note of days and times, then, because I don't think we're fully in step with one another, even allowing for one day in my time being about four in yours. So do you go to church in the morning on Sundays or in the evening?" She had no idea whether it was the custom to attend morning service and evensong back then, so it was relief that she heard Quill answer,

"Just in the mornings. That's when most people go, though the deeply devout go in the evening as well."

"Okay, then I'll steer clear of trying to contact you in the mornings, just in case I happen to hit a Sunday."

There was a lingering silence, neither of them having anything immediately to ad, and yet neither of them wanting to let go, either. Yet within moments there came the sound of running feet on the stairs, but someone much lighter and nimbler than the servants.

"Papa!" a youthful voice called and then Nilmani came charging into the bedroom. "Look what I found!" he exclaimed, holding up a very bemused slowworm. "A snake!"

"It's not a snake like we had in India," Quill explained with amusement, "and I think he'd be better going back out into the garden. Martha might scream rather a lot if she finds it in here."

"But can't I keep him, Papa? I'll look after him and feed him."

Fliss very gently spoke up, "He needs to be outside in the cool, sweetheart. He's not like your Indian snakes who can cope with the warm."

Nilmani spun to face the wardrobe, his eyes becoming even rounder. "The angel!" he squeaked. "You came back!"

"Yes, I found a way to come back," Fliss replied, knowing that her smile couldn't have got any wider. "I'm so sorry that I couldn't help you and Ishwar before now."

"Ishwar died," he said, his face falling into a sad expression.

"I know, sweetheart. You father and I have been talking about that." And suddenly Fliss saw a way to help Quill. "Nilmani, I know you tried to run away, but will you believe me if I tell you something?"

He looked up curiously, but nodded.

"Your papa is telling you the truth when he says that your brother and sisters have died. Like Ishwar, you can't see them anymore because they're no longer here."

His lips wobbled and he asked, "And Amma, too?"

Fliss risked a covert glance to Quill and saw him give a fractional nod. "And Amma, too. I'm so sorry, sweetheart. What made them sick is a terrible thing, and the reason you couldn't go and see their funeral was because it had to be done very quickly. The disease spreads so very fast that the people around your mother and family had no choice but to do it straightaway. They dared not wait even for your father to get there, much less for him to bring you as well. He brought you here to England because there truly was nobody he could leave you with anymore. If there had, he would have just come back here for a visit, and then returned home to India to you all. But even for him, that wasn't a choice he had left."

She saw Nilmani turn and look up at his father with his huge, pleading eyes, and when he saw Quill nod with the tears starting to fill his own, the little boy gave a huge sob, dropped the bemused slowworm, and threw himself into his father's arms. For a while all Nilmani did was sob, but Fliss saw the relief on Quill's face as the little boy said something in Bengali. Clearly Nilmani was accepting what he'd been told for the first time, and Quill silently mouthed, 'Thank you', to her.

As Nilmani's sobs gradually subsided, Fliss asked,

"Are you getting on any better at school?" and saw him immediately shake his head, even as Quill heaved a sigh and said,

"Unfortunately not."

Keeping the hand that was still in her own time hidden, and with her fingers crossed, Fliss dared to suggest, "If it turns out to be possible, would you like me to come and teach you?"

The way Nilmani instantly brightened up was enough to confirm that, but rather more importantly for Fliss, it was the way that Quill's eyes lit up too. With a hand firmly on Nilmani's shoulder, he brought the boy right up to the wardrobe's front, and then lifted his hand up inside his own so that Fliss could touch them both. The moment her hand touched theirs, Fliss felt a jolt like nothing she had ever known before, and it was all she could do not to launch herself through the portal to them. Just about managing to grab a hold of the edge of the wardrobe on her side, she leaned right through and pulled Nilmani to her as close as she dared, giving him a kiss on his cheek. Unlike the response she would expect from a modern lad of that age, he didn't pull away, or pull a face, though he did look a touch embarrassed. But what then surprised her was feeling Quill taking her hand and saying,

"Miss Fliss, I do believe you are the answer to both of our prayers!"

Drusilla 1816

Watching their mother being taken kicking and screaming to the wagon with its barred window and doors was both terrifying and liberating for Drusilla. Of all the things to happen, Uncle Quill committing Mamma to an asylum was the most unexpected, and yet almost instantly a strange kind of calm descended on the house of a kind that she and Lucretia had never known before. For the first time in their lives there was no Grandfather or Mamma reeling around drunkenly screaming, or batting away at things they alone could see, or fumbling at one another in perverse passion. Martha and Mary had stood by and watched the men come and take Mamma away, nodding in approval as she vanished off down the road, and even Walter had been seen to heave a sigh of relief. Yet somehow Drusilla couldn't help but feel that this was wrong. Her basic instinct was that you shouldn't feel this way about your own mother being locked up, however dreadful she might have been.

Rather more worrying were the thoughts which came to her that night, as she lay awake in her bed fretting about the future. What was going to happen to her and Lucretia now? And belatedly she realised that that also included Selina. Their strange little sister – now seven years old, and getting more like Mamma every day – was currently having one of her sickly phases, and spent more time in bed that out of it, but like them, she was nothing to do with Uncle Quill in reality. Only Nilmani was his, as he made perfectly clear in the way he treated them all. So what was going to happen to them?

Lucretia was so broken these days, Drusilla believed she didn't care what happened to herself anymore, and so it had fallen to Drusilla to do all the listening and information gathering that she could. The odd carefully put question to Martha the next day, who of all the servants seemed to be in Uncle Quill's confidence, had her shaking with fear again. A *governess* for them? What kind of dragon might Uncle Quill think suitable for that job? Because Martha had also implied that Uncle Quill thought it was high time that they learned to behave 'properly', whatever he thought *that* was.

Drusilla was horrified.

No, she and Lucretia were too old for governesses, surely, she thought, when she finally stopped panicking enough to think clearly about it. That was probably for Nilmani and Selina. But that equally didn't bode well for her and Lucretia, either. Where was he going to send them? Because it sounded very suspiciously as if he had every intention of clearing them all out of the house once and for all.

That suspicion was confirmed when Quill announced that he was moving both her and Lucretia to the spare bedroom on the top floor at the front. It was done with the excuse of giving their rooms a thorough clean out, and if Lucretia complied without question, incapable of caring any more, Drusilla immediately knew that there was something more behind it. So when they came to her with the papers of arsenic and asked her about them, although she could answer in all truth that she had no idea how they had got there, a chill spread through her soul. Where *had* that poison come from for it to be in her room? She hadn't put it there, and neither had Lucretia, but somebody had.

Was someone trying to implicate her and Lucretia in the death of Ishwar?

It couldn't be Grandfather's ghost, for whoever heard of a ghost being able to go out and buy stuff and then hide it?

Could it have been Mamma in her last raving days? But if so, how had she got hold of the arsenic? Then it came out later that day that Cook had ordered some months ago, but had thought it locked safely away. So again, who had managed to get hold of the keys and put it where the blame would fall on her and Lucretia?

It really frightened her. Especially as she had crept as silent as a mouse up to the top floor behind Uncle Quill, and had heard him telling the ghost about Mamma murdering her real husband. That had been this latest time, when there had been someone else with the ghost, a male ghost with a nice voice. And it had been to him that Uncle Quill had told all about what Mamma and Grandfather had done, though it sounded as if he had already told the lady ghost this not long ago. Both ghosts had sounded horrified, which at least was a relief, because these days Drusilla was finding that, like Lucretia, it was hard to decide who were the good people and who the bad.

Uncle Quill had seemed like their saviour when he arrived, but look at how he behaved now? So she wasn't about to trust the ghosts as blindly as Lucretia did. And with regard to Lucretia, she decided that it might be best to not tell her about the man buried in the staircase for now. Her sister was haunted by enough nightmares as it was. She didn't need to know that she was walking past a corpse every time she walked from the kitchen through to the front door. It gave Drusilla the shivers alright, but she had enough of a grasp on her sanity to realise that this had happened before either she or Lucretia had been born, and that therefore this was one misery which could not be laid at their feet.

But knowing now that Mamma had committed murder, it made her very worried the way Uncle Quill seemed to be looking strangely at her and Lucretia. Did he think that they had done the same to poor little Ishwar? And could he 'prove' anything to a court, even though she knew they were both innocent? Would he even go as far as making something up in order to get rid of them?

It's up to you now, she thought resolutely. *You've got to find a way to protect both you and Lucretia. Nobody else is going to do it for you. You have to tell someone the truth before the lies start coming.* And the only people she thought would believe her were the ghosts. Moreover, the ghosts might be the only people Uncle Quill would believe if they told him that she and Lucretia had done nothing wrong.

So she went into what was called the library – though there were few enough books in there in truth – which was where Uncle Quill had his big desk where he did all of his business. Luckily, Mamma had been prone to taking sheets of paper and scrawling wild letters in French to people who Drusilla had thought were figments of her imagination, but which she suddenly realised had probably been relatives of her Mamma's long ago and back in France. They had presumably all died years ago, because the letters never got sent, but for her it was helpful right now in that Uncle Quill was used to blank paper eternally going missing, and always seemed to have a spare ream or two on the one shelf, one of which had already been ripped carelessly open by Mamma in her last days here.

Taking a handful of the sheets, Drusilla decided that she would have to write in pencil. Getting a pen and inkwell away was just too risky, and she had never managed to learn to write without getting her fingers inky, which would be sure to have Uncle Quill asking questions if he spotted them. So she took a couple of the good pencils from Uncle Quill's desk and the little penknife he used for sharpening them. That would have to be returned as soon as possible, because what he would conclude if he found a knife in amongst her things she dreaded to think. He'd probably wonder if she was going to start stabbing people!

In her room up above the kitchen, she could hear Martha and Mary moving the furniture around, and was just about to go out into the hall when she heard Uncle Quill's heavy footsteps out there, and him saying affectionately,

"Come Nilmani, you can do your lessons in the library with me today."

Damn, damn, damn! she thought, making a mad dash for the deep doorway through into the old hall, only just getting into its shadow in time before Uncle Quill threw the hallway door open and strode in. She didn't fully close the door behind her, instead leaving it ajar, and ducking behind it to move into the arch of the doorway that doubled back to the hallway from the old hall. Luckily, Uncle Quill only came over to shut the old hall's door against the draft blowing through from the kitchen, allowing Drusilla to scurry out into the hallway and past the door he'd gone into the library by without being seen.

But where to go to write all this down where she wouldn't be found? Lucretia was lying down in the room next to Nilmani's, which they were sharing for now, and somehow Drusilla thought she would think clearer if she was alone.

The first-floor bedrooms weren't any good, because the oldest one was right next door to where Martha and Mary were working, and was where Selina was in bed. Of the two front ones, one was Uncle Quill's, which she definitely didn't want to get caught in, and the other the guest bedroom, which would be equally suspicious if she was discovered there, sitting on one of the dust sheets. And there was no way she was going into the room where she now knew that old staircase had come up into, when she knew the body of the Frenchman lay buried there. *It'll have to be the old store room at the top,* she though resignedly. The little window up there didn't let in much light, but if she perched on the chests stacked underneath it, she might just be able to see what she was doing.

Luckily it was a bright if slightly overcast day, so there was a decent amount of light coming into the storeroom. She had peeped around their bedroom door and been glad to see that Lucretia was asleep on the bed. If she had another of her nightmares, Drusilla was close enough to hear her calling out, and to go to her to wake her before the dire dreams left her a shaking mess again. But for now, she would be able to sit on the one chest and lean over to rest the paper on another to write.

But where to begin? That had been what had held her back so far, despite her and Lucretia having decided to try this. How much should she say?

In the end she decided that it would have to be the truth with nothing held back, however, scandalous it might sound, because without knowing about Felicity, how would the ghost understand that they couldn't have hurt Ishwar?

Dear ghost, she started. *We need your help*.

Chapter 29

Monday-Wednesday

By the time Fliss had broken away from Quill and Nilmani this time, there was no doubt in her mind that she would do everything she could to go to them permanently. Thankfully, as she tottered down the stairs on rather shaky legs, she could hear Ed and Bernie still talking technicalities in what would soon be another bathroom again, and so she carried on down to the kitchen and replenished the tea. How long would it be before she could go through, though? She didn't want it to be too long, but on the other hand, vanishing as soon as Ed had got here wasn't kind to either him or Bernie. And of course, there was the matter of signing off the money for her flat. That was due to happen this Friday, and the more Fliss thought about it, the more she was determined to hand that over to Bernie to be used to secure this house. She must find a way to bring that subject up with them both and soon.

Luckily, that opportunity came on the Wednesday when the documents for her to sign arrived by courier. She had already had another conversation with Quill on Tuesday, and had explained what she needed to do, meaning he was fully understanding of her delay, and so now she had to convince Ed and Bernie. Sitting them down in

Bernie's lounge, all of them having a stiff drink at the ready, she carefully began to tell them what had been going on. As she saw Bernie stiffen at the mention of the portals, she gently said,

"You know this happens, Bernie. You may not ever see or feel the portals yourself, but you weren't dreaming back when you came and grabbed hold of me in the old hall that day. And you were right the first time when you said that I faded. I didn't faint, I *faded*! I'd begun fading into another time."

She saw his growing distress and went to crouch in front of him, taking his hands in hers. "I don't fit in here anymore," she said gently, "And I don't mean here in your home. I know I'll always be welcome here. And if you aren't living here, then I know I will always have a home wherever you are.

"But it's what happens to me beyond this point that's the problem. The longer I've been away from that hectic office environment, the more I'm convinced that if I try to go back into it, it wouldn't be long before I crack again. The damage went too far and too deep to ever be just patched over again. But rather worse than that, I can't see me heading out into the dating scene, either. And before you protest that I've not given myself a chance to get fully back on my feet, I need to tell you that even before I'd left London, I'd acknowledged that I wasn't going to meet the man of my dreams in my daily life. So I'd signed up with various online dating agencies."

She shook her head, wincing at the memory. "What a disaster they all were! The clicks or 'likes' I got back on my profile were all the kinds of men I'd always have run a mile from – even the few I exchanged the odd emails with. And yet trawling the same sites for men who *I* would like to approach, I just couldn't find any who seemed to be my type, either."

"Like what, Fliss?" Ed asked, but clearly sympathetic to her problem. "What is your type, do you think?"

Fliss huffed and sat back on her heels. "Someone with good manners for a start off. You know, someone who is actually courteous, probably a bit old-fashioned, if I'm honest, and definitely somebody who is considerate by nature, not because they're trying to hoodwink you into trusting them." That had Bernie and Ed exchanging worried glances. What kind of people had Fliss met that would make her say that? But she was continuing, "Someone who is happy in their own skin, and content to sit down at night with a good book, or just going for a gentle walk in the countryside. I have no desire to go snowboarding down the Rockies, or snorkelling in the Red Sea, with some bloke who's having a mid-life crisis, and trying to recapture his lost youth. And oh my god, are there a lot of those out there!"

And Ed laughed. "Oh, I've heard enough of that from some of the guys I've worked with. They didn't get to do it when they were in their late teens or early twenties, so all of a sudden, they're trying to make up for what they think they lost out on."

"Exactly!" Fliss exclaimed, relieved that he, at least, understood. "But worse even than that, I can't seem to bring any focus to what I'm even going to do job-wise in the future." She leaned in and squeezed Bernie's hands again. "I have so loved doing this current house with you, but as we've gone on, I've realised that it's this particular house that's been the pull for me, not the job itself. I get that restoring old houses is your passion, Bernie, and you do it so well," and she turned to smile at her cousin.

"And Ed, you've got that same drive, too, I could see it in your eyes the moment you started helping your dad. It was like the lights came on inside you – it was great to see. And that's how it should be. But for me, another project would just have me going through the motions. I have no idea why or how, but I think I was meant to come to *this* house at *this* time in my life, and it's because there's something for me there that I'm not going to get elsewhere."

It took a lot longer, and a lot more trying to explain before Bernie finally relented a little, and that was largely due to Ed. With a covert wink to Fliss, he said to his father,

"Look at it this way, Dad. If a week back then is only a day in our time, Fliss could go through and be back within a few weeks if she doesn't feel it's right for her anymore. If she could lean right through and still come back again, there's nothing to say that she couldn't return, is there?"

Realising that the worst thing she could do would be to declare that she had no intention of ever coming back, Fliss forced herself to cheerily agree with Ed, and that seemed to be the turning point for Bernie. He ceased protesting so hard, and she soon tottered off to bed, worn out with all of the emotional wrangling. However, Bernie was surprised to see Ed making covert signals for them to hang back, and once the door to Fliss' bedroom had closed, said softly,

"Dad, we need to talk!"

"Damned right we do! What the hell are you playing at, encouraging her like that?"

"Outside!" Ed hissed softly. "We need to go out to the summerhouse. Somewhere where Fliss can't easily walk back in on us. There's stuff you don't know about, Dad, stuff you need to hear."

"What the hell?" Bernie was now baffled, but trudged in Ed's wake as he led the way out through the kitchen, pausing only to grab a couple of bottles of beer and open them, and went out into the garden. "Why didn't you say anything earlier?" he demanded, feeling faintly daft sneaking out into his own garden like some clumsy burglar.

Opening the door to the summerhouse to let Bernie through, Ed sighed as he followed him, answering him with, "I needed to make things right between us two first. I needed you to trust me on what I'm going to say."

Bernie stiffened and turned sharply to face Ed. "If you're about to start slagging Fliss off, I won't take it kindly. That poor girl has been through enough!"

"Dad …I know, okay? Please sit down and I'll fill in a big gap for you."

Reluctantly Bernie sat on one of the wicker chairs, but was surprised that once Ed flicked on the light, to see him sink into the other chair with a groan, wiping his free hand across his face almost as if bracing himself for another round of arguments.

"Ed? What's wrong?"

"Okay, it's like this – and before I start, I'm not saying this to paint Jonas in an even worse light, alright? I just think you really need to hear more about Fliss, and I can't tell you one without the other."

That had Bernie sitting up and starting to get worried. What else had Jonas done?

"About three years ago," Ed began, "Jonas decided that we needed to do some advertising. You don't need all the ins and outs of that. I'm sure you can guess that Jonas was bigging up the company in a way that you wouldn't have been so pleased about, and I'm sorry that it was done behind your back, because you were still involved if not controlling things. I tried to talk Jonas out of it, but he was already way past listening to me over much of anything.

"Well I suggested that we used Fliss' company. It seemed to me that that would be good damage control, because I thought Fliss would soon leap onto anything which might do our reputation harm, such as making promises we couldn't keep. So you can imagine how surprised I was when Jonas turned around to me and told me emphatically that they were no good. He had it on good authority from someone in the business, or so he said."

"Eh?"

"I know. I was shocked, too. Enough to not let it go at that. In fact, I kept badgering him about it, saying that I wouldn't sign off on this other company doing the work until *I* knew how *he* knew that Fliss' company wouldn't be able to do our job for us properly. Well, these days Jonas can't resist bragging, but by now I suppose you've caught on to that. And it turned out that he'd been going off down to London at the weekends, supposedly with the excuse of business trips to keep Chantal off his case, though I doubt she cares much one way or the other these days. But worse, his new woman on the side down there was some god-awful creature called Imogen, who worked for Fliss' company's main competitors."

"Oh God," Bernie groaned.

Ed gave a weary nod. "The exact words I used when he was telling me! Hardly an unbiased opinion, was it? But Imogen told Jonas that she knew Fliss –

or at least she'd met her in passing, being in the same line of work – and that Fliss was crap at her job."

"I don't think so!" Bernie protested, but Ed was already waving him down with one hand as he took a gulp from the bottle of beer in his other.

"I wasn't taken in, Dad, so don't think I'm about to go on a Fliss-bashing rant. The dreadful Imogen apparently always dresses in designer brands. Is always made-up to the nines, flashes her Jimmy Choos, and carts her Versace bag around with the logo visible. I guess you can paint a mental picture, because I certainly could. And Imogen was the one who had a right slagging session on Fliss, making her out to be this absolute frump who didn't fit into the advertising world and should never have been given the job. Her phrase, which Jonas repeated for days, being, 'how can she brand your product when she can't even brand herself?'"

Bernie was speechless.

"I know," Ed sighed. "And the worst of it is, Jonas never once defended Fliss, and that really annoyed me, so I started digging even harder then. I'm not proud of the fact that I started ferreting around in my cousin's life behind her back, and this is why I needed to make things right with you before I told you this, because I wanted you to understand that I did it because I was worried about her, not trying to drag her down even further if she was in trouble. The way things have been between us three, I didn't feel back then that I could come to you without making it even worse between us, but particularly between you and Jonas, and in fairness, I didn't think you could have told me what I needed to know anyway."

Bernie wasn't happy about that, but he was sensible enough to be able to understand Ed's position. In his place and at that point, he too would have been trying to keep everyone at least talking to one another.

"So what did you do?" he asked.

"Initially just asked Jonas a lot of random questions on those days when he was full of himself and chatty, and what I started hearing made me even more worried. I hate to tell you this, Dad, but last week wasn't the first time in ages that Uncle Graham and Jonas have talked. When his bloody woman started telling Jonas all this stuff, he only went and asked Uncle Graham if Fliss was as useless as Imogen said."

"Oh no! Poor Fliss! He's the last person who'd stand up for her, though God alone knows why."

Ed reached across and grasped his dad's hand. "You see now why I wanted to come out here. Your instant reaction was 'poor Fliss', and rightly too, but there's worse to come, and she'd be bound to hear us."

"Worse? Jeez, son, how much bloody worse?"

"Let's just say that when you next see Uncle Graham and land one on him, I'll be holding your coat for you and then taking my turn."

"Bloody hell!"

"Oh yes. Have you heard that he demanded that Fliss pay him back every penny he paid out for her while she was at university?"

"Yes, she told me that. I have to say that was pretty low."

"Not as low as charging her interest at two percent above the bank rates."

"*What!*"

"Apparently it was 'to teach her a lesson so that she won't come begging to me again!' That was what he told Jonas, and Jonas was laughing over it when he told me. Personally, I was practically sobbing inside for Fliss, but Jonas just carried on, laughing at Fliss for being such a 'fucking idiot' for paying up. He said that he admired Uncle Graham's business sense, and thought Fliss was stupid to have abided by it, but it was further proof of how useless she is. Then he told me that Uncle Graham had actually got Fliss to sign a contract with him set out by some solicitor friend of his just as she was going to uni, so Uncle Graham threatened to take her to the small claims court if she didn't pay on the strength of that."

"But she's his *daughter*!" Bernie exploded, proving Ed's need for them to be out of earshot of Fliss. "What evil bastard does that to his eighteen …nineteen-year-old daughter? At that age she wouldn't have been able to stand up to him – not when she was still living at home, anyway. And no doubt that pair of wicked misers charged her some extortionate rent for being there even before she left."

"I suspect that was the case, because I don't think Fliss had had much of a chance to save anything before she left. But can you see that if Fliss was living in London, paying London rents and subsequently a mortgage, and at the same time was having to pay her father back too, then there's no way on earth that she'd have been able to afford designer clothes and shoes. There's probably some element of truth in what dreadful Imogen said of her being a bit of an outsider amongst her colleagues, but not because she was hopeless, but just because she couldn't afford to join in the high-cost social scene they undoubtedly had."

"Oh, that's awful," Bernie choked, horrified at the way Fliss had been treated. "And bloody Graham must have tied her up legally pretty tightly, because I can't imagine that Fliss is such a doormat that she wouldn't have tried to free herself from that trap."

"I think she did, which may account for why she finally had her breakdown, because the strain must have been terrible. And maybe if she'd had man in her life, someone who could have supported her morally one hundred percent if not financially, then she might have found a way. …Which brings me to what's going on now. I didn't want to argue too hard with her this evening for one very simple reason: I don't think Fliss has ever had someone help her to do the things she wants to do, not up here or down in London. She's a great person, so I can't imagine that she didn't mix with the crowd down in London out of snobbery, or not wanting to, or because none of them liked what little they saw of her. It was because she couldn't go through the motions of keeping up with them, because for years, every spare penny she had that wasn't going on essential living costs was going back to her dad. But if she wasn't socialising, then she wasn't meeting anyone she might have got involved with romantically either. Dad, I don't think Fliss has had a boyfriend in years – probably not since she left uni."

"Now the internet dating makes sense!"

"It does, doesn't it!"

"I couldn't figure that out earlier. When she talks about her university days, that all sounds fairly normal…"

"…and it probably was, Dad! But the thing is, very few people keep close contact with folks from those times. People move away, get different jobs, get married, and within ten years your uni' mates are people you probably keep in touch with with

Christmas cards, and maybe a reunion once every half dozen years, if you're lucky. There's nothing abnormal in Fliss gradually losing touch with those friends, it's the absence of any new ones to take their place that worries me, and all the more so because of what's happening now. And the other thing she's said to me since we've met up again here, is that she never wanted to go into advertising in the first place, but it was the only job she could get where she could start paying Uncle Graham back as fast as he was demanding! So can you see what a bloody awful trap that whole life down there became?"

He took a deep breath. "I'm not going to pretend and say that I fully believe all that she's said about that house. I'll need a lot more convincing about that. But what I do know is that I too can feel a very strange atmosphere in certain parts of it, which I think is what Fliss has picked up on. What troubles me more is what's going on in her head. Dad, I think this man from the past – whether he's a total fantasy or some ghost she really can see – represents something way more to her than you're seeing. To her the past is safe. It's already been written, so she thinks she knows what she's going to. She can check up on people and places before she even sets a foot in there, so she believes that she's got more certainty there. And a man with a lonely child who needs a mum is about as strong a pull to her as it's ever going to get."

"But there are men in the here and now who have kids who need a mum!" Bernie protested. "Sean for one! I know he's helping his sister out after her divorce by letting her live with him for now, and that it gives him childcare for little Daisy while he's at work, but she needs a mum all of her own. Katie dying when Daisy was only three means she's never going to have much in the way of memories of her, and Fliss would be able to fill that gap."

"You old match-maker, you!" Ed teased, and Bernie had the good grace to laugh with him, but added,

"Those two would be good for one another, and Sean's interested – he's already asked me if she would go if he asked her out – he's just not sure if Fliss is, and he's been through enough himself to be wary."

"Dad, I think it's been so long for her that Fliss doesn't even recognise what a man's interest looks like anymore. That's why she's getting all tangled up the wrong way with this man in the past. She's had nobody she can trust for so long she's forgotten what it's like. But worse, she has the innate good sense to run a mile from any man who's an obvious flirt and womaniser, yet no longer recognises normal interest from someone like Sean."

He leaned back in the chair and huffed out a long breath. "But possibly even worse than that, I'm worried that she doesn't even trust herself anymore. This breakdown she's had has crushed what little self-confidence she had left, and again and because of that, someone in the past who she can fully check up on through the records makes her feels safer about trusting him. She's not daft. I'm sure she knows that her judgement is all over the place right now, and when she and I were talking about moving on and getting another job, I can tell you that she's fully clued up over how hard it's going to be for her to find something else, primarily because the jobs she has the experience for are the very ones she can't face returning to, and she's already past the age when most employers would take her on to retrain. So right here and now she sees herself as unemployable, undesirable, and incapable of making the changes she needs to improve any of those things.

"I think she's given up on herself, Dad. I think she's convinced that since there hasn't been a man in her life when she was young enough to have two or three kids, that there's never going to be. That she's already on the scrap heap before she's even reached forty, and with the way Uncle Graham and Aunt Constance emotionally crippled her before she left home, and then piled on the damage when she returned, her future looks utterly bleak."

Chapter 30

Wednesday night – Thursday

"No!" Bernie groaned. "No, she can't give up like that."

Yet Ed shook his head. "She doesn't even recognise that she *has* given up, Dad. And that's why this whole thing about going through time to someone whom she's created the perfect image of is such a pull for her. In *her* mind she *is* moving on in the only way that's left to her, going after the one thing she's always wanted. And *that's* why I didn't want to go against her too hard tonight. I wasn't trying to encourage her. I was just desperate for her not to think that just when she needs us to understand her, that we're going to do what everyone else has ever done, and turn our backs on her unless she dances to precisely our tune and nothing else."

"Christ Almighty!" Ed's words had shaken Bernie to the core. Even during the worst points in his own life, things had never seemed that bad, and he was having a hard time imagining what it would be like to feel so desolate. But on the other hand, he couldn't fault Ed's analysis, either. The revelations about what Graham and Constance Allcock had done to their own child, on the other hand, practically had steam coming out of his ears, he was that furious with them, and it endeared him to Ed even more that he'd said what he had about wanting to thump his uncle, because that was very high on Bernie's agenda of things to do to Graham in the near future right now.

In a surge of affection for his younger son, he reached across and squeezed his hand tightly, the cramped space in the summerhouse making it impossible for both of them to stand up so that he could hug him. But for the first time in a while, Bernie was really proud of Ed. Proud of him for his consideration and kindness, and for trying to do the right things in an almost impossible situation, because Bernie couldn't fault him for trying his best to mend fences with his own brother. Yet knowing all of this now meant that Bernie could foresee a prolonged period where neither of them would want to see much of Jonas – there was only so much betrayal you could stand by and let happen in a family before having to take sides, and it was clear that both of them were taking Fliss'.

"What do you think we should do then, son? You've seen things even more clearly than me, so I'll be guided by your intuition."

Ed's sigh was partly for Fliss, but also in relief that his dad wasn't arguing against him over this. "I think we need to say that we want to meet this man before she does anything. I mean, that sounds reasonable enough, doesn't it? We say exactly what we both feel, which is that we're worried to death about her, and want to make sure that she really is going to be okay. It signals that we're very much on her side while not seeming to shove her harder towards him, so hopefully we can create a bit of breathing space."

"Damned good idea!"

"I think we whole-heartedly support her idea to buy into Sytchampton House with the money from her flat, as well. If nothing else, it will mean that as a part-owner of a prestige property, she'll have a good credit rating even if she ultimately doesn't live with us for long. …Of course that's as long as once the job's done you feel we can do that and for Fliss to still be safe from this pull to the past, and unless Mrs D puts a bloody great spanner in the works, and we end up having to sell the place on after all!"

Bernie grunted. "The Davenports are a couple I'm wishing I'd never damned-well met! I've still heard nothing from either of them and I need to start paying some of the suppliers, even if Kev and Sean are being diamonds over when they get paid."

Ed smiled affectionately at his dad. "They trust you. They know you're good for it, and that you wouldn't be delaying apart from you being out of pocket with the Davenports." Then a thought occurred to him. "How soon is Sean due back to polish up that parquet floor? Can you get him back on any other pretext? Only if he is interested in Fliss, it might be no bad thing for him to spend some more time with her."

"Now who's the match-maker?" Bernie laughed. "But you're right, I think I'll give him a ring tomorrow before we leave and try and work something out. If I explain some of what you've said about Fliss having no faith in herself, and being so unused to anyone taking an interest in her, then he'll understand that the reason she hasn't responded to any of his hints isn't because she doesn't like him, but that she simply hasn't been aware of them."

"Do you think Fliss likes Sean enough?"

Bernie thought for a second. "I think she got on with him very well, and what you've told me tonight explains why she's not even looked twice at him. I don't think it's occurred to her to wonder if she should even go on a date with him. It's nothing to do with Sean, and everything to do with her."

"So let's agree that you'll call Sean, and we'll both offer to meet this man in the wardrobe, or wherever he is, to try and keep Fliss on an even keel."

And so it was on Thursday afternoon that all three of them went up to the top bedroom, Bernie doing his best to hide his incredulity, and Ed keeping Fliss talking about the way she could sense the portals opening. As Fliss jabbed her finger and smeared the blood onto the wood, however, Ed immediately went, '*Oooh*!', but Bernie looked at him perplexed.

"Can't you feel it, Dad? It's like prickly heat all over you!"

"Not a thing, son."

"Don't you feel the room spinning?" Fliss asked, already hanging onto the wardrobe.

"Nope, nothing."

However, Ed was looking faintly queasy, and muttered, "Bloody hell! It's like having motion sickness!" And he grabbed hold of his dad's arm to steady himself, making Bernie stare at him in shock, because there was no way that Ed was faking that faint, sickly green tinge to his face.

And then for Fliss and Ed the room changed and they were looking into the same room, but via the wardrobe's location and with Quill standing there waiting for her.

"Quill, this is my cousin Edmund, but you can call him Ed."

"Pleased to meet you," Quill responded, and with great care leaned forward so that his arm extended through to Ed with the hand held out.

As Ed reached out and grasped it, he and Fliss heard Bernie's, "Bloody hell!"

"My uncle," Fliss explained to Quill, who was looking quizzically at them both laughing. "He can't see through to you, but I think he just saw your ghostly hand coming out of thin air." She turned and looked at Bernie who could only nod.

Ed, however, had grasped Quill's hand in amazement, but now that the room had stopped spinning for him, like Fliss he was more fascinated than scared. So there followed a long conversation between Ed, Quill, and Fliss, with Bernie having to admit that either Fliss and Ed's imaginations were far more synchronised than ought to be possible, with them both responding to the same unspoken thing, or they really could see and hear someone that he couldn't. It was helped by Ed relaying questions and comments to him, and repeating his words back, because it turned out that Quill couldn't hear or see Bernie either.

By the time they broke off and the three of them went downstairs to pack up and go home, Bernie was far from happy, but in a way relieved that Fliss wasn't imagining the whole thing – which might have signalled a relapse in her mental health – despite there being a very real danger that she might be able to do what she had said she wanted to do. It was still a toss-up for him, though, whether it was worse that he was in danger of losing Fliss through time, or that she was cracking up again.

It would have heartened Bernie considerably to know that once they were back at his, Fliss herself was having serious worries over her decision. Taking herself off to bed early, she was praying for the weekend to come around because it would give her two whole days away from the house to get her thoughts straight. When she was there, all she could think of was to go back and be with Quill. Once she was back in Bernie's house, though, the way she was feeling positively dragged towards the past was starting to frighten her. Yet at the same time, she didn't want the only two people who believed in her to start thinking that she was so all over the place that she couldn't make basic decisions for herself.

Of course, in her heart of hearts she knew that neither Bernie nor Ed would ever try and control her the way her parents had. But having been through that meat-grinder of a childhood, where no choice of her own had ever been respected, there was still that ingrained sense of needing to do things her way or lose all sense of her own identity again. This time, though, there was a part of her that was wishing that one of them would stand up and say, 'no, you're not going for your own safety,' and the chances were that she wouldn't protest too hard. Or at least she recognised that she wouldn't if it was said here, but that if they did it at the house, then it might not be fully her who supplied the answers.

Therefore, lying in her bed, staring up at the thoroughly modern ceiling, Fliss knew that she had to avoid saying or doing anything too drastic tomorrow. That would be Thursday, and then she only had to hold on to her sanity – or whatever it was that was pushing her so hard – and then once Friday was done, she could take a deep breath and decide whether she was ever going back to the house. If by Sunday night she was really doubting what she was proposing to do, then she would ask Bernie if she could not go in for a week. By that time, she had the strong sense that she would have passed the worst of the compulsion, if that was what it was, or whether she would be genuinely missing Quill for who he was. Either way, she was not as oblivious to the dangers of the past being more of an unknown than she had hitherto seen as Bernie and Ed feared. It was rather that at the moment she almost couldn't help herself, and she was praying that in that case they would.

In another late-night conference in the summerhouse, Ed and Bernie quietly agreed that they were both of a mind that if Fliss went through, she'd get the shock of her life at how people lived in that far off time. It was desperation which was drawing her there, and when the reality truly kicked in, Bernie at least thought that she would be home the next night. What worried them both rather more was that there had been no declarations of affection towards Fliss on Quill's part. They both agreed that it might well be because such a display of emotions from a man of that time in the company of strangers was not the done thing back then. But Ed, in particular, thought that there was none of the emotional attachment that he would have hoped to see, even if it was never put into words.

"Don't get me wrong, I don't think Fliss has totally fantasised his connection to her," he told Bernie. "But what I heard was a lot about how much of a relief it would be to have a woman in the house whom he could trust with his son. I'm worried, Dad, because I've done job interviews with as much warmth as that – you know, that moment when just the right person walks in through the door, and you're keeping everything crossed that they say yes when you offer them the position."

However, Ed could also see what was drawing Fliss there and tried his best to explain it to his dad. If Fliss was going to be lacking in the modern comforts in this other place, he pointed out, it was equally far from a pauper's life she was heading to, and a much simpler and less complicated one. And he could understand Fliss' utter weariness with the modern rat-race lifestyle, and why she was so despairing of finding someone to share her life with here. Moreover, if she was attracted to Quill, he could understand her subsequent dismay, for if she was looking for that kind of man in the here-and-now, she was potentially going to have a long wait, because the men who were like that and anywhere close to her age were invariably already married and set to stay that way – unless, like Sean, they were widowers, and that at least was a good similarity between the two men which they could point out to her. And so he could empathise with his cousin's despair, and the determination to grasp what she genuinely believed might be her only chance at happiness, even if he wasn't wild about her solution.

"We have *got* to make the comparisons between Quill and Sean!" he told Bernie emphatically. "Both men have lost someone they loved, and are left with a child who needs a mum. If she's so taken with the prospect of a life where she's already aware that she won't be the first and only love of his life, our best bet is to try and turn her around to see what's here, not try and put her off altogether."

When they repeated the strange conversational process the next day, another piece of news that had Quill and Fliss rather more puzzled, however, concerned Lucretia.

"She swears to me that she has no idea how the arsenic got into her closet," Quill told them. "And either she is a very accomplished liar – much more so than I previously gave her credit for – or she is telling me the truth. I confess, Miss Fliss, this is giving me many qualms about sending her away now. I had asked for recommendations for apprenticeships where the discipline was most strict, but I am relenting more than a little now."

"What about Drusilla?" Fliss asked.

Quill gave a shrug. "Again, I am all at sea to know what to make of her. Without Marie around, she is a different girl altogether, and though I have watched her like a hawk, I have been unable to spot any point where I have thought, 'ah, she is lying to me.' Yet somebody put that poison into the closet, and with the way that Marie was so often the worse for the brandy, combined with her illness, makes me question whether it could have been her, even if she was clearly the one who paid for its purchase in the past, since nobody would sell it to a child."

Fliss thought hard. "Could it nonetheless have been Marie hiding stashes of the stuff around the house, and then forgetting where she put it?"

"I did consider that," admitted Quill, "and so I had a quiet word with Martha and Mary, and together we have searched the whole house. I was honestly expecting to find paper packets all over the place, yet we found none except for that in Lucretia's room and some behind the chest of drawers in Drusilla's room."

"And did Drusilla ever protest at you searching her room?"

"No, she did not. In fact, she quite welcomed it once I suggested that we thought that her mother, in her confusion, might have been storing poison all over the place."

Fliss frowned in concentration. "That really does sound as if she had no idea that the stuff wasn't there, doesn't it?"

"That's what I thought."

"But if not her or Lucretia, then who?"

"Precisely."

"What of the odd manservant you said was with your father? Could they be from his time"

"Kenric? No, as I told you, he was long dead by the time I came home and when these packets of arsenic had been made up. They were dated, you see. No, much as I wish I could pass them onto Kenric's guilty memory, of this he cannot be charged."

However, they could find no solution to the problem, and neither could Ed or Bernie when they and Fliss discussed it later on at home.

"It does make me concerned about you going to Quill, though," Bernie declared, finally unable to keep his worries silent. "You've got someone wandering around that house with an obsession for using arsenic on people. You have to admit that that's deeply worrying. If it isn't Quill himself, and it seems unlikely to be Marie or her girls, are you absolutely sure it's not the little Indian lad? Arsenic wasn't unknown in India back then, you know. In fact, I'm not sure that it wasn't found naturally there, if I'm remembering something I read in the past correctly."

"Nilmani?" Fliss gasped. "No! No, Bernie, it couldn't be him! He's such a sweet boy, and he was beyond devastated when his little brother died."

However, Bernie seemed less than convinced, even though he didn't press it further with Fliss. And later on, Ed admitted to Fliss that his dad had voiced serious worries about Nilmani to him after that conversation.

"He thinks you aren't thinking clearly about Nilmani because you want a kid to love and cherish so much," Ed confessed. "He gets it, Fliss. He gets that you have this terrible hormonal burning going on inside you that you can't switch off, and he loves you for it and feels so helpless that he can't take that pain away for you. But it also means that he worries that you can't help but be taken in by that kid – by all of the kids, in fact."

"And you, Ed? What do you think?"

"Having seen Nilmani, I think you're right. I don't think he's a kid who has enough guile to be able to pull something like that off. Oh, I've no doubt that when his grief gives over a bit more, that he'll be a normal mischievous lad, putting spiders or frogs in the servants' beds, or whatever kids of his era do for pranks. But killing someone? No, definitely not that. And when you remember that the person who died was the little brother he adored, that makes it even more certain for me.

"After all, he doesn't know that you are going to find his letters in the future and read them all, does he? What he wrote then was what he genuinely thought his mum was going to read, not you. He still thinks that the letters got posted, not shoved in the old dresser and forgotten about. From what got said, I think even Quill thinks that you just found one or two that got missed, not a whole collection, so he isn't – or wasn't – about to launch a hunt through the house and then have Nilmani rewrite them to fit what will throw us off. No, I think that whoever this is, it's someone who's an accomplished liar, and I don't think that's Nilmani, he just doesn't fit, no matter what Dad thinks."

That made it a rather emotional end to the week for Fliss, for she didn't want Bernie to be worried sick that she was about to be poisoned to death the moment she set foot in the past, but also because on the Friday afternoon, she, Bernie and Ed drove into Worcester for her to sign off on her old flat.

"I can't quite believe it," she said as they headed back to Bernie's, and as Bernie covertly cast worried glances Ed's way, praying that Fliss was now starting to rethink her future. "I'm free! Oh my god, I'm free of that past life of mine! I never need to go back into a big city ever again!"

She was sitting in the back to allow Ed the extra leg room in the front of Bernie's truck, and saw Bernie looking back at her in the rear-view mirror. "Honestly, Bernie, it's such a relief. It feels like this huge weight has come off me. Like I can move on now that I don't have that connection dragging me back to my old life." She exhaled heavily. "*Phew*! The last of my job, all the stresses, all the anxiety, it's all gone. I never have to walk that path ever again. Life looks so much brighter now."

Only Ed heard Bernie mutter under his breath, "Except that you're determined to through some bloody hole in time to a house with a mad poisoner in it!"

Quill 1816

On the other side of the portal, Quill was counting his blessings. However bizarre and otherworldly his encounters with Miss Fliss were, he could not doubt that she was real. And more than anything, what was drawing him inexorably towards the conclusion that she was the right woman to look after Nilmani was the obvious affection she showed for his remaining son. Not since his mother had died had anyone else shown his poor, lost boy that kind of love, and for that Quill would have forgiven her for even being one of the fairy folk as long as she promised to keep Nilmani safe. Granted, her very informal behaviour was not quite what one would expect of a young woman of substance, but then Nilmani had struggled to adapt to the formalities of English life, so someone who could at least unbend with him in private might do much to ease his son's sorrow at having to live here.

Even better, she seemed to have had sufficient experience of the world to have a shrewd grasp of what might be going on with Marie's daughters, yet without being the kind of coarse and common woman he would have reservations about having in the house. If she would countenance coming to live here, and would exercise some level of control over the girls, or Selina at least, then that would be a huge weight taken off his conscience. He had no desire to be cruel to any one of the three of them, but they were not his daughters. His own much-missed sweet girls had been nothing like them in character, and he had found it impossible to warm to any of these in a fatherly way, instead finding himself merely going through the motions of being their guardian. He would do the right thing by them, there was no question of doing otherwise, and he had no desire to inflict the kind of misery on them that his own father had done on him, but he could not envisage a time when he would feel any true affection for them.

Therefore, if he could employ a governess for them, and a woman whom he could leave in charge of the house and children for periods of time, then that would be such a relief. Because in the last six months or so, Quill had found himself being invited out to various neighbouring houses, and there he had met Miss Jennifer Cranford. She was not the prettiest of women, but she had a sweet temperament and a kind nature, though she was not a young woman of great personality. However, Quill could foresee that a life spent with her would be tolerable in a way that he had not considered with any of the other women who had been pushed towards him in varying degrees by well-meaning neighbours. She would not be the love of his life. That woman was dead and gone and in India, but Quill was coming to the realisation that he also did not want to spend the rest of his life alone.

Miss Jennifer would not be coming to him with any great dowry. That was reserved for her older sister, who was already engaged to a merchant's son, and in that Quill felt sorry for Miss Jennifer, because it had to be hard to be so passed over for a sister who was only older by a year. And so he knew that once he was free to pursue Miss Jennifer, that she would be most likely to say yes to a proposal.

Of course, he would have to wait until Marie was dead, but given the state of her health, that could not be long in coming, and thanks to Miss Fliss' suggestion, he had managed to put a respectable distance between himself and Marie. Whatever grim demise she endured would now be done out of the sight of the servants, and therefore not a hint of malicious gossip could be spread around the county – not that he thought Martha and Mary or any others of the household staff were the sort to do such a thing, but you just could not be too careful. So far none of the servants knew that he had had to marry Marie, and none of them ever would now that it would not matter how insane she became, and how carelessly her tongue wagged.

So with Marie safely locked away, and Miss Fliss on hand to take care of her children, Quill thought that he might actually be able to look forward to living a pleasant if not exciting life with Miss Jennifer. Once Marie was dead, and that surely would come soon, might he be able to take Jennifer to somewhere like Paris or Venice for a honeymoon, he wondered? By that time, Miss Fliss would have settled in here, and Nilmani would be comfortable with her presence, meaning he might be able to safely propose to Miss Jennifer and take her abroad for a month without everything falling apart around his ears. Yes, indeed, Miss Fliss was the answer to all of his prayers!

Drusilla's Letter

Dear Ghost,

We desperately need your help. I am Drusilla Spink, and my older sister is Lucretia Spink. We know that you have spoken to our Uncle Quill, but we need you to hear our side of events.

I have heard Uncle Quill tell you of how our Mamma murdered the Frenchman who was her husband. But that was before either of us was born. Yet now we fear that he thinks that we did the same to his dear Ishwar. We did not.

Lucretia and I did everything we could to keep Ishwar safe. We do not know why or how he died. All I know is that Uncle Quill now thinks he was poisoned, but I swear to you upon my dear sister's life that Lucretia and I know nothing of how this happened.

I write to you now in our most desperate hour. Please convince Uncle Quill that we did nothing wrong. We know that we are not the daughters he ever wanted. He has already made that most clear. But that does not mean that we are not deserving of some pity, my sister Lucretia in particular. She has suffered most terribly for no other crime than being our mother's daughter.

Please do not think me improper or vulgar for what I must tell you now, but until you know this you cannot understand my sister's pain.

Thanks to Mamma and Grandfather's behaviour, we have become the pariahs of the neighbourhood. Nobody comes near us. Nobody wants to know us. We are utterly forgotten. Out of sight and out of mind, here in this awful house down a lane that goes nowhere but to the river. And the river scares me, for I think one day we shall find Lucretia floating down there like Ophelia when her pain becomes too much for her to bear.

You see, she was raped by the butcher's boy last year, and though Mamma and Grandfather never took notice of the change in her, she fell with child by that vile act and had a little girl whom we called Felicity. We managed to hide Felicity from Mamma's madness with the help of our gardener Tom and his wife Meg, who took her in as their own. Lucretia thought they would live in the cottage down the lane, and she would see Felicity even if she could not be a proper mamma to her.

But Tom and Meg have left. Tom got another job and they work at somewhere called Whitfield Manor, though we do not know where that is aside from it being in Hereford. Felicity is now gone, and Lucretia is so heartbroken she seems to fade by the day.

Dear ghost, please, please can you fly there and at least tell Lucretia that Felicity lives and is well? We have heard nothing in months and it is killing Lucretia. Her daughter is known as Felicity Miles now. We did not want her to have the wicked name of Spink attached to her, but now it makes it so hard for us to try and find her.

But knowing that Lucretia mourns for her own baby, please can you believe that we did nothing to poor Ishwar? We could not have hurt him, truly we could not. Nor do we know who did, though we fear it was Mamma in her madness.

Caring for Ishwar at least gave Lucretia some purpose to her days, and so his death hit her as hard as it did Uncle Quill in many ways. Ishwar was not her little boy, but he partly filled the hole in her heart. Now with both him and Felicity gone, I believe it will be the end of her if Uncle Quill makes some public accusation against her. I too fear him blaming us, but can only pray that if I am brave and swear upon the Bible that I honestly know nothing of it, that someone will believe me, though I cannot conceive of who that might be when we know so few people around us. Yet I fear Lucretia will be so crushed by such accusations that she will have no will to protest her innocence.

We are as good as in gaol here, but I do not want to know what real gaol looks and feels like. Please Ghost, for the love of God, will you tell Uncle Quill we did nothing but care for his son, and that Nilmani has nothing to fear from us. Nilmani himself tells his father this, but Uncle Quill just looks strangely at us when he does, as if we have some compulsion over Nilmani. We do not.

We are so friendless, you are our only hope.

Yours respectfully,

Drusilla Spink

Chapter 31

Monday

They hadn't long got to the house on the following Monday when Phil pulled up, coming to install the lights that would illuminate the old staircase for decorative purposes, and for that Fliss was grateful. His presence made it impossible for Bernie to carry on fretting out loud as he had done off and on throughout the weekend, and it restored some sense of practicality to the day as they took Phil through the house, and showed him the new decoration. Josh had already installed the new bathroom suite in the room where he would need to lift the boards for the stair lights, and so as soon as that was done, they would be able to seal the ancient stairs for good, and cover the floorboards with a pretty marble-effect floor vinyl. And after her contemplations of the weekend, Fliss for one couldn't wait for that to happen.

As she had both feared and yet dreaded would happen, her absence from the house had substantially quelled her desire to run full tilt through one of the portals, and more and more she was coming to the conclusion that it was more the house itself which was pulling her than any deep abiding love she felt for Quill, however much she wished that that might be the case. Worse, every time that Bernie lifted those boards and opened up the stairwell, she got the shudders. If she was in the old hall only looking at or up the stairs she could cope, but not when the upper access was open, and she wished she could understand why it should be that it would be that bad compared to the other places where the house tugged at her. The only consolation was that it gave Ed the shivers too.

More of a surprise for her was the appearance of Sean, scrubbed up rather smarter than when he came to work, and declaring that he had a day off, and so had wanted to come over and see how the house was getting on. He was actually rather nice looking in a homely sort of way, she thought, surprised at herself for not having noticed that before, along with the fact that he had kind eyes and a pleasant smile, although today that seemed a little restrained.

"How did the anniversary go?" she was surprised to hear Bernie ask in sympathetic tones, and for Sean to answer,

"Grim, but not as bad as last year."

"How was Daisy?"

Daisy? Who is Daisy, Fliss wondered, and seeing her perplexed expression Sean explained,

"My wife Katie died three years ago on Saturday, and our daughter finds it hard. She's only five now, so she doesn't really have any solid memories of her mum to hang on to, especially as Katie was in a hospice for six months at the end, but at the same time she's very aware of her being gone. My sister's living with us at the moment with her two boys while her divorce goes through, but Daisy knows she's not her mum, and anyway, Jess is about to move out in a few days' time, now that the judge has ruled in her favour and said she's to live in the family home with her two lads, not that shit of an ex of hers! I went up to the cemetery to take some flowers today, because it's easier to do that while Daisy is at school. …She …she finds it hard to see her daddy get upset, you see, so I try not to frighten her with my grief."

"Oh!" Fliss was quite floored by that. Sean was a widower? She'd thought Jess was his wife, never dreaming for a moment that she'd be anything else.

However, Sean was saying, "Actually, I was going to ask for something of a return favour, Bernie. Jess is all of a jitter about going back into the house, not least because before Nigel sodded off with his trophy girlfriend, he left it in a right mess. We went to look at it yesterday, and the fuckwit has started painting the main bedroom walls black! Well, the boys' rooms are both small singles, so Jess can't even double them up while she uses one of theirs temporarily, so I was wondering if we could take a day or so and blast through the upstairs to give it a freshen up?"

"No problem at all," Bernie immediately declared. "And not just because I'd have been stumped without you and Kev helping me. I've known your Jess for nearly as long as I've known you. Ed, Fliss, and me will be there with our sleeves rolled up. When do you want to do it?"

"Any chance of this week?" Sean asked with a wince. "It's just that Jess and I think she needs to take possession fast so that Nigel can't claim that she's left the property vacant. Nigel only finally got out on Friday, you see, and that was with a court official watching him go. I've got no choice but to work Wednesday and Thursday, but even so I'm going to go over there in the evenings to work on it while Jess keeps an eye on Daisy."

"We'll go over tomorrow," Bernie announced. "The bloody Davenports can whistle for a few days!

Have we got much of that nice peachy white colour left, Fliss?"

"Err… nearly a full can. I had to start one just for the last coat on two walls."

"Great! Then we'll give the main bedroom two or three coats of trade white which should cover the black – I've got buckets of the stuff in the garage at home – and then a top coat of that. Come on upstairs, Sean, and have a look at how good the top bedroom here looks in it. Fliss did a cracking job of picking out the colours."

Feeling more than a little disconcerted at the prospect of leaving off on this house, and just when she was almost ready to make her own move, nonetheless Fliss had to acknowledge that Bernie was just being his generous self, not trying to deep-end her plans. And it would help straighten her own thoughts out immensely to work on just an ordinary modern house, not one with some weird hooks into her psyche. Moreover, it was typical of Bernie that he would offer to help like that, but it was also something of a revelation that Bernie, Sean, Ed, and Kevin all seemed to have this mutual respect thing going on, and would drop what they were doing to help one another out. That was something she belatedly realised she hadn't had since way back in university, and there was a part of her that suddenly hungered for that support network around her.

Am I doing the right thing planning on going back to Quill? she found herself wondering yet again, because that overwhelming need was the first thought that had come to her being in this house for some days, and it made her feel rather queasy. *Am I jumping out of the frying pan and into the fire? Heavens! Do I even know what the fire really, truly is? Am I just getting swept away by a compulsion and some romantic notion of what the past is really like? Because if so, that's doubly scary! Being carried along on the wave of romantic desire from the books I've read is one thing, being compelled by this bloody house to dive into a past time I'm not remotely prepared for the reality of is quite another!*

I know I don't know all of Bernie's friends and contacts, but at least I know that he has them. And I know that if Sean and Kevin are anything to go by, they're all normal! What if I don't fit in with Quill's? Belatedly she realised that this was something else she hadn't taken much into consideration. *Maybe Bernie is right, and I'm drawn more to Nilmani than anyone? Or rather it's Nilmani's fate that has made me not look too hard at everything else? Oh Lord, what the hell am I doing? What do I do? I'm not sure what I want all of a sudden. …Oh Fliss, wake up and make up your mind!*

Suddenly she was rather glad that with Phil and Sean there, it wasn't the right time to be opening up the portal to speak to Quill again. So she accepted their compliments on the décor with faint blushes, being unused to such effusive personal praise, and kept her inner turmoil to herself.

Coming back down to the first floor, she was less happy when they all piled into the almost finished bathroom, and Bernie pulled up the boards over the old stairs once more for Phil, then hoisted up the ones which made the ceiling of the old staircase.

"How many recessed spotlights do you think should go in?" Bernie asked him. "I don't want it lit up like Blackpool Illuminations but something sophisticated."

"I reckon four will do it," Phil replied, giving Fliss the shivers by trotting down the stairs, oblivious to the sudden chill in the air in the room.

"I'll go down the other way," she said faintly, and was very glad when Ed hurriedly agreed and joined her, followed by Sean.

When they got down into the old hall, it was to see Phil sitting on the edge of the gap, legs dangling into the void with a piece of chalk in hand, and marking where the lights would go on the lifted floorboard as Bernie directed him from just below. But for her, the chill down here was even worse than upstairs, and she began to feel terribly light-headed.

"Oh shit, Ed!" she whispered to him urgently, as Sean went to hand Phil his tool belt up, "I think there's another bloody portal here! And a big one at that."

He immediately wrapped a protective arm around her shoulders, saying, "I feel it too. God, I'll be glad when Dad's got that sealed up! It can't come too soon."

Phil hopped down from where he'd been perched, although Fliss and Ed noticed that he gave a small shiver, as if caught in a sudden draft, while Sean went through into the kitchen to leave his decent jacket on one of the chairs, having volunteered to stay for a bit longer. So it was as Phil asked Ed to pass him the first of the light fittings, which were right beside him, and Ed couldn't really refuse without saying why, that it happened. As soon as Ed's feet were both on the bottom step of the stairs, with Phil on there too, the familiar swimming sensation rose higher and hit Fliss, but this time it was strong enough that even Bernie gulped,

"Oh no! Is this…?"

Up where the bathroom should have been visible, all of a sudden they were looking into a much older version of the room. What was within it furniture-wise they couldn't say, because they were looking straight up at the doorway to the landing, but that door was open and revealing the landing beyond, and on the bare boards of the room a teenage girl was on her knees, another bending over her.

For one awful second Fliss thought that they had caught one of them in the act of poisoning the other, for the girl on the floor was curled in on herself, clutching her stomach and rocking in agony. But the other girl was calling out,

"Uncle Quill! Help! …Somebody, help! *Uncle Quill!*" and as she raised her head to scream, they could all see the tears streaming down her face and the panic in her expression. Going by their ages, it had to be Lucretia on the floor and Drusilla was the one calling for help. But unless Lucretia had taken one of her own concoctions, it was blindingly clear that neither of them could be the poisoner, because Drusilla was incapable of faking that much distress unless she was so mentally ill that she displayed two totally separate personalities at different times.

The sound of someone heavy running up the stairs echoed through, and then Quill appeared as he swung himself around the end of the servant's staircase and took in the scene. But of course, he was in a position to also see that the stair portal was open, and for a moment he was stunned. However, Drusilla probably couldn't see much through her tears, and now she was facing away from the stairs, and so she misinterpreted his pause.

"Uncle Quill, help her!" she wailed. "I know you want us gone, but surely you don't want us dead? She's going like Ishwar did! *Do* something! Uncle Quill, *please* …*do* something!"

Brought to his senses by her cries, Quill dropped to his knees beside Lucretia, and called loudly over his shoulder for Martha to come, but to also to send for the doctor straightaway. His gaze kept going to the portal, though, pleading with his eyes if not in words for them to also help him.

"What the fuck is that!" breathed Phil, unable to believe his eyes, but Ed managed to pull himself together enough to call up,

"Quill, we don't know any cures for poisons. None of us are doctors!"

"Who's not a doctor?" Sean asked, coming back into the hall and taking in the way the others were all clustered at the foot of the stairs. "Has someone had an accident?"

Bernie stood back a little to let him see, but warning him, "Don't ask us how or why this is happening, but we can see into the past."

"Eh?" But then Sean reached the point where he could see too, and this time there was no question that all of them could see up into the other time. "What the…?"

"I know," Bernie choked out. "Fliss and Ed have seen it before upstairs, but I couldn't then. This time it's much stronger than before."

Phil tore his eyes away from the retching girl to ask, "You've seen it before? Like *this*?"

"If you mean a repeat of this," Fliss said, her voice shaking, "then no. But the man you can see is called Quill, and the two girls are his step-daughters."

Taking a few tentative steps upwards, Ed asked, "What has she had to eat or drink recently? It has to be something she's just had."

There was a shriek as Drusilla turned at the sound of this new voice, and saw the group of strangers through a hole in the floor which shouldn't have been there.

"'Silla!" Quill said sharply. "He's right. What did she just have?"

Falling sobbing against him, Drusilla wailed, "Martha had taken some of our fresh strawberries up to Selina. Martha sprinkled them with some sugar because she knows Selina loves them, but the first ones Alfred raises in the frames are not as sweet as the later ones. But Selina has eaten some and she's not been taken ill! We were just taking the bowl back down to Martha and Lucretia had one of the ones left over."

"Sugar!" Fliss gasped. "Oh my God! Are you sure it was sugar?"

Quill looked down the stairs at her. "Of course, it was. We all had some downstairs. It was only because Selina has another one of her headaches today that Martha took some up to her. We all had some from the same bowl."

"Then I hate to say this," Fliss began, "but I think, knowing that her sister might be tempted by the leftovers, that Selina might be the…"

She never got to finish, because a slender shadow detached itself from the room beyond the door and launched itself at Quill's back, a thin knife in her flung-up arm, clearly intending to plunge it into Quill's back as he knelt. Dressed only in a linen shirt, he had no thick jacket to help deflect the blade, and it was Fliss' scream and Ed's yelled warning of, "Look out!" which made him turn just in time. Even then he overbalanced as he tried to push Drusilla out of harm's way, but at least that meant that Selina's stab went far wide of the mark, and she stumbled as she too overbalanced.

"I hate you!" she screamed, a maniacal glint in her eyes. "You betrayed Mamma! You brought those filthy native boys here where they don't belong! You locked up dearest Papa! You deserve to die! Then Mamma can come back home, and she can live with me here. You'll all be dead! Dead like the filthy rats you are!"

"Why?" was all a horrified Quill could ask, crabbing backwards on his hands and knees to avoid the wild stabs that she was making towards him. "Why hurt your sister?"

"*She's* not my sister! And neither is *she*!" the knife made a swipe towards the floor and Lucretia, then flashed back in Drusilla's direction, and Quill grabbed the middle sister and flung her towards the doorway and safety, the blade luckily only making a gash in the skirt of her dress as she fled. "*They* were not Papa's! Only *I* am his! I was the *only one* he let in with him and Mamma to play his special games!"

"Oh God, no!" wailed Fliss, suddenly realising what this meant, as did Quill by the stunned horror on his face. God help her, but Selina was probably as ill as Marie, and just as mad because of it.

But then she realised that Ed was crawling up the stairs on his hands and knees with visibly gritted teeth and determination, taking each of the stairs as the swaying Selina sporadically turned her back to him. And Quill putting his arms around Lucretia and pulling her back towards the door was enough to distract Selina, especially as there now came the sound of at least one of the servants running up the stairs.

"There's only 'Silla left, and soon she'll be gone!" Selina laughed manically, and the full impact of that hit Quill, who yelled,

"Nilmani!" and with a surge of desperate strength, hoisted himself and Lucretia up, practically throwing her into the arms of the male servant who appeared in the doorway and staggered backwards as the full weight of Lucretia was thrust into his arms. And then Quill charged out, frantically shouting his son's name as he ran.

"*Noooo*!" screamed Selina, crazily laughing as she danced in manic glee, "You won't save him! You won't save any of them!" but made the mistake of getting too near the top of the stairs.

Like a striking snake, Ed's hand shot out and grabbed her ankle and hauled hard. As he told them all later, he only ever intended to make her fall down into his arms so that he and Phil could pin her down, but what happened had him frozen in shock. As Selina plunged down into the stairwell she changed. One moment Ed was holding onto flesh and bone, the next she was toppling beyond him because he was already holding only mainly dust!

The speed with which Selina went from a living girl to a pile of bones clattering against the bottom treads froze everyone in shock.

"Ch…Ch…Christ!" Ed stuttered, stumbling himself as the force he'd been exerting suddenly had nowhere to go, and he found himself toppling over towards Phil. "No! …She wasn't supposed to *die*!"

Luckily Phil managed to break his fall, but then both of them couldn't get off the staircase fast enough, jumping past the tumbled collection of bones huddled at the bottom tread before the stairs turned to the hall. Wide-eyed and shaking, everyone could only gawp at the bones.

"What the hell happened?" Sean asked, barely able to believe his eyes.

For a moment none of them could answer, but it was Bernie who recovered first and said,

"Sadly, I think she became what she would always be in our time – nothing but an old skeleton."

For Fliss, that was the final straw, and she felt her legs giving way under her and the room fading, because if Selina couldn't fully exist in this time, then could she have ever existed in their time? Might she have become nothing even as much as old bones, if she had never existed back then? Just vanishing in the proverbial puff of smoke?

When she came to, it was to find herself with Sean and Ed kneeling beside her, her feet up on Phil's tool box, and Ed fanning her with a piece of card from one of the light's boxes, and a glass of water standing beside her at the ready. The others had all moved away from the staircase, and were listening intently as up above an unfamiliar male voice could be heard saying,

"Master ran out calling for his son, Mary, but where Miss Selina has gone, I don't know. She must have run outside. I put Miss Lucretia in the next bedroom, but it don't look good. Martha says she don't think the doctor will be here in time to help. Miss Drusilla don't look any too good neither, but she says she d'ain't have anything but one tiny bite of the strawberry, so there must'a been a lot of poison on it."

But then in the distance they heard someone sobbing inconsolably.

"Oh no," a woman said, whom the man must have been speaking to – a local woman by her voice – since they seemed to be unaware of those in the future listening in. "That sounds like she did for poor Master Nilmani!"

"Poor Master," the man said. "To lose both of his boys like that."

"Maybe 'tis for the best."

"Mary! What do you mean! You can't have wished the poor lad gone?"

"Walter, no! The very thought!" the woman replied, clearly appalled that he should have thought that. "No, I just means that becoming mother to him was all that was holding back Miss Jennifer from making her feelings for him clear. He said he had a governess lined up for the lad and Miss Selina – a decent, educate woman and someone he could trust – and was going to send Miss Drusilla and Miss Lucretia away to some place where they could work and live in. But even so, Miss Jennifer's maid told my sister that she still weren't sure about having an Indian step-son, not least 'cause it might affect her older sister's chances of a match with that man from Bristol. Seems he thinks the lad's sort are only fit for servants."

Walter's snort of disgust was audible even to Fliss. "Damned nonsense. He can't be much of a catch if he believes daft stuff like that. Anyway, they'm not just natives plucked out of the gutter, they'm Master's sons!"

"Maybe," Mary agreed, and now they could hear her and the man moving away, "but that man's rich, and her father needs her to marry well to save the family's fortunes."

The two must have gone further away, and when Phil dared to stick his head around the end of the stairs to look up, he said with relief,

"The bathroom's back!"

But Fliss was now shaking all the more. What an idiot she'd been! Or had she been blinded by the compulsion? Had she simply been abnormally susceptible to the house because of being so off kilter when she arrived?

A man like Quill and in his era wouldn't see her as his equal – not when she'd been so open about having to work for her living. What woman of quality did that in his time? It was one thing to love and marry a native woman in India – or had he even married the boy's mother? Had it been in a Hindu ceremony, but one which the British authorities out there would never have recognised as legal? Had he always been free to marry in their eyes had he found a Western woman he loved, and had he only lived with the boys' mother because he chose to?

Yet here in England he would have to behave according to his station, and all the more so because of how his father and brother had been. There'd be no just living with him in his day and age. That would be unthinkable – it would have to be marriage or nothing, and could he do that if he and his legal man knew that Marie was still alive? Even worse, he had clearly thought already about his future plans for once Marie had died, and they didn't include Fliss beyond her being left in charge of his child.

Oh God, what an idiot I am? she mentally berated herself. Why would he do anything more than invite her to live in the house! That was probably a little informal and maybe a touch impulsive, but nothing suggestive of anything more than anyone would offer a governess, because Quill would believe he couldn't possibly offer her anything more. And did he even want to? Who was this Miss Jennifer, and was she a woman of his own class whom he could eventually marry without becoming the talk of the town? Had his relief at finding a practical solution to all of his problems been mistaken by herself as romantic interest in a woman from the future? What an absolute idiot she'd been!

Worse, she was now alert to the fact that all the desire to go back in time had vanished. So had that urgent need been for the truth to come out about the death of Henri, and of Selina as the previously unknown poisoner? Was that the secret which had to come out so badly after all this time that it had sucked her down into the whirlpool of the past? Or even worse, was there something about the house which tugged people who were mentally vulnerable to it, and then twisted them so that they did the unspeakable?

Thought about like that, she could see that maybe Marie-Janneton had been a woman with mental health problems which these days would have been recognised if not cured, and that they had made her behave irrationally in the eyes of her contemporaries? And poor sickly Selina, what of her? Having been born in this house, had she always been vulnerable to its warping of her mind? And at that Fliss dissolved into tears, sobbing her heart out in equal measure over both her own gullibility, and at having yet another chance of a new life crumble to dust before her eyes – this time quite literally!

Chapter 32

Monday onwards

Luckily, Sean and Phil took her falling apart as pretty normal behaviour, given that they had all seen a girl effectively die in front of them. Meanwhile Bernie, as the least affected by any of the portals, took the chance on going back up the stairs and reaching for Phil's tools, also handing down the floorboard which they'd marked up so that Phil could fit the lights into it without having to work on the stairs.

Mercifully it didn't take Phil long to sort the lights out, and by the mid-afternoon they were able to slot that board from the ceiling of the staircase back into place along with its companion, and the floorboards above it in the bathroom back as well. There hadn't been so much as a twitch from the portal, but that left them with the awful decision of what to do with the skeletal remains of Selina.

"We can hardly bury them in the garden!" Ed protested when Phil suggested taking them outside. "What if some poor unfortunate buyer digs her up? There'd be all sorts of questions then." He for one was already thinking that it would be unlikely that his dad would want to keep the place now.

"And we can't ask that nice archaeologist lady to take care of her," Bernie added morosely, "because how on earth could we explain how we came by them? Discovering one body is bad enough, but two is just asking for the police to get involved. After all, we don't know how well she'd stand up to any dating science we have now. She might turn out to appear as if she died much more recently!"

In the end Sean and Bernie carefully wrapped the bones up in one of the dust-sheets, and carried her upstairs to the top bedroom.

"If we can still get the bedroom portal to open up," Ed had suggested, "then the best thing we could do is send her back to where she belongs," and so that's what they were hoping to do.

Yet what put the final grim touch on the day happened just as they were locking up. A smart car pulled into the driveway, and a suited man got out declaring,

"Ah! I'm so glad I've caught you!"

"And you are?" Bernie asked rather less politely than he normally would have.

"Tyson Newbold, from *NewHomes4U* estate agents," and the man thrust out a hand with an oily smile which he obviously thought would charm Bernie. He was wrong.

"Do you represent Mrs Davenport?" Bernie asked frostily.

"Err, yes, I do. Is there a problem?"

"Too bloody right there's a problem! Mrs Davenport has done a flit without paying me for the work that's been done on this property, and if you contact my solicitors, you'll find that there's a legal claim against any profit from the sale to reimburse me."

The smile faded into shock. "Oh! …Oh dear. I had no idea that there was that sort of a problem."

"Well there is," Bernie said sternly. "Now I don't

have any problem with you marketing the house, but I want you to know that your client has tried to defraud me and the police are aware of the situation."

"Police? …Defraud? …Oh? Err, right."

Bernie gave him his best gimlet stare. "So would you like to come back on Wednesday, and I'll take you through the house so that you can measure it up and take photographs? At that point I'll present you with my bill for what's been done, and the estimate for what it will take to finish the place so that it's sellable."

"Could we not do it now or tomorrow? My client is most anxious to get things moving swiftly." Young Mr Newbold was looking more fretful with every passing minute, no doubt anticipating fireworks from Mrs Davenport, but equally not wanting to anger the man standing in front of him, who right now was doing a good impression of a very annoyed bear.

"I bet she bloody is, and no, we could not," Bernie told him firmly. "I need to add on the work that's been done today to the bill, even if we could stop right now and do nothing more – which we can't – and I'm busy tomorrow. And if you think you're getting the keys to this place so that that conniving bitch can sell it without me knowing, you've got another thing coming! Don't bother trying the old keys, we upgraded the locks for valid security reasons, but there's no way I'm trusting *you* with a set of keys! You can have them all once my solicitor confirms that I've got my money!"

With his tail between his legs, Mr Newbold got back in his car and vanished off down the road. As he went, Bernie turned to Fliss.

"If I drop you off at Jess' house tomorrow, can you make a start with the white emulsion?" he asked. "Ed and I will go and get a hire van, and move those bits of furniture we wanted to keep to somewhere out of the way, though where we'll put them is another matter. Might have to be my garage for now. But I'm not letting that bloody woman have a cent from the sale of any of that, so it's better if her tame agent never sees them. If anyone is going to get that it's the Chandlers! It was theirs to start off with anyway."

Once they were back home, Bernie and Ed were all sympathy for the shock that Fliss had had, and not once did either of them say the dreaded words, 'I told you so'. Yet they could have, Fliss knew, because both of them in their way had tried to warn her that the past would not work in the ways she was used to, especially not socially. Feeling an utter fool and totally drained, she took herself off to bed early, actually more than glad that she had the perfect excuse not to go back to Sytchampton House tomorrow. Painting a nice, ordinary bedroom, regardless of any lack of choice in terms of colour, suddenly felt a lot safer and more normal.

Meanwhile in the lounge, Bernie and Ed indulged in a large malt whisky each, and softly agreed that however harshly today had crushed Fliss' illusions, actually things had worked out for the best.

"And what a good way of getting Fliss to go to Sean's sister's on her own," Ed said with a huff of relief. "If we've got to lug heavy furniture around, she knows she can't help much, and going to help Jess makes her feel wanted and useful."

"All I need to know is whether she wants to keep that painted wardrobe now, after all of this," Bernie agreed. "Hell's bells, son, I hope that you can get that damned portal thing to open without her there tomorrow, so that we can send that poor child's remains back to where she belongs. But Fliss associates that painted wardrobe with Quill and the past, even though it's not the one that's opened a portal apart from her first seeing the boys. As for the carved one, once those bones are safely back in the past, hopefully we can send it to auction, don't you think?"

"God, yes! We don't want that thing opening up on some other unsuspecting soul," Ed agreed, "Although to be honest, I don't think it will work once it's away from that house. You don't still want to keep the place, do you, Dad?"

"God almighty, no! I don't care if it goes to auction or what as long as I get what I'm owed. I still might sell this place and buy somewhere which we can convert into three parts for you, me, and Fliss, but that place? Not on your nelly!"

And so in the morning, they dropped Fliss off with more dust sheets and two huge buckets of trade white emulsion, introduced her to Jess, who had just come from taking the children to school, and left them to get acquainted.

Hiring a decent sized van, they went back to Sytchampton House, and brought the first load of furniture back to Bernie's garage. But as they were about to go back for the second load, they got a phone-call from Fliss.

"I've put a coat of white over the black," she told them. "But I think I need to come over to the big house and get some of the cleaning stuff to tackle the boys' rooms. Jess says that her ex decorated them the last time, but they're a right mess, Bernie. I don't think I can put new paint on without getting a lot of half-peeled-off paper off first."

Therefore having agreed to pick her up on the

way, Bernie sighed, "Oh well, so much for saving Fliss from the misery of confronting Quill again. But unfortunately, it's going to have to be done today if that damned estate agent is coming back tomorrow."

And so the three of them trooped up to the top floor and stood looking at the wardrobe, trying to summon up the courage to try opening the portal again.

"I feel such a bloody fool for having thought this was going to have some fairy-tale, romantic ending," Fliss said gloomily, as she stood staring at the wardrobe.

"You're not a fool," Ed said firmly, reaching out and pulling her into a hug. "There's nothing wrong with what you wanted, you just need to look for it a bit closer to home, that's all. You didn't need to go to the past to find a nice, normal bloke who'll think the world of you – I know lots of them who I can introduce you to, and without you going through the hell of online dating!"

"Thanks," Fliss replied, having to resort to snuffling into her handkerchief again, but managing a watery grin back at his conspiratorial wink. "Come on, let's get it over and done with."

She retrieved the hatpin and jabbed another of her fingers, having been careful to not keep on using the same one all the time. But this time, even though she smeared her blood on the inside of the wardrobe, there was only a faint shifting of the portal, and they couldn't see fully into the other time. It was there, but everything was blurry, to the extent that they couldn't even see if anyone was in the room.

"Oh heck, what do we do with the body now?" Bernie fretted, but Ed took a deep breath, jabbed his thumb with the hatpin, and smeared his own blood over the top of Fliss'. Briefly the portal seemed to flare into life, and grabbing the sheet with the bones in, Bernie and Ed rather unceremoniously shoved it through.

No sooner had Selina's remains fully reached the other side than the portal winked out of existence.

"Good lord, that's weird!" Ed exclaimed. "Whatever's made it do that?"

"I wonder if someone has tried to travel through before?" Fliss wondered. "Maybe Selina dying in the here and now sort of redressed the balance?"

"Possibly," Ed agreed, "but don't you think in that case there would have been more reports of this place being haunted?"

"Hang on," Bernie gasped, suddenly reaching beyond Fliss and Ed. "What's this?"

He lifted out something which looked like a folded bundle of paper.

To the Ghost was written on the blank outside fold, making all three of them gasp and stare at one another in shock.

"That wasn't there before," Ed said firmly.

Fliss agreed. "I went through the whole interior of the wardrobe when we first found it. There's no way that those papers could have lain there and me not see them."

"And I think they're addressed to you," Ed said, handing the bundle to Fliss. "You're the one – indeed the *only* one of us – who anyone in the past has been able to see up until this last time. So given that it's addressed to the 'ghost', not the 'ghosts', I think that means it has to be you."

Finding her hands shaking all over again, Fliss took the papers and went to the window where the was better light to read them by. As she read Drusilla's letter out loud to Bernie and Ed, all of them frequently gasped or groaned as it dawned on them how wrong they'd been.

"Those poor kids," Bernie said as Fliss folded the letter back up. "What a bloody awful life they led. Growing up in a house where your mother is totally nuts, and doing God alone knows what with your grandfather… Hell, that's the kind of thing that these days has Social Services swooping in and taking all the kids into care for, and a damned good job they do too!"

"Why didn't I feel her, though?" Fliss fretted. "Drusilla. Or even Lucretia? I mean, I get that Nilmani and Ishwar were always going to tug at my heart-strings, but the lack of love and care those two older girls in particular went through? That rings horribly close to home to what I went through."

Yet Ed wondered, "Perhaps you did connect? You just didn't know it? Didn't you say that you felt as if a voice from the past kept prompting you? Well, what if that was actually Drusilla and/or Lucretia? And it's one heck of a strange coincidence that Lucretia called her baby girl Felicity. That hints that they were being tugged to you as much as you were to them."

Bernie nodded thoughtfully. "And I know this is going to sound contradictory after the way I've been so sceptical over everything, but I find it a lot easier to believe that the fate of two distressed young girls – even the spirits or ghosts of them, if you want to call them that – would call to you far more than some romantic notion of running off into the sunset with their uncle. I may tease you about your romantic novels, Fliss, but I credit you with enough sense to know the difference between fiction and real life.

That's what I think bothered me so much about the idea of you trying to get back to that man. It just wasn't you! You've got too much common sense, even when you're buckling at the knees from stress."

"Thanks, Bernie …I think," Fliss said with a faint laugh. "But yes, I do understand what you mean. Looking back, I think that obsessiveness was starting to frighten me more than I was willing to admit."

And the more she thought about it, the more Fliss thought that Ed could well be right. That voice, or whatever it had been had felt sufficiently female that she had mistaken it for her own subconscious. *But why me?* she now wondered. *Why did it pull me, of all people, in so strongly?*

There was only one thing for it, she was going to have to try and find more out about Drusilla and Lucretia. And not only for her own sake. Having read Drusilla's letter, she found herself desperately wanting to know if she had survived. Had at least one of the innocents caught up in that dreadful time made it out and gone on to live something like a normal life?

After the rest of the day peeling off half painted-over wallpaper at Jess' house, she gratefully sank into a chair at the dining table, and while Bernie and Ed were engrossed in the sport on TV in the lounge, she turned again to the genealogical site on her laptop. Knowing now what era the two boys had lived in, it made it a lot easier to search, but also having the full names of Drusilla and Lucretia when their forenames were so unusual for the time. She freely admitted that if they had been typical family of the time full of Elizabeths and Anns, then it would have tested her limited research skills harder.

Yet once again she got lucky and discovered that someone had already made a fairly comprehensive tree, and this time she was resolved to take more notice of any modern connections. This was partly because with the portals gone, it was almost as if she was waking up from a dream. She felt more like her old self than she had in a very long time, and part of that reawakening was her own moral compass kicking in strongly. If there were valuable antiques at Sytchampton House, then given the way they had spent years if not decades in the upstairs store room, the chances were that they had been there even when the Chandlers had bought the place thirty years ago. And in Fliss' mind, that meant that morally they belonged to any descendants of the original family who might be around.

So she sat and read carefully through the online family tree, copying it out on some of Bernie's printer paper so that she could keep a physical version for herself. That wasn't retaining some morbid link, but the practical means of showing Bernie, Ed, and whoever those rightful owners were, just what their connection to the place was. But because she was working from the past forwards, she therefore didn't focus on the modern names until she got to within a couple of generations of the present, and then she sat back with a gasp as she saw the person's name who had made the tree.

"Saskia Bailey! That's mum's cousin! What's she doing creating this tree? Or is that just a coincidence of names?"

Scarcely able to believe her eyes, Fliss scrolled down one more line.

"Bloody hell, it *is* Cousin Saskia!"

There they all were, her mum and her sister Margot, and their two sets of cousins – one by her grandmother's next sister, and another by the youngest of the three sisters in that generation. Feeling badly shaken, Fliss could only stare at the tree for a moment, taking in that Saskia had even put in that her brother had died, leaving her as the only surviving member of the youngest family, while the middle sister of Fliss' grandmother's generation had never had children.

Dear God, Fliss thought, *we're a bit thin on the ground now! Just me and Ben from mum, and Ed and Jonas from Margot in our generation*, because Saskia's only daughter had died in a car crash a couple of years ago. Indeed, it had been that which had made Saskia obsessed with the past, to the extent that she had rung Fliss' mum up every week or so for months with the next exciting find, though only Saskia had had any enthusiasm for it at the time. But Constance Alcock had been glad enough to have a copy of the family tree to stick up on the dining room wall once Sheila had found that they had a landed gentleman in their past. That this should turn out to be Aquillia Spink was just too weird for words.

Fliss had walked past that framed family tree many times without ever really looking at it, revolted by it as a symbol of her parents' pretensions to grandeur, and so it was no surprise that she hadn't recognised any of the names. Now, though, she felt an urgent need to speak to Saskia and find out what she had managed to uncover. There was no point in her going digging if a simple call to Saskia would answer her questions about what had happened to the Spink family, and Drusilla in particular. And for once Fliss felt she could approach Saskia, because she could tell her about the letter which put Lucretia's illegitimate child on the tree after all these years. Also, Saskia had always been a lot more lively and considerably more fun to be around than either Constance or Margot, and so Fliss thought she was unlikely to snap her head off for having the temerity to ring up and ask questions.

Making sure she had enough charge in her phone for what might be quite a long conversation, Fliss went to her room and called Saskia. In total contrast to her own parents, Saskia was delighted to hear from Fliss, and the first half hour was taken up with Fliss having to fill her mum's cousin in on all that had happened leading up to her being here with Bernie. And to her surprise, Saskia was full of praise for Bernie and at the same time distressed that Fliss had gone through all of that without coming to her for help.

"Goodness me, Fliss," Saskia said, audibly choked up, "I'm beyond disgusted at Constance. What in the world was she thinking not standing up for her own daughter? My dear Ralph would never have behaved as Graham has, but if he had there would have been strong words said on my part, you can be sure of that. To treat your own child like that! You poor soul! And God bless Bernie for coming to your rescue. I always said he was far to good for Margot. And how are his boys, by the way?"

That was all the opening Fliss needed to get into the full story of why she was calling, and by the end Saskia was utterly gripped.

"So can you help me?" Fliss asked her. "Do you know what happened to Drusilla?" She'd had to be a bit careful about the whole portal thing, instead sticking very carefully to the letters and other objects, and the discovery of Henri's skeleton. She had altered the facts very slightly by saying that they had discovered Selina's bones in the process of clearing the extra soil out, because she didn't want Saskia thinking that she was some weird fantasist. However, Saskia was far more broadminded than Fliss had expected.

"You do know there is a curse on our family?" she said as the first thing after Fliss had finished her tale.

"A curse?"

"Oh yes! And I can tell you exactly what happened to Drusilla!"

Amazed, Fliss begged her, "Tell me, please!"

"Well," Saskia began with great satisfaction, delighted that at last she had someone to tell the family tale to. "I found a newspaper article from back then which revealed the terrible scandal of the death of the little Indian boy."

"Which one? Ishwar or Nilmani?"

"Oh, I think it must have been Nilmani. I'll dig out all of my papers and bring them over to you, but the name Ishwar doesn't sound familiar at all, whereas Nilmani faintly does. There was a coroner's inquest, you see, and as poor Drusilla feared in her letter, she was accused as being an accomplice to her sister Selina. It wasn't helped by the fact that Selina had seemed to vanish into thin air. Aquillia Spink testified to having heard Selina confess to poisoning Nilmani, but because Selina had always made great play of being an invalid, he couldn't believe that she had done it alone, even though Drusilla had been utterly distraught over the death of Lucretia."

"I can imagine!" Fliss agreed, thinking back to the almost frantic pleas for help in the letter.

"And this is where it gets very muddy," Saskia said with relish, "because Aquillia's two sisters were called upon to give testimony. Now Elizabeth sounded every bit the battle-axe you describe from her letters. A real nasty piece of work. She took the stand and readily blackened Marie-Janneton's name, though from what you've said, most of the locals didn't need much convincing by then. But the sad thing is that she tarred Marie's daughters with the same brush.

"However, the younger sister, Marjorie, also insisted on giving her version of events, and thank heavens she did. You see, she'd been keeping a much closer eye on things than your letters have led you to believe, and certainly more in person than Elizabeth had. Once Aquillia came home from India, she'd made a point of coming to see him every month – no small journey for a middle-aged lady having to travel by pony and trap. And it turned out that she had long been saying to her brother that the two oldest girls were suffering by being kept in the house the way they were. At the time, she didn't know about poor Lucretia being raped, but by the time of the inquest, she had come and scooped up Drusilla and taken the poor girl back to live with her, and it was she who spoke up for Drusilla."

"Good for Marjorie! I knew I liked the sound of her!"

"Me too, Fliss. Marjorie comes across even in the newspaper reports as a thoroughly decent and kind woman. So it was thanks to her testimony that the court grudgingly decided that there wasn't sufficient evidence to prosecute Drusilla, but bloody Aquillia refused to let her ever cross his threshold again!"

"No!"

"I've got a copy of the newspaper article from Worcester court, which I'll make another of and bring it over to you. But yes, he pretty much washed his hands of her. The poor girl would have been out on the streets if not for Marjorie. Rather worse, Aquillia and Elizabeth took against Marjorie for taking Drusilla in."

"Bastards!"

"Exactly my thoughts. It turned out that Aquillia wanted shot of Sytchampton House, and since Elizabeth, it transpired, was actually rather better off than she made out, she sold her house and moved into Sytchampton with her son and daughter and their spouses, who I think must have had to sell wherever they were living to make up the short-fall in cash. What they thought of the arrangement wasn't on record, and with a mother like that, I can't imagine that their other halves were any too thrilled at being cooped up with mum-in-law! Aquillia married that Jennifer what's-her-name you mentioned, and they end up going back to India, where although he initially made rather a lot of money, it all went bad for him."

"Ever serve him right," Fliss said darkly. "If he'd opened his eyes a bit, Lucretia might never have died, and neither would Ishwar and Nilmani. I suppose it was easier to blame a girl who would struggle to defend herself than admit that he'd been too stupid to see what was in front of him."

"Probably," Saskia agreed. "But where it gets juicy is what happens to the rest of the family. You see, Elizabeth and Aquillia cut Marjorie out completely. She never got a penny out of Sytchampton House. Aquillia got paid two-thirds of the value of the house and its grounds, and Elizabeth would keep all of the income from it from then on, but Marjorie never saw any of it. Elizabeth didn't even let her have any of their mother's jewellery, which is pretty bitchy, don't you think?"

"Downright mean, in my books."

"It was. But to Marjorie's credit, she took Drusilla to live with her, and by the time Marjorie died, and then Drusilla was an old lady herself, they were pretty much broke. However, Marjorie and Drusilla didn't take their exclusion lying down. I found an account of Elizabeth calling upon the local rector or vicar, or whatever he was at the time, to come and get rid of the 'family curse'."

"Oh, my goodness. A curse?"

Saskia laughed. "Whether it was true or not I don't know. But first of all, Elizabeth's son was killed having been thrown by his horse right in the driveway of the house. That was seen as dreadful bad luck, but nothing worse. But then the oldest daughter's husband and son were killed in a freak accident when a tree fell on the trap they were in."

"Blimey! That must have started to feel a bit as though someone had it in for them."

"Especially as the pony attached to the trap got away without a scratch!"

"Wow!"

"By the time every male in Elizabeth's family had died, and some in some pretty odd circumstances, you can understand why she and her daughters felt they were on the end of a hex. Now whether that was real or not, you can understand Drusilla for making a meal out of it, can't you? She claimed that she had cursed every male in the family unto the tenth generation."

Fliss was aghast. "And how far are we in that ten-generation thing?"

Saskia laughed. "*We* aren't. We're descended from Drusilla herself."

"Really? Drusilla is my ancestor? …So she married?"

"Eventually, yes, though to a very ordinary man – a relatively poor farmer's son by whom she had just the one daughter. But listen to this. That daughter's name was Felicity. And from what you've just told me, she probably would have liked to call her Lucretia after her own sister, but knew that it would dog the poor kid all of her life after the scandal that rocked the neighbourhood. So she did the next best thing, and called her after Lucretia's daughter. Your own grandmother was Felicity, you know, and she insisted that you be named after her to 'keep the curse away', though your father wasn't happy about that. Every other generation going back to Lucretia's daughter has at least one Felicity in it, the belief was that strong."

"Well I never," Fliss said, sitting back in amazement, and understanding for the first time why her mother had been so insistent on her name – possibly the one and only time she had stood up to Graham Allcock over anything, and he had often grumbled about Felicity's name, which was why she knew even that much. "So what happened to the direct line?" she thought to ask Saskia.

"All gone by the 1900s," she said. "There weren't even any for the First World War to wipe out, and that's pretty unusual. Drusilla got her revenge alright, and given that she lived until she was an old lady of eighty-three, she saw a fair few of them go before her."

But she didn't live to see justice for her sister done, Fliss thought, *and that's where I came in.*

Chapter 33

When she finally got off the phone to Saskia, Fliss went to tell Bernie and Ed what she'd found out.

"Don't you see?" she said to Ed with a grin. "That's why *you* felt the portals as well – you and Jonas are linked to Drusilla the same as me through our mums. But it's why Bernie didn't feel a thing."

Bernie added thoughtfully, "And I wouldn't be as sure as Saskia that Drusilla didn't curse *all* the men of the family. I remember looking at that family tree on your folk's wall, and even within that line, there wasn't a boy surviving to adulthood to have kids of his own until Ed and Jonas. It really all has come down through the female line."

Yet Ed had a more profound thought. "Could it be that by sending Selina back to where she belonged, after all this time, is what was needed to bring this all to a close? After all, to all those generations in between then and now, she sort of got away with murder. Okay, I'm no scientist to give you even what they know about how time works, and you could argue that Selina's bones went back very quickly, and so have always been there in the past.

"But what if you were right, Fliss, when you wondered whether Selina's bones made it back intact? Because if they crumbled even more by a second trip through the portal, there might not have been much of anything for anyone back then to find. Cousin Saskia said there was never any mention of them burying Selina, whereas they did Lucretia and Nilmani. And wouldn't you have thought that since Quill had Nilmani buried with his brother, but had the family grave opened up for Lucretia, that there would have been mention of Selina being shoved in there with her?"

"Yes, it's odd, that, isn't it?" Fliss agreed. "Every reference that Saskia came across implied that they all thought Selina had run off and might one day turn back up. When she didn't, they just seem to heave sighs of relief and been glad to forget about her. But to Drusilla it really mattered, because until someone proved that Selina acted alone, then Lucretia's name would forever be tarnished, not to mention her own."

She thought for a moment and then said tentatively. "Please don't think I'm obsessing or anything, but do you think we could inquire how much it would cost to have Lucretia exhumed and put into a grave of her own?"

Immediately Ed said, "I think that would be a really good way of putting the past to rest."

While Bernie mused, "I wonder if that archaeologist lady could help with that? She must dig up bodies and have to have them reburied, so she would know the procedure if anyone would. I'll give her a ring in the morning and tell her about the letter we found. It doesn't mention your name, Fliss, so it's safely anonymous from that point of view, and thanks to Saskia, we have more of the family story to fill it all out for her."

In the morning, Bernie duly rang Dr Sylvia Warrener while Ed drove them over to the house, all of them braced for arguments with the oily Tyson Newbold, but it was a top of the range Jaguar which pulled into the drive an hour later, and a very different man got out. Easily a generation older than Newbold, this man was all professionalism. Yet what had Fliss having to take several deep, calming breaths was the uncanny resemblance to Quill. Much darker in colouring, to the extent that he might even have mixed blood – compared to Quill's very English fairness and freckles – it was in his bone-structure that the resemblance was most striking.

"Jason Kaur," he introduced himself, extending a hand to Bernie. "I own *NewHomes4U*. You'll be dealing with me from now on."

"No Tyson Newbold?" Bernie asked innocently.

"Mr Newbold is taking time to reconsider his position with us," Kaur said in the kind of tone that implied that Newbold was lucky not to have been booted out of the door. "We don't take on clients like the Davenports. He should have done a credit check before signing any agreements with them, because that would have sounded alarm bells straightaway. And if it wasn't for the fact that the courts have us tied to this now with regard to the sale, I would have shed this commission at speed and let that woman find someone else to launder her money for her."

As Ed murmured, "Money laundering? Blimey!" Fliss couldn't help but notice that Mrs D was another female who people referred to as 'that woman'. How strange that that was something else which seemed to have come full circle connected to the house.

Bernie was already leading Jason Kaur away, and obviously feeling more comfortable talking with a proper professional. By the time they had given him the full tour of the house, Kaur was very much on their side.

"I have to say, I think you've done a superb job of showing the very best of this property," he said with admiration. "I specialise in marketing period properties which, if given a modest facelift, can fetch considerably more than the initial assessment would lead you to believe."

"Fliss deserves the credit for the colour schemes," Bernie told him generously, though Fliss demurred and pointed out that Bernie had the knowhow regarding which kinds of plasters and paints would work best.

By this time, Sean had come over and joined them, and to Fliss' surprise he was the one who jumped in when Kaur said,

"You should have seen the one house we marketed only last year. Some fool had thought it a good idea to put bottle green paint on the lounge walls. It looked bloody awful! Like spending your days trapped inside a dingey old wine bottle. God knows who thought that was a good idea, and whoever did the job for them – because the couple who owned it wouldn't have – made a right mess of it, since the paint was already starting to bubble and lift less than a year later." He suddenly looked more keenly at Bernie. "…Hang on, didn't you say *your* name was Cartwright?"

Before he could say any more, Sean declared "Yes, I know exactly the property you're talking about, because I was one of the men who worked on it. And yes, although *this* Mr Cartwright was the founder of the company, it was his son, Jonas Cartwright who insisted we cut corners and use cheaper paint on the job. It did look dreadful, even when we'd first done it, but you should have seen the original job that Jonas was copying. That was Bernie's work, and that was incredible. It wasn't bottle green but a deeper, softer colour, and it was only used for highlights. So just as you don't want your firm tarnished by Newbold's attitude and ethics, please don't judge Bernie by what his estranged son has done."

Kaur looked rather startled at the tone Sean was taking, while Fliss looked at him with new eyes. Clearly there was a lot more to Sean than she'd first thought, and it was then that she realised that Ed had beaten a tactical retreat, just in case Kaur started asking who he was, because Ed would have been part of Cartwright & Sons at the time of the botched job, even if he hadn't overseen it.

By now they were back outside, and it was as he was about to go that Jason Kaur turned back to Bernie saying, "Do you know the strange thing? Although my grandfather came from India, he always told me we had family connections to here, and a house by the river. Something about it being on his mother's side. I might even consider buying this place myself, because something is really pulling me to it."

Fliss managed to keep a smile glued on her face, as did Bernie, while Sean once again rescued them by saying, "Well if you do, it would make things a lot easier for Bernie. He'd know he was going to get paid from a reputable business man like yourself."

Kaur gave a faint smile at the compliment, but warned them, "It could be a very long while before that can happen. I've investigated what's going on here, and unfortunately both Mr and Mrs Davenport are registered as owners, so both will need to sign off on the sale. …but in the meantime, there might be a way for me to pay you some of what you are owed before the sale goes through. You see, I could do with someone like you. Someone who knows how to deal sympathetically with old buildings and bring out the best in them without going to the expense of a full restoration. I could find you regular jobs which I'd pay you for."

Even as Bernie frowned dubiously, clearly wondering how doing yet more work for which he'd certainly get paid, but still not for the stuff he was owed for, Fliss felt that it was about time that she stuck up for Bernie, and immediately said,

"We'd work *with* you but not *for* you. We'd remain independent and come on board as consultants, because we would want to retain the ability to decline a job if we honestly thought that we could bring nothing to the job. Not be having to do it because we were on retainer to you," silently thinking, *and certainly not paid a wage by you! I made the mistake of thinking Quill was going to be generous to me, and if you are a descendant of his from his second time in India, then you could be cut from the same cloth!*

Kaur was obviously not used to people standing up to his wishes, but after a bit of to and fro, agreed that he could work with that. As he drove off, Ed appeared from around the corner and said,

"Way to go, Fliss! You drove a hard bargain there."

She grinned at her cousin. "Just remembered a heap of stuff we used to use at the agency."

"Well you're bloody good at it," Ed complimented her, while giving his father a covert glance, both of them thinking about Jonas' slur on Fliss' abilities and how wrong he'd been.

"What are you going to trade as, though?" Sean wondered. "With Jonas still playing silly buggers, you can't really trade as Cartwright & Son without giving the little shit reason to say you're undercutting his trade."

"Oh, I think we can do better than that," Fliss said with a smile and an airy wave of her hand. "BEF Consultancy & Restorations aims a little higher, you know."

"Eh?" gulped Bernie. "Who the heck are they?"

Fliss grinned back at him. "Bernie, Ed and Fliss, of course – BEF. Just sounds a bit more upmarket once cut to the initials," and they all laughed.

That evening they got a phone call from Dr Sylvia Warrener, the archaeologist, who agreed to help them with Lucretia's remains, and so a month later they were all on hand at a graveyard in Stourport-on Severn to see the grave being opened up. Not surprisingly, Cuthbert, but also his father, William, had declined to be buried at Ombersley, and had instead bought a family plot in one of the other nearby graveyards. It probably hadn't endeared the family to the local rector, Fliss thought, but then the Spinks had possessed a veritable talent for pissing people off. And while they stood back and let Sylvia supervise the exhumation, they were surprised to find that DI Scathlock had come along too, until he broached his news.

"I'm afraid you might have to wait even longer for your money, Bernie," he said sympathetically. "There's now a police search on for Eric Davenport."

For a horrible moment Fliss wondered whether he might be someone who had vanished through the portal, and was also nothing more than a pile of dust. However, Bill Scathlock was saying,

"His car was found abandoned, you see, but with blood on the driver's seat which we've matched as his from his army records. We don't know that he *has* died, but he's probably not in a good way if he hasn't, and Mrs Davenport is the one person with a clear motive for harming him. That would all be easier to clear up if we could find her, but she's gone to ground. We know she was at her cousin's at the time when it was announced on the local radio down in Hampshire that his car had been found, and that there were appeals to find the driver. Yet that night she walked out of her cousin's house while the family were asleep, and hasn't been seen since.

"Doesn't help that the search for her was late in getting going, and there's a strong possibility that the grainy photo we have of a woman matching her description, but with dark hair and glasses, is her getting on the ferry to Bilbao with a false passport. Once there she could have stayed in Spain or easily travelled into southern France, and from there on to pretty much anywhere in Europe. Mrs Davenport seems to have thought out how she was going to do this long in advance, and was well prepared. The only thing that went wrong with her plan is that she didn't get her hands on the money from the house."

Their conversation stopped then because Sylvia was calling them over. The grave had produced another surprise.

"This really is shocking," she said but with distinct relish. "In the grave you have two coffins which we presume are Cuthbert and Nenius Spink, and I think I can see what might be an earlier coffin beneath them which could be William Spink's. But there are two bundles in winding sheets on top of the coffins! He didn't even give poor Lucretia a proper coffin! But half underneath her is another bundle of slightly smaller bones. I shall have to get them back to my lab to try to identify them, but I would say they're of someone younger."

"Selina!" Fliss gasped. "If they're of a girl of about eight or nine years old, then they're Selina – the youngest of the three girls."

"Can you still test for arsenic poisoning?" Bernie wondered, but Sylvia shook her head.

"Unfortunately, arsenic degrades quite rapidly. Even in modern cases, you have only a short window where it remains detectable. After this length of time, I'm afraid I wouldn't be able to tell you if that was the cause of death."

Fliss suddenly gasped. "Oh my God! No wonder Drusilla cursed her uncle! She must have known that he hid Selina in the same grave as Lucretia," then realised that she couldn't babble on about the portal here in front of strangers. But in the car as they were driving home, she, Ed and Bernie all agreed that Selina's bones must have been found in the wardrobe where they had shoved them through the portal while it had opened for the last time.

"We scooped up what remained of her shoes and clothes," Ed said shakily, "so I guess Quill must have realised that those were what Selina had been wearing. …Oh God! And there was a locket too. A locket around her neck. I never looked in it, but what's the betting that that sealed her identification?"

"But Quill couldn't have *told* anyone that that was Selina," Fliss reasoned, "because she would have reappeared within days of going missing, so how could he have explained that her body was far beyond the normal rate of decomposition? Don't you see? If he found her four or five days afterwards, she should still have been flesh and blood – well, okay, not blood, but you know what I mean. A full *body*, certainly not a desiccated pile of bones. So I fully get that he couldn't go to the authorities, and he must have had to hide her somewhere until Lucretia and Nilmani's funerals, when he could slip her into Lucretia's grave. There really wasn't anything else he could have done, grim though it is."

"Agreed, but what a terrible thing to do to Drusilla," Bernie said with a huff of disgust. "It makes it even worse that he allowed those implications to stick to her. He, if nobody else, knew that Selina would never reappear to stand charged with her sister's murder and that of Nilmani and Ishwar, so what was the point of dragging Drusilla through the dirt?"

"To make someone pay," Ed said sadly. "I'd guess he thought someone ought to pay, and heavily, for the murder of his two boys. I can sympathise with that. If one of my kids, let alone both, had been killed by someone within the family, I'd damned-well want that person to stand trial. But the real killer was gone. He could never see her hang for what she'd done. Poor Drusilla was the one person left out of all the family he could take it out on."

"What a miserable sod," Fliss said in disgust, but privately thinking what a narrow escape she had had. But on the bright side, Mr Jason Kaur was the kind of almost-handsome man she would once have fallen for …well she sort of had, hadn't she, if she could see his resemblance to Quill that fast? The old Fliss would have wanted to impress Jason Kaur, but after all this, Fliss was immune to his charisma. In fact, she was downright repelled by him and his macho pushiness, which she now realised wasn't the kind of manly behaviour she'd been looking for at all. Oh he'd been all politeness and good manners – the very things she'd told Ed she thought were important – but there was more to being a proper man than that, as she'd discovered just in time.

Instead, she found herself thinking a lot more about Sean, especially after the way he'd stood up for Bernie. He was someone whom people she trusted vouched for over and over again, so it wasn't just down to her and the instincts she still didn't quite trust to get it right. Sean was right in *all* the ways that mattered to her. In fact, she was well on the way to fancying the pants off Sean, she belatedly realised.

Over the course of the weeks leading up to the exhumation, the finishing touches had been put on Sytchampton House, and now a valuer came out to inspect the contents of Bernie's garage – because nobody quite trusted Jason Kaur enough to admit that they'd removed all the things the Chandlers and Davenports had abandoned. To everyone's surprise, some of the pieces turned out to be worth a lot more than they would have thought, but others far less so. Best of all, he pronounced that the painted wardrobe was virtually valueless in terms of going to auction.

"It's very rustic," the man declared. "Poor workmanship, probably done by a local man. Alright if someone wants to collect artisan furniture, but it's hardly going to fit into any place of quality. Now this one," and he pointed to the one which had opened the portal in the same room, "…*this* is very nice indeed! We won't have any shortage of buyers for this. In fact, I have a businessman who wants to have his newly acquired Bristol townhouse furnished as an English gentleman of the day would have had it. He doesn't actually live over here all the time, but comes over from Europe often enough to be fed up with living in hotels, and anyway, he wants to impress his associates when they come to stay, you see. He'll snap this up before it even goes to auction, and pay you a good price for it."

"Well he's welcome to it," Bernie said with feeling, but also with a sneaking relief that he could hold onto this money and offset it against what he'd had to pay out, just in case he ended up waiting years to get what he was owed. After all, until they could declare Eric Davenport dead, and therefore that Mrs Davenport could not profit from its sale by her crime, the house sale was going nowhere fast; whereas Bernie had now paid everyone out of his own money and was seriously out of pocket.

And so with Lucretia now reinterred in a fresh grave with a suitable headstone declaring her innocence, thanks to Bernie's generosity, and Selina properly reburied with the other Spinks, there was a feeling that they had somehow righted the wrongs of the past. The auctioneer agreed to send a van to collect virtually everything, meaning Fliss, Bernie, and Ed felt a huge sense of closure on everything related to Sytchampton House. From now on, Bernie's solicitors and Jason Kaur could argue the toss over the money, but at a personal level they were well out of it.

"It's rather nice that you can keep the painted wardrobe with a clear conscience, though, isn't it?" Ed replied with a grin.

Yet they were standing outside in the late afternoon of a few days later, watching the auctioneers' men loading up a huge van, when Sean turned up, a little girl practically bouncing up and down with excitement as he got her out of the car.

"Unc'e Bernie!" she squealed, and launched herself at him.

"Hello princess!" Bernie laughed, picking her up and swinging her around, bringing on peals of laughter. "What have you been doing at school today?"

As she chattered on, swinging happily on Bernie's arm, Fliss could hardly take her eyes of her. What an adorable little girl! And then Bernie was saying,

"And this is Fliss. She's the one who's been painting your cousins' bedrooms."

Huge cornflower-blue eyes turned on Fliss. "Wow! Will you paint mine? Can I have a unicorn on the wall? Daddy? Can I have a unicorn? *Pleeeease*?"

Behind her Ed whispered in Fliss' ear, "What on earth did you do to the boy's room?"

But it was Sean, laughing along with Bernie, who answered, "Oh, she painted a football pitch with a goal on Ruben's wall, and Darth Vadar on Elliot's."

"It's a good job he didn't want the *Millennium Falcon*," Fliss confessed. "There are limits to my artistic abilities. …I might just be able to rustle up a unicorn, though. …Oh, that's if you're okay with that, Sean?"

However, Sean was nodding already. "She hasn't had an upgrade in her bedroom since she was tiny, I'm afraid. For a while there were other things taking priority over decorating," and Fliss knew he was referring back to his wife dying, "And then Jess moved in, so it was all a bit too cramped to be doing any decorating. If you're happy to do it, I'm glad to hand the job onto you."

"There you go, Fliss," Bernie said with a grin. "You wanted a new career. Well there's no shortage of kids who would love to have murals on their bedroom walls. You don't have to have the skills of Leonardo da Vinci to do that, and we can give you any technical advice you need on paints and stuff. You provide the arty talent and we'll back you up. It's a nice little sideline for you in between using your talents to make old houses magazine worthy."

Feeling like a huge load had shifted off her, Fliss found she could smile along with them. Yes, making little kids happy was a job she could really throw herself into, and one she felt was within her abilities, as was using what she's learned at the agency to help Bernie and Ed grow a new business.

Then from within the garage they heard an excited, "*Daddy*! …Daddy, come *look*!"

"Oh lord, what's she found now," Sean laughed. "Honestly, I don't know where she gets her energy from, but I wish she could give a bit to me."

When he, Bernie, and Fliss joined Daisy in the garage, it was to find her wide-eyed and staring adoringly at the painted wardrobe.

"Isn't it *boootiful*!" she cooed, completely entranced.

"I think we've found the perfect owner for this, don't you?" Bernie said with a knowing wink to Fliss, who couldn't have agreed more. Taking this wardrobe to a house that had only been built ten years ago was the ideal solution. Nothing there would connect to its past, and if it wasn't valuable, then there was no reason why a little girl shouldn't have it and enjoy playing with it.

Picking his daughter up in his arms, Sean told her, "So when Fliss has finished painting your bedroom, then Uncle Bernie will bring it over for you," and got a shriek of excitement in response.

"What a relief," Fliss gasped, and meaning it, for the wardrobe would be nothing more than a piece of furniture in Sean's house.

I am so glad that I'll be painting unicorns on little girls' bedrooms from now on, she thought, as she and Bernie went in to start cooking dinner for them and Ed, who was bringing the last of his stuff over tonight. *Much safer! Much, much safer! And especially when it's for a little girl called Daisy*, she though happily, remembering the lovely hug they had shared before Daisy and Sean had left. *Yes, Sean and Daisy are very real and here, so maybe there really is no time like the present? I didn't need to go back in time to be happy after all.*

The only time she would be getting involved in the past from now on would be working alongside Bernie and Ed on redecorating houses with no connections to her or her family. And taking a deep breath, she broke the news to Bernie and Ed that Sean had asked her out on a date, and that they were going out for a meal tomorrow night. McDonald's might not be the most romantic of places, but with Daisy coming along, as far as Fliss was concerned it was just perfect.

Thank you for taking the time to read this book. Before we get on to the author's notes, I would like to invite you to join my mailing list. I promise I won't bombard you with endless emails, but I would like to be able to let you know when any new books come out, or of any special offers I have on the existing ones.

If you sign up I will send you free material to read, which includes free books and other offers.

Also, if you've enjoyed this book you personally (yes, *you*) can make a big difference to what happens next.

Reviews are one of the best ways to get other people to discover my books. I'm an independent author, so I don't have a publisher paying big bucks to spread the word or arrange huge promos in bookstore chains, there's just me and my computer.

But I have something that's actually better than all that corporate money – it's you, my committed and loyal readers. Honest reviews help bring them to the attention of other readers (although if you think something needs fixing I would really like you to tell me first!). So if you've enjoyed this book, it would mean a great deal to me if you would spend a couple of minutes posting a review on the site where you purchased it.

Thank you so much.

Author's Notes

Sytchampton House is in part based on a lovely old house I stayed in for holidays with my parents when I was very young. That house was down in North Somerset, and it did have a Georgian frontage tacked onto an older back half. This was the house where the two eras didn't quite match up – the later Georgian frontage having much higher ceilings than the Jacobean back, and so there were only a couple of extra steps up to the bedroom floor of the older part from the tall rooms of the later ground floor. When I returned there many years later with my husband for another holiday, I knew somehow that I would write about the house one day!

There are many lovely houses of the same era in that part of Worcestershire, and Ombersley is a lovely village with a Victorian church (St Andrews), and many black and white half-timbered buildings, and is worth a visit. *The Crown & Sandys* hotel is a former 17th century coaching inn, from the English Civil War period, but which got substantially rebuilt around 1810, while *The King's Arms* is a lovely 15th century, black and white half-timbered pub. Both would have been in existence at the time of the historical story in this book. Ombersley Court was the seat of the Sandys family until 2017, and is the grandest house in the area (privately owned), but as you drive around you will see many gentleman's country houses of the

Georgian era in the vicinity which will give you an idea of the frontage of my fictional Sychampton House.

Then as now, the River Severn cuts through the countryside as you go north from Ombersley towards the real hamlet of Sytchampton, meaning that many lanes in that area lead only to the river and no farther, making it even now a very quiet place to live. However, Sytchampton House as written does not exist, and certainly not matching my description and location, which is north and west of Sytchampton itself. However, you can walk the Severn Way long-distance footpath, which runs on that eastern bank of the Severn along that stretch.

A parliamentary report in 1770 recorded three parish workhouses within Worcester. St Clement's (which would undoubtedly serve the western side of the city) had accommodation for twenty inmates, St Martin's in the city centre could hold forty, and St Nicholas' thirty. By the time of the 1797 survey there was a new workhouse built at Tallow Hill on the eastern side of the city and it records that before 1792 there was provision for ninety-six inmates, while two to three hundred poor souls received what was called out-relief – which in a city as small as Worcester was at the time, represents a substantial number of poor. By 1795 the creation of the new workhouse on Tallow Hill had allowed the number of inmates to swell to two hundred and twenty-one, and the report mentions that they were well fed and given what was probably small-beer to drink but of a good quality.

On the western side of the river, St John in Bedwardine had its own workhouse from 1816 until 1837, but the building remained for much longer having been re-let, and was described as having a frontage of 86 feet and going back 89 feet – so quite a large building for a small parish. At the time that this story is set, there was also a workhouse at Hallow which served a wide rural community, including Martley, Claines, Warndon, and Wichenford. After 1834 this changed when there was a new workhouse built at Martley to cover a wider area and cater for more inmates, but the Hallow workhouse would have been Quill's first option for Maria, and then the Tallow Hill one.

Arsenic has a very short traceable life in a body, and even today, modern forensics only have a limited time in which to prove arsenic poisoning. Therefore in the early nineteenth century, proving that kind of poisoning after any length of time would have been impossible – hence Selina getting away with killing Ishwar. (I promise you I know this form research only!)

By the time of this story, the famous East India Company was indeed little short of being a government holding. The days of its hold over trade in the east were fading, and nothing like they had been in the previous century. Yet this was not quite into the days of Queen Victoria being Empress of India either, and a resourceful man like Quill could still do very well for himself out there if he could survive the climate and the living conditions.

About the Author

L. J. Hutton lives in Worcestershire and writes history, mystery and fantasy novels. If you would like to know more about any of these books you are very welcome to come and visit my online home at www.ljhutton.com

Also by L. J. Hutton

Witches' Brew

Angelo is bad news, the kind Fleur doesn't need. But is he truly evil, is the past leaking into the present, and is he acting alone?

Cataloguing Angelo Vance's latest acquisition is the last job Fleur wants, but his mother insists that it's her and her alone he wants for the task. Yet arriving at *The Rookery*, alongside the books Fleur discovers a treasure trove of old grimoires. Worse, something is very wrong in this old house. Who is the shadowy figure she keeps catching glimpses of, and hears? If it's, Angelo he's not just bad but mad, and if it isn't, is he in danger?

As Fleur digs into the family who owned *The Rookery*, ever darker secrets start coming to light and worryingly, seem to be impacting on the present. Could the lethal recipes from the grimoires be still in use, and if so, why? As violence towards her and others erupts, the police get involved and Fleur needs all her skills to make sure the wrong man does not get arrested ...and the right one lives to tell the tale!

A Gate to Somewhen Else

Kat's boss has vanished. The police suspect her. But they'll never find him where he's gone! Only Kat can help him.

Interior designer Kat is broke and desperately needs this commission restoring the Edwardian mansion of Fownhope Priors, but her employer Scott's wife and mother-in-law are a nightmare. Yet when they are killed in suspicious circumstances, and she is the last person to see him, she can't help but be drawn in to the family's feuds. Where has Scott Hawkesmoor vanished to? Is it back to Yorkshire where his wife and mother-in-law died? Or is it somewhere far stranger? And how can she ever explain it to anyone – especially the police – let alone how she knows?

Enlisting the help of Scott's solicitor and friend, Drew, seems like a good idea, but is complicated by finding herself confusingly attracted to him. Could he be the fresh start she needs in a relationship? Then her own family's dark secret rears its ugly head and an over-eager detective jumps to the wrong conclusions. Can Kat convince Drew and the police that she's not a murderess? Why won't Drew trust her, and what is his own strange past that he's hiding?

Yet above all, once she discovers where Scott is trapped, can she find a way to send him a message that will show him the way back home, and can he go through the right gateway? Or will he end up somewhen else altogether? And will the experience of the portal reveal whether Scott or Drew is the man she's been looking for?

House of Lost Secrets

Some people keep secrets, this house hides them for generations. Can Cleo dig back in time to save the present?

When genealogist Cleo is asked to investigate the family of Upper Moore House as a favour to her estate agent friend, it's a different commission to the ones she's used to. And right from the start she feels there's something not quite right about Mrs Darcy D'Eath Wytcombe. What is Mrs Wytcome's real motive for digging so deep into her late husband's family? What secrets does she think Cleo will uncover? And is she prepared for what else might be revealed?

As Cleo discovers increasing numbers of old letters, some of which have been buried for over a century in hiding places within the house, a strange web of deceit begins to appear. What was the family's connection to Georgian and Victorian Croatia and Italy, and just how closely related to one another were some of the Wytcombes? More urgently, who have been the real heirs to the house down the generations, and have others been willing to resort to blackmail or even murder to keep it from them?

With Mrs Wytcombe pushing for a swift sale of the house, Cleo must work against the clock to find the true heirs to Upper Moore House and prevent a terrible miscarriage of justice.

Printed in Dunstable, United Kingdom

75248309R00313